Love of the Blossoming Hills

Other Works
by Johann M. Moser

Verse

Most Ancient of All Splendors

Late Autumn at Dumbarton Oaks
And Other Poems

Farewell … and If Forever
And Other Poems

Prose

The Ivory Fount
A Novel

Tutelary Presences
And Other Stories

The Song of the Eternal Aeons
A Phantasmagoria

Translations

O Holy Night
An Anthology of Classic Nativity Verse

Devoutly I Adore Thee
Prayers and Hymns of St. Thomas Aquinas
(with Robert Anderson)

Johann M. Moser

Love of the Blossoming Hills

New England Stories and Sketches

The Diamond Ledge Press
Sandwich, New Hampshire

For more information, please contact us at:
https://diamondledgepress.com/

978-1-964001-00-5 (hardback)
978-1-964001-01-2 (paperback)
978-1-964001-02-9 (ebook)

Library of Congress Control Number: 2024904677

Contents

“Head for the Hills!”

Our newly purchased house was situated in what geologists, I'm told, describe as a "cirque"—a high upland pasture, reasonably level and almost perfectly round and surrounded on all sides by steep, wooded embankments. You couldn't imagine a more picturesque location for a late eighteenth-century farmhouse, soon to be painted a fresh white, with an adjoining natural-timbered barn and the usual jumble of outbuildings and sheds common to this region. The house sat directly in the middle of the cirque; a dirt road led out from one side of the cirque, passed directly in front of the house, and disappeared back into the woods on the other side. It cut the round grassy enclave into two half circles.

The forest on all sides of the cirque was made up largely of lofty spruce, hemlock, and pine trees, the dark green of the woods contrasting sharply with the summer yellows of the meadowland below. A brook curled out into the cirque at its southernmost border, flowed past a rise at the far edge of the meadow opposite the house, and arched back into the woods, where a thin gap in the embankment allowed the waters to escape from the cirque and ripple down into a series of ponds in the low-lying woodlands to the north.

It was an idyllic locale, a natural amphitheater of verdant hill and golden field, with the house at its center, one day to be like a sparkling white jewel aglow in the midst of its vibrant setting. We saw, in our imaginations, white fences that would someday enclose separate parts of the meadow and a small herd of chestnut horses, their manes tossed about in the autumn winds that would blow down from the neighboring ranges of the White Mountains. In our search for the ideal New Hampshire farmstead, we'd never expected to find anything nearly so fine.

To be sure, the house needed work. Its powerfully built post and beam frame and its granite foundation would last "till doomsday," we were told. That was a curious sort of prediction, now that I think of it in retrospect. But neglect of a century or more had taken its toll on many of the minor features of the house.

Several central heating systems had been installed over the years, one crudely and cheaply superimposed over the other, with rusty pipes and bent ductwork punched through walls here and there in odd places and at odd angles. Old plaster, paint, and wallpaper peeled off the walls and ceilings of every room; huge yellow-orange stains of peculiar shapes and sizes looked like strange antique maps etched on any flat surface one could find; the floors—their original pinewood boards showing through the cracks of paint and missing shards of a linoleum so worn that its original colors and patterns were indecipherable—creaked and buckled under one's tread; windows were stuck firmly in their frames and couldn't be budged; doors, many of them missing knobs and latches, were swollen shut or were so warped they couldn't be closed; exterior screens were ripped or just dangling idly at the windows' edges; and the cut-off ends of tangled, brittle electric wires stuck ominously out of holes in the wall like the black legs of dead, shriveled spiders.

Outside, the clean colonial lines of the house's facade were disfigured by the leaning, rotten bulk of a grotesque late nineteenth-century front porch. In front of the porch, a makeshift drainage ditch had been gouged out of the earth, for no ostensible purpose that we could see.

But we were not daunted by any of this. With some professional help and plenty of time, we could fix the place up to meet our expectations—Marilyn and I. Our three children, of course, were too young to help.

But there was one thing we couldn't fix. It defied all ingenuity, all hope, all thoughts of a visionary re-creation of an original colonial dwelling. For a decade while the house was on the market, refusing steadfastly to be sold, embarrassed real estate agents did everything in their power to get potential customers not to notice it, not to make some irreverent joke about it, not to be unduly depressed by it, not to stand before it too long with open mouths and horrified expressions before being ushered into an adjacent room.

But how could anyone not notice it? How could anyone not take it seriously (no matter how funny the jokes—and they never were really funny)? How could anyone not be profoundly depressed by it or not drink the dregs of horror to their last bitter drops in its stupefying presence? It was, without question, the ugliest thing that I or my wife or anyone had ever seen in a house.

Midway during the nineteenth century, when it became the fashion to do so, someone had removed the original colonial-period central chimney and replaced it with four small chimneys, each coming out of a separate fireplace on the first floor and linked to a fireplace just above it in a bedroom on the second floor. Three of these chimneys and their fireplaces were still there—in the dining room, in the living room, and in a kind of office or library.

But in the second living room, or second parlor (many of the old farmhouses around here have what might be considered two parlors—one on either side of the front entry and hallway), the nineteenth-century fireplace had, in turn, been replaced by an early twentieth-century hearth. It was not just a hearth; it was a most extraordinary wall constructed of gigantic, irregular stones. A small, black, semicircular aperture, gouged out of the massive wall and utterly disproportionate to it, helped to identify the edifice as what it was, a stone hearth with a tiny fireplace hollowed out in front. Just over the fireplace, a shelf of flat, shale-like rocks, arrayed in a line to form a kind of jagged mantelpiece, projected out of the edifice.

The rest was just a solid wall—rising from floor to the ceiling and stretching across one whole end of the room—made of immense, ill-fitting stones of different colors and textures, all clashing with one another so cruelly that it practically hurt the eyes to gaze upon it.

On the corner of each stone was etched a small number—from 1 to 48. Number 1 looked pretty much like a typical piece of New Hampshire granite; it was positioned in the corner on the floor as first in a sequence of stones along the bottom of the wall that numbered up through thirteen.

Everything else was built on top of those thirteen base stones. Number 48 was mounted rather prominently just above the mantelpiece, as if it finished off the monumental composition with just the right flourish. It looked like a large hunk of wood; but it was not. It was a piece of petrified wood from the state of Arizona. And high on this unspeakable horror of a wall, right over the center of the mantelpiece, was another very tiny hole. We were told that at one time this hole was used to support a small flagpole that projected out of the stony monstrosity, and that an American flag—back in the days when the flag exhibited only forty-eight stars—used to dangle from the pole.

And that was the key to the mystery. In the late 1920s, the owner of the house, the last and somewhat batty scion of the otherwise stalwart and rational family that had built the house, lived in it, and farmed the cirque for generations, decided to make several forays around the entire continental United States in his wobbly old Ford truck in order to pick up, in each state, a large stone for his new fireplace. It took quite a bit of work and several years of effort to accomplish this task. Luckily, at the time—or unluckily, depending on your point of view—Hawaii and Alaska were not yet joined in statehood to the United States, for then, perhaps, such a project would have been discouraged as too difficult, or maybe and more relevantly, as pointless. But the project was completed with a pertinacity that surprised everybody who knew of it, and the edifice was built. An enormous amount of concrete was used to hold together the ill-fitting stones, and a foundation was built in the cellar underneath that was strong enough to support the Statue of Liberty. The owner of the house was not a stonemason; nor could his sense of pattern and form be recommended to anyone in the world. But there was no question that the dragging in, mounting, and sealing of the stones in place was a cyclopean labor, worthy of a race of giants—especially a race of giants facing the prospect of imminent extinction.

The fireplace was regarded locally, for a while at least, as a kind of wonder of the world. If there was anything to admire about it, at least you could admire the sheer labor that went into its construction, even though the rest of the house was allowed to disintegrate around it, and the farming operations associated with the house—once the pride of the region—were abandoned. Even more, the great wall was regarded, in its time, as a most remarkable and eccentric expression of patriotism in a locale that's given to rather peculiarly remarkable and eccentric expressions of patriotism.

I find it curious that it never got listed somehow as one of the tourist attractions of central New Hampshire; things much less significant than that have been thus listed and have drawn thousands of gaping, if somewhat bewildered, eyes each year to view them, wondering all the while what exactly there was to look at.

The problem for us was: How could we get rid of it?

It required a conference, and a conference it got. After we'd closed on the house, Marilyn, the children, and I decided to "set up camp" inside the house for the summer—and literally that's what we had to do—so that we could get the restoration underway. One early June morning, I brought together the tradesmen whom I had contacted about doing various jobs. My primary purpose was to coordinate their activities and to set up a timetable for doing things. I didn't know yet that, in the local area, there are no such things as coordination or timetables. Things get done when they get done, and that's all there is to it.

But my second purpose was to discuss the question of the wonder of the world sitting there so imperiously in that second parlor. Ezekiel the carpenter was there, Septimus the electrician, Job the mason, and Agamemnon the plumber. If there was something about them that inspired the most immediate sense of personal confidence, there was also something about them that should have inspired the most immediate sense of professional distrust, but we were too addled by our initial country giddiness to take proper note. Marilyn presided over this conference; she had her own special ideas of how things should get done—not that any such ideas would matter anyway. Once again, things get done the way they get done, special ideas or not.

The conference took place around the kitchen table.

I suppose that the first joint resolution made by our conference was that nothing should proceed in the restoration of the house until the colossus of the second parlor was expeditiously removed. As I reflect back upon this decision, I wonder what really motivated it, though I certainly had intimations at that time of various possibilities: of course, such a decision could obviously delay matters, and given the nature of the obstacle, delay them indefinitely.

I discovered that in the minds of the local tradesmen, something like two established and irrevocable principles always hold: any delay is a good delay, and the longer a delay, the better.

I also wonder if this decision was not made out of a certain generosity—I use the word "generosity" here somewhat guardedly. A recent incident at a local hardware store, where the storekeeper had talked me out of several items I had come in to buy, was a case in point. He said I didn't need them and showed me, in some detail, exactly why I didn't need them. Perhaps Ezekiel, Septimus, Job, and Agamemnon were trying to tell me that, once having removed the monstrosity from the second parlor, I might no longer want or need their services. I should have taken more account of these implications than I did.

The most dramatic point in our conference was when we all moved together into the second parlor to examine the structure we were discussing. We were like a small knot of Mongolian tribesmen standing in front of the Great Wall of China. It looked unshakeable, imperturbable, solid, impenetrable. Talk ran from pickaxes to jackhammers to everything imaginable. The men took the discussion very seriously, only to break out now and then in some inexplicable laughter.

The combination of glorious incompetence and eccentric audacity that had gone into the building of the wall both awed and amused them. It was, in its way, a quintessential expression of the world they lived in. If Greeks had their temples and medieval guildsmen had their Gothic cathedrals, they had this monument to their own unique spirit of putting up something without the slightest regard for its comeliness or beauty.

The early generations of New England craftsmen and architects have left behind them innumerable exemplars of their ingenuity and tastefulness, if such monuments were left reasonably alone and managed to survive. But, by some great unwritten law of generational decline, their progeny could no longer sustain such standards. Just as peoples who enter into the late phase of their cultures love to deface and even destroy what was most dear to their ancestors, these same peoples seem to be more than happy to erect monstrosities whose sheer pretentiousness shall stun and amaze all who come to gaze upon them.

Here, in this wall, was just such a sublimely paradigmatic memorial of this effort. But how, how indeed to get rid of it? After a long and indubitably meditative silence, Ezekiel made a solemn pronouncement, which was echoed by Septimus, Job, and Agamemnon. There was only one solution: the solution was a fellow by the name of Elvin Nab.

We returned that fateful day to the kitchen and resumed our positions around the kitchen table and at our coffee cups. Ezekiel, abetted now and then by the remarks and consent of the other three men, filled us in on the details concerning Elvin Nab, according to the way that Elvin himself—as they made certain in an evasive sort of way to inform us—was accustomed to tell it.

He was, it turned out, the member of an old-line Philadelphia family and the graduate of a Harvard engineering program in mining and metallurgy. He had become familiar with the Lakes Region of New Hampshire when, as a student, he had spent many productive summers at the Harvard engineering camp on Squam Lake. His career in mining engineering came to a premature end when, a few years after graduation and in a silver mine in Colorado somewhere, he had tripped on a wire and fallen down a deep shaft where his fall was broken and his life was saved, ironically, by his splashing down into a vat of sulfuric acid. Nearby miners managed to fish him out of the vat before the acid killed him.

In any event, it was years before he could even walk again. He was partially paralyzed on one side, one eye was missing, and his brain was severely injured. A few years later, when he could take care of himself again, he moved back to the Lakes Region and settled into a small hut by a pond in the woods near the National Forest. Here he lived alone amid a graveyard of old engines and appliances and other junk, a broken hulk of a man, but still containing within him, like a smoldering flame, the young and brilliant engineer of bygone years. And though he rarely practiced his trade, he made it known that he retained all the scientific expertise that he once had, for Elvin Nab was considered a demolition expert. He could do anything anyone wanted him to do—with dynamite. Ezekiel declared that he was the man for the job. Septimus concurred with a brisk nod of the head. Job clucked somewhere deep down in his throat, "Yup!" and Agamemnon added curtly, "Yuh bet!"

Two days later Elvin Nab appeared at our door. I don't quite know how he got there. No sound of a truck or car entering the cirque had announced an arrival. He just stood there suddenly and silently on the other side of the screen door, an immense shadow filling the entire doorway. He said nothing. But I ascertained who it was, for this was clearly an injured man. His left arm hung loosely at his side; his head was crooked over his right shoulder. His enormous hulk seemed to encase him in a heavy and intolerable burden.

"Elvin Nab?" I said.

A thick, deep, rumbling voice growled slowly: "Yuh got it, boss."

I showed him in, and Marilyn offered him a cup of coffee, which he politely refused. In the light of the kitchen windows, we could see more clearly his ravaged and dewlapped face, all hanging to one side, with one eye socket revealing through its half-closed opening a moist surface of creamy yellow. Obviously, he had not shaven in a while, but the stubble of beard appeared in only a few places, especially in the folds between the jowls. He wore a long smock that hung down from his massive, bent shoulders and looked as if it had been roughly sewn together from a bunch of old coats. It was shredded and dirty. Beneath the smock, woolen trousers drooped down in folds and dragged along the floor, and only the broad tips of soiled leather boots appeared from underneath them. A crushed red hunting hat, so stained with oil that only here and there was it possible to see the original color, sat precariously balanced on the top of his head; its brim was partially torn off. When he removed his hat, he seemed to have hair on only the right side of his head. The left side looked like old sunburnt leather.

We wasted no time in marshaling this strange wreck of a man into the second parlor to examine the great fireplace. Elvin, who had said practically nothing up to this point, examined it carefully, running his one usable hand tenderly over its surface and talking to himself all the while in scarcely audible but rumbling tones coming from deep inside him. At one point he broke out into a curiously soft and childlike smile that revealed a jagged band of yellow teeth almost as impressive in their own way as the fireplace wall he was now studying. The smile disappeared, and again he was serious. He asked, in his low, deep growl, to be taken to the cellar so that he could examine the foundations of the wall. Other requests followed, and both Marilyn and

I found ourselves scurrying about at his behest like the ephemeral servants of some primeval beast that had survived the last ice age. Meanwhile, he withdrew from a baggy pocket appended to his smock the stub of a pencil, a soiled shred of what had once been a paper bag, and a wrinkled-up cloth tape measure. With these and using his lame left arm as a brace, he managed to take and write down some measurements and even drew several crude pictures, despite the fact that the pencil hardly fit in his massive hand. When Elvin had finished his assessment of the situation, he stood before the great wall and turned to us.

Then the most astonishing thing happened. His whole body jittered and shook, and his large, twisted mouth melted once again into that soft and childlike smile. He opened his mouth, and a voice came out — not his usual voice but the high-pitched yet smooth and sing-song voice of a young man, still green in years but confident and wise, voluble and eloquent, spelling out in precise terms the dimensions of the problem we faced and the steps that needed to be taken in order to solve it.

With scientific exactness it spoke of pressures and force, dynamics of thrust, lines of fracture, explosion and implosion. It assured us that, with just the right placement of devices and with accuracy of timing, the great wall of stones could be reduced to a neat, removable pile without injury to the house or its surroundings.

When the discourse concluded, the soft smile reverted back into the great twisted orifice of a mouth and the voice resumed the taciturn, growling texture it had before. We could hardly believe what we had heard. After he had left — limping heavily off into the woods like a wounded cave bear — Marilyn broke down into tears. It was the saddest thing she had ever seen — the voice of the young genius still alive in a man who was so physically ruined. I also, presuming that our great urban wastelands harbored the ruins of potentially brilliant and talented men in countless skid rows across the nation, couldn't help but be moved by the appearance of so similar a tragedy in a rural setting.

We decided to use his services, and through Ezekiel — Elvin himself seemed to be impossible to reach through any modern system of communication — we made the appropriate arrangements. Ezekiel suggested that the job be done as soon as possible—which was a curious kind of suggestion for Ezekiel to make. Late June had already come around, and thus early July would be best. In fact, Ezekiel thought, why not have it done on the Fourth of July? Wouldn't that be in keeping with the original patriotic intent of the great fireplace itself? So I agreed. But I should have given that matter just a bit more thought.

Other events that occurred soon after that should also have given me pause. A few days after making arrangements with Ezekiel, I tore a pair of trousers on an old barbed-wire fence that was concealed by a dense growth of ferns behind the barn. This fence was only one of many "booby traps," as I came to think of them, remnants of the old farming life that were hidden all over the place and that sprang up from time to time to threaten both life and limb. I took the trousers to a seamstress named Temperance Dawkins, who lived not far from us. After settling what needed to be done to the trousers, we began talking about a number of other matters, and she asked me how we were getting along in the house. She was a spare, thin, pleasant woman who had the curious habit of tilting her head, closing her eyes, and smiling blissfully while she talked and subsequently fixing her eyes on you like a nervous sparrow while she listened. I discussed with her some difficulties we were having.

She seemed to be very knowledgeable about such things and didn't abstain from predicting—with a certain irrepressible delight, I must say—further complications we might expect to see arise in connection with these matters. My comments about the help we anticipated from the various tradesmen in the town were invariably met with some degree of bemused skepticism.

In the course of our conversation, I mentioned Elvin Nab. Her mouth dropped with surprise. This time she didn't tilt her head or close her eyes or smile blissfully while she spoke. "Elvin Nab—why, fur goodness' sake, don't be lettin' that rascal through yowah front dowah!" she declaimed.

She told me her version of Elvin's story. "My word, Elvin wern't no Hahvard student. He nevah graduated from eighth grade. But he comes from a township ovah ta thuh othah side a' thuh lake so nobody knew 'im heyah-abouts. Somehow, he got a maintenance job up ta thuh ol' Hahvard engineerin' camp ovah ta Squam (ain't theyah anymowah). He were set ta rakin' leaves an' cleanin' up thuh bunkhouse an' thin's like that.

"Well, up ta thuh Hahvard camp theyah's this young scamp — his name were Parkah Winthrop; I nevah sore 'im, but I heard that he were small an' well-spoken an' had a sweet, childlike smile an' a baby face that would'a bewitched anyone who evah looked at 'im. He come from some wealthy family down Philadelphia way, an' maybe they thought that by sendin' 'im ta Hahvard they could get rid a' 'im or at least cure 'im a' likin' so much ta blow things up. He blew up most a' thuh toys he got fur Christmas, includin' some fancy electric train set.

"He got kicked outa' some prep school fur puttin' a firecracker in thuh candle that thuh headmastah lit up durin' one a' thuh chapel services. When he got ta Hahvard, I guess he settled down a bit, but up ta thuh camp, when he found out theyah were a shed with dynamite in it, he became big buddies with Elvin an', usin' Elvin's keys ta thuh shed, would steal sticks a' dynamite, an' thuh two a' 'em would run off inta thuh woods an' blow 'em up somewheyah. He were a smart fella, all right, an' seemed ta know what he were doin', despite thuh fact that he shouldn't-a been doin' it.

"Then one day he an' Elvin are foolin' 'roun' in that shed, an' Parkah Winthrop screams, 'Head fur thuh hills!' an' dives outa' thuh dowah. Elvin wern't so lucky. He managed ta get mostly out befowah thuh shed blew.

"Well, Parkah Winthrop got thrown outa' Hahvard fur that, an' I dunno what became a' 'im. Elvin were badly injured, as I guess yuh know. He were away from heyah fur a long time aftah that, prob'ly bein' put back tagethah on Winthrop money. But whatevah they did, it didn't work all that well. He came back ta thuh area. I can tell yuh, he ain't good fur practically nothin' yuh can think a'. Ever' once an' a while some crazy fella gives 'im a job an' gets some explosives inta his hands an' he blows somethin' up, but not always thuh somethin' he's supposed ta blow up, an' ever'one thinks that's kinda funny. Thuh fellas 'roun' here also think he's funny 'cuz he does great imytashuns a' folks' voices an' can sound like anybody yuh want 'im ta sound like."

When I got home, I called up and convened our building committee. Ezekiel, Septimus, Job, and Agamemnon arrived within the hour. I told them what Temperance Dawkins had told me. They broke into laughter. Ezekiel spoke: "Pay no heed to what Tempy Dawkins tells yuh. She were sweet on

Elvin once, an' he spurned her. 'Hell hath no fury,' as they say." The other men guffawed and slapped their thighs.

Agamemnon went on to enumerate various jobs that Elvin had done: the demolition of the old railroad crossing, blowing out a hole for Hosea Hall's fishpond, exploding Edna Stone's defunct well, blasting Hiram Mulrooney's henhouse—the list went on and on. Every reference to one of these jobs elicited another storm of laughter, as if the incident mentioned involved something more than what was being revealed. Ezekiel interrupted this litany by bringing up the story of the cemetery.

"Why, heck," said Job, "that were thuh best a' 'em all. Ol' man Turnus had just gone on ta his well-deserved eternal punishment when thuh grave-yard crew found they couldn't dig out his grave 'cuz they hit a huge, flat stone jus' two feet undah thuh surface a' thuh groun'. So, in comes Elvin ta do thuh job. Natur'lly ever'one is a little worried 'bout thuh Methodist church, which is right close ta thuh gravesite, but Elvin assures 'em theyah won't be no problem. So early one fine mornin', ever'one clears outa' thuh graveyard, leavin' ol' Elvin theyah ta do his work. Suddenly, thuh next thin' they see is Elvin runnin' as fast as he can—which ain't all that fast—an' hollerin' like hell, 'Head fur thuh hills!' Then he dives inta a gully by thuh side a' thuh church, an' theyah's this huge blast, an' a piece a' flat rock sheers outa' thuh groun' an' goes hurtlin' up an' through thuh air, slicin' off thuh tip a' thuh church steeple as clean an' cleyah as if t'were a knife blade passin' through a hunk a' bacon."

"An' that ain't thuh best a' it, neythah," Septimus chimed in. "Thuh rock goes sailin' ovah thuh village like one a' 'em flyin' saucahs ever'one keeps yammerin' 'bout, an' comes crashin' down right through thuh roof a' Jesse Mugthorpe's house, through his attic, through his bedroom on thuh second flowah, an' inta his pahlah on thuh furst floor. So, we all went a-runnin' over theyah ta make showah ever'thin' were okay, an' we find Jesse still a-lyin' theyah in bed, chokin' on all thuh plaster dust in thuh ayah, gapin' at thuh hole in thuh ceilin', an' gapin' at thuh hole in thuh flowah right close ta thuh bed itself, an' sayin', 'Now what thuh hell?'"

The four men could hardly contain their hilarity and laughed and laughed while Marilyn and I looked at each other nervously. Ezekiel noticed this and remarked, "Now don't yuh worry 'bout nothin'. Thin's'll go jus' fine. Anyhow, thuh church needed a new steeple."

"An' Jesse Mugthorpe were spendin' too much time in bed!" Septimus interjected. "He don't do that no mowah." There was more laughter.

"That's fur showah," Ezekiel concluded.

Septimus concurred with a brisk nod of his head. Job clucked somewhere deep down in his throat, "Yup!" and Agamemnon added curtly, "Yuh bet!"

As they turned to leave, I asked the men if Elvin Nab was good at doing imitations. The question initiated a whole new round of laughter. "'Course he is," Job responded. "Yuh should hear his imitation a' Tempy Dawkins. Sounds exactly like her, complainin' an' fussin' about everythin', especially about Elvin." More laughter followed, and they left.

I had to pay an advance to Elvin so that he could buy the materials he needed. On the third of July he came over to the house, this time brought by Ezekiel in his truck. With Ezekiel's help and that of a large electric drill, which he cradled quite skillfully in one arm, he sank several deep holes in the great stone wall, cutting through a piece of Florida coral reef and some Wyoming sandstone. After several hours, he seemed to be satisfied with his work. He unpacked several thin sticks of dynamite and readied them for the following day.

The event was planned for the early evening of July 4. Marilyn, the children, and I carefully removed everything we needed from the house and made a little encampment on the shallow rise at the southern end of the cirque. We planned to watch from there. Meanwhile, Elvin Nab was back at work inside the house, doing more last-minute drilling and hauling in box after box of explosives. Since I had thought that all the preparations had been made already, I found this additional round of armaments to be somewhat alarming.

About seven o'clock in the evening, we were troubled by the arrival of the volunteer fire department with three rather old engines chugging across the cirque and gathering in a foreboding, though distant, circle around the house; they ran their hoses down into the stream. But we were assured that this was a "precautionary" measure only.

We were even more troubled when hordes of people began to arrive. Cars and pickup trucks by the dozens entered the cirque, bounced slowly and unevenly over the fields, and parked around the perimeter. The crowd was clearly in a festive mood; children carried little American flags, men had cartons of beer, and women had metal pots filled with fresh doughnuts and pitchers filled with cider. The town band showed up — an unruly group with bent brass instruments and an old torn drum mended with duct tape — and played a snatch or two as the crowd continued to swell.

By eight o'clock, the sun had gone down far enough behind the hills to leave the cirque in deep shadow. At the far circumference of the cirque, a crowd of vehicles and people faced inward to the lonely house at the center. At some signal, they turned on the headlights of their vehicles and bathed the house in an almost magical luminosity. A great hush settled over the crowd as the countdown to eight forty-five began.

At exactly eight forty-four and fifty seconds, the screen door of the house flew open and Elvin Nab leapt out onto the old Victorian front porch. In one great blood-curdling yell, he shouted, "Head fur thuh hills!" Then, with all his enormous hulk, he dived, as gracefully as a great northern whale, into the ditch at the base of the house.

I'm not sure I can remember clearly what happened after that. It was all over in a few seconds, but it also seemed to go on forever. It looked as if the house took a deep inhalation, one last, deep breath, pulling everything into its center, including all those windows, which I could never open, being sucked out of their frames and swept almost noiselessly into the interior of the house. The next thing I saw was the roof open up like two great flaps, as if tilting neatly backward on hinges, and a column of forty-eight boulders rose out of the house and directly into the sky.

As the column rose higher and higher, it splayed out against the sky and formed an almost perfect rectangle, now higher than the rim of the cirque and catching the rays of the setting sun. Like stars resplendent against the dark blue of the encroaching night above, the forty-eight boulders whirled and blazed in the flaming golden yellows of the sun, and their star-spangled wonder was framed by the red and white stripes of the clouds along the western horizon.

The crowd gasped in astonishment as the sound of the explosion finally passed over us like the front of a violent summer storm. The earth shook beneath our feet, and the immense cataclysm ricocheted back and forth in thunderous shocks from one side of the great natural amphitheater to the other. And there it was, Old Glory itself, suspended in the eternal heavens above us, the most wonderful living sculpture and the greatest expression of patriotic sentiment that history has ever witnessed.

After an infinitesimal, but interminable, moment of this miraculous vision of forty-eight glittering boulders caught in the evening light, and just as neatly as a film run in reverse, the boulders gathered themselves again into a straight column and fell down into a huge pyramid on top of the house, which meanwhile had collapsed in on itself and had formed into something like a neatly stacked platform several layers deep. Not a shard of glass or wood, not a stone or brick or piece of plaster had blown outward into the cirque. When it was over, the smoldering heap lay as still as an ancient monument in the center of the great semicircle of lights formed by the surrounding vehicles. A vast, dusty silence hung over the cirque like an evening mist.

The crowd broke the silence with a rousing cheer and suddenly swept inward from the circumference of the cirque and, according to some unwritten rules of salvage, scrambled over the pyramid, carting off the stones while the band played "The Star-Spangled Banner," and the children ran about with their little flags and the men popped the tabs on their beer cans and the women spread little portable picnic tables with the doughnuts and the cider. It was the finest Fourth of July ever. Fireworks began going off all over the place, and the hoses of the fire trucks were aimed straight up as the spray rose like enchanted fountains over the cirque, catching the final rays of the sun as it set in the west.

Marilyn and the children and I just stood on the rise, too dumbfounded by the rapidly evolving spectacle to speak or to move. Few people noted the dark hulk of a man emerge from the ditch beside the ruins of the house and lumber off into the woods, his left arm dangling heavily at his side.

Before the summer was over, we'd contracted with a firm in a nearby city to build a new house for us. They did a beautiful job. Using antique wood from the old barns that were left behind, we created the glowing white New England farmhouse of our dreams, with a small herd of chestnut horses in pastures surrounded by white fences, and some white wooly sheep in our yard, and some white ducks and white geese floating on our newly dug pond, and a big vegetable garden, bordered by a white picket fence, behind the new house. It worked out very well for us, and we had, after all was said and done, no regrets.

The following June, after our new house was finished, Ezekiel, Septimus, Job, and Agamemnon came over on a Saturday morning to have a cup of coffee and inspect the work. It was flawless, they conceded, with a humility rare for local tradesmen when commenting on the work of competitors. They knew, of course, that they were "fix-up" men and quite incapable of the sort of advanced techniques exhibited in the construction of our new home. When I asked them if they approved of what they saw, Ezekiel remarked, "That's fur showah." Septimus concurred with a brisk nod of his head. Job clucked somewhere deep down in his throat, "Yup!" and Agamemnon added curtly, "Yuh bet!"

Gradually, the men went off to other appointments, except for Ezekiel, who lingered for a while beside his pickup truck in the yard and turned to me with a smile and said, "Yuh know, that ol' Elvin Nab certainly did yuh folks a big favor, in his own sort a' way."

I was a little stunned by this remark. "What do you mean?" I asked.

"Well," Ezekiel replied, "theyah are some a' these ol' houses that can be restored an' some that can't. Thuh best are thuh ones got left mostly alone ovah thuh course a' time; thuh worst are thuh ones wheyah folks did lots a' little thin's—often tempo'ry thin's—ta 'em, an' none a' those little thin's evah worked, 'ceptin' ta make 'em worse than theyah evah were.

"Yuh did right by buyin' this place, 'cuz it's thuh sweetest piece a' land in twenty miles or mowah. But thuh house would'na been nothin' but a drain on yuh. It couldn't be fixed. It would'a taken a lon' time befowah yuh realized that it needed ta be stripped ta thuh groun', an' by that time yuh couldn't-a done it 'cuz yuh would'a already done so many othah thin's ta it. Thuh moment we set foot in it, Septimus an' Job an' Agamemnon an' I knowed that. What made it even a biggah headache were that thuh original post an' beam frame were as sound as evah, an' a division a' Sherman tanks couldn't-a pushed it down."

"So it took Elvin Nab to do what Patton's army wouldn't be able to do," I said.

"Yuh bet it did. Problem is that Elvin knows his explosives all right. When yuh asked us 'bout Elvin, we gave yuh his version a' who he were, 'cuz we figgahed that were all yuh might want ta be knowin' at thuh time. But Tempy Dawkins were mostly right 'bout what she tol' yuh, 'ceptin' that Elvin ain't as entirely useless as he seems ta her. I dunno what he learnt from that fella Parkah Winthrop ovah ta thuh Hahvard camp, but that fella were a genius a' some sort, as they say.

"An' Elvin got it right. I figgah that were thuh most perfect exploshun any human eyes have evah seen. It was thuh finest thing I evah sore, risin' straight up like it did an' all those forty-eight stones just a-shimmerin' 'gainst thuh evenin' sky like thuh stars an' stripes furevah. It showah beat any Fourth a' July fireworks we evah had 'roun' heyah."

"You mean, he meant to blow up the house?"

"Not d'rectly. Elvin Nab didn't blow up yowah house."

"Who did?"

"Why, that fella Parkah Winthrop did."

I was too astonished to say anything.

"Don't ask fur no explanashuns," Ezekiel continued. "But yuh know, 'cuz yuh sore it an' yuh heard it yuhself, that Parkah Winthrop kinda lives deep down inside a' Elvin Nab, an' thayah's no controllin' when an' how he comes outa' 'im now an' then. I guess it's some kinda brain damage or somethin'. Elvin can even talk jus' like Parkah with a high-pitched voice an' a soft an' childlike smile. Devil knows!

"Anyhow, whenevah Elvin does one a' his jobs, somethin' un'spected always happens, an' that somethin' is always mowah amazin' than what were planned. That's why folks always come ta see, jus' so long as they can be at a safe distance. Yuh see, it were Parkah Winthrop that blew off thuh steeple a' thuh Methodist church an' woke up Jesse Mugthorpe aftah he'd been sleepin' too late that fine mornin'. An' both a' them thin's needed gettin' done, if yuh ask me. Parkah jus' gets inta Elvin's hands an' brain an' makes 'im do thin's jus' a bit differently than Elvin planned ta do 'em. That's all. When Elvin realizes that Parkah has taken control an' it's too late ta be changin' that, why, he runs away full speed ahead shoutin' his — or maybe it's Parkah Winthrop's — 'Head fur thuh hills!' But yuh don't need ta head fur thuh hills at all. Theyah's no danger. Everthin' happens jus' thuh way it's supposed ta happen. 'Course, thuh results ain't always what yuh 'spect 'em ta be. That Parkah Winthrop showah were some prankstah, as I guess."

"Did you know this all the time?"

Ezekiel swung himself upward into his pickup truck and closed the door. He looked at me with a grin. "I guess yuh can be supposin' that," he said. He drove off down the dirt road with a flourish of dust behind him.

As for Elvin Nab, I sometimes think the restless spirit of Parker Winthrop has departed him, as if finally put to rest by this last and greatest feat of detonative artistry. For example, Elvin seems to have lost interest in explosives. Even more, he's now gainfully employed — from time to time — and that, at least, is a change for the better. He comes to my pastures twice a week to do mowing and other odd jobs. Yet I wonder about that, too.

Some days I see him resting a bit on that rise at the distant edge of the meadow. He stands there, gazing toward the center of the cirque where the old house once stood and where the new house now stands. His one good eye tilts upward to the heavens, and his face, still filled with jowls and bearded stubble, is lifted in a soft and childlike smile.

Is he remembering his great feat?

Or is he thinking about something new?

It makes me tremble just thinking about it.

Obsequies for a Tightwad

I teach history in a rural high school. During the summer, I work at odd jobs in order to make ends meet. Mostly they don't. I once had a neighbor named Larry Monroe. He had retired to his old family homestead, which was down the road about half a mile from me. He was short and stocky and had a huge belly that hung down over his belt. His eyes were tiny blue dots under pale and virtually nonexistent eyebrows, and his forehead, which seemed to stretch all the way to the back of his head, always looked as if it was severely sunburnt. The skin often flaked on his forehead, which was not protected by the baseball hat that was perpetually tipped back so far on his head that the visor stood straight up in the air.

Before his retirement, he was a stockbroker in Boston. Often, he liked to boast that he was worth, as he would put it, "a million, a couple of times over." Then he would lean back, laugh, show his perfectly even, yellow teeth, and shout "Eee-yah!"

When he died, I buried him. It was the least I could do. *I mean, the very least.*

Larry had a way of showing up at dinnertime on Sunday. Again and again, over the years, his shabby pickup truck would rattle up our dirt road in a puff of dust just as my wife was pulling the diminutive weekly roast out of the oven. It was difficult to send him away. He would look sad, rather like a stray dog, until the inevitable invitation was offered. Then he would beam. We learned to make do with small portions, as Larry energetically speared piece after piece from the platter with his fork, exclaiming "Eee-yah!" as he landed them on his plate. Then he gobbled down remorselessly what we'd hoped to serve as leftovers for most of the coming week. I never knew him to bring anything to supplement the dinner, as guests so often do. A bottle of wine, perhaps, or a six-pack of beer would have been nice. But no—he never brought anything. He was always "unexpected" in a sense and came empty-handed. Also, since we didn't have dinner at a fixed hour of the day, we could never quite figure out how he knew when to come. "He can smell Sunday dinner all the way over at his house," my wife used to say. She hated him.

He was a lonely man. His wife, a Boston woman, had divorced him so long ago that she was scarcely a memory anymore. They had no children. His mother had died when he was in college, and his father, after many years in an old-folks home, had finally passed away. This had happened fairly recently—in the past decade or so—and Larry was relieved. He used to complain that the old-folks home had cost him "an arm and a leg." That was one of his favorite expressions, by the way. Everything had a way of costing him "an arm and a leg." He had some distant relatives who lived in Florida, but they never came to see him. I think I was one of the few people Larry actually knew.

In all my years of running errands for Larry, of listening to the endless, self-congratulatory chatter about his financial dealings, and of helping him in the dozens of little emergencies that rural life has a way of producing, I never knew him to give me anything—except once. It was half a bottle of beer, and the beer was flat. This happened on an unusually hot late-April afternoon. I had received a panic-stricken telephone call from him asking me to rush over to his place to help him bring a brush fire under control. I jumped into my car with my two fire extinguishers, a shovel, and a rake and drove as fast as I could. After I arrived, I spent the next forty-five minutes in a desperate struggle against the widening circle of flames that crept ever closer, on one side, to his house and, on the other side, to a dry stretch of woodland. Meanwhile, rake in hand, he ran back and forth around the outer perimeter of the fire and jumped up and down in the smoky background like an enormous ruffed grouse protecting its territory and uttering incomprehensible cries. Of course, he did nothing to help me fight the flames.

When it was all over, he thanked me.

My clothing was ruined, my shoes were burnt, I was wet and grimy with sweat and ash, and I was choking on all the smoke I had inhaled. But I had prevented his house from burning down. I also had prevented a potentially quite serious forest fire. I told him he should have called the volunteer fire department, but he told me that he had started the brush fire without a permit, in which case he would have had to pay for the expense of the fire department in putting out the fire, as well as pay a substantial fine to the local fire warden. That would have cost "an arm and a leg." Then he leaned back, laughed, showed his even yellow teeth, and shouted his triumphant "Eee-yah!"

Afterward, he fetched the half-consumed bottle of beer from the refrigerator in the house. He conferred it upon me with the utmost solemnity. As I said, the beer was flat. He did offer to have my fire extinguishers refilled, but he never came through on his offer.

I received another call from him one night. School starts at six-thirty each morning, so I need to go to bed early. I was already in my pajamas when the telephone rang. Larry's voice had a peculiar tone to it, as if he was about to embark on some clandestine mission of the greatest urgency. As it turned out, he was ... and I had been, without my consent ... recruited to be part of it. He told me to wear old, dark clothes. I didn't ask any questions—I don't know why; over my wife's protestations, I dressed in the appropriate clothes and drove to his house. It was an unusually bright, moonlit night.

When I arrived, I was astonished to see him decked out in what looked like some old army fatigues that must have been used in the First World War (which his father had served in), and his face was covered with oily-looking camouflage. He insisted that I smear my face with the same gruesome concoction. He also had a sack filled with implements. Then he lifted an old coffee tin ceremoniously out of a wooden box and showed it to me, saying, "Look at this!"

"It's an old coffee tin," I said. The brand name—I think it was S. S. Pierce—was hardly recognizable.

"Ha!" he said, grinning with all his even yellow teeth. "That's what you may think! But you're wrong. This is my father."

I was a little stunned. He explained: "My father's ashes are in this coffee tin. I've never buried them."

"Why not?" I asked.

"My family has owned a burial plot in the cemetery at Piper's Landing for three generations. I want to bury him there. He's been dead these past ten years. So, I figured it was about time."

"Why tonight?"

"Because the moon is out. It will give us the light we need."

"But why do it at night in the first place?"

"Because I don't want anyone to know I'm doing it."

"Why not?"

"Because there's a fee involved for a burial. Also, they'll hold me up for thirty years of unpaid maintenance costs. And they ..."

He hesitated.

I pressed my inquiry. "And they ...?" I repeated.

"They'd charge an arm and a leg," he responded.

I knew that that settled everything. Please don't ask me how I got involved in what followed. It's all like a dream. Sometimes I wonder if it really happened. But since it would all happen again at a later time, and, I regret to say, at my own initiative, I know it was real.

We drove in Larry's truck to an area of woods near the cemetery. When we arrived, Larry unloaded some pine boughs from the back of the truck and arranged them around the truck in order to "disguise" it. I didn't see why this was necessary, but he was intent upon following each step of the process exactly as he had planned it. My job was to carry the coffee tin and a flashlight, though the flashlight was not to be turned on unless an emergency called for it. We walked the rest of the way through the woods around to the back of the cemetery. At the cemetery, we lay down on the ground and crawled along the turf on our stomachs. Larry gave me little signals as we went along to stay flat and be less noisy. He obviously took this "operation" very seriously and must have envisioned us as commandos of some sort penetrating an enemy camp. I had been aware that he was fond of war movies.

We arrived at the family grave. We looked off into the moonlit distance at a house that stood at the far end of the cemetery. This was Widow Carberry's place. She had a reputation for sitting in her rocking chair by an upstairs window and exercising her rather morbid sensibilities by staring out all night over the cemetery. The opinion in the neighborhood was that she was making sure that the spirit of her deceased husband was not up to some sort of untoward shenanigans. Other than the occasional passing automobile on the nearby road, she was our major worry.

At the gravesite, Larry produced a rather long hunting knife from his sack and cut a small, square, deep incision into the turf. He lifted the turf carefully off the soil beneath it, being sure to keep the matted root structure intact. He did it so skillfully that I wondered if he had been practicing this procedure for a while. He drew a trowel from the sack and dug a hole in the ground, placing the dirt in a plastic sandbox bucket he'd brought in the sack for this purpose. He took the coffee tin from my hands and slid it down into the hole, replacing the dirt and packing it in solidly around the tin. "Six inches down," he whispered. "Hardly six feet, but at least I don't have to rent a backhoe to do it." I didn't bother to ask how much that would cost, for his answer would have been predictable: "An arm and a leg." Meanwhile I watched Widow Carberry's window with some anxiety, since the light was on, but I could see no sign of her. I could only make out the high back of her rocking chair. Finally, Larry refitted the piece of turf into its place. It was a perfect job. No one would ever know there had been an interment that night. We crawled back to the woods. When we arrived at the truck, Larry put the pine boughs into the back and leaned against a front fender. I couldn't see him clearly in the darkness, but I could hear him exclaim, with obvious satisfaction, "Eee-yah!"

Several years passed.

One year my wife threw him out of the house during Sunday dinner, so he never came back for that again. I forget what he did to merit this summary dismissal; I think that, in a moment of forgetfulness, he forked the entire roast, as yet uncarved, and dumped it whole onto his plate. His "Eee-yah" was cut short by my wife's infamous "wild Indian" shriek. The next moment he was gone.

Another year, Larry did an unlikely sort of thing by joining up with a citizens' group; however, the purpose of the group was not so unlikely for him. Its job was to get the school board to lower teachers' salaries. I suppose, as a teacher, I should have been offended, but I wasn't. I knew better than anyone how wasteful the school was and how most of the teachers had given up trying to teach the students anything. But the citizens' group didn't know this and wouldn't have cared if they did. All they cared about was their tax bills. In fact, I sympathized with them, knowing how poor many of them were. But Larry wasn't poor.

Through all this, he acted as if I were not in any way involved or affected by the activities of his citizens' group. In fact, he would sometimes say directly to me, "These damn teachers cost an arm and a leg!" His greed was wonderfully innocent.

Then one day he died. I don't know how it happened. Mrs. Cormier said that she saw him driving his truck along the landfill road when he stopped, got out of the truck, and walked crazily through a nearby orchard until he came to an old grazing pond. Mrs. Cormier pulled her car over and followed him into the orchard. Amid the cattails and pussy willows, he plopped down dead in the shallows of the pond. Mrs. Cormier went off for help. The volunteer emergency squad took over from there.

What happened after that is hard to say. People claim his relatives from Florida showed up, put his property on the market, made a fortune, and took off with his money. It was millions — there was no question of that. There were no visiting hours, no funeral, no memorial, not even an obituary in the local paper — nothing that I ever heard of.

A few months later, I got an angry telephone call from Reardon's Funeral Parlor over in Rollinsville. They told me they had three things: my telephone number, an unpaid cremation bill, and some ashes. What was I going to do about it? I came to an agreement about the bill — yes, it cost me some money. They wanted to sell me an urn for the ashes, but I told them I couldn't afford it. It would cost — well, *it would cost an arm and a leg*. What should they put the ashes in? "Anything you've got around," I said.

When I came to fetch the ashes, they had them placed in a coffee tin. I think it may have been Maxwell House.

One moonlit night in early autumn, attired in dark clothes and with camouflage on my face, I drove to the cemetery. Once again, I crawled in on my stomach, carrying the coffee tin and everything else I would need for the interment. I arrived at the gravesite. In the distance I saw the auspicious figure of Widow Carberry rocking back and forth in the dim light by her window. I cut the turf carefully away, dug the hole using a trowel and a plastic pail, and buried the tin, replacing everything exactly as it had been. I knew that Larry would have been pleased.

I patted the turf once again in a farewell gesture as I turned to crawl out of the cemetery. It was the closest I could come to some sort of ceremony, a eulogy even, befitting the occasion. "Goodbye, Larry Monroe. You were a fine old fellow after all, weren't you? *Weren't you?*"

Somewhere, somehow, in the back of my mind, I heard in reply, "Eee-yah!"

A Good Neighbor

"He is not, in any case, what could be called, even in the most attenuated sense of the term, 'a good neighbor,'" Prof. Polson concluded, taking a deep draw on his carved briar pipe and exhaling a cloud of richly aromatic smoke.

Prof. Polson's face glowed like a pipe bowl full of fiery embers. His rotund, red-cheeked face was surrounded by a flaming scarlet mass of beard and hair. He wore a bright-red hunting jacket and trousers and leaned against a red brick mantelpiece, under which a cheery orange-red fire blazed in the hearth. A silvery-red Irish setter slept at his feet. Outside the windows, the wind gently whirled the bright ruddy leaves of a Vermont autumn across the front yard. Prof. Polson's wife, Doris, sat in a chair near the fireplace and gazed absentmindedly into the flames. She had heard the story at least a dozen times in the past few days. Even more, she had lived through it. She was dressed in green.

Prof. Polson pointed the end of his pipe at me and continued: "Of course, my observations on the behavior of the much-flaunted northern New Englander have led me to the view that any sensible talk of 'neighborliness,' or of what it means to be 'a good neighbor,' is largely unintelligible to the locals. The failure of the northern New Englander to understand—at any level, mind you—what it means to be an active and participating member of a community is as marked as it is in the marginal, even the criminal, elements of a more adequately socialized populace. Yes, I should even go as far as to say that Jeff Kearsarge, in any other setting, would have all the antisocial propensities of a common criminal."

"Oh, that's going a bit far, isn't it?" Doris suddenly exclaimed. "I mean, all he wanted to do was shoot my horse."

Doris originally came from Georgia. She didn't like Jeffrey Kearsarge any more than her husband did, and any critique of the "Yankee" found a sympathetic ear with her. It bothered her that sometimes she felt she understood these contemptible "locals," precisely because, somehow, she was from Georgia. But Doris was not only bored with the story. She was equally bored with the lecture that inevitably followed it.

Prof. Polson was, as usual, unperturbed by his wife's interruption. He took another draw on his pipe, exhaled slowly, and appeared to sink into a period of thoughtful silence. Having known him for years, I realized that it was probably more a reverie than a thoughtful silence that occupied his mind—a reverie perhaps of Irish setters and flaming hearths surrounded by the lavish beauty of a New England autumn. It's strange how, even when some dreams are fulfilled, you continue to long for them anyway. I suspected that was the case with Prof. Polson, who had attained all that he had dreamed of—the degree in sociology from a world-famous university, a job for the rest of his life at a prestigious rural college with a picturesque campus located in the adjoining township, a white "colonial" house overlooking pastures and fieldstone walls with the Green Mountains in the background, a wife who shared most, though not all, of his self-consciously fashionable convictions, a hearth blazing with applewood in the autumn, and an Irish setter at his feet. He had everything—even a horse, a sprightly Appaloosa mare, to adorn his front pasture, to occupy his newly constructed stable, and to provide his wife with something to look after.

But Prof. Polson, for all that, was a disgruntled man, and the horse incident had simply brought to the fore what had gone irrevocably wrong with his dreams: his New England paradise was filled with people he didn't like.

"Jeffrey Kearsarge," he blurted out. "Now he's as good an example as one could find of the kind of regressive, reactionary mentality of the locals: 'Give me my land, give me my gun, and the hell with the rest of the world!' There you have it—Jeffrey Kearsarge and all his kind wrapped up in a nutshell."

Again, he pointed his pipe at me.

I assumed it was something he did rather regularly in his classroom. There was passion in his voice. "But Kearsarge is even worse. Who else in this town would even get close to Pete Sorbor, the worst scum turned up — or rather, turned out — by the families who live up in the Notch behind the Abenaki range?" Prof. Polson shuddered.

I was accustomed to the kind of abhorrence for the rural poor shown by Prof. Polson. The summer visitors, the skiers in winter, the colony of the urbane who lived scattered about the college in various townships, the well-heeled students at the college all shared this abhorrence. They interpreted the awkward, inarticulate cheerfulness of the people "from the Notch" as an arrogance that was calculated and threatening.

Pete Sorbor had been seen as the worst of the lot because he had been a loner who no longer lived in the Notch but, rather, in a small, rubbish-filled shack by the river and who often drove around in an old pickup truck without any apparent purpose. He was mentally handicapped, an alcoholic, and a bent figure of a man who had lost his teeth and whose gums were perpetually inflamed by some grotesque disease. He had died of cancer — cancer of the jaw — the previous year. Jeffrey Kearsarge's association with him during the last years of his life had been a mystery to all the townspeople.

Prof. Polson emptied his pipe into the fireplace by striking it against his cupped hand and placed it in a pipe stand on the mantelpiece. He looked at Doris and said, "Well, my dear, you still have the horse. We can consider ourselves fortunate for that."

It was midafternoon when, having heard the full account of what had happened between the Polsons and Jeffrey Kearsarge, I left the Polson place and drove down the road about a half mile to where Jeffrey and his wife, Edna, maintained their small farm. My property was immediately adjacent to the Kearsarge land; we'd been neighbors for almost fifteen years and had always had a good relationship. Since a fairly sizable area of woodlands, belonging mostly to me, separated our two houses, I granted permission to Jeffrey to hunt on my land. He did this, usually with some success, bringing me a haunch of venison each year for Christmas dinner and, more importantly, keeping other hunters away. There could be no question but that encountering

Jeffrey in the middle of the woods during hunting season would be — and, indeed, had been for a number of unwitting trespassers — an intimidating experience. I was glad I was the one to benefit from it, since, after a few years, the inexperienced and often incompetent hunters from downcountry were disinclined to come anywhere near my woodlands. In many other ways, Jeffrey has been an important help for me; he taught me a great deal about living in the mountains and in the cold winters. Under the circumstances, I was a bit surprised by Prof. Polson's story and by his assessment of Jeffrey's character.

I pulled onto the dirt road that led up to the Kearsarge farm. I was interested in hearing the other side of the story. But my ostensible reason for coming was to renew, as I felt we should each year, our understanding about the hunting arrangements. I saw Jeffrey out behind his barn, firing arrows from his new compound bow into a nearby tree. He was a short, lean, bony man, as taut as the bowstring he was pulling back to discharge the arrows that, clustered closely together in the knot of a severed bough, attested to the accuracy of his aim. Edna was not far away. She was watering the horse, the pony, and the donkey that lived in the small stable nearby. The farm looked like an actual farm, not like the peculiar simulacra of farms that Prof. Polson, and even I, had created, which corresponded more to calendar or glossy magazine pictures of country homes.

Jeffrey, as ever, was glad to see me. He put aside his bow and walked out to greet me. We always shook hands. Edna waved at me from the stable. We talked a bit about the weather — the degree of frost achieved during autumn nights never failed to be a matter of some conversation among people in the area. Then we talked about hunting, and soon our usual agreement was bound and settled for another season. I was uneasy about broaching the question of the Polsons' horse, so I began by asking about his own livestock.

He answered, "Well, they survived, but it took some doin' ta make 'em survive. Look at thuh pony!"

I looked. I saw that the pony had several deep cuts in his side, and one leg, being held up off the ground as the pony stood in the field, was seriously bruised.

"That ain't nothin' compared ta thuh donkey. An' thuh horse is thuh worst hurt a' all. I couldn't get thuh Polsons ta understand what was goin' on. He refused ta believe it. Doris had a lot more sense 'bout it. That horse is a devil. Yuh wanna beer?"

"Sure," I answered.

Jeffrey brought two beers from the farmhouse, and we drank them while we talked. He let me know that he would have to be off in a few minutes to meet one of his cousins at the local gun shop. He often went bear hunting with his cousin up in the Abenaki range.

After a long swig of cold beer, he continued with the story: "I tol' thuh Polsons that theyah horse didn't need no sheltah this time a' year, at least not fur a couple a' weeks yet. As long as they had a fenced-in pasture, thuh horse would take care a' herself 'til thuh stable got finished—an' t'were almost done, wern't it? But no, they insisted thuh poor crittah needed a roof ovah her head durin' thuh night, and would I look aftah her 'til thuh stable at least had a roof on it? Well, yuh know me—I agreed, 'gainst my bettah judgment, an' we brought her ovah heyah an' put her in my stable."

Jeffrey looked at the ground a bit, and then he said, "Quickah than yuh can shake a fist at it, all hell broke loose. That horse began bitin' an' kickin' thuh dickens outah mine. My crittahs are ol' an' not so likely ta fight back 'gainst a windstorm like that. So, I call Prof. Polson an' ask 'im ta come an' take her away. Theyah wern't no hard feelin's or nothin' like that. Horses are horses, an' they don't always act thuh way we'll be wantin' 'em ta. That were all.

"But I still can't figgah what else Prof. Polson thought that I or anyone else could do. Yuh can't set a bunch a' livestock down tagethah an' say ta 'em, 'Now come on, yuh guys, let's jus' talk ovah what's botherin' us an' get this settled once an' fur all.' Horses ain't humans, an' they jus' ain't goin' ta go in fur that kinda thin'. Yuh can scare 'em, or force 'em, or jus' plain make 'em do what yuh want 'em ta do, but yuh can't bring in some damned consultants with some kinda degrees in management or somethin' like that, an' manipulate 'em inta doin' what yuh might happen ta think is best. That's fur humans, or at least fur humans who let 'emselves be pushed 'roun' without wantin' ta know they're bein' pushed 'roun'. But that's not fur animals."

I was a little surprised at that final observation, but it was typical for Jeffrey. I often thought that his world was defined by four or five townships in the local area, and not much beyond that. But, again and again, he astonished me by what he had read and what he knew about. His house was littered with books and magazines, often tumbled together in stacks, not lined up, on bookshelves. Hunting magazines, *National Geographic*, rifle catalogues, and other well-thumbed periodicals were mixed together with books about history, about travel, and even about economics. He also treasured a number of items he had brought back with him from Japan when he was stationed there with the service. One day I unexpectedly called at his house, only to be ushered by Edna into the living room, where I saw Jeffrey sitting cross-legged on a floor mat dressed in an elaborately embroidered robe. I joined him on his floor mat, and we drank warm sake together and discussed the news, but never with any allusion to his unusual attire or why he had it on at the moment.

"But thuh Polsons nevah came ta get thuh horse," Jeffrey went on. "Finally, aftah a couple a' days a' askin' again an' again, I called up an' I jus' plain tol' thuh Polsons that they would have ta come ovah an' get theyah horse, once an' fur all. I asked 'em as nice as I could. But no result. Prof. Polson still says ta me on thuh phone, 'Now c'mon, Jeff, ain't yuh bein' just a bit touchy 'bout this? Them horses'll work it out 'mong 'emselves.' Then I had it. I says, as calmly as evah, 'Prof. Polson, yowah horse is out ta kick my crittahs ta death. Now eithah yuh or Doris gets ovah heyah within fifteen minutes a' this call, or I shoot dead yowah animal.' 'Yuh're kiddin',' he says. I says, 'I'm goin' out an' sittin' on thuh ol' stump in thuh middle a' thuh pasture with my Winchestah on my knees an' a couple a' cartridges, an' in fifteen minutes I shoot.'"

Jeffrey smiled. He finished off his beer in one great draught. "I don't like ta make a joke outa' this. It were serious business, an' I wern't lyin' when I said what I were aimin' ta do. An' I don't like ta shoot what could be a mighty fine horse if someone would make thuh effurt ta look aftah her properly. But I got my own ta look aftah, an' Prof. Polson jus' wern't like as ta mind that at all. Still, I think it's funny how a lot a' people think that make-believe thin's are real an' real thin's are make-believe, an' how confused they are when thuh real thin' gets in front a' 'em. Like a gun. Like someone plannin' ta use it. Like thin's havin' results. I mean really final results, which sometimes means somethin' bein' dead aftahward. All a' that jus' ain't supposed ta be real. But it's thuh most real thin' theyah is.

"Well, thuh two a' 'em got ovah heyah in no time at all, Doris carryin' a haltah ta lead thuh horse back an' bein' pretty seriously worried. She's no fool. But Prof. Polson were all smiles, an' says, 'Now, Jeff, I know yuh'd nevah do nothin' like that.' He looks at my rifle like it were some kinda copperhead snake I was holdin' in my hand with a life a' its own.

"I says, 'Yuh bet I would.' I cocked thuh Winchestah, pointed it up inta thuh aiyah, an' fiyad. Hell, thuh two a' 'em musta jumped ten feet off thuh groun'. They didn't say anothah word; they went as yellah as fresh Guernsey cream in a pail, an' within a minute or two, they were in that pasture tryin' ta get hold a' that crazy horse. It practically kicked 'em ta death, too. Actually, I got ta admit, it were kinda' funny watchin' 'em runnin' 'roun' aftah that hoofed whirlwind, an' then runnin' away from her when she charged 'em an' tried ta trample 'em. Remembah 'em ol' Buster Keaton movies with 'im dartin' in an' outa' one place or anothah? Well, it were jus' like somethin' you would a' seen in that. But Doris did get control a' thuh sity'ashun, finally, while Prof. Polson spent most a' his time hidin' behind a tree an' a-quakin' in his boots. Fine boots, too; I wondah where he bought 'em. Not thuh kinda thing fur steppin' inta a pile a' horse manure, I'd say. Fine horse as well; it would 'a been a shame if anythin' had happened ta her."

"You would have shot it?" I asked.

" 'Course I would. Would yuh have preferred me ta be a liar?"

"No, I wouldn't."

"I figgah Prof. Polson would. I think he thinks that's thuh way ta get thin's done in this world is ta lie 'bout 'em. Naturally, he then figgahs ever'body must lie. I wondah what he teaches 'em students at thuh college 'bout these things. I figgah not much. They probably know all a' that already. That's prob'ly how they got inta that school in thuh furst place. Anyhow, if I had gone an' made an empty threat, it would a' jus' made Prof. Polson even more ornery than evah, 'im thinkin' that, with jus' thuh right words an' thuh right tone a' voice, he could wiggle outa anythin' he evah wanted ta wiggle outa."

At this, Jeffrey excused himself. He urged me to take my time and finish the beer. Then he drove off in his pickup truck. I watched the dust curl up behind his back fenders as he disappeared down the dirt road.

Edna came over to me. She shook her head. "Jeff ain't an easy man, my husband, but he's a good 'un," she said.

I turned to her. "Edna, you know him best. I don't suppose you might think it was too nosy if I asked you something about Jeff that maybe you could answer and that I've been wondering about for a long time?"

"Well, yuh can try, an' if I think it's too nosy, I jus' won't ansah," she laughed.

"I've been wondering about his friendship with old Pete Sorbor, who died last year—you remember Pete, the man who lived down next to the river by himself?"

"Who could evah furget Pete? I guess a lot a' people been wonderin' thuh same thin' yuh been wonderin', but Jeff always asked me not ta get inta it too much with othahs. But fur yuh—being as close as yuh'are—I think it's all right. Anyway, theyah wern't no friendship between Pete an' Jeff. In fact, Jeff didn't like 'im much at all."

"But why was he down at that cabin so often in the final year of Pete's life?"

Edna replied, "Well, Jeff had done a lot fur Pete—tryin' ta get 'im work, an' even givin' 'im work 'roun' heyah off an' on, though theyah wern't much Pete could do, or would do. Then Pete got sick, so sick he couldn't move, an' Jeff took him ta thuh hospital in Hanovah a bunch a' times an' even down ta a clinic in Bahston. But nothin' would help. Cansah spread all through Pete's jaw an' throat an' gums. Jeff jus' took care a' him through that final year 'til thuh day he died."

"He must have really felt sorry for poor old Pete," I remarked.

"'Poor ol' Pete' nothin'! Jeff nevah felt sorry fur 'im. Pete wern't too bright an' all that, but theyah's many a good man an' many a good woman in this world who ain't any brighter than he were who made a decent life fur 'emselves. Jeff always said that Pete brought down upon himself his own troubles. Heck, he didn't feel sorry fur Pete at all!"

"Then how could he have liked taking care of him like that?"

"Liked?" Edna looked at me in a puzzled way. "He nevah liked what he was doin'. He jus' did it. He may've seen that he were thuh only person 'roun' heyah who could a' done it. I know I couldn't a'. I once tried ta walk inta Pete's shack ta find where Jeff were, an' it smelled like a slaughtered pig had been a-hangin' in theyah fur thuh last month. Jeff were thuh only one 'roun' heyah who had a strong enough stomach, as I guess."

"But then why did he do it?" I asked. "Why did Jeff do all of that?"

Edna looked at me again. "'Cuz he had ta, that's all," she said. "Theyah are certain thin's folks gotta do whethah they want ta do 'em or not. I'm surprised at yuh."

"Surprised?"

"Don't yuh know what it means ta be a good neighbah?"

"I'm not sure I really know. Prof. Polson up the road seems to know all about what it means to be a good neighbor."

"Well, I'm not showah he really knows, an' I'm not showah I really know eithah, least not in thuh way yuh can talk 'bout it. Jeff's not much of a talker, but I figgah he knows what a good neighbah is supposed ta do. An' that's jus' what he went an' did. I don't think theyah is anyone in thuh world so foolish who wouldn't know right off about Jeff."

"Know what?" I asked.

"That Jeff is everthin' that's meant by bein' a good neighbah."

The Coming of the Lord

D amn Sir William! Damn his cheeses and all the fuss he makes over them! Damn his squinting eyes, his meddling chitchat, and all the rest! He probes me the way he probes his cheeses with that double-tipped cheese knife of his. I don't care what he thinks of me. In fact, I don't even really *know* what he thinks of me. But I do care what Mrs. Quimby thinks of me, or at least what Sir William says she thinks. And you, Laetitia Brownlow, how could you have done this to me, even from beyond the grave? You and your outlandish stories!

First of all, I have to say that contrary to what some individuals would like to believe about me, *I am not some sort of religious fanatic!*

It's just the opposite, and that's what caused the misunderstanding in the first place. I've spent a good deal of my life running away from zealots, fanatics, all-too-eager proselytizers of every stamp. I hate to admit it, even to myself, but there is something about me that *attracts* them. Yes, *attracts* them! I'm sorry about that. I don't doubt for a moment their good intentions; I also don't doubt for a moment that maybe I overreact to some things and perhaps am too hasty in my judgment of others.

But I've been accosted once too often in airports by saffron-robed Hare Krishnas; I've pretended to sleep in Trailways buses to keep a Seventh-day Adventist in the adjoining seat from trying to secure a throne in heaven for me; I've hid in closets when the local committee of the Jehovah's Witnesses knocked at my door; I've had to hang up the telephone quickly during a multitude of solicitations to celestial bliss because I realized that my house was suddenly discovered to be burning down and I needed to call the fire department.

Frankly, there is no end to my list. I was once chased an entire city block by some Hasidic adolescents who were collecting for a summer camp on the Golan Heights. Rosicrucians, Baha'ists, Moonies, Sufi mystics, Enneagram enthusiasts, denizens of witch covens, EST seminar people, and a multitude of others have in turn assaulted my peace and quiet. At college, now so many decades ago, a Mormon who lived in the next room in my dormitory constantly shoved leaflets under my door, usually in the middle of the night. I was even once bashed on the head with a placard carried by an angry Catholic nun protesting something or other in Nicaragua.

But the crowning experience of my life was many years ago in New York City when I was trapped in a stalled elevator for three hours between the sixty-fifth and the sixty-sixth floor of the Empire State Building with a Salvation Army band aboard. They were fine people, all of them, and they were just as nervous as I was about the imminent opportunity of getting to meet our Maker. Besides, there was not much to do in the elevator for those hours but to wait for it either to be fixed or to fall sixty-five and a half stories to certain oblivion. So I understand why they began to play their instruments and continued to play until the elevator was repaired. I understand; but, given that it was all in rather close quarters, I will never forget, I will never forgive, and, most importantly, I will never recover.

All of this explains—to some extent anyway—what happened at Mrs. Quimby's. Sir William simply had no justification to regard it, as he eventually would, with such apparent and sardonically repressed amusement. What he didn't understand is that I've developed something of what the psychologists call a "phobia." There is, indeed, a great deal that I can tolerate. I have no difficulties with Handel's *Messiah* sung at Christmas, or visiting great basilicas in Italy, or looking at Raphael's Madonnas. I have no difficulties with people's ordinary pieties and beliefs. In fact, I share them. It's just something else, a certain something I can hardly define, that does the trick. And then my hands begin to tremble. I break out in a sweat, my feet begin to jerk uncontrollably, my heart beats with such a force that my ears are practically deafened with the thumping, and I often have to … well, I'll confess … run for it.

Sir William, of course, could hardly have known this, in spite of how long we have been associated. And as for Mrs. Quimby—poor Mrs. Quimby, I would be inclined to say, if she were not perhaps one of the strongest persons I've ever met, and if I were not aware that she used that word "poor" to describe me—well, I'll have to apologize to her. I'll have to set things straight.

Not more than a week before all of this happened, Mrs. Quimby's husband, Carl Quimby, had died. Carl had been a caretaker on Laetitia Brownlow's estate on Squam Lake in New Hampshire. In fact, he outlived Laetitia Brownlow by only a week or so.

Carl was a familiar personage to me, traveling as I often did during the summer months from my law offices in Boston to consult with Mrs. Brownlow on her various investment and legal matters. While employed by Mrs. Brownlow, Carl must have spent most of his time raking the pine needles that accumulated on the long gravel drive that curved down through the hemlock woods to the stately lodge that Mrs. Brownlow had built in the decade after her eminent husband's death. Carl would lean on his rake and wave to me as I passed by.

A visit to the lodge was always a pleasure, and Mrs. Brownlow would inevitably entertain me on her screened porch overlooking a broad expanse of the lake. She loved to serve a lunch of poached salmon with egg sauce before discussing business. She also loved to talk for hours, telling what seemed to be a never-ending stream of marvelous stories about her life, about her friends and enemies (mainly imagined, but sometimes real), and about her family. I knew she tended to exaggerate things a bit, but that was what made the stories quite as marvelous as they were. Sometimes she talked about Carl. Here she didn't exaggerate. She knew that Carl had a weak heart but that he insisted nevertheless on working. Light gardening and the patient raking of the driveway were as much as he could handle. She also knew Alice Quimby, his wife, who sometimes came over to help in the house, especially when there were guests. Mrs. Brownlow insisted, and I made the arrangements, to include the Quimbys as beneficiaries in her will.

The death of Mrs. Brownlow, followed so quickly by the demise of her faithful gardener, is what brought me to New Hampshire in the late autumn of that year. The lodge, or "camp," as Mrs. Brownlow had always called her rather commodious establishment, in keeping with the prevailing custom around the lake, had just been closed down for the winter. Soon thereafter, Mrs. Brownlow died quite unexpectedly at her home in Winchester, just outside Boston. Her only daughter, Lady Beatrice, and her husband, Sir William, too late to be at the bedside, came from England for the funeral. Lady Beatrice had to return quickly to England in order to attend some important social engagements. Sir William decided to remain behind to look after the proper arrangements for disposing of the Brownlow properties.

Sir William, it might be said, was your typical American's image of a typical Englishman, especially of the gentleman sort. And Sir William never was at pains to disabuse anyone of his or her cherished stereotypes and played his role in fulfilling them to something like perfection. He even managed to find in Boston a London-style "club" where, on his frequent visits to the States, he could take a room overlooking Boston Common and invite guests to dine with him in impeccably polished elegance. I had not known that such clubs existed on this side of the Atlantic, and I still can't figure out how he managed to find the place. I often suspected, in my more delirious moments over an after-dinner glass of port, that he had invented this "club" in his imagination, and that I had inadvertently become the victim of some astonishing act of hypnosis on his part.

It was at the "club," late on Sunday evening, that Sir William first received the news that Carl had passed away. He called me and asked me to visit Mrs. Quimby as soon as possible. He was delayed by several appointments with real estate agents in Winchester, but he would make the effort to attend to her when he was free of these obligations. He urged me to hurry. I telephoned Mrs. Quimby at once, only to be somewhat surprised by her own resoluteness and calm. She certainly didn't see any cause for hurry and invited me to have lunch with her later in the week.

On an overcast and gloomy Wednesday, with a vague threat of a late autumn snowfall in the air, I drove northward from Boston. My task was to console Mrs. Quimby in her bereavement, to assure her of the immeasurable gratitude felt by the Brownlow family for her and her husband's services over the years, and to inform her that she was generously provided for in Laetitia Brownlow's estate.

I had never met Alice Quimby before. I was aware that the Quimbys' house lay not far from the entrance to Mrs. Brownlow's driveway. It was a small white house, very typical of that part of New Hampshire and probably very old, having been in the Quimby family since the early 1800s. A short, sandy driveway led from the road around a cluster of lilac bushes to the house. Behind the house was an old, rough-timbered barn.

Mrs. Quimby greeted me at the door. She took my coat and hung it on a hanger by the door. I saw immediately in her that kind of woman I can only associate with the hill country of northern New England. She had short gray hair, a slender figure, a face of the most extraordinary clarity and kindliness, and deep eyes that were both lively and serene. I certainly didn't find, as Sir William must have imagined I would, a distraught woman overcome with grief and isolation. To the contrary, she was very happy to see me and eager to bring me into her home.

She led me into a parlor that was small and yet supremely comfortable. Of course, one might find a great deal to complain of: the room certainly was overfurnished, the windows full of glassy knickknacks that on a sunny day would have filled the living room with a multitude of bright colors, and the tastefulness of the braided and hooked rugs scattered everywhere might be questioned. But still it was comfortable in the best sense imaginable. It seemed to come out of some childhood fantasy, some buried memory of what an ideal "grandmother's" domicile on a modest rural farm should be like. The air in the house was sweet and fragrant, filled as it was with the aroma of fresh-baked bread. There was only one discordant note for me: over the mantelpiece was an especially appalling reproduction of Leonardo da Vinci's *Last Supper* painted in garish colors against a background of black velvet. I felt my heart thump one mighty beat, and my hands trembled for a moment.

Soon I was sitting back on a spacious sofa with a cup of tea in my hand, well at my ease. Mrs. Quimby went to the kitchen and then rejoined me. She spoke calmly of her husband's death and assured me that all the funeral arrangements had gone well. She and her husband had been lifelong members in the local Congregational church, and the church group had helped her out in every way possible. I recognized in her one of those people whose often difficult life had been led in such an unassuming and generous way that the regrets, which are such an important part of our grieving for the dead, were simply not present for her. She had loved her husband. Her husband was gone. Her faith told her, and her convictions confirmed, that she would one day rejoin him. It was as simple as that.

I finally decided to speak my piece and had just begun when she interrupted. She looked calmly and steadfastly into my eyes and told me that she knew everything already. I was a little surprised. Without thinking to inquire what it was she knew about, I asked, "How did you know?"

She smiled graciously at me and said with unfaltering words, "The Lord told me so."

I admit there was something of an embarrassed silence on my part. "*Who* told you so?" I asked.

"The Lord," she answered with a delighted smile.

My hands trembled momentarily. "Oh, really," I said. I laughed a bit. "The Lord has his ways."

"He does indeed," she replied, again smiling resolutely at me. "He came last night. He sat right where you're sitting now, and he told me that everything was taken care of."

"Right where I'm sitting?"

"Exactly where you're sitting. He comforted me. He told me all would be well."

My hands began to tremble again, but now the trembling became violent. My heartbeat began to echo loudly in my ears. I quickly placed the teacup, now rattling noisily in its saucer, on a side table, but not without spilling some of the tea on my lap.

She rose from her chair and raced into the kitchen to get a dish towel. When she returned, I was still sitting. I looked nervously at the da Vinci reproduction and then at her. She was as unflustered as ever.

"We must clean you up before the Lord returns," she said with a chuckle.

"What do you mean — returns?" I gasped.

"He's coming for lunch. You see, I've set a place for him."

I looked at the dining table. There were three place settings. Meanwhile, she went to the window and looked up into the sky. "I hope he won't be delayed," she said. "The clouds look so heavy in the sky."

My feet jerked compulsively under me. Great drops of cold sweat ran down my neck. My heartbeat thumped in my ears like the sound of a huge tuba playing bass to "Rock of Ages" as some invisible elevator seemed to drop through a dark, interminable shaft of airports, buses, street corners, placards, doorbells, leaflets, and millions of friendly, pleading, importunate eyes.

She looked again at me. "The Lord is eager to see you. He has something to say to you."

Then I broke.

I don't know the precise moment. I don't know how I went from sitting to standing. But I do know what happened after I was standing.

"Hallelujah, sister!" I shouted. I raised my arms and waved them frantically around. "The Lord is coming! The day of the Lord has come!"

"But I don't think you—" she tried to say something, but I wouldn't listen. I was beyond listening.

"We shall see the glory! Yes, sister, we shall see the glory! Hallelujah!"

"But ..."

Meanwhile I was running for my coat, which I grabbed from the hanger, and bolted through the door. I continued to scream, "Praise the Lord, sister! Make ready for the glory. He will trample out the vineyards ..."

My car lurched violently out of the driveway, practically skidding into another car that apparently was attempting to drive in. I drove for thirty miles before I calmed down at a rest stop on the thruway. I could hardly sleep that night.

The next morning, I received a telephone call at work from Sir William. He invited me over for lunch at his "club." I could hardly refuse. There were certain things he should know before he made the drive to New Hampshire.

The luncheon was as pleasant as it ever was. The dining room of the club was decorated with paintings and carvings of clipper ships and was a celebration of Boston's maritime past. Each table was adorned with a small brass ship's lantern. Sir William sat opposite me dressed in a fashionable gray tweed suit. His lean and now elderly face sported a wiry mustache that quivered significantly whenever he had an important point to make and whenever his gourmet's palate was touched by a particularly appealing flavor. The food was excellent, especially the delicately seasoned New England chowder, followed by baked scrod in lemon-butter sauce. After a dessert of hot Indian pudding (Sir William always had hot Indian pudding for dessert at least once when on a visit to America as a kind of tribute to the American "aborigines," among whom, I had the suspicion, I was included), he insisted on his usual cheese platter. I was accustomed to Sir William's cheese platters and was prepared to suffer through the tiresome protocols it inevitably involved.

Our conversation was deftly held in check by Sir William during the meal. My efforts to bring up my experience with Mrs. Quimby the day before were always diverted back into a discussion of Mrs. Brownlow's properties. Sir William maintained that the house in Winchester should be sold in pretty much the ordinary way. The lodge on Squam Lake would need special considerations: though Laetitia Brownlow had not so specified in her will, she had often expressed a desire to leave the property with its unparalleled view of the lake to an institution of some sort — a college, a charity organization, or whatever. Lady Beatrice was in full agreement with this sentiment. But what sort of place? That was the chief concern.

When the cheese platter arrived, the conversation took a noticeable turn. Sir William began his painstaking probing of the cheeses with his double-tipped knife.

"You are aware, of course, that I finished with the realtors a bit earlier than I had expected on Tuesday and decided to drive to New Hampshire in my rented car somewhat sooner than anticipated. I spent Tuesday night at a motel near the lodge — after a few social visits, of course."

"Oh," I said, being rather surprised at this news.

"Indeed," he replied. He twisted the knife into a slab of brie and bore a small hole into it. He looked into the hole and sniffed the small sample of brie that he had extricated. He put it aside.

"You know, *Mother* was a most remarkable woman," he continued. He always referred to Laetitia Brownlow, his mother-in-law, as "*Mother*," but with such an overtly sarcastic pronunciation that it was quite clear that Mrs. Brownlow was not actually his mother and that he was imitating his wife's form of address and pronunciation. "She loved to hold court on that screened porch of hers looking out on the lake and tell the most delightful stories."

"I know. I've heard many of them."

"Delightful and preposterous. Most of them were made up, you understand. I mean, not made up purely—just exaggerated beyond recognition. But I mean no criticism here. I loved those stories just as much as anyone else did." Sir William was now working on the Gruyère. He poked a little hole inside one of its bigger holes.

"My fondest memories of the lodge are those stories," I said.

"Indeed!" Sir William examined disdainfully the green peppercorns on a piece of chèvre. "You Americans certainly have a thing about peppercorns these days! What a perfectly abominable way to ruin a good piece of cheese," he remarked.

He looked up at me. "You know, old fellow, that it's not easy being an English baronet here in the 'former colonies'—I use the expression 'former colonies' not because I think it's clever to say, nor do I subscribe to some sort of idiotic eccentricity implied by an Englishman using such an expression, but because Americans just adore to hear it said. They worship me and everything I represent. Few Englishmen do anymore, you know. For better or for worse, they have adjusted quite well to living in a democratic society, though we do love to export our postmortem imagery. It so enhances our tourist trade.

"In any event, nowhere in the world have I found such obsequiousness before a title. And what a title, I might add! It has been in my family for only four generations. My great-great-grandfather led some kind of charge in the Crimean War—well, I should say, *may* have led some kind of charge, because there is a measure, should we say, of ambiguity about it. The dispatches may have characterized what was actually a retreat as a charge, except that it was, as it were, in the wrong direction. Luckily (for us), our not-so-hapless Russian adversaries had already abandoned their position, not because they couldn't hold it but because they figured out, apparently, that it was not worth holding, so that whatever it was my great-great-grandfather did looked rather wonderfully victorious. He was not quite ready to own up to exactly what did happen. But there are some rumors about a deathbed recantation. It's all quite potentially embarrassing, but let ambiguities stay ambiguities, I always say."

The Gruyère not having passed muster, he was now turning and prodding the Stilton, sniffing it with his exquisitely practiced nose.

Sir William went on: "Now, this thought brings me back to *Mother*. She did so love the idea that her daughter, her only child and the treasure of her life, had married into — well, we will call it, to use *Mother's* terminology — the 'British aristocracy.' That means, in case you have missed the point, Beatrice married me."

"Ah," I said. But I hadn't missed the point.

"And many of those preposterous stories she told had to do with me. In fact, purely on her own, without consulting any historian, any genealogist, and certainly without either the knowledge or the consent of the British royal family or whoever it is that exercises authority over such matters, she had extended my ancestry back to William the Conqueror and had elevated me to the peerage of the realm."

"The peerage?" I asked, weakly.

"The peerage," he replied with a little nod. "You know, the House of Lords and all that."

"The House of Lords?" I piped again, my throat constricting into a tight little knot.

"Indeed," he said.

He shifted the Stilton to a special part of the plate. Apparently, it had passed some kind of test and was to be reconsidered at a later time. He went on to the Camembert.

"Now, among those who might be expected to ask some impertinent questions," Sir William went on, "*Mother* knew where to stop. But among the local people, whose families had come from Northern England two centuries ago and whose memories, however confused, preserved really a great deal of their historical roots, she knew no limits. It developed into quite a mortifying experience for me to find myself, among the local people in New Hampshire, elevated to something like a duke. I tried to stop it, but to no avail. The people were too kindly, too simple, and too generous to allow what they took to be my excessive modesty to deflect the reverence justly conferred upon me by my unimpeachable ancestry."

Sir William now began to prod a slice of Italian provolone. "Did you know what those people became accustomed to calling me? In fact, they still call me it today."

"No, I don't," I said nervously, though I could already guess what it was.

"Well," he replied, looking sideways at me from his provolone, "they call me, 'the lord.'"

"The lord?" I stammered.

"Thou hast said it."

"Oh dear," I said.

"Oh dear," he echoed. "Oh dear, dear, dear. You know, old fellow, we did so miss you for lunch yesterday. It was a wonderful lunch. Mrs. Quimby, as imperturbable as she is, was upset to see you dash off like that. Did you know that you almost ran into my car on your way out? Hertz Rent-A-Car should not have appreciated that very much."

I sat in silence. I had lost my appetite. All that cheese, now poked and bored with a dozen holes, looked revolting. Sir William seemed to have settled on a wedge of Pont-l'Évêque. He jabbed the knife all the way through it, lifted it from the cheese platter, and transferred it to his plate, but without withdrawing the knife.

"But the worst of it, if you don't mind my saying so, is Mrs. Quimby's impression of you. She had always heard such wonderful things. *Mother* used to say you were the most rational and level-headed person she ever knew." He squinted momentarily at me, his wiry mustache quivering ever so slightly. "I told you she had a way of exaggerating things a great deal."

He returned to his meticulous scrutiny of the Pont-l'Évêque and murmured, "And now, Mrs. Quimby thinks ..."

He hesitated. The wedge of cheese was being readied for some kind of ceremonial *coup de grâce*.

"Yes, thinks what?" I asked.

"It appears that she thinks you are ... what with all that shouting and arm waving and hallelujahs and the like ..."

"Yes?"

"I mean, she was most sympathetic. She even referred to you as a 'poor man.'"

"Go on! What does she think?"

He looked up at me out of the corner of his eyes, suspending the entire wedge of cheese momentarily in front of his anticipating lips, and uttered, "Well, old fellow, since you insist ..."

"I do."

"Well, she thinks you're some sort of religious fanatic."

The entire wedge of cheese disappeared with one great shove into the voracious cavity of his mouth. His mustache contorted into a grizzled arch tilted ominously to one side. His left cheek became monstrously distended. His eyes glittered sarcastically at me.

I fled from the club as soon as I could. On Beacon Street I was followed by two college girls dressed in God knows what, shaking rattles, beads, and bells as they sang Apache chants, passed out leaflets, and asked for money!

Damn Sir William! Damn that cheese! I'll call Mrs. Quimby this afternoon from my office. I'll fix it up with her. She will understand. I know she will understand. As for you, Laetitia Brownlow, tell your stories wherever you are, in Heaven or Hell or Nirvana or in the Third Bardo of the Great Buddha or in the Happy Hunting Ground! Make up whatever you want, but leave me out of it! If you must include me, at least don't tell *this* story. Bad as it is, what would it look like when you got finished with it? After all, I don't want to be too hopelessly embarrassed *before* I get there (assuming, of course, that I get there). And as for the rest of you, I mean all the rest of you, I'll try to get there one way or the other, thank you very much, without your help! If you don't leave me alone, you know what will happen! I mean, now, you do know, don't you?

A Happy Man

Vladimir Orsolov lives in an old farmhouse down the road from us a bit. On warm summer evenings he likes to sit, crossed-legged and motionless, on the lawn under the maple tree in front of his house. The crest of thick silvery hair on his head glows like a medieval helmet in the evening sun. His massive chest is bare. His narrow-set eyes peer over a large angular nose at some mysterious thing in the distance, as if he were a hawk gazing at some far-off prey. His lips are just slightly pursed, as if he's waiting for something, yet the wrinkles around his eyes are smiling. I don't know what he's thinking about when he sits there, or what he's looking at, and I never thought it would be polite to ask. But I do know one thing: he looks as if he's a very happy man.

Vladimir came from Russia many years ago. It's said that he was once a member of one of the great Russian ballet companies—I don't know which one—but that he emigrated to New York (the fellas up at the dump like to say that he "jumped ship"). Eventually he came to our village with the other ballet artists to spend summers here in the White Mountains, performing at the various festivals, rehearsing with the others, and teaching—for he seemed to do a lot of teaching.

Then one autumn, after the summer season was over, he didn't return to New York. Instead, he bought the old Lansdowne house, which had come up for sale. The house was in pretty bad shape and needed a lot of work. But he bought it anyway, and he stayed.

He just stayed. He rebuilt the house. That took him years to do. I don't really know why he stayed—nobody else ever knew either—and I never thought it would be polite to ask.

As I said, the old Lansdowne place was in sorry shape at the time. It's one of those farmhouses from the early part of the 1800s that grew with each successive generation into a series of rambling "ells" and sheds and barns, all connected with ramps and mudrooms, where different branches of the same family could work together yet live in the privacy of their own quarters. In recent generations the farming operation declined, and many family members left the village for the western states. The great flat meadows that once stretched across the entire width of the intervale—with the exception of a few acres immediately around the house—were sold off, and the house became a boarding establishment run by old Nettie Lansdowne herself and occupied by a few aged men living out their lives largely at the expense of the village poor fund. When Nettie died, the elderly men were moved to the county home, and the house was put on the market. It's the sort of place that the local real estate agents—and I think especially of Nestor Barnes in this regard—like to advertise as a "village colonial" in hopes of snaring someone from outside into buying it at an outlandish price.

Vladimir didn't fall for any of that, though. He saw the place—wreck that it was—and offered what it was worth to him, which was about one-fifth the price being asked. The offer was taken, not without some little protest, I suppose. But we still get a laugh about that when the fellas meet at the dump, because Nestor Barnes was so angry.

Now, it would be wrongheaded to think that the local people, myself included, haven't gotten used to the New York dancing crowd when they come up for the summer, because they've been doing it for a long time. What got them coming in the first place, of course, was that the huge wooden hotel on the mountainside just outside of town closed down sometime after the war. It used to cater to people coming up through the Franconia Notch in horse carriages and later in trains. Now they got expressways and just about everything else going through here, and so most of the big hotels this side of the Presidential Range also closed down. I never quite figured out why.

Now everyone has second homes, and skiers have condos, and I guess who really needs those old hotels anymore?

But then the dancer people discovered our hotel and took it over. It was a good place for them to be during the summer, and, as I said, we got used to them pretty quickly. Naturally, it brought a lot of money into the town — not as much as the hotel did in its heyday, but it was welcome.

Vladimir was different, in the first place, just because he stayed. In the second place, we didn't especially expect to see one of the dancer people take to living in the north country the way he did. I don't know how Vladimir learned to handle an axe the way he could, but he put up his wood for that first winter faster than I've seen any of my neighbors ever do. You forget how strong these dancer people are — and Vladimir was strong, as strong as some of the lumbermen who still work the forest reserves up past Lake Umbagog. And then he started working on that house. Did he ever work! I don't know when he slept and when he ate, but, piece by piece and part by part, he put that whole place back together again.

Even long before he was finished — in fact, in the very first summer — he rented out rooms to some of the dancer people who passed through the village at various times. It turned out he was something of a chef, too, and he served up an odd sort of cuisine to his guests — not like Nettie Lansdowne's cooking, I can tell you. And he taught. He fixed up a ballet studio in one of the old milking sheds — they said it was perfect for the job. Beginners, advanced students, even professionals came to work with him for a week or two at a time, lived in his house, ate his meals, and danced. At the end of August they all left, except for Vladimir, who went back to work on his house.

Winters passed. Barns, sheds, outbuildings of every description were hammered and sawed and nailed and painted and divided up into small, comfortable chambers, which were warm and scented with the aged wooden beams and planks. Another studio was built, and some music practice rooms were constructed where the old sheep pens had once been located. The large carriage shed was turned into a dining hall with a special summer kitchen attached to it. Here Vladimir, helped during the summer by a staff of local high school girls, served out his soups made from the fresh cabbages and beets he grew in the gardens behind the house. His place was always rich with the aromas of exotic coffees and teas, brewed at unusual times of the day and served to his guests in shallow cups and tall glasses. We all came to understand, as the years went by, that to lodge at the house of Vladimir Orsolov was considered a privilege of a rare kind and was sought out by people from around the world. I think that every language spoken in the world has been spoken in that house at one time or another.

Curiously, or perhaps not so curiously at all, no else made the same kind of decision that Vladimir made … except for, well … there was Anton, who came from Romania, but he really doesn't count. He stayed for a while in our village — by "a while" I mean for several years. He, too, bought a house — a beat-up old cottage at the edge of the village. But he never did manage to get it in order, despite all the talking he did about what he was going to do. He was friends for a while with Vladimir, but then he bought a pickup truck and began to wear a baseball hat and hang around with the fellas at the dump. He sure did have a lot of good stories about the times back in Romania, and the few things we ever really learned about Vladimir we learned from Anton. But then one day he left, and his house was put up for sale, and that was the last we saw of Anton.

Besides Anton, there was — there is — Titania. She came from Russia. I guess she must have "jumped ship" too.

She came to the hotel one summer. The next summer she stayed for a few weeks at Vladimir's. A year later she stayed the entire summer at Vladimir's — but not just as a guest. She was helping him out. The next year she spent the summer and stayed into the fall. In early November of that fall, she left. In February she returned. She has been living at Vladimir's ever since.

Titania is like so many of the lady dancers — very thin, lithe, and beautiful at a distance, but not so beautiful close up. That's when the taut — maybe the too taut — skin begins to affect you and when the strange glow of the eyes begins to look somehow unhealthy. But I'm no judge of this sort of thing. All I can say is that she's a quiet and elegant lady. My daughter took lessons from her and loved her. They all — her students, that is — love her. That's good enough for me.

I've never known why Titania decided to come back that February. My friend Joel up at the dump said she had a big fall in a performance and felt too ashamed—or maybe was too spooked—to go back to the stage. But how would he know? Joel doesn't know anything: for him, going over to Portland, just because it's in Maine, is like traveling to a foreign country. It makes him nervous.

Others whispered—well, they didn't really whisper, but you know what I mean—that Titania was "romantically involved" with Vladimir. It's strange how in a small village this is all people ever talk about, especially since not a word of it is ever true. I don't think it was true in Vladimir and Titania's case either. I just think that they were too occupied with other things to be all that much occupied with one another. I just think that whatever it was that brought either of them to our village, it had something to do with not wanting to be "involved" anymore with things that made life too complicated. That's what I think it was all about, but I don't really know, and, frankly, I never thought it would be polite to ask.

In any case, Titania stayed. At first, she lived in the old central house with Vladimir. She helped him repair and outfit a wing coming off the first "ell," and here she took up residence—a house, in a sense, of her own.

Then she set up her dancing academy. She called it—now get a load of this name—The White Mountain Institute of Ballet. Isn't that something? I mean here in this little village of ours! You have to understand that this really is "country," in order to get the message of how strange this was—to set up an academy of classical ballet in an area where there are more deer and moose and fox and bobcat around during the winter than human beings—more bear even, but you don't see them in winter.

Anyway, it worked.

The girls—and the boys, too, if you can believe it—came from all over the county to take lessons at her academy. Pretty soon every high school in the north country had some connection with her institute. She taught people around here something that they hadn't known since their grandparents' generation and that the local schools have given up on for a long time now: how to get something done and how to do it right. I mean, if the young folk in the north country are going to learn how to do things the best they can do them, they're going to learn it from Titania and no one else. A few of the girls actually went to schools of dance in New York on scholarships after they had finished with her. But everybody she trained got something special out of it. Meanwhile the parents waited for their children in a room warmed by a gigantic porcelain stove of a type they had never seen before and had strong tea served to them from a huge brass samovar that bubbled in the parlor. There were hot soups and bowls of steaming kasha and even slabs of black bread and cheese served on nights of the cold winter storms, and free lodging for them if the drive home had become too perilous. Vladimir saw to all of that.

It's hard not to think that Titania wasn't the best thing of all for Vladimir, no matter what you want to figure about it. Vladimir's establishment was most active in the summer, as it still is today. But during the winter it did seem kind of empty, even though Vladimir enjoyed his solitude and his work of restoring and building. Eventually that was finished. It needed another tenant—someone who would bring life to it during the other seasons of the year. That Titania did—and does to this very day. I never knew anyone in our village who so completely fills out the times of year with just the right ornamental touches—Christmas and Easter, Halloween and Thanksgiving, the Fourth of July and Flag Day and Columbus Day, the planting and the harvest, and some days we had never heard of, probably from the Old World, I guess. All of these are celebrated in the windows and porches of the old Lansdowne house as if the whole earth somehow had taken up lodging in that place. It's a place filled with the music of peoples and nations and with dancing that never seems to end. For the children of the village, it's a second home—a place of enchantment that never goes away, like one of those fairy-tale ballets that's more like a dream than anything else. For the adults, it reminds them of things they had forgotten about—I don't really know what sorts of things it reminds them of, but they're things that mattered once, back when everything mattered much more than it matters today.

I know that Vladimir likes all this because the wrinkles around his eyes are always smiling. When I drive down the road on summer evenings, I see him sitting there, cross-legged, bare-chested, on his lawn under the maple tree. He seems to be looking into the distance with a contentment I can hardly describe. Often, I've wondered what it is that he's looking at—but I never thought it would be polite to ask. Still, sometimes he notices me when I drive by, and he waves.

I think he's a very happy man.

Two Sisters

This is the story of two sisters whose names were Marcia and Constance. They were tall, slender girls with fine features, and though Marcia was born three years earlier than Constance, they almost looked like twins. I can tell you that more intelligent, more accomplished, and more lovely girls you couldn't find anywhere in the world.

But things didn't turn out too well for them, as you will see. All of this happened quite some time ago. I must warn you that this is an unhappy story—a very unhappy story. If you don't like unhappy stories, you shouldn't read it.

Marcia and Constance grew up in Newton, just outside Boston, back when the town still had a vaguely rural quality about it. Their father was a distinguished lawyer who died while the girls were still children. Their mother was a beautiful woman, remote and elegant, who managed her household in an old-fashioned way. She rarely left her house. Over the years she maintained a small staff of domestic servants—butlers, maids, chauffeurs, gardeners—who performed the various errands that kept the household well supplied or took her daughters to church, or to school, or to the various lessons that girls of that time needed in order to acquire the appropriate social graces. Though she never accepted engagements outside her own home, she did bring many guests into the house and entertained them in regal fashion. She insisted, all of her life, on dressing in the long, beaded, corseted gowns stylish several decades earlier, at the time of her courtship with her late husband. It made her something of an oddity in the social circles of Newton in the 1920s — but, I should add — a pleasant oddity, a living memorial to what so often the young assume to have been a more settled, more ceremonious, and less demanding age.

Marcia and Constance had many friends who enjoyed coming over to their house. To catch a glimpse of their mother moving like an apparition through a distant hallway was considered something of a privilege. It would be talked about for days afterward.

Newton was a wonderful place to grow up in. Tree-lined, shady streets; fine houses adorned by well-groomed gardens and lawns; the succession of seasons, each with its own inimitable charms and delights; the various little village centers here and there throughout the larger township whose pharmacy soda fountains made ideal destinations for leisurely bicycle rides: all of these surrounded the girls with what can only be described as a kind of domestic paradise. The years revolved slowly and dreamily, marked by events that, however commonplace they might be for the experienced eye, were a source of boundless excitement for the girls. Their mother was always there, somewhere in the background, ordering and cherishing their lives with an aloof but patient tenderness. And they got along splendidly together, Marcia and Constance: in their childish games when they were younger, and in whisperings and flutterings when they were older and began attending country-club dances, involving themselves, as they inevitably would, in the whimsical stratagems that so enthrall adolescent hearts.

Their college years were just as good: Marcia went to nearby Wellesley, and Constance, three years later, packed off for what was regarded as somewhat distant Skidmore College. Those years were filled with interesting courses about things such as Gothic cathedrals, French poetry, and Russian novels, and with sporting events and dances on weekends and occasional trips to New York or to other college campuses throughout New England. Warm, golden summers were spent on Cape Cod, when their mother sent them off with half of the domestic help to occupy their old but sunny house perched on a grassy dune overlooking the beach. Things couldn't have been better for them. Never could the future have held out more fecund promises, more assurances that the blissful, dreamy years could go on forever.

It's too bad it didn't.

When Asherton Bricklawn first appeared on the scene, it seemed like the confirmation of everything the girls had ever anticipated. He was handsome, rich, well educated, robust, and full of derring-do—well, with too much of this latter quality, as it would turn out. He went to Harvard, where he was a catcher on the varsity baseball team. A goodly crowd would turn out on sunny afternoons in the spring to see the team play, and especially to see Asherton, because of his dramatic leaps after bunted balls, his playing perilously close to the swings of the batter, and his daredevil pursuits of pop flies. One time, in pursuit of just such a pop fly, he ran full speed into a post of his team's dugout and knocked himself unconscious. He was borne off the field like a slain warrior or like a knight felled in a joust, and the crowd applauded loudly.

Marcia was in that crowd. She could, verily, have swooned. Six months later she was engaged to be married to Asherton Bricklawn. He was certainly the most dashing, the most wonderful man she had ever met. He was so much like the adventurous men you used to read about in the weekly magazines back in those times—who flew open-cockpit aircraft over desert wastelands, who traveled to the heart of Africa, or who climbed the Himalayas and visited the Dalai Lama.

Constance couldn't have been more excited about it, too, or happier for Marcia. The two of them began laying the most detailed plans for an elegant wedding—knowing full well, of course, that their mother would finally plan it all in her own way, in her own house, and do a much better job of it than they could dream of doing.

The engagement turned out to be a long one. Asherton, having graduated from Harvard, was trying to get established in a brokerage firm in downtown Boston. His intelligence and vitality naturally recommended him highly to his superiors, and the way looked clear for a meteoric rise in his profession. But delays occurred. In his first year of work, he was in an automobile accident and was hospitalized for two months during his recovery. He broke both legs the following winter by trying to ski Tuckerman's Ravine in New Hampshire at a time when few attempted to do it on those old-fashioned wooden skis. In the spring, he took up airplane flying and flipped a small biplane upside down on the runway while trying to take off, though he emerged miraculously unscathed by that adventure.

Marcia spent a lot of time that year in hospital rooms and guiding Asherton around in wheelchairs as he urged her continually to run with the wheelchair and send him careening off down a hallway or a lawn or a steep sidewalk. He once even tried to persuade her to let him loose at the top of a staircase in the wheelchair. He would lift his arms and wave his hands and fingers around as if trying to clutch the air above him and cry out, "Marcia, push me, push!"

His lively spirits were irrepressible — irrepressible indeed! Often Marcia, keeping faithful watch at his hospital bedside, had to hear him talking for hours about how unfortunate it was that there was no war for him to go to. He dreamed of charges into hails of machine-gun fire. At his job he did get into serious trouble when he lost a small fortune for an important client of the firm by investing funds in an extremely risky venture, one that his superiors had vigorously warned him against. It's fortunate that he didn't lose his job at the time, for his supervisors decided to give him another chance. New clients were drawn by his verve and good looks. Of course, Asherton didn't really need a job — he had a trust fund that made him independently wealthy.

The wedding finally did occur. It was just as glorious as one could expect, except for when Asherton, grasping a bottle of champagne in one hand and a tall-stemmed glass in the other, climbed up to the roof of the porch and jumped, with a great shout, into the garden fishpond from there. The guests were horrified — most human beings could not have survived such a jump, but Asherton stepped, dripping and laughing, out of the pond still grasping his bottle of champagne, though the tall-stemmed glass had vanished somewhere in the murky waters. A tangle of lily fronds was wrapped about his neck. Marcia tried to laugh but could not. She decided it was time for them to be on their way, and after the bride and groom had changed their clothing, they departed with much fanfare in the open Pierce-Arrow coupe that Asherton liked to drive at breakneck speeds. They were driving north to Maine for their honeymoon at Boothbay Harbor.

Several hours later, they pulled up at a scenic outlook where some rocky cliffs dropped rather abruptly into the sea below. It was early evening, and Asherton said he needed a short rest from the driving. The couple stood at the side of the cliff, arms around each other's waists, and watched the easy rolling of the sea and the breaking of the surf on the rocks far beneath them. Marcia couldn't have been happier; she knew that Asherton, now a married man, wouldn't take so many risks and would settle down to a more reasonably tranquil way of life. Suddenly, Asherton lurched out in front of Marcia, stood teetering at the very brink of the cliff, and raised his arms into the sky, wildly waving his hands and fingers. He cried out, "Marcia, Marcia! Push me! Push me! Push me!" Marcia was terrified; these were words from the wheelchair games he had liked to play, but now the circumstances were too real, too dangerous. She lifted her hands to grab hold of his shoulders so that he wouldn't fall, but, as she made contact with his shoulders, it was like touching off a powerful spring or trap. He was not there anymore — just the sea and sky in front of her. Instantly she heard a thud from the depths below.

It was good that Marcia had Constance to look after her in the first few years after Asherton's death. Marcia was convinced that she had killed her husband on her wedding day. In another way, of course, she knew that this was not true. She had not pushed him; he had jumped. But it didn't matter. She sat for hours on the porch, looking into the distance. Often she imagined Asherton rising up out of that fishpond with a shimmering skein of wet water lilies wreathed gruesomely around him; the image would make her tremble violently. Her life was crushed under a load of remorse and suffering. The girls' mother was as gracious and as remote as ever; she was able to do little to alleviate her daughter's grief.

Then came Bob.

Who could forget Bob? His full name was Bob Shreveman — a graduate of Colgate University and an aspiring estates lawyer. Constance met him at a "mixer" while in her junior year at Skidmore. I don't think anyone ever liked Bob, except for Constance. If there ever was a man who preened himself, it was Bob. He combed his hair; he straightened his tie; he made sure his cuffs came out of his coat sleeves just exactly the proper length; he looked into the mirror at himself from several angles and worried and fussed about himself constantly.

Whenever he was about to sit down, he examined the chair to make sure there was nothing there to stain his suit. He had a clean handkerchief that was perpetually in use, patting this or dusting that or insulting any number of mortified hostesses by wiping their silverware and the rims of their glasses and cups before he would deign to use them. He also went in for extravagant clothing and was fond of long silk scarves that he would sweep dramatically around his neck and let drop almost to his knees on both sides. But Constance had an absolute passion for him because he was so good-looking, so well spoken, so courteous almost to a fault.

Bob gloried in her worship of him; she was his fan club, his adoring audience. He could parade himself up and down in front of her and know that her attentive eyes would appreciate every detail, every finely attuned color and line in his invariably matchless attire.

An occasional doubt about Bob, however, sometimes flickered through Constance's mind. He almost never touched her. He held her hand once after a date, but when her hand became a bit sweaty, he released it abruptly and wiped his own hand with his handkerchief. There were a few kisses now and then, to be sure, but Constance quickly realized that if there were the slightest hint of moisture on her lips, the kiss would be met with repugnance. He also didn't like contact with lipstick—he regarded it as "slimy," which was an important word for him and which he used to describe anything he didn't like. Practically everything was "slimy" for him—and especially anything bodily, wet, warm, earthy, protoplasmic. His obsession with clothes was to keep things covered up, disguised, and out of sight. She also felt hurt sometimes when he wouldn't drink from the same cup she had drunk from or take a bite of a sandwich or cake that she had previously tasted. He was constantly afraid of "germs."

Just about any woman in the world would have dismissed Bob without further ado, but Constance loved him. Perhaps he reminded her of her mother somehow—so reserved, so elegant, so detached. There must be passion, somewhere, under all that reserve, she thought.

They got married. It wasn't a big wedding such as Marcia had. Bob had no friends to speak of, Marcia was just coming back to something like an active life again, and their mother had retreated deeper into the recesses of her aging household. Constance, for her part, was more than ready to depart the household and make a life of her own.

On the wedding night Bob emerged from the bathroom in the hotel suite dressed in a pair of red silk pajamas with a black silk bathrobe. He exuded the most powerful fragrance of *eau de cologne*. After studying himself for some time in a full-length mirror, he walked proudly about the room, turning and posing like a model and basking in his own admiration. Constance knelt on the bed and clapped her hands and giggled. She was practically jumping up and down with excitement. She was dressed in a short nightgown. Her slender arms and legs were bare. She felt so supremely glamorous, as if she were a girl in an advertisement. She just knew that Bob's reserve would turn into the passion she had been longing for so long.

But there was no passion. He wasn't even looking at her. He removed his bathrobe, got into bed, and fell fast asleep.

It was not until two years later, after the marriage had ended, that Constance was able to confide in Marcia about what had happened. She had a difficult time putting it directly. She said that Bob just didn't like anything—well, messy; anything "slimy"; anything that involved getting too close; anything that was not ... not ... sufficiently dressed. She said all of this in tears, in a stumbling and humiliated voice. But Marcia got the message; there had never been a marriage in a physical sense; it had just never happened. Constance, whatever she thought of Bob, could no longer live with his ever-present disgust at her physical existence.

The saddest thing about Constance was that she didn't get over her adoration of Bob for quite a while. For the next three years, Constance lived by herself in an apartment in Boston that overlooked Kenmore Square. She did this solely to be able to see Bob every morning punctually at 8:35 driving his car down Commonwealth Avenue to work. She loved it especially when he would stop at the red light at the intersection of Commonwealth and Beacon Street so that she could have a minute or so to gaze at him. The same viewing was repeated every evening at 5:35 when he returned home from work.

Some seasons of the year were more difficult than others in this regard, for the early winter nights and headlights often made it difficult to see him. But he was always so impeccably dressed, and Constance found it a matter of great curiosity to see what he would wear each day. She came to know all of his various outfits and was delighted to see a new one show up from time to time. In the summer he would drive to work in his convertible, often with one of his long silk scarves trailing in the breeze as he drove. He was so gallant! She organized her entire life around this effort to see him drive by twice a day.

One morning on his way to work, one of those long silk scarves was blown to the side by a gust of wind and got caught in the left rear tire. It reeled in like a fishing line and grabbed hold. It snapped his neck as it yanked him out of the driver's seat and down onto the road. The convertible bolted around to the right and drove into the large front window of a beauty parlor, dragging poor Bob behind it. Luckily, the beauty parlor had not opened up for business yet and no one was hurt.

Constance noted that he didn't appear that day at the intersection, but she was accustomed to his occasional failure to show up. When she read about his accident in the newspapers the following day, she was very sad about it—but not too sad.

In later years she would come to interpret her momentary relief at the news of his death as an expression of satisfaction that some force of destiny had finally exacted a just revenge on the person whose vanity had cast such a malevolent spell over her life. As she grew older, this "spite," as she came to understand her relief, would become a source of endless self-reproach.

In the meantime, the girls' mother had passed away, and Marcia was living alone in the house in Newton, attended by a now substantially diminished staff of domestic servants. Things were getting a bit shabby at this point; the gardens were overgrown with weeds and shrubs; and the fishpond, no doubt deliberately, was allowed to vanish under a heap of dead vegetation that had accumulated on top of it through the years. Despite all this, Constance decided to give up her apartment in Kenmore Square and to move back to live with Marcia. Both were still young women, and it was unfortunate that they resolved to withdraw so prematurely into an isolated life. Financially, they were well off. Inheritances came to them from their mother, as well as from their deceased husbands. Marcia and Constance let themselves be known to the outside world, respectively, as Mrs. Bricklawn and Mrs. Shreveman. Like their mother, they retired into what seemed to be a dignified widowhood, though neither of them — and rightly so — had any sense of having ever actually been married.

As they saw it, they had wounds to heal, though the measures they took to heal them ensured that these wounds would remain open for the rest of their lives. Shortly thereafter, they decided to sell the house in Newton and to live year-round in the old beach house at Cape Cod.

How can I describe the mode of life that they lived now in that tall, lonely beach house in all seasons of the year? Mostly, of course, it was very good — at least good for a decade or so. They inhabited a kind of tense but unreal postscript to a life that had never happened — or more accurately, since most of their conversation dwelled on those beautiful childhood and adolescent years whose memories were made most poignant by recalling the dreams of the future that they once had, it might be proper to say, as paradoxical as it sounds, that they inhabited a prelude to a future that was irrevocably past.

For all of this, they managed to live well together, to enjoy long walks on the beach, the flowers and vegetables they cultivated, their care of the house (for they no longer had servants), their literary excursions, the occasional guest from Boston or New York, the unusual and imaginative cooking they did, their boundless fascination for the seabirds that flew overhead and for the schools of whales that sometimes passed along the coast. Winter, of course, was bleak, but it had its consolations in the cheery fire that burned in the hearth, in the hot cocoa they loved so much, and in the endless stacks of novels they read with passion and discussed from week to week. Curiously, the only season that posed any real difficulty for them was summer, when tourist traffic clogged the local villages, and the beach in front of their house was overrun with bathers carrying noisy radios and leaving behind rubbish strewn over the dunes. In fact, in a moment of what we might call lavish eccentricity, and partly as a reaction to the summer crowds, they decided to have a spacious sundeck built on the roof of their house. Since the house was three stories tall, the venture would involve a rather costly and skillful feat of carpentry. They could use it during the summer, watching the sea from there when it was not so pleasant to go down to the beach. The sundeck finally was built. They called it their "widows' walk" and were amused, initially, by this ironic appropriation of a relatively harmless architectural term to fit the circumstances of their lives. The "widows' walk" was reached by a long wooden staircase and gave a superb view over the dunes to the sea beyond.

In quite another sense, things were not so good between the sisters. The tragedies of their marriages, the remorseless ambiguity of having been, and similarly of not having been, married, occupied their home and their life together like great blocks of silent granite around which they had to move and squeeze and scrape themselves day after day—a vast, unfathomable vacancy as immovable, as impenetrable, as stone.

Because they lived so much in the past, they kept that unspoken vacancy, that unfulfilled promise, continually in mind. At times it would produce tension that would explode in a hail of bitter words between them. But they quickly brought things back under control and were easily reconciled.

Perhaps the most injurious development, however, was their beginning to make jokes about each other's predicament. At first, such a practice might have looked salutary; they were being lighthearted, jocular about matters that preoccupied them too seriously. Certainly a few jokes now and then, some kindly teasing, would help to deflate the burden of those somber feelings that still dominated their lives.

Marcia would express either discontent about things in general, or disapproval about Constance in particular, by invoking the language of Bob and using one of his favorite terms, such as "slimy." She would dress with inordinate attention to detail and press Constance, in a jovial way, to admire and flatter her for her achievement.

Or Constance would dare Marcia to do various things, more ostensibly than actually risky, or act as if she herself was about to engage in some monstrously daredevil act. Then both would laugh and think it was terribly amusing and call each other Mrs. Bricklawn and Mrs. Shreveman in ways that mimicked the voices of the former husbands.

As the years passed, however, such exchanges became less amusing. Marcia began to act and think like Bob and to relate to Constance in the way that Bob had. She began to hate anything bodily, putatively unclean, "slimy." She began to detest her younger sister's physical presence. She would do everything to avoid any contact with her. Personal items belonging to or associated with Constance, such as a toothbrush or a comb or a stray hair, became objects of loathing for her. Marcia also grew inordinately protective of her eating utensils, segregating them meticulously from anything that Constance ever used. Finally, she became almost unbearably timid—afraid to swim, to climb a stepladder, or even to drive a car.

Constance, in turn, became intolerably reckless, taking on the personality of Asherton and acting toward Marcia as he had done. Marcia's abandonment of car driving gave Constance the opportunity she wanted to drive irresponsibly, sometimes spinning the car out onto the beach, getting it stuck in the sand so that the local tow truck would have to recover the car while the rising tide came ever closer and closer to it. Sometimes, when driving with Marcia along the causeway that passed over the salt marshes to the local village, she would bring the car to a screeching halt, leap out of the door and onto the railing of the causeway, and dive from there into the shallow murky waters below with a shriek of delight. On these occasions, Marcia not only would be painfully reminded of similar episodes with Asherton but also would be terrified for Constance's safety.

Even more, Constance took to frightening Marcia with slimy crabs and spiders and garden snakes. She did everything, too, to make herself unpleasant: walking around the house in torn clothes or leaving wet underwear to dry over the kitchen sink. But, worst of all, she would suddenly dare Marcia to push her anywhere, anyhow—from chairs (which she had climbed on specifically and solely for this purpose), from door stoops, from sand dunes, from boating docks—as she grappled the air with wildly twitching fingers.

One summer, an unbearably hot, humid, overcast day settled over a sea as flat and colorless as a tile of gray slate. Not a single breeze stirred the grass on the dunes, and the seabirds were nowhere to be seen. A few knots of tourists dotted the beach here and there, but they seemed as listless and as torpid as the sea. A single radio blared its thumping cacophonous music across the length of the beach. In the midst of this heat, Marcia and Constance decided to mount the wooden stairway to their "widows' walk" in the hope of catching any cooling breeze that might come their way.

Marcia climbed the long flight of stairs with some trepidation, as she now usually did; she held tightly to the railing and wouldn't look down. At the top she lay down on a lounge chair with her eyes closed and rested for a while. She wore a kind of red terry-cloth robe which made her even hotter than she was, but she insisted on wearing it. Body exposure had become repellent to her.

Constance, on the other hand, virtually danced up the stairs and flung her robe aside, sitting down somewhat precariously on the broad railing of the sundeck in her bathing suit. She was sweating profusely. She took a plastic bottle of suntan lotion out of her beach bag and, squeezing some of the lotion into her hand, began rubbing herself all over with the white, oily substance. Marcia opened her eyes for a moment and watched. "Ugh," she said, "how revolting! Do you have to use that stuff?"

Constance shot back, "Begging your pardon, Mrs. Bricklawn, but it's well-known that hazy days like this can give one serious sunburns."

Marcia groaned. "How intolerably hot and slimy you look today, Mrs. Shreveman! Do you have to offend my eyes this way? It's making me feel sick." She closed her eyes again.

"Go ahead and feel sick!" Constance retorted.

"And your body—you're too old for swimsuits like that, Mrs. Shreveman! I would rather look at a decaying fish whose eyes have been plucked out by the gulls!"

Constance glared at Marcia. Tears flooded her eyes.

Suddenly, she tossed the suntan lotion back into her beach bag, jumped up from the railing, and skipped over to the head of the long wooden stairway, and, looking out to the sea, she shrieked, "Push me!" She lifted up her arms and waved her hands and fingers around in the gray sky. "Push me! Push me, Marcia! Marcia, push me!" To make it even worse, she began to teeter back and forth on her heels and toes at the brink of the stairway.

Marcia opened her eyes again. She stared at Constance's glistening back with its streaks of white suntan lotion mixed with sweat. She thought how slippery and gruesome it would be to touch. But an inexplicable rage overwhelmed her. The image of her husband at the edge of the cliff that had so haunted and obsessed her all these years took furious possession of her mind. Even more, though, she was gripped, as so often happened, by a terror for her sister's safety, of seeing her sister tumble off that dangerous perch. Unaccountably, and to her own shock and surprise, she bounded from the lounge chair and tried to grab hold of her sister's shoulders and pull her back, but the momentum of the bound and the slippage of her hands downward on Constance's oily back resulted in a push. It was an unintentional but an actual push this time.

After the thumping and screaming and banging were over, everything was silent. A few bathers on the beach in the distance stood up and looked with astonishment toward the beach house. They were not sure what they had observed and didn't know, at that moment, what to do. Marcia sat at the top of the stairs. She had shrunk into a little ball, her legs pressed up beneath her, her face buried in her knees, her arms wrapped over her head, and her hands tearing at her hair. At the bottom of the stairs, Constance lay sprawled and motionless. Her head was tilted in the coyest, sweetest way. Her neck was grotesquely broken.

Marcia spent the rest of her life in a mental institution. She would spend the day — day after day — weeping and moaning and butting her head against the walls and floor of her room. But it was a very nice place just outside Boston, with courteous and mindful attendants, with flourishing trees and well-tended lawns, with rose gardens and fountains, and with twittering birds fluttering through the trellised arbors, and ... and ... well, enough of this.

I told you that you shouldn't read this story.

Heathertop

"We're going to climb it someday," Robinson would say, gazing out from his veranda at the distant mountain that dominated the northern horizon. "We're going to climb Heathertop."

He would stand by the low stone wall that bordered the veranda, one leg up on the wall itself, his elbows on his knee, and a corncob pipe in his mouth. He would bend around to me, pull the pipe from his mouth, smile in his funny, sideways fashion, his eyes cheerful and just a bit mischievous, and jab the stem of his pipe repeatedly in the direction of the mountain and then at me. "We're going to climb it together someday."

This was our secret, our project, our plan worked out laboriously over the decades, the enduring foundation of our friendship. Robinson's pronouncement on such an occasion was merely a repetition of what he had said a hundred times before; it was the renewal and confirmation of an understanding we'd arrived at years ago. But he always said it as if he had just thought of the idea, as if the idea was as fresh and ingenious and daring as when he first proposed it back in our college years. As it turned out, we never did climb it together. When I finally climbed Heathertop, I climbed it alone.

Heathertop! It still excites me just to utter that word. Almost a century and a half ago the huge mountainous massif at the end of our long valley was given the name of Heathertop by Robinson's great-grandfather, who, it is said, was translating an original Algonquin name for the mountain. It was called Heathertop because the summit of the massif rises just barely above the timberline, and, instead of exposing an outcrop of rocky crags, as might be expected, it's covered by a vigorous alpine heath that blooms throughout the summer with a variety of wildflowers, and, in the spring and fall, glows with the purple-pink hue of spiky heather. In the winter the meadow is encased in a dense white carapace of snow. From the distance where an observer ordinarily views the mountain, this alpine meadow looks like a ceremonial toque or hood of unusual shape whose brightly variegated colors change from week to week, and even sometimes from hour to hour as the bend of the sun in the sky, with its angling rays and deepening shadows, displays ever new shades of color within the changing contours of the meadow. The variation gives the mountain an aura of something alive — of something constantly shifting and ebbing and yet remaining the same in its unalterable repose.

In the autumn, the predominant evergreen of the mountain forests becomes variously streaked and dotted with hues of the pale rich gold and brilliant red and flaming yellows of the deciduous woodlands. In the winter months, Heathertop's flat and icy dome of snow glows a pristine, ferocious white against the piercing blue of a winter morning, or a fiery red and amber during the long, cold twilights when everything else in the landscape has already succumbed to the darkness of the polar night.

During the spring, rains drifting in from the North Atlantic swell its innumerable streams and rapids with racing waters, and mist floats through its upland crests, revealing, even to the experienced eye, depths and hollows in the face of the mountain that one never knew were there before.

On bright summer days, the prevailing westerlies blow billowy clusters of clouds over the great massif, their shadows dappling the vast forested domains in the valleys below. Summer storms sometimes rumble down from its lofty ranges, crackling with thunder and lightning while turbulent gales howl through the gorges that skirt the massif as it blends into the lower valleys. But most of all, when summer breezes are tranquil and filled with the calls of crickets and night birds, of owls and the loons that nest in its mountain ponds, Heathertop is bedecked with its ever-changing coronal of bridal flowers.

From year to year, it summons us. "Come to me," it says. "Be nurtured in the beauty of my days." To live close to Heathertop is to allow your eyes to be drawn up again and again to contemplate its mysteriously changing moods and tones. It's no wonder that the Indian tribes that once hunted and fished in this region regarded it as a sacred mountain. For Robinson, Heathertop was the most important thing in his life.

I first came to know Robinson—everyone, even eventually his wife, always called him simply by his last name—when he lived down the hall from me in my dormitory at college. He occupied a rather spacious room by himself which he outfitted in the most extraordinary way: two sets of antique snow shoes were hung crisscrossed on opposing walls, along with maps of the Allagash wilderness, ski poles, canoe paddles, hunting knives, old knapsacks and canteens, a bow and a quiver of arrows, geological surveys, fishing rods and baskets, frayed posters showing moose and bear, an Indian headdress and a stone-tipped spear with feathers attached to its neck, a tangled cluster of well-worn pitons, carabiners, and climbing ropes, and other odd assortments of outdoor paraphernalia, most of which were decidedly well-worn and looked as if they belonged to a previous age. There was no bed in the room. Rather, there was a tent set up—a brown canvas army tent, with a sleeping bag unrolled on an aluminum camp cot positioned inside. A camp stove stood in front of the tent, and several battered paraffin lanterns were slung from hooks that had been attached to the ceiling over the tent's entrance. On both sides of the one window in the room was a set of crudely fashioned shelves that rose all the way to the ceiling. These were filled mostly with canned goods of all kinds and with books and catalogues about wildlife, botany, American Indian ethnology, geology, wilderness survival, and mountaineering memoirs. Many of the books looked as if they had been published in the early part of the 1900s. Stones were piled up here and there among the books and canned goods. A sizable collection of Indian arrowheads was displayed in little boxes. One shelf housed an array of huge old leather boots, all of them scratched and worn, some with hobnails and others with sharp but rusty glacier spikes still attached to their soles. The highest shelf on either side of the window was surmounted by several not-altogether-respectable exemplars of the taxidermist's art: a moth-eaten beaver on one side stood up and looked over its right shoulder with a distinctly goofy expression on its face (one of its eyes had fallen out);

on the other side was a Canada goose, but its neck was broken, so its head hung down limply at its side and its beak almost touched the surface of the shelf. Opposite the window, a pair of whitetail antlers was mounted over the door that led into the hallway.

One would think that Robinson, in outfitting his room this way, had violated most of the college rules about dorm-room furnishings, especially with all those hooks and nails and pegs driven in everywhere—even into the floor to affix his tent. But a relative of his, in some far-off time, had given the college an enormous land grant in the northern woods, and so I supposed he could get away with anything he wanted. One would also think that, with the canned food, hunting apparatus, and cooking utensils in the room, Robinson fed himself in the midst of this bewildering habitat. But there was no evidence that he did. In fact, he ate at the college cafeteria quite regularly; I don't think that he ever, in his whole life, cooked something for himself. Moreover, I never knew him—despite all his hunting gear—to kill anything other than mosquitoes and blackflies. I heard that he did run over a chipmunk once, by accident, but that he almost overturned his Jeep in the effort to avoid it.

Robinson dressed to fit the scene he had designed in his living quarters. He wore—in any season whatsoever—hunting boots, plaid flannel shirts, and woolen lumberjack pants held up by a pair of bright-red suspenders with shiny brass clasps. He even wore this distinctive garb under his graduation gown at the college commencement. His physique was short and narrow, wiry and taut, nervous and fidgeting all the time, with a swath of molasses-brown hair that was combed sideways over the narrow crest of his head and swung down loosely on the other side. His small eyes always glowed with the look of a little boy who either has done or is about to do something self-consciously naughty—a look that was intensified by his strange smile, which twisted around to the left side of his face, as if he were secretly revealing his smile to one person while concealing it from another. Wherever he went, he had with him a corncob pipe whose mouthpiece he constantly chewed, when he was not using it as a rapidly jabbing pointer, but whose bowl apparently never had tobacco in it and which I never saw him actually smoke.

His conversation was always about the outdoors, about trails and cabins and canoe portages, about camping equipment, about the latest hiking gear, about the habits of wild animals, about great exploits in the wild by adventurers and explorers, about harrowing mountain expeditions and trips to the North Pole and ascents of Mount Everest.

I was interested in all of these things too, though perhaps not as much as he was. I urged him again and again to join our college outing society and to come with us on our various excursions deep into the Maine and New Hampshire wilderness areas. I thought we could benefit from his expertise. But, for some reason, he never had time for this, though I suspected, at least in those early years of our acquaintance, that our club might be beneath such an experienced and dedicated outdoorsman as he so obviously was.

I had images of him going off alone into desolate and lonely wastelands to meet the challenge of survival by himself in the most difficult of circumstances. Yet I was often confused about that; if he went off on such ventures, I didn't know when and where he went, for he always seemed hunkered down in that "wilderness" domicile of his in the dorm, and he never failed to answer when I knocked on his door. Whenever he answered the door, however, he always had the breathless, excited look of a person who had just returned from, or was about to set out for, some remote and invariably untamed locale in the depths of the forest.

His college subject was hydrology—water management—and he planned a career around being a hydrologist in the national forests and timber reserves, though, once again, frankly, I don't know when and how much he studied the subject. When I would ask him a question about some fairly simple matter related to hydrology, he always found some reason to deflect the answer, such as by saying, as he always did: "Research on that matter hasn't attained any definite conclusions yet." Then he would shake that pipe at me and smile his devious and delighted smile. What he did professionally after he graduated from college I could never quite ascertain.

He married, in later years, a schoolteacher named Marion, and she once intimated to me that their primary source of income came from her teaching and from rents derived from leases and easements that Robinson renewed with various timber companies. Most of these agreements had been arranged at least two generations ago, so not a great deal of work was involved in their renewal. I guess Robinson had inherited a lot of land in northern Maine.

My friendship with Robinson survived our college years for two reasons. First, while we were in college, we "concocted a plot." Those were Robinson's words, or at least the sort of words Robinson would be inclined to use. We would climb Heathertop together. But why this expedition was considered a "plot" and why it was a kind of wonderful secret between the two of us I'll never understand. Nevertheless, I went along with his curious pretense and participated in his secret, though it was never really a secret at all. Anybody who knew the two of us knew that one day we would climb Heathertop together, that this was our abiding intention. Secondly, it just turned out that my own professional work brought me into the same valley where Robinson lived and which faced toward the great massif of Heathertop. Heathertop became part of my life, as it would for anyone who lived there. But having entered into Robinson's strange conspiracy, I couldn't climb it until he was ready to accompany me. He was not ready for years. He was never ready.

Robinson's great-grandfather, a geographer and land surveyor of distinguished reputation, not only gave Heathertop its name but was also the first to climb it. Back in those days, this was quite a feat, involving, as it did, a major wilderness expedition that took weeks to prepare and a month of canoe travel and portage and difficult trekking over uncharted terrain to bring to completion. Having conquered the mountain, he decided to remain in the area. He built a cabin in the foothills of the long valley facing the mountain from the south and used this as a base for his extensive lifelong exploration of the massif and its surrounding territories, which he surveyed in detail and of which he produced geological maps that were a model of such study for his time.

Well into his midlife, Robinson's great-grandfather convinced a young lady from Portland to share his life in the wilderness. From this marriage were born Robinson's grandfather and a whole lineage of men remarkable for their woodsmanship as well as for their accomplished professional lives. As a boy of ten years old, his grandfather was introduced to the rigors of wilderness life by being taken on the long hike up to the summit of Heathertop, a journey now reduced to four days: one day to a base camp at the foot of the mountain and a second day for the ascent of the mountain itself, where it was necessary to camp out at the summit; two more days reversed this process. The going was arduous because there were, as yet, no established trails or lumber roads that made things easier.

With this venture a kind of tradition was established, a way for a father to pass on a special inheritance to the son and a rite of passage for the son, whose initiation into the active life of the wilderness was accomplished by this momentous and consummate excursion. Robinson's grandfather, in turn, took his only son, Robinson's father, on the same journey at the age of ten. In keeping with the tradition, Robinson's father likewise prepared to take Robinson himself on that journey at the same age.

As had happened previously, years were spent telling the young boy about it and getting him ready for the event. Father and son would linger for hours during the evening on the porch of the old cabin facing the mountain, as the father would impart, carefully and tenderly, the stories that had gathered over the generations about the Maine wilderness and especially the lore about the great mountain massif itself whose imposing presence so touched every aspect of their lives. But at the age of nine, Robinson lost his father, who died in a lumbering accident. The promised event didn't take place. The tradition was broken. Robinson was left to himself to carry it out, and he would spend the rest of his life planning for just that.

After our college years, my vacations would frequently bring me to the Maine woods and into contact with Robinson once again. Then we would sit on his porch, gaze at the great mountain, renew our pact, and lay our plans.

When he married Marion, he decided to build a modern house on the site of the old Robinson cabin. It was a bit uncharacteristic of him, in a way, but he did it for Marion's sake. As a substitute for the original porch, he constructed a spacious flagstone veranda with a low stone wall surrounding it. To be sure, some of the rustic quality of the original dwelling had been lost, but he made up for this by adding a large, two-story room to the end of the house. It was called his "study" and was built in the shape of an A-frame tent. The entire front of this addition was made of glass and gave a perfectly framed view of Heathertop. Into this room he moved all the contents of the cabin and of his college room of old. In one corner of the room was an old rolltop desk and a clumsy oakwood swivel chair. The desk's many miniature compartments were stuffed with papers and knickknacks of every description. I imagined that the presence of this desk was the reason for calling this room his "study." Over the years he would add more and more items to his enormous collection of outdoor equipment, presumably on the pretext that such items might be necessary for the ascent of Heathertop. He was especially proud of two old dogsleds he had acquired somewhere. He claimed that they were the actual sleds used by Admiral Perry on his memorable expedition to the North Pole. I couldn't quite figure out whether he imagined us making the ascent in winter with these sleds. In any case, no live dogs ever showed up to pull the sleds, though he did begin collecting brass statues of sled dogs famous in northland history, including the husky who took the serum to Nome, Alaska—a story of which Robinson was especially fond. These bronze huskies were lined up along a shelf with his arrowhead collections.

Not many years later, when I finally moved to the valley of Heathertop, I saw a great deal of Robinson. My wife and I often went to his house to have dinner with Marion and him, especially in the summer, when he would fire up that barbecue of his and stand there, dressed in his plaid flannel shirt and lumberjack pants and boots, jabbing his pipe in every direction, while Marion grilled fresh brook trout (which Robinson purchased at the village market). Robinson would babble on about the moose that roamed occasionally through his backyard and some black bear that had scrambled into a dumpster at a local restaurant and couldn't get out until rescued by the volunteer fire department, who, in turn, for all their pains, got growled at and lashed out at before the bear ran off into the woods.

I would see Robinson from time to time pull up in his Jeep at our local diner, where he would stop for a cup of coffee and a doughnut after running a few errands. He was always apparently busy, always amused and cheerful, always fussing nervously about something or other but in a good-humored sort of way, and always adding some little but fascinating detail to our plans for the great expedition. The only kind of vehicle I ever knew him to drive was a Jeep. He needed this, he said, for his occasional forays into the deep woods on unpaved roads; yet the only unpaved road I ever knew him to negotiate was his own driveway. In any event, a Jeep would be most useful when the time for the great expedition finally rolled around.

But the great expedition never came; it was always delayed by one thing or another. There was the long-term weather pattern to be worried about—and Robinson seemed to be something of an expert about long-term weather patterns. Questions of health—Marion's health—came up, though I'm not aware that she had a sick day in her life. One year Robinson had to visit a distant relative in Arizona; another year there was a lawsuit with a lumber company over a stand of prime oak located on a hillside somewhere close to Moosehead Lake; yet another year Robinson needed to break in a new pair of boots before he could use them on a long hike. Sometimes the mosquitoes were too bad, or the rivers too high, or a drought had created a forest fire alert, or it was too hot, or it was too cold, or some equipment—such as a cookstove—had failed at the last moment.

In all of this, Robinson still imagined that the ascent of Heathertop would require a four-day trek over demanding terrain with all the gear and provisions such a trek would necessitate, though even in this respect one would have thought that he was contemplating a journey to the proverbial ends of the earth. Either he had no idea how thoroughly everything had changed in the mountains—and in the Heathertop massif itself—or else he pretended that he didn't know. For now, even in the depths of winter, snowshoers and cross-country skiers traversed the high ranges of Heathertop with little hazard to themselves or to their small children who came along with them, and snowmobilers skidded up through the wintry gorges on their noisy machines with no more provisions than the six packs of beer they carried with them in the compartments under their seats.

Robinson died at the age of forty-six. He became numb in his hands. After being shunted around to every hospital in northern New England, each one providing a different diagnosis, it was decided to send him to Boston. But beforehand he got too sleepy to be moved. It was over in two weeks.

I saw him the day before he died. He was in bed at home, next to a window that looked out over the valley to Heathertop. He woke just long enough to see me. He managed a bit of his sideways smile, his little glint in the eye. If he could have lifted his hand, he would have been jabbing the stem of his pipe in my direction. He said, "Climb it for me; climb Heathertop for me." He rolled his eyes in the direction of the window and looked out at the distant mountain. It was strange: there was no sense of loss in his voice, no sense of tragedy. He was as cheerful as ever.

"Of course," I said. "I promise I will." But, at the time, I didn't think he had heard me. He was asleep again.

A day after the funeral I went over to the house to ask Marion if I could be of any help. She told me that everything had been left in perfect order. She had been surprised by this, for somehow she had always had the impression that Robinson was not too well organized. That rolltop desk in his study with all the paper spilling out of its compartments didn't present a welcome challenge to anyone unfamiliar with its contents, as Marion had been until several days before. But in fact, once the pattern of organization was recognized, everything was in its exact place and all schedules of things to be done, payments made, and obligations met had been scrupulously observed. Robinson had left a clean slate on everything, except for …

"It's a shame," I said, "that Robinson never climbed Heathertop. It was the great dream of his life."

"It's not a shame actually," she replied. "It was more than the great dream of his life. That dream was his life. If he had climbed Heathertop, there would have been no dream left. His vitality, his humor, his graciousness came out of it. I'm glad he had that dream, and I'm glad he never lost it. And, you know, it gave him something to pass on to you, something special, your 'secret.' He died content, knowing that he could count on you to carry it out."

"But I don't think he heard me make my promise."

"He heard you. He told me so later. Even if he hadn't, he would have known anyway. He could rely on you."

"I appreciate that," I said.

Marion took me to his study. "Do you want any of this?" she asked.

I surveyed the collection briefly and turned my gaze to the view of Heathertop so perfectly framed by the window. "I don't think so. But there are collectors for these kinds of things — someone who would be overjoyed to have them and who would take good care of them."

She nodded. "But you'll take this, won't you?"

She went to his rolltop desk and drew something out of one of the small drawers at the edge of the writing area. It was his corncob pipe. Its mouthpiece had been practically chewed off. She handed it to me. I grasped the bowl and felt the curious impulse, which I managed to refrain from doing, of jabbing what was left of the mouthpiece in the direction of Heathertop and saying in a half-secretive, mischievous tone, "I'm going to climb it someday."

I climbed Heathertop the following autumn. A modern highway brought me to the base of the massif, and a gravel road, actually well-kept and service-able even for ordinary vehicles, penetrated deep into the woodlands of the massif itself and terminated in a nicely appointed parking facility equipped with a National Forest hut that provided information, maps, and the most recent dispatches concerning weather and trail conditions. Even from this point, the trek, while long, was nowhere near as difficult as we'd surmised. I left early in the morning. The trails were well marked and trodden, indicat-ing that this was a popular hike. It did take me six hours before I was at the summit—a long hike, as these things go, with a number of descents as well as ascents before it was over. It felt so strange to be there at last, for there was so little that was strange or mysterious about it—one more mountain like so many others I'd climbed in my day, except that the alpine heath at the top was unique, even if showing no little ecological damage by the hordes of hikers who now tramped routinely over its surface.

I found a comfortable niche among some rocks in which to have my lunch. Nearby, a young couple with a dog was sitting on a tuft of grass and having a heated argument about something—mainly about having brought the dog, I think. Each one blamed the other for the idea, and for the dog having chased a bear cub, a porcupine, and countless chipmunks on the way up. Elsewhere a party of campers, boys and girls, was strewn about the summit, greedily eating potato chips from little plastic bags, drinking soda from brightly colored aluminum cans, and generally ignoring the immense wilderness that stretched off in every direction from the mountain.

Several campers were talking to parents and friends on their cell phones. One orotund little waif was commanding his mom to watch the television at home and keep him informed every few minutes by phone of what was happening on *The Adventures of Pillowman*. Meanwhile the dog kept running around and pushing its dripping muzzle into the plastic bags of the campers. They would yelp in protest and snatch the plastic bags away.

I noted that neither of the young couple, though involved in a quarrel about the dog, would initiate any effort to stop the dog from further foraging among the campers. Another knot of climbers, young men and women, looking as if they had purchased most of the items from L.L. Bean's latest catalogue, were sitting in a tight cluster on a boulder, discussing the relative merits of white versus dark chocolate in making gourmet mocha coffee. At the edge of the heath, six huge crows were perched in the limbs of a stunted balsam pine, waiting patiently for the hikers to leave so that they could clean up the shreds of processed ham and bread crusts and cookie crumbs that would be left behind.

After lunch, I took Robinson's pipe out of my backpack and buried it in some loose rubble not far from the peak. I should feel a little guilty about this, I suppose. I did it a bit furtively; I didn't want to give any of those campers with their aluminum cans the wrong idea. The motto these days is "Carry in, carry out." I believe in it. But this was an exception.

This was Robinson's mountain. It belonged to him. If anything ever belonged here, it was something of Robinson. Also, Robinson would have appreciated the secretive touch, the sense of doing something just a bit risqué.

Then I drew from my pack a pair of binoculars I had borrowed from a friend. I wondered if I could see Robinson's house from the peak. The binoculars were powerful, but after lining up landmarks I thought I could recognize, I finally saw little more than a tiny white dot pressed in among the far distant ridge of hills to the south. I guessed it must be Robinson's house, but I wasn't sure.

It's strange how one place can so dominate your view from another place, which place, in turn, from the opposite direction, is scarcely anything to see at all. I could imagine Robinson down there, looking up at this peak, planning his climb, thinking of it from season to season, year to year, jabbing the stem of his pipe in this direction.

The pipe got here anyway. Part of him got here anyway. Maybe that's all he ever wanted.

The Biggest … in the World

There are stories in this life that, all sagacious counsel would agree, are simply too adventitious to be told. To be sure, who doesn't thrill to the coincidental, the semi-miraculous, the outrageously impossible, no matter how far these may stretch our credulity in a hundred subtle, and sometimes not so subtle, ways?

Yet the simply adventitious — the concurrence of events too real and yet too remarkable to comply with our ordinary canons of logic — so amply fills the course of our daily lives that, should we even care to notice it, we don't regard it as suitable for the raconteur because, I suppose, it's the extraordinary in life itself that we are least disposed to believe.

All of this is a roundabout way of restating the common maxim that truth is sometimes stranger than fiction and that some real things in life are simply too improbable for the often-unreal probabilities demanded by successful mimetic representation. That master of mimetic precept, old Aristotle himself, would admonish us to avoid precisely that which is possible — because it did, after all, happen — but which is, at the same time, too improbable for anyone to believe. Better the "impossible probable," he infamously contended, than the "improbable possible." But I shall not be deterred by such recondite reservations. If I incur such a risk in telling the story of "The Biggest . . . in the World," I gladly do so. Such acute ironies as mark, more often than we think, the larger banalities of our existence should not, in their time and season, be left unsung.

A little background is in order. My wife, Sophie, and I moved to northern New England when we were in our early thirties. Yes, it was a flight, if you want to call it that: a flight into rural seclusion from overbearing urban ways; a flight into simplicity; a flight into gardening and splitting wood and firing up the woodstove sometime in October and keeping it going until late April. Now, I know that I've conjured up already some idyllic image of northern New England — the one that's portrayed in the numerous photography magazines that exist expressly to promote just such an image: little villages sequestered in wooded valleys with the white spires of village churches rising elegantly from groves of elms and maples and with the surrounding hills and mountains drawn to seem rather significantly larger and closer than they really are. For this, of course, we can thank the magic of the telephoto lens that distorts the natural landscape as much as those engravers and painters of an earlier century were constrained by fashion to do, making northern New England look like one of the lesser-known cantons of Switzerland. Such a picturesque landscape, of course, is understood to support an old and landed rural folk, frugal in their ways and tenacious in the observance of the yearly round of picnics on the village green and the celebrations of harvest abundance.

Sure, it's there — minus a bit of the pictorial grandiosity. But that's not *all* that's there. The great four-lane highways that now slice ubiquitously through valley and hill both disguise as well as augment the more complete picture of the terrain. Many decades ago, the great expatriate poet T. S. Eliot, traveling southward through New England and confined, as one necessarily was in those days, to local roads, could find only one word to describe the endless sequence of small mill towns he encountered with suffocating monotony on his way. It was that rare, Latinate word "sordor." I shall let you scurry to the dictionary for that one, though I warn you that only a rather comprehensive dictionary will do.

Of course, T. S. Eliot may have been on some pilgrimage of pain: he usually was, wherever he went, but he was not far off the mark on this one. The word itself virtually rings with the shabbiness, the disorder, the bricky grime of these little municipalities that dot the landscape; and the roads that lead into them, as well as lead out of them, are alleyways through dunes of industrial rubbish spun off by the larger factory towns and have nowhere else to go. As I've already indicated, nowadays you can bypass all of this on those thruways whose lofty detachment affords immediate and breathtaking vistas of wooded mountains but whose convenience has simply accelerated the speed with which an industrial civilization can deposit its waste, though momentarily unseen, in the surrounding countryside. I spoke earlier of the things that Sophie and I conceived of us as fleeing toward; what we were fleeing from has followed us with the relentless pursuit of a hunter closing in on its quarry: I speak of shopping centers and suburban developments and parking lots as vast as the devastated acreage of Verdun soon after the Armistice was signed.

As for the rural folk, who and what they are can be most deceptive. I'm unable to supply a sufficient sociological hypothesis for what has happened, but perhaps the agricultural and industrial impoverishment of northern New England earlier in the twentieth century made it the depository for all the dispossessed of the earth—that is, for anyone who had to get out of or away from wherever they were and whose resources were inadequate to get them much more than several hundred miles from their original port of entry. The result has been a multi-tiered, multi-ethnic society whose complexity could challenge New York City itself, though its contours are infinitely more hidden and hence more surprising than the great city would exhibit.

Thus, it's not at all unusual to discover, after knowing her for many years, that the lady running the bed-and-breakfast down the road is a dispossessed Hungarian countess who delights in serving up, to her flabbergasted guests, the most pungent paprika omelets, accompanied by slabs of spicy cabbage strudel.

Hungarian?

Yes, I'm serious about that, as outlandish—even as conventionally outlandish—as it all sounds, though I could have spoken even more pertinently of my Finnish neighbors, of the Irish, Lebanese, French-Canadian, Portuguese, Slovak, Polish, Armenian, Greek, Korean, Pakistani, Italian, and a dozen others. In fact, the Yankee, right from the start, has been a mixed breed—always has been, always will be.

While I'm on this matter of ethnicity, I would like to point out that Sophie and I, in our early stage of settling into the New England way of life, went through a prolonged and intense "Japanese" period. This was not such a strange thing: like-minded people in our locale have Japanese gardens and Zen pavilions and Japanese decorations of all kinds in their homes, drive Japanese cars, and devour their fair share of sushi, garnished with seaweed and rice balls.

The local potter, of Scots-Irish descent, who produces a plethora of what he calls traditional New England, back-to-the-earth pottery, received his ceramics training during a two-year apprenticeship in Japan itself. That his Japanese ceramics are identified by unwary tourists as old New England ceramics is not his problem, so he says. His work, however, is exquisite, whatever you take it to be.

We northern New Englanders are also not unaware that the distinction of our spectacular autumn is shared with only one other place on earth — northern Japan, which shares a climate and landscape similar to ours.

Sophie and I, however, had an interest of a different kind. We learned to pass long winter nights engorging ourselves on Japanese movies — to be more specific, everything samurai held us in thrall, and we could never get enough of it. We purchased books about the samurai and discussed Miyamoto Musashi's great island duel with the redoubtable swordsman whose weapon was several inches longer than the traditional sword. We hankered for every new Kurosawa film that we could purchase for our home entertainment system. I tell you this, for it's a vital part of what is so distressingly adventitious in my story.

I would like to return to the word "picturesque" for a bit, for it's here, in some curiously perverse sense, that my story really has it origin. Now, I know that various antiquarians, art dealers, social historians, and the like scour our derelict countryside, rather like old-fashioned brigands engaged in looting expeditions of various kinds, with the purpose of scaring up esoteric forms of "folk" art in order to fill up museums, private collections, antique shops, and, most significantly, their bank accounts. So even now, as I embark upon this effort to describe what may very well be the most abominable art form to appear in the history of the world, this same art form has already been heralded by the cognoscenti as bearing a quintessential northern New England "voice" and demeanor, and hence as worthy of being enshrined in the annals of great regional art.

Let them do what they must; at least they have not—not yet anyway—erected some sign somewhere, executed in a style commensurate with the mode it celebrates, that announces that, within an adjoining enclosure, you can find "The Biggest County Fair Sign in the World."

If all of this seems hopelessly obscure, allow me to expatiate a bit. T. S. Eliot's presumed pilgrimage of pain would have been all the more gratifyingly painful, and his vocabulary all the more proportionally strained, if he had had the opportunity to visit a northern New England county fair. Such fairs have their "picturesque" side in the good and proper sense of the term: impeccably groomed sheep displayed by rosy-cheeked farm girls blushing at the brightly colored ribbons bestowed upon their charges; long rows of trestle tables displaying bottled relishes and maple syrup; and quilts whose gaily colored motifs depict little barns and pastures and frolicking dairy cows.

But if we step a few feet over to what is often called the "midway," we are greeted by a spectacle so grotesque that few of the worst urban enclaves in this sorry world devoted to vice in all its forms can be as appalling. And most appalling of all are the huge, lurid signs proclaiming that, within the adjoining enclosure—ever so secretive, ever so tantalizing—you can see "The Biggest ... in the World."

Fill in the appropriate term at your leisure. Rat. Pig. Lady. Man. Mongoose. Skunk. Snake. Head. Tail. Neck. Ear. You name it. For fifty cents, you get to enter the secretive enclosure and gawk at this biggest thing in the world of its kind for as long as you would like.

I tell you right now, I've never walked into one of these places, though I've never been able to interpret the enigmatic expressions on the faces of those who exit them. Are they satisfied with what they saw? Are they disappointed? Do they feel taken advantage of? They betray nothing. They say nothing. Their faces are blank, though a sly smile plays about their lips as if they, too, are now in on a secret—a secret that nobody, by the way, needs to know.

Meanwhile, I focus my attention on the sign.

It shows a picture of the aforesaid object in monstrous, lugubrious, frightening contours. I sense that I might faint, or have a nervous breakdown, if I saw the thing in question: the picture is morbid — it suggests the psychotic, the diseased, the abnormal.

I wonder who paints these pictures. They all look the same — every fair I've ever been to, every "biggest" thing in the world that's thereby proclaimed, has the same dreary, macabre look. Do I exaggerate? Or is it more a question of my own excessively neurasthenic sensibilities that confer upon these rustic images their aura of psychopathic deformity?

I don't know. I don't think so.

So what was I supposed to do when, on some errand or another one day, I was driving down a back road in the hills that surround the nearby mill town and I happened upon an immense corrugated steel shed, almost sixty yards long, by the side of the road with a huge sign on it that said "The Biggest Collection of Samurai Swords in the World"? This was not in the middle of a fair; it was not in the middle of anything except tangled second-growth woodlands that stretched for miles in either direction, interrupted now and then by an old shack or a decaying barn or a field littered with rusty machinery. The sign was executed in that customary ghoulish style: it showed two gigantic samurai swordsmen squaring off against each other with the most distorted gestures and horrific grimaces I've ever seen. One of them must have been stabbed somewhere, for a geyser of blood spurted out of a chink in his laminated armor.

Now, I'm aware that there is a classic Japanese pictorial style that depicts such violent scenes, and such a style may well have served partially as a model for this sign. Yet whatever influence may have been exerted from this source, it had been thoroughly transformed into the morbid and distended hues of the equally classic northern New England midway sign.

And here it was in the woods, by a huge shed, advertising exactly what, at that time in my life, I would most like to have seen, if that was what actually was in there.

A few cars had parked in the dusty lot that surrounded the shed. Otherwise, there was no sign of activity.

I drove by in contempt. Is there anything that people will not leave alone? Is there anything sacred anymore? What could be in that building except for a few specimens of Second World War Japanese officers' swords, clanking loosely in grayish-brown steel scabbards, objects not unlike the rusty German helmets brought back as trophies by returning servicemen and ending up as odd items in every junk collection put up for sale? Hardly worth the charge of admission! Hardly worthy of the outrageous claim made about it in that great sign that stood by the road!

When I got home, I told Sophie about it. She concurred. There were many traps we'd fallen into in our lives; this was one that we could well avoid. That night we ate our rice balls and dreamt of Miyamoto Musashi tramping across the stony hills of New England, his great sword tucked in his sash and its gilded pommel catching the glint of the evening sun.

The exact temporal sequences involved in my adventitious story are no longer known to me. All I vaguely remember is that I passed that same immense shed a few more times in the following years, ever with the same shock of disgust and contempt. The monstrous sign grew somehow worse as it weathered. No one was called in to touch it up or refresh its gruesome details. The surface became chipped and faded, while the faces of the warriors gradually vanished into the original boards upon which they had been painted.

Nor did the collection ever seem to attract many customers. One year I saw a small group of bored motorcyclists emerge from the shed, mount up their Harleys, and spin off through the dust toward town. They had those usual enigmatic expressions on their faces that I always associated with such exhibits.

Six months later I happened to see a long black limousine parked in front. A delegation of Japanese dignitaries, meticulously dressed, was gathered by the door. I cringed to think of their reaction to the lurid sign. I hoped they wouldn't notice it. But how could they not notice it? And what fraudulent claim in what tourist handbook brought them thus to our own beloved boondocks and to this monumental sham? Another year I saw an old, stooped man emerge from the building and limp heavily toward the road. He had a mass of silver-white hair on his head. After I passed him, I watched in the rearview mirror as he crossed over the road to a rural mailbox on the other side.

Then one year I stopped.

I don't why. There were no cars parked there, and I was just driving by when I found myself unaccountably slamming on the brakes. I practically slid into the parking lot, all tires screeching in a cloud of dust. I pulled up to the front of the shed, where an admission booth announced a fee of five dollars.

I was ready to spend it. I was ready to go in. My curiosity had finally gotten the better of me. I tried to ignore the gruesome sign.

But the place was closed.

I should have felt relieved. It's always nice to have an irrational and somewhat degrading impulse checked by an unforeseen obstacle.

But I didn't feel relieved. I knocked on the door.

After a few minutes' wait, an old lady, with her gray hair tied in a knot at the back and wearing a knitted sweater fastened in front by a set of coin-like buttons, answered the door. I knew at once that she was foreign, educated, deferential, a woman of old-world culture. She informed me, courteously — if officiously — that the "museum," as she called it, was closed. In fact, it was closed permanently.

I recognized at once a habit of speech marked by a German accent and by an occasional lapse into the *Muttersprache* itself. Ah, so there we are: you never know what or whom you're going to encounter in the hills and dales of northern New England.

But still, it struck me as odd. Why was a woman of this sort connected to a great metallic shed and a sign of such portentous squalor? To keep the conversation going, I asked her, as politely as I could, if she came from Germany. Just as courteously she said no. She said she came, instead, from "the ancient and honorable Kingdom of Bavaria." I didn't want to argue about this, even if that kingdom has been part of Germany for well over a century now. I let it pass. I asked if I could see the collection anyway.

"*Ja*, you can see for yourself that you can no longer see it," she replied, raising her arms in a gesture of futility. She ushered me into the shed, and I saw a huge space, almost the size of an airplane hanger, filled with crates and boxes. Everything was to be shipped out in several days. I looked at the addresses on the boxes: several locations in the United States, many in Europe, quite a few in Japan — most of which were going to national museums in Osaka, Tokyo, and elsewhere. My heart sank.

"It is a shame you haven't seen my husband's collection," she said. "You know, *natürlich*, who he was?"

"No."

"His name was Heinrich Schlemmer. He has died only a month ago."

I remembered now the obituary that appeared in the local newspaper, as well as in the *New York Times* we received on Sunday. Heinrich Schlemmer! Was that the silver-haired old man I saw crossing the road? Was that the man who, in his youth, in the early decades of the last century, was considered one of the greatest concert violinists in the world, until a collision with a truck outside Carnegie Hall crushed his hands, his body, and his career forever? Was this the man whom Sophie had crooned about last month as she read the obituary and exclaimed that he had lived, all this while, so close to us?

Frau Schlemmer didn't expound on his virtues. She only made the point that nowhere in the world had her husband been so idolized, so praised, as in Japan. He had brought Beethoven to the Japanese. The First Violin Concerto, with its great cadenza, had been his route to national idolatry and international fame. And the Japanese had repaid him regally for a boundless enrichment of their national life.

I knew all of this already. Again, my heart sank. I felt sick.

"Before the accident," she continued, "he has worked hard on his collection, some of which he bought, much of which has been given to him as gifts. They were national treasures, *wissen Sie*. After the accident, there was nothing left in his life but this collection. It was the testimony to his greatness as a musician. He could not let it go, even though we were now impoverished. Then we set up this museum. It brought in *ein bissen* money—not much, you know. Not many people are come here, but a few people from all over the world are come—the few who have known what we had." She nodded patiently, grasping her hands together.

"But now you're sending it away," I said.

"No other choice have I, no other way to live, and I cannot continue to live here *ganz allein*. I return next month to my family in Bavaria. Some of the collection goes to Sotheby's in New York, the rest all over the world, but most of it is returned soon to Japan. That is good, yet a great shame is it, in a way."

"Why is that?" I asked, fearfully.

"Because never again, *ich glaube*, is it all in the same place at once. *Das tut mir leid.*"

"You mean . . ." I trembled. I was now so heartsick I could have used one of those swords in some dramatic hara-kiri enacted on the spot.

"*Ich meine* it was the biggest collection of antique samurai swords in the world. *Und das war nicht alles*: armor, archery, saddles, war banners, we have had it all—all packed here now in these crates. Our finest exhibit was the sword of that great poet-painter and sage, Miyamoto Musashi himself, though that has been returned to the Imperial House of Japan only last week."

I sputtered, "Just as the sign says . . ."

"*Ach Weh*, that sign! Dreadful, dreadful! *Furchtbar war es!* But we had no other choice. We had so *wenig* money, and Heinrich would not sell anything to raise it. And the local people said it would draw the public. Such signs work, they said, at county fairs. But I don't think it ever worked much for us."

Further conversation was hardly necessary. After exchanging a few more words with the melancholy Frau Schlemmer, I drove home and told Sophie the terrible news. My prospective hara-kiri almost became mutual. In the following days I mentioned the "museum" to friends and acquaintances, many of whom shared our interests. None of them had even been aware that it was there, though several mentioned driving by and having had, pretty much, the same reaction as I did.

The curious reader may now be impelled to ask if I've reformed my notions about the folkloric artwork of the county fair; if I now go in to see the colossal rat, the gigantic pig, the ant as large as a Labrador retriever, the lady with the longest nose, the man with the flappiest elephant ears, the biggest, the absolutely biggest . . . in this whole, wide, ever-loving, prodigy-producing world!

No!

The answer is no!

I still hate those signs. I will always hate those signs. I hate them now more than ever.

If any antiquarian of the future insists on featuring those signs along with weathervanes, old lanterns, broken wagon wheels, homemade crockery of a dozen different sorts, and other ragged appurtenances of the rural life, I shall tell him exactly what I think about it. After all, such a sign kept me, positively kept me, from seeing the biggest ...

No, it hurts too much to think about it.

In fact, it hurt so much at the time that soon thereafter, Sophie and I lost all interest in samurai and like matters. It was a kind of denial syndrome, I'm sure. We just couldn't face the calamity of our obtuseness.

Or were we obtuse?

Don't chuckle, Miyamoto Musashi, smirking down at us from your perch on that eternal lotus bloom! The adventitious — isn't that what you Zen masters said that life is all about, anyway? Play the cosmic game, and dance the cosmic dance, and smile the ineffable smile that celebrates the foibles of our daily dreams.

But this little irony — did it have to work that way? After all, I'm bound to probability — probability in the least. My old master Aristotle would, minimally, consent to that. Again, I say, don't chuckle! As for T. S. Eliot and his sundry pilgrimages of pain, of penitence perhaps — I would be all too glad to accompany him on the biggest of them all, the biggest in the world, to slog up the terraces of Dante's *Monte Purgatorio* with Old Possum himself dogging my heels, as long as, just as long as, we have within our purview the biggest, yes, the biggest of the biggest ... in the whole wide world and beyond it, steadfastly transfixed before our eyes.

(None of those signs please! Please, please, please!)

Aunt Jennie's Christmas Pie

I t's generally held that every family has its secrets—little mysteries of one sort or another that it discloses to the rest of the world, if ever, only with the most obstinate resistance or in a language intended, by virtue of its recondite phraseology, to confuse and obfuscate, as much as to illuminate, any potential auditor.

In one sense, certainly, I intend—and flagrantly so—to violate such a generally held principle, for the revelation of family secrets will be my stock-in-trade. In another sense, I'm bound to the principle in spite of myself, for the deepest mystery of all is as mysterious to the family members themselves as it would be to anyone from the outside who endeavored to plumb its shadowy depths.

That's why it would be futile for me to attempt any description of that sumptuous pastry so notable in my family's history—futile and possibly self-defeating as well, for the enigma of Aunt Jennie's Christmas pie itself has, assuredly, been part of its charm and part of the reason why the Ballankirk clan has treasured its memory so deeply, even as it has tried to fathom its inscrutable contents.

Suffice it to say, in the present context, that Aunt Jennie's Christmas pie is a curious combination of candied fruits steeped for several days in the appropriate spirits and covered with a thick cream, or possibly custard, flavored with nutmeg and other spices, and chilled in a rich pastry crust. That much is known; what is unknown are all the specific choices and measurements of these various ingredients. What, for example, are the "appropriate spirits"?—a subject which, in any event, is dear to the Ballankirk heart regardless of its relationship to the confection under discussion.

Endless attempts over the last century and a half have been expended in the effort to determine what the original ingredients of the pie might have been—on the supposition that Aunt Jennie's prototype had a flavor whose sublimity couldn't be surpassed; and a traditional feature of the great Ballankirk Christmas gatherings is the submission of at least a dozen variants of the pie for the discrimination and judgment of the clan members. Needless to say, none of these submissions ever passes muster, and all are ultimately—though politely—rejected as not being "quite the real thing," though I've never really understood what standards are being applied in rendering such a judgment, since no one, for the last century and a half, has, to my knowledge, ever tasted "quite the real thing," though there is one candidate for this honor, and he, a complete stranger to the family and of unknown provenance, has disappeared altogether from the annals of gods and men. To this fortunate one, though profoundly unfortunate in another sense, I shall return later on in my tale.

Indeed, the quest for the pie's ingredients might be thought of as having assumed a role, within the hermetically enclosed (though soon to be disclosed) world of the Ballankirk clan, analogous to the search for the Universal Elixir among alchemists of old, or for the restorative waters of the Fountain of Youth among enterprising conquistadors of all stripes.

These analogies are more than capricious; the quest for the recipe is driven not only by a gastronomic hunger but also by a distinctly spiritual desire that no Ballankirk would ever confess to having and yet which all of them have in one way or another: a deep-seated though rarely articulated longing for something we might vaguely call "reconciliation." I know that such a claim is apt to appear a bit odd at the moment, but that's what, finally, the pie is really all about, as I shall endeavor to explain, though my explanations require precisely the sort of family secrets I will purport to divulge.

As a final note, in all deference to whom I hope will be my patient reader, if I did know the actual recipe of the pie, I certainly wouldn't tell it. I'm prepared to tell a great deal, much of a deeply personal nature about my family, but of such a monumental betrayal of family confidences, I am not, and, God forbid, never would be, capable.

Aunt Jennie is a person whose stature in family history is almost as remote and as mythical as the pie itself. She lived her brief but memorable life sometime in the early to middle part of the nineteenth century—that is, about five or six generations ago. The Ballankirks had recently resettled from Canada to the hills of northern Vermont, and Aunt Jennie, a younger member of the clan at the time, was a sprightly girl who married a young farmer not far from the parental household and who died at the age of twenty-two when giving birth to twin boys in the middle of a particularly bitter winter. Within a day or so, her two sons followed her to the grave, and all three were buried in the same coffin together, Aunt's Jennie's arms tenderly wrapped around each of her deceased children.

Aunt Jennie was noted for, among other attractive features of her personality, her cheerful and generous disposition—a quality of character not especially prevalent among Ballankirks but prized by them nevertheless; for in every generation since the demise of Aunt Jennie, Ballankirks have eagerly sought out the traces of Aunt Jennie's character in fellow family members, a quest that's not, I must confess, easily rewarded. Yet every generation or two, an Aunt Jennie does seem to appear, though such a solitary figure tends to be acknowledged as such only in retrospect—that is, after he or she has ceased to be of any possible living challenge to the complex play of hostilities that animates the mutual life of the Ballankirks and gives such infinite, if transitory, joy to their hearts.

Aunt Jennie was also noted for her culinary skills. Once again, this made her unusual for Ballankirks whose tastes in food and drink can best be described as execrable, though they like to talk a great deal about such matters; and, if talk were a guide to what is real, you'd imagine that all Ballankirks were gourmet chefs and connoisseurs of fine cuisine with the most impeccable credentials. Nothing could be further from the truth; all Ballankirk cooking, even if it's spaghetti with tomato sauce or lobster bisque or roast duck, ends up tasting like some version or another of burnt oatmeal.

But Aunt Jennie was different, so it's said.

Her greatest contribution to family history, however, was her invention, or rediscovery, of a pie recipe especially designed for the festive Christmas season. You must recall, at this juncture, that for people like the Ballankirks, even into the first half of the nineteenth century, Christmas was a time of year to be rigorously shunned as tainted with the vestiges of medieval idolatry and papist superstition.

Aunt Jennie must have been quite a rebel in this regard; or perhaps living in the proximity of the French inhabitants of Canada had exerted all too subtle an influence in bringing the Ballankirks back to at least some of the customs of their own ancestors many centuries before, so that they were, by Aunt Jennie's time, receptive to her startling innovations. For Aunt Jennie's pie was redolent of something sweetly and succulently medieval — as rich and full as an illuminated manuscript, as light and gracious as Gothic tracery, as joyous and colorful as a stained-glass window. Aunt Jennie restored Christmas for the Ballankirks, and her pie succeeded in giving the tone (or I should say, more properly, the final tone) to the season.

If, as we shall see, a Ballankirk Christmas is not always as merry an affair as it might be, it's precisely Aunt Jennie's pie that brings such a festive occasion back to what Aunt Jennie, in the goodness of her heart, had seen as its proper purpose. I might add, incidentally, that the endemic culinary handicaps of the Ballankirks, mentioned above, are surmounted only in relation to this pie, for the multiform efforts at reconstruction, though inevitably off the mark, are nevertheless tasty enough concoctions to satisfy the most exacting gourmands.

The central fact is that, as I've intimated several times already, the Ballankirks are not, by any standards, a peaceable folk: and, though they spend much of their lives fighting anybody, at any time and at any place, for any reason whatsoever, they mainly fight among themselves. I've little doubt that, when some Roman legionnaire, fresh from the fragrant hills of the Campagna, looked northward from Hadrian's Wall in horror at bands of naked, blue-painted warriors (of both sexes, incidentally), twirling axes in their hands and shaking spears tipped with venom, he was viewing the remote ancestors of my illustrious clan. Both extra- and infra-clan warfare kept them happily occupied for the centuries that followed, to say nothing of holding back the "Saxons" from the south, as well as raiding Saxon cattle herds and burning down their granges, whose burgeoning storage bins argued for all too unseemly a devotion to industry and skill.

It's no accident that the first Ballankirks showed up on the North American continent in the mid-eighteenth century to fulfill any number of variously combative roles: to take on Indian tribes as warlike as they were, to ambush French explorers and settlers, and to march southward from Lake Champlain with General Burgoyne's British army against the rebellious thirteen colonies, though the Ballankirks were no more loyal to the English crown than the insurgents against whom they fought. If poor old General Washington had had more ready cash on hand, the Ballankirks would have traded sides in an instant.

As it was, their English paymasters didn't have much ready cash on hand either, but the Ballankirks were amply rewarded for their service, even despite the defeat, with substantial land grants in Canada. As soon as real estate prices had peaked (and Ballankirks always know when prices of any kind have peaked), these lands were sold, and the Ballankirks moved to Vermont and later spread throughout New England, where they mostly reside today.

To be sure, things have become somewhat more genteel with time. The verbal challenge, the insult, the stinging reproach have always been uppermost in the arsenal of the Ballankirk character; but the days of the accompanying claymores, dirks, poisoned goblets, studded war clubs, and burning strongholds are over; a later age of canes, broken whiskey bottles, hairpins, darning needles, and other instruments of assault have also been replaced with more ostensibly civilized methods. For example, no truly serious hair-pulling incident has taken place since Great-Aunt Bertha's wedding, eighty-five years ago (by "truly serious" I mean a situation in which the hair-puller successfully uproots a substantial fistful of hair from the hair-pullee). I should mention that kicking, scratching, and biting are reserved for interspousal conflicts and enter into larger family rows only when a husband and a wife happen to find themselves on opposite sides in a major clan split—which is rare but is likewise fruitful in providing some fascinating, if delightfully vicious, ancillary skirmishes and ambushes.

Even the language of reproach has undergone subtle alterations through the years. For example, it's reported that a great-great-grandfather went to the Pacific Northwest in his early years as a trapper and "mountain man" and returned to eastern Canada fifteen years later with two girls said to be his daughters by an Indian woman whom he had married in the west and who later succumbed to smallpox. The two daughters became the progenitors of the so-called western division in the Ballankirk clan structure, which could claim Amerind ancestry and which adopted a strange propensity to resort to a kind of "westernese" in its linguistic habits, especially when tempers were blazing hot, as they frequently were.

Thus, expressions such as "warpath," "firewater," "wampum," and "bad hombre" (applied to both sexes) gave vent to outrage and provocation. Referring to a fellow family member as a "paleface" was generally regarded as an especially opprobrious charge—a curious enough reproach given that all Ballankirk visages are as blanched, if not bleached, as the most proverbial linen sheet ever was, since they all scrupulously avoid any direct contact with sunlight (for a variety of sinister reasons, no doubt; though some have to do with superstitions regarding the notorious "noonday devil," but we'd better not get into this matter). That such "westernese" phrases were actually picked up from dime-store novels and early western films (and that everyone seemed to know pretty well that they were) didn't deter either their forcefulness or their usage.

Another example of linguistic change can be illustrated by the ability that all Ballankirks in the past claimed to have: an ability, that is, to discern with spiritual acuity who is, and who is not, a member of the "elect" in quite a theological sense. To be able to make such a discernment was itself obviously a sign of being "elect," and it just so happened that anyone with whom one was in conflict at the moment was one of the "reprobates" and needed to be rather urgently and persistently reminded of this fact.

We don't need to worry about the inconsistencies that may have arisen in this discernment, given that one's antagonists shifted from time to time and hence membership among the predestined "damned" was subject to correlative revisions as well.

Nor do we need to worry about the sources of this extraordinary charism, nor the mode of its characteristic expression as derived from the lore of many a learned divine; but I think that even John Calvin himself would have trembled in his grave if he could have heard the earth being rocked by some Ballankirk pronouncement of eternal damnation. For in every Ballankirk, male and female, there lurked a fire-and-brimstone preacher poised perpetually to leap out, even if the setting was in a playpen and the protagonist was a four-year-old Ballankirk girl precociously declaring that her antagonist, in this case her three-year-old sister, was a "daughter of Jezebel" and a "whore of Babylon."

But those days are over.

Freud has replaced Calvin as the arbiter of salvation. The "loony bin" and "the funny farm" have replaced Hell as the place where one definitely, as well as indefinitely, deserves to be. And the language of theology has been replaced by the language of "fixations" and "complexes": "neurosis" and "schizoid" and "obsessive behavior" and "bipolar" and other psychological terms whose implications are taken to be as deadly and their effects as permanent, incurable, and irredeemable as adverse theological predestination ever was.

Of course, no Ballankirks have ever had training in scientific psychological observation, but this doesn't in any way impede the certainty with which they make their diagnoses of other family members, nor the authority with which they enunciate them.

It's not uncommon, for instance, for one Ballankirk to accuse another of having an "inferiority complex." Such an accusation is an absurdity to begin with, because whatever gene in the human chromosomal makeup allows people to have inferiority complexes, such a gene is utterly lacking in a Ballankirk. It's as impossible for a Ballankirk to have an inferiority complex as it is for an elephant to be a giraffe.

But the charge itself is guaranteed to put its receptor into a towering rage, for the mere suggestion that one would think oneself somehow inferior to others is enough to put one's sense of inexorable superiority to a most severe test. This set of facts holds true even despite the not infrequent practice among Ballankirks, especially the females, of engaging in prolonged bouts of verbal self-flagellation and accusation. The function of these bouts is purportedly to elicit compassionate denials from its audience, but such denials are not, and never will be, forthcoming, and the self-flagellator knows this full well from the start. Hence, the silence of the audience is taken to mean its tacit consent to the self-accusations, which therefore now become *its* accusations, for which it will be held, for the next century or so, to be responsible.

Since I'm speaking of linguistic usage here, I should conclude by mentioning that no Ballankirk ever uses obscenity in verbal engagements; such a practice would be regarded as intolerably beneath a Ballankirk's ability to score a hit with a more precise and wounding locution than the hopeless vacuity of obscene language could ever hope to accomplish. "Obscenity is stupidity": that's the Ballankirk view, and the case is closed.

And no Ballankirk, unfortunately, is stupid; in fact, they just about all have what are called genius IQs. If they could ever learn to use intelligence for constructive purposes, they would be a formidable force in this world. But don't worry. That will never happen.

At this point the inquisitive observer might be prompted to ask: "What, after all, are they fighting about?" Everything and anything is the answer, except for the two things that most other people tend to fight about: money and politics.

Ballankirks never fight about money because they all have much more than they need. The proceeds from the original sales of the Canadian land grants have proliferated over the last two centuries into multitudes of bulging investment portfolios that support virtually all the Ballankirks very handsomely without their having to work, except at the management of their own accounts—a task for which all Ballankirks seem to be particularly well-suited. An inexhaustible ingenuity for buying and selling, for hoarding and evading and hiding, has resulted in an enormous accumulation of wealth over the years.

This talent is compounded by a stinginess so profound that no one, except a Ballankirk, can understand either its boundless range or its abysmal depth. For example, Ballankirks live in old, simple if spacious houses, passed down through the generations and sparsely furnished in the interiors with monumentally fashioned porch furniture which is as indestructible as it is grotesque and uncomfortable. They drive shabby cars, twenty to thirty years old, whose mufflers sometimes drag along the ground and send up showers of sparks, even though the typical adult Ballankirk could afford, if he or she wanted, to buy out the entire inventory of a local car dealership by writing a check on the spot. They never go to hotels or restaurants and never travel, except to visit one another — and they do a great deal of this, if for no other purpose than to nurture their feuds. Occasionally, a Ballankirk indulges in an eccentric hobby that might engage some infinitesimal percentage of his or her total assets, but no other extravagances are evident. Hence, concerns about money are rarely at the focus of quarrels.

Ballankirks never fight about politics, either. It's true that college-age Ballankirks sometimes go through a brief Marxist-Leninist phase when they think that their allowances are insufficient to ferret aside enough cash to start their own stock portfolios.

But that phase, usually terminated at the age of twenty-one, never outlasts the first, and inevitable, dividend remittance (which, of course, is immediately reinvested).

Beyond that point, Ballankirks share one political conviction: that is, once the legal age is reached and whatever perpetual trust targeted at a certain individual kicks in, all thoughts of a social utopia pop like a bubble blown out of a child's little wire hoop; and whatever it is that, long ago, made them want to keep the Roman legions out of their viper-ridden fens, the "Saxons" away from their wind-blasted moors and dales, and everybody else as far away as possible, unifies them into a cohesive group vis-à-vis the outside world.

"Hands off my stuff!" says it all.

Then what do they fight about?

They fight about "making sacrifices" and "being slighted." First, about "sacrifices": no Ballankirk ever makes a sacrifice. It's just not in their nature. But for some reason they think they're constantly making them. In fact, what they're doing is making fairly risk-free investments of time or energy in others, for which they expect to receive about a 200 percent return — a return that they always get, by the way, but not with gestures of the appropriate gratitude and the groveling flattery that all Ballankirks feel is due to them but which they would never confer upon each other.

Even though what would constitute an adequate response is subject to the most capricious standards, it always follows that the "sacrifice" has been unappreciated. If you were to believe what you'd hear during one of those massive, multifaceted family confrontations, you'd imagine that such a den of snarling lions represented the highest concentration of sacrificial lambs in the world.

Second, about "slights": such slights can take an infinity of forms, and that they be unintentional, of course, is utterly irrelevant to their being slights. Even more important is the memory of slights. All Ballankirks have prodigious memories; and the capacity to produce, at a moment's notice, an exhaustive litany of slights received from a given adversary over the years is one of the most treasured, if not indispensable, accoutrements of any successful combatant. There is a certain irony here, of course. To remind an adversary of his or her insults over the years is both to flatter their pride and imagination as well as to instigate aspirations for even higher levels of achievement. It's also to invite a rejoinder such as, "Well, I was right about that, wasn't I?"

Ballankirk slights arise from many factors. One important source is pets; Ballankirks have some of their most ferocious quarrels about pets. A sacred Ballankirk rule, for example, is that all pets, whether dogs, cats, horses, parrots, fish, lizards, turtles, boa constrictors, or tarantulas, may do whatever they want to do, wherever, whenever, and to whomever they want to do it, without the risk of incurring even the mildest complaint, either explicit or implicit, by anyone other than their personal masters. Any infraction of this rule will be taken as one of the worst of slights to the personal master of the pet in question, even when, and especially when, that pet has long since departed to its Happy Hunting Ground.

I should mention in this regard that even the suspicion of complaint, though never validated, can count as a serious slight. Every Ballankirk has some animal or another that he or she worships and expects the rest of the world to worship with at least equal devotion. Sometimes—yes, I hesitate to mention this—these animals are not domesticated. Ferocious and long-lasting wars have been fought over any number of bears, chipmunks, birds of all kinds, mice, otters, raccoons, foxes, deer, moose, frogs, bees, possums, woodchucks, daddy longlegs, skunks, dragonflies, butterflies, porcupines, coyotes (also known as "feral canines" or "coydogs" in our neck of the woods, depending on your social status), and other creatures that have won a place of endearment in some Ballankirk heart.

My mother even had a third cousin, once removed, who dedicated her life to doting upon spiders—creatures with which she obviously identified because she was always crocheting long, thin, woolen afghans that she drooped like spider webs all over her house. Molesting an actual spider web, or a spider, in her presence could provoke a dreadful retaliation.

In any event, such quarrels extend, I regret to say, even to plants, a cardinal Ballankirk principle being that any plant over which you can claim proprietary rights is to be regarded as an irreplaceable miracle of natural beauty (no matter how loathsome it may actually be).

Further, any plant over which *someone else* can claim proprietary rights is to be regarded as a horrifying weed (no matter how lovely it may be) and should be, according to all reasonable protocols of man and nature, summarily stomped upon or uprooted, or both. Such stompings and uprootings have borne consequences that have lasted for decades.

Another important source of slights, real and otherwise, is the giving of gifts—but we will put off our somewhat detailed account of that until a bit later because that will bring us back to Christmas and to Aunt Jennie's Christmas pie, for Christmas is the proper setting of this marvelous pie, and the role it plays in the life of the Ballankirk clan is so utterly different from anything that I've been thus far describing. It's the one thing that manages to dampen fury and, miraculously, to bring out the more positive side of the Ballankirk temperament—and that's no small accomplishment, given that there is close to nothing about the Ballankirk character that's positive.

But before we advance to explicating this rather "miraculous" phenomenon, we must switch our attention to an incident remarkable in family history for its specific violation of the connection between Aunt Jennie's pie and the Christmas season. This violation was perpetrated by Great-Aunt Gwendolyn, who was perhaps her generation's candidate for the most Aunt Jennie–like person in goodness of character and kindness of heart. It's she who probably came closest of anyone in Ballankirk history to rediscovering the actual recipe of the original pie.

But she didn't make the pie at Christmas; she never submitted it to the judgment of the clan; and she destroyed the recipe soon after the pie was made, without even having tasted it herself. It's a deeply, deeply tragic story, and I warn my thus far (presumably) indulgent readers that they shall shed many a tear before it's over.

If it's true that Great-Aunt Gwendolyn was the recipient of the rare and gracious Aunt Jennie strain in her character, it's likewise true that she gave birth to a son in whom all the most surly and contentious traits ingrained in the Ballankirk heritage were distilled to the point of — shall we call it? — perfection. His name was Ossborough. He was also known as Ossborough the Terrible and, somewhat more affectionately, as Ossy of the Baleful Eye.

Ossy was, to use the expression commonly applied by Ballankirks to any child other than their own, "not a particularly lovely child," except that in this case the description, even if a gross understatement, had a certain veracity about it.

Indeed, Ossy was a very ugly child.

Except for a head quite a bit too large for his body, no particular feature could be pointed out as being especially repellent. But a protracted, malevolent, venomous glare emanated from his eyes with such power that it somehow gave the impression that Ossy had three, rather than two, eyes in his head, all of which were lined up in one straight row beneath a single, shaggy, menacing eyebrow that stretched across the entire width of his face. It was as if nature, frustrated in its ability to provide a sufficient outlet for such reserves of boundless animosity in a single soul, had endowed him with three vehicles with which to express what couldn't have been otherwise expressed with two.

Ossy's father was one of the many innocents who married into the clan but who, unlike most of those innocents, was not instantaneously transformed into a 100 percent, full-blooded Ballankirk. Testimony to this is the fact that he continued to perform productive labor even after his marriage to Great-Aunt Gwendolyn. The nature of his work as a sea captain, of course, and its entailment of long absences, may have assisted in maintaining his purity. Then there was Great-Aunt Gwendolyn, who was so unlike a Ballankirk and who would have exerted little pressure on him to conform to family standards.

As a result, Great-Aunt Gwendolyn and her husband, contrary to Ballankirk tradition, lived a somewhat luxurious life consonant with their fortune, occupying one of those stately mansions that surround Louisburg

Square on Beacon Hill in Boston and furnishing it with fine antiques and a small collection of old master paintings. They exercised, within prudent limits, that ancient virtue of "munificence," sharing resources generously with others and patronizing judiciously the practices of elegant craftsmanship and studious service. The only difficulty in this arrangement was Ossy, whose horrifying manners began to occupy more and more of Great-Aunt Gwendolyn's time and devotion.

Anyway, his father had noted with some vague alarm the peculiar three-eyed effect while Ossy was still of "tender" age (though the epithet here is merely conventional, I can assure you). But he had not found it especially troubling until a second cousin of Gwendolyn was invited over for tea and rather pointedly called it to his attention.

The second cousin began by referring to Ossy as "such a cute little thing" —again, another standard Ballankirk expression intended to mean its opposite and followed inevitably by a wide, teeth-baring grimace known to exist only among Ballankirks and among certain breeds of East Tanzanian mountain baboons. The relative continued to praise that "marvelous third-eye effect" which gave such "distinction" and "character" to Ossy's visage. The poor father and sea captain spent several sleepless nights thereafter, as he wrestled with the memory of a grotesque three-eyed idol he had once seen in Malaysia, and which had haunted him during a long bout of malarial fever while riding at anchor off the steamy coast of East Timor. Now, whenever he gazed upon his own son, he saw that idol, and his physique was once again racked by malarial tremors.

Not long afterward, on a bright, sunny day, with sails flapping merrily in the wind and the ocean raising joyous white-capped waves on Massachusetts Bay, Ossy's father piloted the last great clipper ship out of Boston Harbor, bound for the far reaches of the earth, the "Antipodes" of song and legend. Neither he, nor the ship, nor the ship's crew were ever seen again, though it's said that a derelict seaman, presumably a member of the vanished crew, appeared many years later among the waterfront taverns and boarding houses of Boston Harbor and spoke of some earthly paradise where the crew had settled down to live in the South Pacific. Nobody believed the foolish old man—except for those who had ever had a run-in with Ossy and who knew that half the watery earth was scarcely enough space to put between him and his distraught father.

Meanwhile, good-hearted Great-Aunt Gwendolyn settled down to a life of pampering her son. She came to the conclusion, as many parents do, that the way to a child's heart is through desserts — the richer and more sumptuous, the better. Accordingly, she devoted herself to preparing a dessert that Ossy would finally appreciate and that would, consequently, temper the burning fury in his youthful heart. The only problem was that Ossy abhorred all desserts, with the sole exception of chocolate ice-cream cones, and all his mother's efforts were in vain. Even more, she failed to grasp, through all those years, that her efforts had precisely the reverse effect they were intended to have — the more refined, the more exquisite a dessert was, the more Ossy was provoked by it into an unspeakable rage.

Every afternoon, the same scene was enacted in the dining room of the old mansion in Louisburg Square. The room itself was ornate in a simple and tasteful manner. Oak paneling, tall, sunny windows, and a great glistening mahogany table surrounded by high-backed chairs gave it a tone of mellowness and serenity. On the side of the room facing the windows was a fireplace with a mantelpiece of carved ivory upon which graceful nymphs and satyrs danced as they held up bunches of grapes and sheaves of wheat. Over the mantelpiece was hung a large Van Dyck portrait. It depicted the sixth Duke of Hallingforth standing in a regal pose, with one gloved hand on his hip and wearing a gilded cuirass embossed with a picture of Mars. Between the painting and the mantelpiece was a sizable scar on the wall, where the oak paneling was bruised and splintered. This is where Ossy, with deadly accuracy, always threw his desserts.

When lunch was over, Great-Aunt Gwendolyn would bring in the dessert that she had spent most of the morning preparing for Ossy. She would place it in front of him and watch anxiously, but with ever indefatigable optimism, to see how he would react. He would prod the dessert with his spoon, pushing it down against the surface of the mixture to explore, with all three eyes, what suspicious fluids might ooze out of the concoction. After turning the spoon and scooping up a small amount of the dessert, he would lift it slowly to his lips.

But before it even touched his lips, he would let out a great yell, spit violently, start choking and gasping and clutching his neck as if being strangled, grab his dessert, dish and all, and pitch it clear across the room, where it would smash into the accustomed place on the wall, showering the dancing nymphs and satyrs with broken pottery and sticky clumps of whatever dessert it was that day.

Ossy would leap from the table, screaming that he was going to run down to the pharmacy on Charles Street to get a chocolate ice-cream cone. He would exit the house with an enormous slam of the front door. The domestic staff would enter the dining room to clean up, and Great-Aunt Gwendolyn would return to her cookbooks.

She tried everything.

She scoured every cookbook of every nationality and every age to discover a delicacy that would finally appease Ossy's taste. She tried Austrian strudels and French crepes and Russian tarts and Sicilian marzipan and honey cakes from Tehran.

Nothing worked; and, of course, Great-Aunt Gwendolyn, who never could and never would doubt Ossy's judgment, always concluded that the dessert must indeed have been just as bad as it seemed to be to merit Ossy's treatment of it.

Then, one bright day, she remembered Aunt Jennie's Christmas pie. Of course, at the time, the Christmas season was still far off, but she was impatient for results. She was also determined that this pie, with all its succulent memories and promises, would be the thing that finally worked.

For a period of time, her regular parade of desserts went down in quality somewhat—not that it would make much difference to Ossy anyway—as she devoted most of her energy to a vast research effort to recover the original recipe. Under her tireless supervision, hundreds of old cases were opened, attics and closets from Maine to Connecticut were ransacked, thousands of old letters were read, and interviews with all living Ballankirks were conducted. Finally, by putting together hundreds of clues and scraps of information, she was able to estimate, with a relatively high degree of certainty (so she thought), how the pie should be made. She even managed to unearth the original pie pan that Aunt Jennie had used so long ago.

The fateful day arrived.

Great-Aunt Gwendolyn woke her staff at 4:00 a.m. so that the pie might be ready for lunch at 12:30. At 11:00, the pie had been completed and was prepared for serving. Great-Aunt Gwendolyn forbade her servants even to lick the spoons or bowls that had been used in making the pie, though several servants ventured to sniff the precious mixture, and they simply ululated with pleasure; never had they sniffed anything so good. It inspired in them momentary hallucinations of gastronomic paradises. The elixir had been found; the magic key had been discovered. Even Great-Aunt Gwendolyn didn't taste the pie. That joy of discovery was to be Ossy's and Ossy's alone.

As usual, she brought in the dessert and placed it on the table. Ceremoniously she cut a slice of the pie and placed it on Ossy's plate. Then she put the plate in front of him. The servants all peeked from the pantry door to see what would happen.

Ossy lifted his spoon. He bent low over the dessert. His lips curled. Three rays of cold, bitter light seemed to emanate from his eyes at different angles and to fix the dessert in their crossbeams. Even he couldn't help but notice that there was something very special about this dessert. His mother clasped her hands in delight as he prodded the surface of the pie with his spoon. No suspicious juices oozed out. The first test had been passed.

Great-Aunt Gwendolyn beamed with pleasure. Ossy scooped a tiny bit of the creamy yellow filling with his spoon and lifted it cautiously to his lips. Great-Aunt Gwendolyn held her breath. Suddenly an ear-splitting scream tore the serenity of the dining room from top to bottom, causing the servants at the pantry door to fall violently backward into the pantry.

It was followed by the most ghastly swish as the plate flew toward its accustomed place, and the entire pie hurtled after it. The plate smashed home, the pie dish clattered directly behind it, but not before its contents had risen from the dish and ended up as a bright yellow swath across the Duke of Hallingforth's cuirass.

Ossy scuttled out of the dining room at full speed, screeching for a chocolate ice-cream cone and slamming the front door with more than usual ferocity as his mother collapsed in shame and horror.

Part of the tragedy of this story is that Great-Aunt Gwendolyn came to her usual conclusion: the pie must indeed be detestable, even despite her servants' intimations to the contrary. The consequence was that she destroyed the recipe, as well as many of the clues she had found—so deep was her humiliation at the failure of the pie. Later generations would mourn, quite aptly, this loss to family tradition, though by now much of their attention had shifted to what she had discovered—a mystery in itself as inexplicable as the one her investigation set out to solve.

There was one person who did taste the pie prepared that day, but, as I've already indicated, he has passed into ignominious oblivion. His story is noteworthy for the international controversy it aroused at the time. First, we must give an account of the events that led to such an extraordinary occasion as that of a complete stranger partaking of the joys of Aunt Jennie's pie.

As we have been at some pains to illustrate, Ossy was an unpleasant enough fellow, and several decades later, his unpleasantness went to the point, as it does unlaudably in some Ballankirks, of conspiring to remove from this lamentable vale of tears any elderly personage whom one might finally construe as being an obstacle to the rightful and timely passage of a bountiful legacy. In this case, it was his own mother, who, even if Ossy had been able to forgive her for all those unwanted desserts pressed daily upon him, was considered to have lived quite long enough.

Now, there was a standard procedure for this kind of thing in the family: it was to take your intended victim out for a drive (formerly in a horse carriage and, of more recent vintage, in an automobile) that turned out to be so harrowing that only the sturdiest could survive it.

If you were really serious about this procedure, you loaded your victim into the back seat of a drafty convertible and set off for Florida in the dead of winter. As we all know, Florida is warm and balmy in the winter months, but the twelve or so states you must traverse in order to get there are locked in a vast North Atlantic chill that gets a bit milder, if not a lot damper and clammier, the farther south you go.

Remember, we are speaking of the days before superhighways, glossy motels, and restaurant chains laced together the regions of the country in their dreadful monotony: but the local color of bumpy roads looking like endless back alleys extending through miles of piney hills and plains and little corroding towns was scarcely more attractive; and what could a pair of tired New England eyes think when confronted by plate after plate of that old Southern roadside food with its pale, leprous mound of grits inexorably simmering in a puddle of hot, pungent grease?

The outcome of all of this is too clear to need mention. After a week of hard travel, the corpse is returned to Boston by way of railroad car and lugubrious cortege and is laid to rest in the family grave in Mount Auburn Cemetery in Cambridge.

So it happened to Great-Aunt Gwendolyn.

I've seen the actual farewell photograph. Ossy hugs the wheel of his monstrous Pierce-Arrow, with all three eyes burning holes in the photographic paper. A glint of satisfaction plays about his mouth as if he were anticipating the biggest, and indubitably the best, chocolate ice-cream cone in his life. Great-Aunt Gwendolyn sits in the back seat, optimally placed for catching the worst drafts, despite the masses of fur in which she's bundled and which makes her look vaguely like an Eskimo about to be led forth to her demise on the icy tundra of the north.

Three weeks later the funeral was held in Boston. It was a typical Ballankirk funeral replete with wailing, gnashing of teeth, quarreling, blaming, confessions of guilt (not to be believed, by the way), and the dreadful Ballankirk custom of the entire clan following the casket up the church aisle while walking on their knees, keening and ululating, the whole penguin-like procession wobbling and bumping into each other—a practice that it's thought (though in vain) will placate the assuredly angry spirit of the deceased.

After the funeral, Ossy collected his spoils and did a most unlikely Ballankirk thing: he detached himself for good from the clan, moved to California, and never, to the contentment of everybody, was seen again. The house on Louisburg Square was sold and all its furnishings and adornments auctioned off at Sotheby's to sundry art collectors of the world.

The Van Dyck portrait eventually found its way to the Fogg Art Museum at Harvard, where it became the object of a long and bitter academic controversy. Papers were written, scholarly symposia were held, and heated arguments conducted — all of which were to explain the glowing yellow band that stretched across the Duke of Hallingforth's cuirass.

Two major schools of thought evolved in regard to this question.

Prof. Eselkopf of Yale contended that the band was a golden ribbon added by Van Dyck to commemorate the duke's participation in the great battle at Tumble-Up-and-Down-on-Tweed between the Cavaliers and the Roundheads.

Dr. Gerhard Schwarmer, however, firing his scholarly salvos from his well-fortified bastion in Princeton, argued against this position, claiming that the duke's participation in that notable battle was one of unmitigated cowardice and that the yellow band had been added by an unknown, though hostile, painter and was intended to underscore the duke's headlong flight from the thick of the fray.

Both schools of thought conceded that the band indeed was a later addition to the painting.

The progenitors of these positions, and their rabid followers, fought out the question for years, doing everything in their power to block academic appointments, deny tenures, and destroy both the reputations and careers of their adversaries.

Then one day, a famished and lonely Harvard freshman, having nothing in particular to do with his time (as is often the case with Harvard freshmen), wandered into the Fogg Art Museum, found himself mysteriously attracted to the painting with its delectable band, and picked off and ate the entire thing before a custodian managed to catch him in the act and turned him over to the Harvard judicial committee.

This committee, retaining the self-righteous rigor of its Puritan origins, but not the latter's sense of moral principle, and directing its ire not so much at acts of immorality as at acts of indiscretion, summarily dismissed our young man from the school.

He, in turn, didn't help his case by having declared a complete lack of any repentant attitude. He asserted boldly to his judges that he would do it again under any circumstances; it had been worth it.

Ballankirk matrons are fond of citing this final part of the story to reassure themselves that the pie is truly a gastronomic wonder, even though they have never, to their knowledge, actually tasted it. Also, the members of what is called the "egg" (or sometimes the "custard") party use this story to argue that the recipe does contain eggs because the band had stuck to the painting rather remarkably like tempura. Apparently, it had even deceived the scholars (not all that difficult a thing to accomplish in most circumstances).

Efforts to reach the poor evicted freshman with the intent to probe his memory have failed because he, like so many expellees of Ivy institutions in those days, had disappeared permanently into the impenetrable mazes of the Amazonian rainforests.

Meanwhile, the academic controversy about the painting dissolved into mutual recriminations, just as bitter as ever, between the two schools of academicians, each charging the other with having perpetrated a monstrous hoax on the scholarly world. The duke of Hallingforth's descendants launched international lawsuits against just about everybody for the defamation of their august ancestor—though the proceedings uncovered new information that proved that the duke may have been an even more cringing defector than anyone had previously suspected (though an alternate hypothesis also developed claiming that the duke actually abandoned the field in order to meet, munch, and mate with his newest mistress).

Despite such dishonorable revelations, the royal family, cravenly bowing to the Hallingforth family and to public opinion (as created and conveyed by the news media), insisted on an apology from the president of the United States.

The president of the United States, cravenly bowing to the royal family and to public opinion (as created and conveyed by the news media), gave it, though the president had never heard of Van Dyck, nor of the Roundheads and Cavaliers, nor, for that matter, of the royal family; and art museums around the world, cravenly bowing to curatorial hysteria and to public opinion (as created and conveyed by the news media), significantly tightened their security by denying all famished-looking visitors access to their collections.

The Ballankirk quest has continued nevertheless, for Aunt Jennie's Christmas pie is the bond that unites them. Of course, the clan gathers, either in part or as a whole, quite a few times a year at various familial domiciles around New England.

The Fourth of July is an important event, despite the original Ballankirk contribution to the "other side" and despite the opportunity afforded by the holiday to provide untoward "incidents"—often involving fireworks used to stun pets into more or less permanent states of zoological imbecility—that can be cited as grounds for conflict for years into the future.

Labor Day is spurned, and that's good—the very idea of Labor Day puts a typical Ballankirk into such a foul mood that it's just as well they don't convene. Instead, they mope around throughout the designated day in the isolation of their homes and sedulously cultivate their throbbing migraine headaches (migraine being the only impairment Ballankirks are subject to). In any event, how could one celebrate Labor Day if one doesn't believe that those who work for the companies one holds equities in shouldn't even get Sunday off? (And since the Ballankirks, collectively, own equities in virtually every American corporation, this conviction encompasses pretty much the entire industrial workforce of the United States.)

Thanksgiving, on the other hand, is permeated by an atmosphere of late-autumnal somnolence. The clan retires from a presumptively sumptuous repast in a calm and tranquilized mood. Indeed, despite all the burnt turkey and dried-out stuffing that makes sawdust taste wonderful by comparison, they resemble a roost of great roasted turkeys themselves, stuffed and bulging and basted in the juices of contentment. Moreover, the day subsides into the implacable boredom induced by the menfolk snoring and nodding before the television set, where a dazzling play or a sudden touchdown in a seemingly endless sequence of collegiate football games occasionally pops open their bleary eyes.

But Christmas, alas, is different. The New England winter has set in; one's spirit is alert and poised as it contemplates the onset of some great meteorological Battle of the Somme against an indomitable and wily foe. One's parsimonious propensities have been exacerbated into a paranoiac frenzy by the incessant barrage of Christmas catalogues, by armed sorties into glittering department stores and malls, and by children well advanced in the stages of holiday pandemonium; and one's greed has been assaulted at every street corner by a host of Santa Clauses ringing bells and collecting money for one cause or another—after all, what is wrong with all those dimwitted and indolent Santa Clauses? Why don't they go out like anyone else with a brain in their head and inherit fortunes? But above and beyond any such trivial considerations, Christmas means two things to a Ballankirk, each as deadly as the other: the ritual of gifts and the ritual of drinking.

I shall grant for the moment that whoever gave the first Christmas gift—one of the Magi, I presume—had only the very best intentions in mind. But history has changed, and Ballankirks have reversed much of that.

To begin with, Ballankirks, by nature, have little or no inclination to give gifts to anyone for any reason at all, but if social convention forces them into such an unwelcome procedure, as lamentably it often does, then they have a genius for turning the act into something more or less contrary to its accepted purpose.

Second, all Ballankirks have the congenital trait of being born with a full-scale cash register wedged in their cranial cavities somewhere between the two lobes of their brains, along with a permanently updated price list of all merchandise made and sold on the face of the earth.

Ballankirks, it must be known, are fond of memorizing sales catalogues (in fact, mountains of them)—they're the only sort of thing they do memorize, and once memorized, nothing is ever forgotten. This enables them to identify almost instantaneously the provenance of any gift—i.e., from what discount catalogue or bargain-basement sale it came and how much it cost.

In addition, Ballankirks are aware from birth that a complex set of rules applies to all acts of giving gifts in order to avoid giving offense: needless to say, it's important that these rules are *not* observed. We can itemize some of these rules as follows:

First, the value of a gift received must be equal to the value of a gift given. The only allowable method for determining in advance what the value of a future gift might be is psychic clairvoyance.

Second, no gift may duplicate anything the recipient of the gift has already in his or her possession, even if it has been hidden away in an attic for the last half a century and even if the recipient doesn't know he or she has it.

Third, the gift may not touch even remotely upon any disagreeable experience that the recipient has had in his or her past. For example, since Cousin

Beatrice was once stung by a bee on the end of her nose while sniffing a daffodil, it would be most unwise to give her a teapot with daffodils painted on it (it would be otiose to mention that she has received, nevertheless, innumerable gifts over the years with daffodil motifs engraved thereon).

Fourth, no drinkable or comestible gifts are allowed; an upset stomach or momentary indigestion caused by it is bound to elicit an immediate and irrefutable charge of poisoning.

Fifth, no gift can be too useless to its receiver ("What am I going to do with this thing?") or too useful ("I had to get one of these anyway").

Finally, the color of a gift must match the color of any possible thing in the recipient's household that the recipient could conceive of matching it with—a task made rather difficult by the Ballankirk inability to match a color with any other color anyway.

Well, none of these criteria could ever be met, but they're useful guides in knowing how best to fine-tune the offensiveness of the gift to its recipient. What a joy it is to see a full-blooded Ballankirk—and all Ballankirks are full-blooded Ballankirks, no matter how remote or exotic the origin of their non-Ballankirk ancestral lines may be—cautiously removing the wrapping paper from a gift (wrapping paper, I should add, that has been recycled at least a dozen times and that the recipient will use again).

And then there is that first shock of chagrin and derision, the mind whirring and clicking with the alacrity of a thousand IBM computers matching, pricing, remembering, comparing, plotting revenge. This is followed by a tilting of the head, a long, languorous turtle-like blink of the eyes, and a high-pitched, quavering wail: "Eeeooo, thay-yank yeeeuuu seeeuuu mooch!"—the final "mooch" being pronounced with a loud and ominous snap of the teeth.

Ah, yes, the ritual of giving lays out the battlefield.

Now for the ritual of drinking. Once again, I wouldn't want to disparage any venerable tradition of the Christmas season, least of all the fine old customs of wassail and good cheer. But I must admonish all who would attend a Ballankirk Christmas that a martini in the hands of a momentarily gracious Ballankirk matron is like a high explosive in the hands of a well-trained terrorist. How often have I watched those tilted glasses, the olive with its glowing pimento like a red-hot fuse, the chilled gin laced with vermouth like pure nitroglycerin about to be poured down into the entrails of a seething volcano! And those portly Ballankirk gents saturating themselves in heavy spirits so that their progressively addled faces appear like a hybrid of a brandied peach and a live hand grenade ready to burst! All it takes is just the right spark to get things going! And how they can get going!

There comes to mind one particular occasion that, to this day, is called The Battle of the Railroad Crossing. It all started over the high-speed collision of a freight train with the 20th Century Limited — a collision that resulted in the total derailment and partial destruction of both trains. No, this disaster didn't happen in the state of Kansas or someplace like that, where trains apparently go zooming about and crashing into one another; it happened on my brother's electric-train layout.

I was a child at the time. The clan decided to gather at my family's house for Christmas; all sixty-five extant members converged on our roomy domicile in southern Massachusetts for the festive occasion.

As usual in this season, we dragged the electric trains up from the basement and set them up in the library so that visitors could play with them. There was no difficulty about the children sharing them with adults, since children usually find electric trains insufferably boring after a short while, whereas male adults can play with them all day long.

As could be predicted, several of my uncles spent rather a considerable time at the trains, both before and after dinner — which was usually consumed in midafternoon, the dessert being put off until late in the evening. They drove the little trains around and around and around, and while they were doing this, they drank and drank and drank. Finally, only two uncles were left at the train set.

Uncle Henry, at that time in his life, was going through his riverboat phase. Though he lived on a bluff that overlooked the Connecticut River as it bends down from Hartford into the Long Island Sound, and occasionally ventured out on the river in his small cruiser, he came to fancy himself for a while as a Mississippi riverboat captain and as a dashing gambler enjoined by some unwritten law to wear a red silk vest with a small derringer tucked away in one of its pockets. He had dressed accordingly for the Christmas gathering and was now preoccupied at the train set in constructing an extraordinary network of tracks, switches, crossings, embankments, tunnels, and signal lights.

Across the table from him was Uncle Matt. He watched Uncle Henry's activities with no little irritation. He was also enormously "steeped," as they say.

Uncle Henry began to run a freight train carefully through his network to see if it would hold up; Uncle Matt determined that it would not. Just as the freight train was about to reach a crossing, he gave full power to his 20th Century Limited and brought it careening around a side track and broadside into the freight train as it arrived at the crossing, knocking down the entire network that Uncle Henry had spent so much time in building.

Immediately, Uncle Henry pulled his derringer on Uncle Matt. He did it to frighten him, of course. It was only a replica, anyway, without the power to shoot. But, simultaneously with Uncle Henry's little gesture, there was a short circuit on the track caused by the tangle of electric equipment and accompanied by a bang, a flash of light, and a puff of smoke.

Uncle Matt, who had just finished his eighth bourbon on the rocks, slipped underneath the table and lay silently on the floor.

Since it was now about seven in the evening, and everyone was sufficiently fatigued and "steeped," the scene was ripe for plenty of action. The whole company jumped from their armchairs, sofas, piano stools, and little circles around the fireplaces or in the pantry or by the liquor cabinet and dashed into the library. Uncle Henry stood by the train layout gaping in a rather bewildered way at his derringer and wondering if it had actually, for some utterly inconceivable reason, gone off.

Uncle Matt's legs protruded from underneath the table.

It is significant that Aunt Lizzy, Uncle Matt's wife, either jumped to the conclusion that her husband was dead or didn't care too much whether he was dead or not, or was engaging (as her enemies would, in later years, contend) in a bit of wishful thinking. Instead, her sole concern, at the moment, was to launch a full-scale verbal attack on Uncle Henry, reminding him vociferously of the devious and violent ways he had exhibited throughout his life, ever since the time he threw sand into her lemonade at the beach when she was three years old.

It became instantly clear that she really wanted to fight about the lemonade incident once again, and the apparent murder of her husband was merely a pretext for doing so.

Meanwhile, Uncle Matt was dragged from underneath the table, and everyone noted the rather silly smile on his face. His face was doused with a bucket of cold water (a therapeutic procedure learned from cowboy movies and, along with pouring whiskey over a wound and into a mouth, a standard Ballankirk way of dealing with any medical emergency). He opened his eyes and gazed upon the crowd gathered about him.

You can just imagine the disappointment when he was discovered to be alive. When Ballankirks get riled up over a tragedy and then find out there is no tragedy at all, they feel personally cheated. But this opportunity for a good row would not be allowed to slip by.

The clan immediately fractured into two warring groups. The fault lines of such fractures, as I've discovered over the years, are utterly unpredictable and utterly inexplicable. Each great quarrel has its own distinctive structure of hostilities. Even the size of the warring groups can differ dramatically. In this case, the groups were about equal; but sometimes minorities take on majorities of various dimensions and convictions.

I would like, at this point, to make special mention of my grandmother, of whom I, and everyone else, was especially proud. Like the great champions of ancient epic lore — Achilles and Roland and Aeneas and the Cid — she could advance into the fray and destroy anything or anyone who was in her way.

Even more, not unlike the redoubtable Cúchulainn of the Ulster Cycle, she could distort her body in the most terrible ways as she fought, sucking in one eye until it disappeared into her forehead while the other eye expanded into a bloodshot whirligig the size of a wagon wheel, and her hair meanwhile would change its color from fiery red to lethal yellow to deathly black and back again.

I mention her in this context because there was one occasion — it was her birthday party, and someone (we will never know who) put an extra candle on her birthday cake — when she took on the entire clan and fought them all to a standstill. She reminded me of one of those samurai swordsmen I've seen in Japanese films who single-handedly mow down small armies of a warlord's household retainers. The side fortunate enough to get her support in a family brawl was usually victorious.

She's deceased now, poor dear, but in her prime there was no warrior who could withstand her assault. I can't help but imagine that to this very day she assists old Charon himself by harrowing the hapless hordes of the dead into his flimsy craft and across the tumultuous waters of Styx.

The Battle of the Railroad Crossing followed the usual procedures, and it would be tiresome to go into all the details—for example, the tendency of the quarrel to move from room to room, to spread out at times into minor engagements, and subsequently to reconverge into major conflicts; the appointment of heroes and heroines from either side representing their group in individual combats conducted before the drawn-up hosts; the "fast draw" phenomenon when daring adversaries matched up for quick verbal exchanges of a particularly vicious nature; and the taking of hostages—i.e., shepherding your opponents' children together and pretending to whisper to them "dreadful secrets" about their parents (I've said "pretending" here because there are some depths to which even a Ballankirk will not descend). Indeed, the art of whispering is considered one of the most potent weapons, and a well-timed whisper can obliterate even the strongest man or woman.

Of course, in the midst of this there is the usual slamming of doors, stamping of feet, walking up and down staircases as if trying to make them collapse, running off for short periods into the wintry night without a coat (so as to punish an adversary by proposing—in theory, at least, though never in practice—to freeze oneself to death), threatening to leave and the angry bundling up of children in snowsuits, only to unbundle them again just as angrily (to demonstrate defiance), and the solemn promises, of immeasurable verbosity and length, never to speak to a certain person again.

It's also the custom at regular intervals for warring groups to break off and retreat into a place of privacy so that they can recoup their forces, plan strategy, and take nourishment to "settle the nerves"—primarily liquid and primarily very strong, of course.

These respites are particularly interesting because this is when the "spies" become active, circulating surreptitiously from one group to another, gathering information, and generally having the effect of heating up the situation to ever new pitches of excitement by telling people what others in the adversarial group are saying about them. There are also "double agents" who work for both sides. All of this ensures that the combatants will return to the attack more charged up and ferocious than ever.

In this particular battle I recall how Cousin Adele at one point ran screaming and wailing from the living room into the hallway and then stopped in front of the large mirror to admire herself because she thought she looked especially beautiful when her eyes were swollen and glistening with tears. Actually, Ballankirks in general take enormous pleasure in observing themselves in mirrors while in the throes of some passion.

They also use mirrors in the same way that a few especially deranged Roman emperors did — that is, to observe others indirectly — and that's why any Ballankirk house is filled with strategically placed mirrors. However, it's unclear to what extent the typical Ballankirk understands the optics of reflection by virtue of which to be able to observe another indirectly in a mirror is, in turn, to be able to be observed indirectly by that same person in that same mirror while in the act of indirectly observing, though such optics must be understood and even cherished, for such mutual indirect observation occurs frequently and is transformed instantaneously into mutual indirect glaring by way of the mirror — a particularly delightful variation on the normal mode of glaring at another.

The Battle of the Railroad Crossing ended as abruptly as it began — as is true of all Ballankirk conflicts. Cousin Karen of sweet and tender temperament (our most recent candidate for the Aunt Jennie of our generation) stepped into the no-man's-land between the entrenched foes and announced very demurely that coffee was ready and that fourteen of Aunt Jennie's Christmas pies, each prepared by a different family member, had been arrayed on the dining room table and were ready for the annual tasting.

All hostilities ceased instantaneously as if there had been no quarrel at all. Bitter enemies were transformed on the spot into old and intimate friends, as the clan filed slowly into the dining room to study the pies and commence the conversation that inevitably would ensue. Of course, there were differences of opinion, but the differences were amicable.

"Yes, this is superb," someone said as he or she delicately dipped his or her fork into the pie for another mouthful, "but it could use a touch more cinnamon." Another appreciated the candied fruits, but indicated that sherry, not rum, was the proper spirit for the fruits to be steeped in, and that more raisins and fewer currants were desirable. The "egg" party had its say; a recent Devonshire cream group had formed and advanced their cause with any number of compelling arguments.

The atmosphere was genuinely hearty and genteel. Though one could reasonably partake of only a few samples, given the richness of the pies, all the pies were genuinely good and rewarding to the palate.

Meanwhile, any outside guests or nonfamily members who had been invited for this particular occasion and who had been so unfortunate as to have witnessed the former altercation had to be coaxed, gasping and quivering, from closets and other hiding places and drawn, incredulously, into the merriment that now prevailed.

The tasting of the pies brought with it, as it always does, the funny stories that Ballankirks like to remember and recount for the millionth time as if no one has ever heard them before. Favorites are The Sinking of Aunt Ruth's Picnic Basket, The Revolt of Cousin Bill's Septic Tank, Who Put the Brick in Uncle Geo's Birthday Cake? (a still unsolved mystery, but evidence is still being gathered — or made up, as if that made any difference), and the time when Uncle Harnet had a nervous breakdown (so he claimed) when he discovered that someone had dumped scrambled eggs on top of his compost heap.

The story of Ossy of the Baleful Eye was rehearsed once more, and the loss of Great-Aunt Gwendolyn's research was appropriately lamented.

Again, speculations about the Harvard freshman abounded, one old fellow actually claiming to have seen his face in a background crowd in a newsreel filmed in Rangoon. No one believed this assertion for an instant and took it, rightfully so, as a sign of the old fellow's advancing senility (after all, no one had ever known what this mysterious person looked like in the first place).

But, for all this, the old house rang with laughter and goodwill.

Farewells are always lengthy affairs among the Ballankirks and may take hours to complete, as if dozens of important things to talk about are suddenly remembered only after the galoshes have been put on and heavy coats wrapped around the departing ones. Plans are made for summer visits on the Cape or in the Berkshires, or up in Maine somewhere, or by the New Hampshire lakes. Children suffer through these parting ceremonies with heroic patience and sometimes fall asleep in the back seats of cars as they wait for garrulous parents to start the engines, turn on the headlights, and drive off into the snowy December darkness. So it was this very night. Only two aged and rather inebriated bachelor uncles bedded down in the basement game room until they could safely leave on the following morning.

Now, I should remark that an outside observer, witnessing these terminal rituals of a Ballankirk Christmas, would be led to conclude that nowhere in the world could you find such a cheerful and happy group.

Certainly, as we know too well by now, such an observer would not be in possession of all the relevant facts. But then again, might not such an observer be right about this in some sense — that is, when all is said and done?

I mean, where would you find a group of people who have — let's face it — everything they want, and supremely so, and nothing, in the final analysis and according to their own lights, to regret?

We shall defer making a summary judgment about such a matter, as we must, I'm afraid to say, defer so many other similar judgments, to a time and a place somewhere well beyond our ken, somewhere well beyond what we can reasonably understand in this sad and sorry hither side of time.

And somewhere, too, I like to think that, under those frozen Vermont hills, under those wintry New England stars, Aunt Jennie hugs her infant sons closer to her breast, awaiting in her long hibernal sleep to be awakened to an infinitely more Hospitable Kingdom than the one she knew in her brief and gracious life so long ago, a Kingdom of Festivity, a Kingdom of Peace, like that once and future Christmas pie she bequeathed to us all — yes, to us all — so full of promise, so full of wonderment and joy.

Thunder-Egg

P lunge a spade into the soil of northern New England, and you will, inevitably, hit a rock. Force, directed from whatever center in you such force comes from, will pass through your shoulder, down through your arm, along the spade handle and, with a deadening metallic clunk hit the rock, whence, by whatever law determines these matters, it will return instantaneously as an unwelcome shock, which will rebound in reverse order up through the spade handle, into your arm, and, arching painfully over the muscles of your shoulder blades, will terminate in the source whence it originally came.

Let's call that source your "heart," for lack of a better term — "heart" both literally and metaphorically. For the problem, of course, is not simply the rock *per se* but, rather, your instantaneously formed hypothesis about how big it might turn out to be.

The initial shock of hitting it is the same, whether the stone is the size of an egg, of a loaf of bread, or of a hefty footlocker, or — to envisage one of the worst possible scenarios — of a Dodge four-wheel-drive pickup truck with an extended cab and a plow attached. You simply don't know how big the rock will be until continued digging gradually reveals the answer.

The demands that are about to be made upon your heart — understood both as the organ that supplies energy as well as a metaphor for that state of mind that may, or often does, encompass such moral entities as gumption and endurance and despair — can vary considerably.

The smaller rocks soon resolve the issue, much to the satisfaction and ease of the digger (though only temporarily, for the subsequent plunge of your spade will hit another rock and will renew the problem once again). The larger rocks, the boulders, are a different matter; for, in a sense, they start small—like an egg, as I have said—and keep growing bigger and bigger as you dig around them, until, exhausted after an afternoon's labor, you concede victory to a monstrous protrusion that could very well be the tip of a volcanic cone, extinct as of about half a billion years ago, whose granite foundation penetrates deep into the earth.

Some of my compatriots here in the northern woods refer to such underground, gradually emerging phenomena as "thunder-eggs." I don't know how common this expression is, even in our neighborhood. Such a lexical idiosyncrasy differs substantially from the western, or Oregonian, nomenclature conferred upon apparently abundant small, ball-sized igneous rocks with colorful mineralogical deposits inside a shell-like crust, and I don't wish my use of the term to look like some zealous effort to appropriate what could be construed, by some prior right, as belonging to those quite exquisite, Fabergé-like productions of nature.

Our local usage, of wholly independent provenance, I'm sure, is grounded in some kind of meteorological metaphor. For, sometimes, what starts in our northern mountains as an innocuous breeze can churn itself up, suddenly and unpredictably, into a thunderous summer squall. Our summer hikers, under such conditions, can discover that what was a limpid brook traversed in the morning's ascent of a mountain has been transformed, by the afternoon's descent, into a raging and dangerous torrent.

Thunder-eggs are like that, starting small and getting bigger, sometimes growing rapidly in front of your eyes with each subsequent thrust of the spade. I suspect, moreover, that the euphonious relationship between "thunder-egg" and "thunderhead" may account for some phonemic, as well as semantic, elision that generated the former term out of the latter.

Be that as it may, thunder-eggs can be every bit as perilous as thunderheads. Back in the old days, before mechanized backhoes made dealing with thunder-eggs much easier than it once was, farmers used to try to rid their fields of them by digging enormous pits adjacent to them, using levers to roll them down into these pits, then covering over the pits with loam so that the fields would be level. It might happen that not everyone participating in this process was out of the way when the dirt beneath the thunder-egg sometimes unaccountably collapsed and the massive rock rolled down into the pit, impelled by its own gravitational pull. Whatever was squashed beneath the giant boulder was scarcely worth digging out and reburying someplace else.

I say all of this because I know—though actually more *know of* than really know—a fellow who's referred to in our locale as Thunder-Egg. I don't suppose that the proud parents of this prodigy conferred that name upon him; and I equally don't suppose that anybody quite remembers who first applied the expression to him or what specific event, if any, may have warranted the application. I'm also, even to this day, puzzled as to whether the designation is to be understood as honorific or derogatory—for another cognate expression, "dunderhead," may have contributed its own impetus to the curious phonetic and semantic blend involved here.

This latter expression, decidedly not honorific in any event, is arguably a legacy of our Dutch forbears, "donder" simply being Dutch for "thunder." Others contend for an ultimately Spanish origin of the phrase—something having to do with the processing of sugarcane.

Leaving such recondite issues to the etymologists in my audience, I, or anyone else, for that matter, could entertain little doubt as to who Thunder-Egg is and why the name seems to fit. If you had heard the name without prior knowledge of the person, you would scarcely hesitate for a moment, when confronting him for the first time in the post office or outside the general store or at the annual town meeting, from gasping, "O my God, this must be Thunder-Egg!" (or, as it's frequently said, "*the* Thunder-Egg!") And *the* Thunder-Egg it would truly be, bestriding the world (as the Bard of Avon once eloquently and memorably remarked about someone else) like a colossus, like the colossus he is in all his ambivalent glory.

Okay, there is, to begin with and as you can well surmise, nothing small about Thunder-Egg, nothing even remotely egg-like about him—unless, of course, you first behold him somewhere at a distance. In such a circumstance it will not be long before what could be taken to be small will swiftly become as huge as it is. And I mean huge—a gigantic, muscular bull of a man pawing the earth with his hooves and revolving a great wedge of a head that certainly, by all rights, should be surmounted by a capacious span of horns.

Then, as you get to know him better, he just keeps getting larger and larger. Like a thunder-egg, there's no predicting when he will stop becoming even larger than he already is. Of late he's grown a beard—a massive, unkempt beard that, along with his lion's mane of hair, has swollen his head to about twice the size it normally is. His physical stature is rendered even more imposing by the shaggy, loose-fitting clothes he likes to wear: in summer, a voluminous canvas smock covered with stains, which flaps about in the wind like a mainsail on a square-rigger; in spring and autumn, a woolen fleece that assuredly required the sacrifice of a dozen doughty rams to have provided a girth of such amplitude; and in winter, what looks like the shaggy hide of some gargantuan bear that would, unquestionably, have been the terror of the north woods in his prime.

But his affinity with thunder-eggs (and maybe even with thunderheads) of field and woodland is as much moral as it's physical. He has a way, again and again, of suddenly and violently emerging out of nowhere. He bursts through doors, erupts from tangled thickets, crashes through dense underbrush, bulges up and breaks through the surface of snowy drifts, splashes out of rivers, roars into shops and stores and gasoline stations, and startles and overwhelms and jars and terrifies.

Many a serene fisherman has had his vacation seriously impaired by an unexpected confrontation on stream or lake with this embodied specter of the primeval forest. All lowland hunters, nay, all hunters of any stripe, have long ago learned to make as wide a detour as possible around his hallowed acres, for though he seems to inhabit, as an omnipresent spirit, all the upland valleys, venturing upon his personally owned land not only risks—it guarantees—an encounter.

But why? Why be fearful of him?

Nothing, for the most part, ever happens. He just wants to say hello and make sure that everything is okay. If, well after his departure, you're still trembling, that's not as much his fault as it is your own.

For another part of his bigness is the bigness of his character. And he just keeps getting bigger and bigger, too, in that respect and in the most surprising and unexpected ways. You have a dangerously sick cow, and without ever having summoned him or without even being able to figure out how he would know about it, you're astonished to see him plunge through the portals of your barn and take the situation quickly in hand. (The cow, I can assure you, has no objections and finds immediate solace in his elemental but practiced grasp.) Or lose a cat: guess who, a day or so later, scratches his way through the nearby brambly copse cradling the purring critter in his massive arms!

A doe is grazed by a car; its fawn lingers there, sniffing at the stunned and bruised body of its mother. A moment later Thunder-Egg is on the scene! Does he know everything that goes on in heaven and earth? He hoists the injured doe up on his shoulders and, with the fawn trailing behind, carries it — miles, if necessary — to a shed attached to his barn, dresses the wound, cares for both creatures, and releases them back into the woods as soon as they can fend for themselves. And, of course, I make no mention here of the dozen human crises that invoke his assistance, month after month, year after year.

That's part of his being a thunder-egg — he comes unbidden, unasked for, out of nowhere, bigger than ever, especially to the recipient of his ministrations. He's a kind man, generous, openhanded, tender to all living creatures, never crude, never uncouth — until ... unless ...

Well, he is, everyone claims, a stickler for rules, and sometimes that gets him and others into trouble. He insists that folks abide by what they agreed to do, even if that agreement, as it often is, is made by agreeing that others have been delegated to make agreements that are binding upon them. The fishermen and hunters, I noted earlier, can occasionally find themselves recipients of a rough-hewn justice if they're caught violating rules set down by the state for the protection of wildlife as well as for the safety of humans and of domestic animals. Not a few unwary and imprudent poachers who hunt by blinding game with high-beam spotlights at night have found themselves with their spotlights fixed on the angry face of Thunder-Egg himself, with all the attendant consequences.

It must be admitted that, in this respect, his tumultuous intrusions are not always welcome, and this is why some of the village folk — mostly those caught justly in malfeasance but refusing to admit it, even to themselves — would like to elide his name yet again at the bidding of their own self-protective instincts and call him "dunderhead."

It's a mystery, as I've already mentioned, how Thunder-Egg knows the things he knows. He rarely seems to be around except in those impulsive entrances he makes from time to time, yet when he's around, he seems to know everything that's going on. For example, the ordinary citizen hereabouts takes him, at least to all appearances, to be an illiterate man, a man alien to paper and pen and book and balance sheet and computer and all those documentary accouterments of civilization that we assume are indispensable for conferring intelligible order upon our lives. He, by contrast (and in keeping with his name), appears to be the product of some geophysical shifting of the tectonic forces beneath the earth, or, better yet, something deposited at random, like those actual lapidary thunder-eggs, by the passing glacier of a recent ice age.

Yet such a citizen must reel in astonishment—yes, *reel* in astonishment—when he or she learns that, on a winter morning not long ago, he burst—as he's wont to do—into the town offices, demanded to see the financial records of the past few years, and several hours later had pinned a serious charge of embezzlement on the town treasurer—an elderly, bespectacled lady best known for the oatmeal-raisin cookies she gives, or used to give, to children on the various holidays of the year. She mirthfully denied the accusation, chuckled demurely, and offered him an oatmeal-raisin cookie.

To no avail! The allegation led to a conviction, a substantial fine, and a short prison term for the lady in question (commuted, in any event, because of her age).

As a consequence, Thunder-Egg's stature grew once again, positively for most, though negatively for some. That he could even add a few figures together was a surprise to all; even more surprising was that he had acquired whatever hunch it was that led him to barge into those town offices that chill morning. Had something suspicious emerged in an oatmeal-raisin cookie that his daughter had brought home one day and he bit into? Nobody, to this day, has figured out what set off that peremptory investigation.

Of course, the elderly lady has had her defenders—still does. All miscreants have their defenders; in this case, the lady's defenders don't contest the charge, which they know has been thoroughly verified; they just hold to the position that if one is nice enough (i.e., if one makes and distributes enough oatmeal-raisin cookies), and if one had intended all along, as the lady in question claimed, to return the stolen—or putatively "borrowed"—funds (along with interest, of course), one should be allowed to get away with it.

Thunder-Egg, as is obvious, observed no such fine distinctions. For him, as he said—using one of the malapropisms for which he was well-known—the "crutch" of the matter was that theft is theft; and, anyway, he didn't want to see his property tax monies, or anyone else's, siphoned off to support what turned out to be the lady's annual visits to the Foxwood Casino in Connecticut, entailing the loss of substantial town funds, oatmeal-raisin cookies or no oatmeal-raisin cookies.

In any event, the incident has made everyone since then *scrupulously* honest in their financial dealings, at least of a public nature. The prospect of Thunder-Egg, of *the* Thunder-Egg, lurching through their door in an ill-disposed frame of mind is most disagreeable.

Yet, sometimes, being tumultuous in all things he does, Thunder-Egg has been hasty in his judgment about what rules have been broken and by whom. This has led to a smattering of incidents that have involved the innocent and that those village folk, adverse to him anyway, like to cite in further defense of referring to him as "dunderhead."

Now, as I'm sure you noted (with raised eyebrows, no less), I just mentioned a daughter. That, obviously, implies a wife. Immediately, I suppose, the most extraordinary pictures crowd your potentially feverish imagination. Who, or what, could possibly be a soulmate for the Thunder-Egg, and what sort of progeny could the Thunder-Egg and such a soulmate possibly spawn?

Dispel from your mind at once an image of some ungainly clan of trolls, dwelling fitfully amongst the higher crags of our mountainous retreats. It was really quite an ordinary family after all, living in an old farmhouse—a bit remote, to be sure, but similar to all the other farmhouses around here. Mrs.—hmm … Thunder-Egg? … I'm sorry, but I don't remember her name —is a reclusive woman, rarely seen in town. Some of her berry preserves, brought to the annual town fair by her daughter, have won prizes and brought good prices from visiting tourists.

But, as far as I know, her seclusion has never been claimed by the village folk to be the result of eccentricity or waywardness. She's simply too busy stoking the voracious fires of a household where chickens, cows, eight sled dogs, a family or two of quasi-feral cats, some belligerent hummingbirds and other assorted wildfowl, a small herd of shaggy Icelandic ponies, a team of oxen, a vivacious daughter, a perpetually fired-up wood-burning range, and old Thunder-Egg himself must be constantly provided with the appropriate fodder. This is to say nothing of the innumerable berry and fruit trees, flowers, and garden vegetables, all of which make their own imperious alimentary demands.

She lives a lifetime of devoted feeding, and even more than a lifetime (so time-"consuming" is the task — no pun intended), but no one ever had a sense that she receives anything more, or anything less, from all this effort than persistent happiness. Abundant feeding yields abundant harvests — though that requires a great deal of work too. Anyway, as the good folks justly contend, with *the* Thunder-Egg in her life, there could be room for little else.

Except of course, for their daughter. Who's not reclusive at all. Medusa — yes, that really is her name — is tall (over six feet), large-boned for a woman, but classically beautiful with fair skin and a stupendous braid of steely black hair that swooshes down to her waist like the banded tail of a thoroughbred mare. From her childhood on, she has participated in all the town and school activities — clomping into town on the back of one of those Icelandic ponies (until she was too tall to ride them without her feet dragging on the ground), or walking, or biking, or being driven by Thunder-Egg in his rattling pickup truck.

Vivacious? Indeed!

Energetic, independent, domineering, charming, the one who organizes everything that goes by the name of school activities, and much too terrifying to be approached by any of the local boys once she reached the bloom of adolescence, especially with the shadow of Thunder-Egg looming ever so precariously in the background.

Now, generally Thunder-Egg is not — because he doesn't need to be — protective of his daughter; if anyone can take care of herself, it is she. But an incident did occur, when she was about sixteen, that put a penumbra of protection around her that no one has dared to violate ever after. Unfortunately, it was based on a misunderstanding and involved the person perhaps in all the world least likely to be a source of offense. Whether or not the incident redounds much to Thunder-Egg's merit will be for posterity to decide; though he made, in the end, the appropriate apologies to the offended party (who's a forgiving sort of person anyway) and old wounds have been healed.

The village folk, however, have never forgotten. Village folk never do forget. But since the story, in any event, adds, in some way, to the dimensions of Thunder-Egg, it's well worth recounting.

At the center of our village, magisterial among the colonial houses that line the street, is an old Congregational church, painted white, with an exquisite steeple (acquired rather late in its history, so I understand) that rises high above the roofs of the houses and the trees of the village green and gives the village so much of its charm. Next to the church is a small white cottage where the minister, the Reverend Mr. Benson, lives. A more kindly man one couldn't find anywhere in the world. The cottage and the church are surrounded by a well-trimmed lawn that, at the back of the aforesaid cottage and church, is bordered by a small mountain river that flows out of Beaver Pond Notch just a few miles upstream. Thunder-Egg and his daughter have a curious relation with the church and with Mr. Benson.

Thunder-Egg is not a churchgoer, but, by some quirk of destiny, he has acquired the function of bell ringer. Like a latter-day Quasimodo, he has the dexterity to scramble up into and through the narrow confines of the steeple and, applying his massive strength and vitality to the ropes, can clang the bells on a Sunday morning with such vigor and persistence that few dare to stay abed with the tolling of the Sabbath so obstreperously impaled through the delicate membranes of their eardrums. Even dwellers in the upland intervales catch the echoes of the bells as they reverberate from the mountaintops.

Medusa is not a churchgoer either, strictly speaking, but the church is, along with the school, another center of social activity in town, so she made herself present for that. She also became quite good friends with the Reverend Mr. Benson, who, though advancing into early middle age, was not married. She enjoyed helping him with his garden and with some of his social activities. She also enjoyed conversation with him — he was, after all, a learned man who could tell her all about the ancient classical world, which she had come to love in her studies at school. He even taught her to read the Greek alphabet and to construe a few simple sentences in Greek, drawn mainly from the New Testament.

Well, one might inquire whether or not there were those who looked a bit askance at this budding friendship. Of course there were; there always are and always will be gentlefolk inclined to nurse the worst suspicions about anything. But between the older Mr. Benson and the young girl, both as innocent as the day they were born, there was nothing but goodwill and affable sociability, something comparable to a beneficent and playful uncle-niece relationship. But one can't always expect others to understand such matters, and malevolent gossip is as much a product of small-town life as are quilts, strawberry-rhubarb preserves, and pumpkin pies. Thunder-Egg once got wind of such gossip and dismissed it as the malevolence he knew it was, though not without getting slightly upset by it. He mentioned it to his wife, who brushed it away like cobwebs on a windowpane and gave it no further thought.

The incident was initiated, one day in early May, when Mr. Benson invited Medusa into his cottage after school in order to help with some redecorating of the "parsonage," as he called it. Especially, he needed her height and steadiness to assist him in repositioning some pictures on the walls and over the mantelpiece. She was glad to oblige.

It was a bright, sunny day, and melting winter snows from the Notch still gurgled, lively and fresh and icy-cold, in the mountain river at the back of the house. Mr. Benson left the front door open so that a fresh breeze could pass through the old house and waft away some of the stale air trapped during the long winter months. Medusa's task was to hold up the pictures against the walls and move them about until Mr. Benson decided they were positioned correctly. Then the spots would be marked, the appropriate nails driven, and the pictures hung.

It all went quite smoothly until it came time to mount a rather large painting over the mantelpiece. A sturdy woodstove stationed on the hearth and partially under the mantelpiece required a reach for mounting the picture that even the long-limbed Medusa couldn't quite make, so Mr. Benson fetched a wooden box from his woodshed that she could stand on. But as she stood on it, the box splintered and broke. Medusa found herself lurching backward, still holding on to the painting, while Mr. Benson rushed forward to break her fall (this was a heroic gesture, given that Medusa was about twice the size of Mr. Benson). In any case, Medusa and Mr. Benson tumbled down on the carpet together, tangled and laughing heartily as they pushed away the painting, which had come down on them both. Luckily there was no damage sustained by persons or painting.

Luckily … yes.

But unluckily, too, for who just happened to be standing at the open door at that moment, clutching the electricity bill and the monthly *The Voice of the Spirit*? It was the rural delivery man—the very worst possible person to be standing at that door witnessing pastor and maid sprawling over one another and laughing on the rug together. This rural delivery man's name is Rover (his parents, once upon a time, named him after the family dog, but we won't go into that curious issue). He's known in the village for little else than his perpetual raising of alarms and predicting imminent dire events (which never happen, of course). He collared me once by the village green and warned me that the biggest hurricane since '38 was about to hit New England—a false prediction, as it turned out. No hurricane of any kind came, though he did succeed in panicking a significant number of village folk into buying more alcoholic beverages than they could use for months (that's what people around here rush out to buy before a big storm).

If, true to his name, Rover had, by some chance, actually been a dog, he would have been one of those dogs that are constantly barking at shadows. Unfortunately, the nature of his job gives him an unusual opportunity … well, to rove … about town and spread his fanciful conflagrations. There's an ancient Persian proverb, I understand, that says that a dog that barks at shadows will soon set all the other dogs in a village to barking at what is even less than shadows.

So, without further ado, Rover was up to his usual thing—darting at uncanny speed throughout the town, baying and howling, spreading the word, raising the alarm. You don't need to imagine long in order to imagine what kind of story he was telling. And you don't need to conjecture long in order to conjecture with what alacrity and delectation the story was absorbed by the good village folk and passed along to others.

The pastor!

And Medusa!

Could anything, could absolutely anything else be more delicious than that? In the parsonage, meanwhile, Medusa and the pastor picked themselves up, straightened out the carpet, and having fetched a proper stepladder for the job, did succeed finally in hanging the picture over the mantelpiece. Medusa departed; she had volunteered to be a referee at an elementary school basketball game scheduled for later in the afternoon. As it turned out, it was for poor Mr. Benson a most unpropitious departure, for, not long afterward, another presence exploded through the gaping parsonage door. Thunder-Egg!

The rough-hewn meter out of justice was about to mete out his rough-hewn justice once again. We don't know how and from whom the story reached his ears, and we know few details of what happened. We do know that Mr. Benson countered the accusation with a mirthful denial, a chuckle, and an offering of a cookie—an altogether fortuitous but exact replication of the lady embezzler's initial response to what was a serious charge brought against her. There's no way under the smiling heavens or over the deep-furrowed earth that poor Mr. Benson could have known that this precise sequence was imprinted into Thunder-Egg's brain as a ploy tantamount to an admission of guilt.

As the village folk scurried from every direction to see what momentous events would unfold at the parsonage, they beheld perhaps the most extraordinary sight ever recorded in the oral (and now written) history of the village. For there, standing up to his knees in the mountain stream was Thunder-Egg, grasping Mr. Benson by the ankles, holding him upside down as he dunked his head up and down in the freezing waters of the stream, and attempting to elicit from him the promise never again to (another of his malapropisms) "truffle" with his daughter.

All of this put poor Mr. Benson into a distinctly awkward position—I mean, not just of being held upside down and being dunked in the water, which, admittedly, was awkward enough, but of having to promise not to do something again that he had never done.

Is it morally permissible to make such a promise—in effect, a false promise—a promise you know you can't keep because you haven't ever done what you're not ever supposed to do again?

Between dunks, sputtering and gurgling, Mr. Benson tried to review in his mind how his ethics textbooks in the seminary might have addressed the issue, and, accordingly, he tried to make his case with Thunder-Egg as best he could. As it turned out, he never had to make that morally reprobate promise. For at this moment who should show up but Medusa.

Medusa? O my God, Medusa!

Having heard what was going on, she sprinted from the school gymnasium to the parsonage, bounding over split-rail fences and stone walls as she went, with her steely black braid twitching furiously behind her like the tail of a hissing dragon. As you know from experience, I'm sure, there are moments in the lives of a parent and child, when, in strenuous conflict, they become most like one another, most truly a parent and offspring glaring into mirror images of one another.

At this moment, Thunder-Egg, for the first time in his life, confronted another veritable human thunder-egg, a thunder-egg in the making for a long time and now fully revealed as the thunder-egg she was and has been ever since: his daughter.

With flashing eyes that could turn any man to stone (of whatever size and shape, and no classical allusion intended here), Medusa quickly set things straight and reproached her father, in no uncertain terms, for his precipitous judgment and rambunctious methods. She pounced into the icy river, clasped Mr. Benson's dangling arms by the wrists, and attempted to hoist him ashore.

Thunder-Egg, still not fully convinced of Mr. Benson's innocence, continued to hold on to his ankles, so that a not-altogether-seemly tug-of-war ensued, with Mr. Benson squirming uneasily in the middle and wondering intermittently if his arms and legs were about to be pulled out of their sockets. He was also still passing in review the moral implications of the kind of promise that he had almost been forced to make.

Soon enough, Thunder-Egg relented, Medusa prevailed, and Mr. Benson was back in the warmth and privacy of his parsonage. The dumbfounded village folk dispersed to home and job, glad to have their gossip batteries fully charged and happy to have been witnesses to this ungodly "baptism," as the local wits who hang around the dump were eventually inclined to call it.

Naturally, there was something of a mess to be cleared up after all this. To his credit, Thunder-Egg responded as fulsomely as possible to the damage he had done and, entering into a church function for the first time, made a truly contrite apology to the assembled congregation. In doing that, he became even bigger than he ever was before. He still calamitously rings the church bells on Sunday mornings.

Medusa, likewise, made it very clear that the congregation need not entertain any doubts about the integrity and virtue of their pastor. She has since gone on, by the way, to be an Olympic high-jumper and gives the Russian and Romanian women some pretty intense competition in that regard.

And Mr. Benson, as I said before, was a forgiving man and held no grudges. He has since written an essay on the ethical issues involved in promises made under unusual pressure and circumstances. It will be published soon in *The Voice of the Spirit*.

I wish I could conclude my account of this notable event by saying that all ended sweetly and happily ever after. But it didn't. For not long afterward, another person — in this case, the importunate Rover — was subjected to yet another ungodly "baptism" conferred upon him in the same river, with the same method, and by the same temporarily self-appointed divine. I don't think I need to go into the details of this occurrence, but rest assured that no one, at least no one I'm aware of, felt much in the way of sympathy for Rover's plight. Let us hope that the poor man, rather forcibly "washed of his sins," as it were, has duly reformed his unacceptable deportment in spreading false news about local emergencies.

I initiated my brief disquisition on Thunder-Egg by talking, generally, about thunder-eggs, about those unwieldy stones that keep growing as your spade keeps digging. And I hope that the application of the term to the specific personage under discussion has become clear enough. But having done that, I would like to return to the level of generality with which I began by turning my attention from stones in general to human character in general.

I should warn that those who welcome, as well as those who deplore, the practice of tacking a presumably pithy moral to the end of a story are about to have their expectations fulfilled; but I should also warn that, however pithy the moral might or might not be, it will not be of the sort to provide sweet maxims for sentimental calendars, nature posters, or high school yearbooks. For I guess that, in my general experience of human beings, all of them (or, I should say, all of us) are, in a way, thunder-eggs. Human beings just keep getting bigger, the more you dig around them—and along with that, more unwieldy, more difficult to move or shove around or place where you want to place them, more inscrutable as to who and what they are, more unpredictable, and, accordingly, more likely to erupt into our lives with a force we could never have foretold, sometimes calling us to account and possibly dunking us in an icy-cold river, either justly or unjustly, either for good or for ill.

Each of us is a world (as the poets have sung in the past) waiting to be discovered or revealed (as the case may be), but waiting mostly in vain, for very little will be discovered and even less revealed, no matter how much digging goes on. I don't say all of this to promote some sanguine view of mankind, correlative with a summons to universal benevolence and complacent acceptance. Much of what is hidden in us can really be quite awful, and it's just as well that it stays hidden (though the Reverend Mr. Benson, I'm sure, would be quick to counsel us that such a state of affairs, either to our advantage or to our disadvantage, won't stay that way forever; and all, someday, will be made known).

Moreover, our being thunder-eggs underscores how really lonely we are, how, in some respects, "underground" our human condition really is. The universal complaint—that we are not understood by others—is always legitimate and, as such, always irreparable. We just need to remember that it's not only others; it's also ourselves that we can hardly ever understand.

As some ancient sage said so long ago, "Who can enter into and understand himself?" That, of course, is not all that needs to be said about such matters, but that much does, indeed, need to be said, if we are going to make any sense out of what can be appended to, or what can sometimes be posited to transfigure, validly or invalidly, this account.

And here I keep my peace for the moment, for even observations such as these are themselves thunder-eggs, getting bigger and bigger and more complicated, the more we pursue them, and sending corresponding shocks up and down through our spiritual sinews as we proceed to dig into and around them.

I pause, but pause only momentarily, before the spade again clanks against the hard surface of a stone whose intractable edge tells me, if nothing else, that what I have before me is life itself; that life in all its monumentality, is real, is substantial, makes demands upon me, is an incalculable thunder-egg poised inexorably against the incalculable thunder-egg who is me. There, too, we find the biggest thunder-eggs of all, the past and the future, only the tiniest contours of which we shall ever be privileged to see, or to touch, or to turn with the probing edge of our spade, delving ever deeper and deeper to where we hope to find what has counted most in the lives we have lived and what will count most in the lives we have yet to live; striking ever harder and harder until we hit what we have always sought, until we strike what we have always recognized, as our sole and proper home.

Maura Briscoe

If life was anything for the girls at St. Mary of Cleophas Academy, it was one of eager anticipations, a solemn and joyous procession of sacred festivals and complex ritual activities of all kinds. Not only were the high holy days of the ancient Church preserved with all due ceremony; a multitude of others were likewise celebrated: Candlemas, St. Joseph's feast day, the feast of the Annunciation, and rogation days, to name but a few. (If school was in session on Gaudete Sunday in Advent and Laetare Sunday in Lent, these feasts, too, were honored in ways truly worthy of their names.)

In addition, this girl's boarding school in rural New Hampshire could boast a full roster of those celebrations common to all schools: the usual sporting events, Christmas and Spring proms, drama performances, parents' days, homecoming weekends, and assorted field trips. Some events were reserved for particular classes: there was, for example, the freshman ascent of Mount Cardigan every fall and the canoe trip along the Contoocook River for sophomores in the late spring (a trip more renowned for its encounter with the burgeoning population of blackflies than anything else) and the junior trip to Quebec to visit, among other places, the shrine of St. Anne of Beaupré and to mourn, yet again, the British occupation of French Canada.

For the girls of St. Mary of Cleophas, there was no lack of exciting events to look forward to, adventures to have, entertainments to share — from week to week, season to season, and year to year. But as delightful as were all of these great occasions, the grandest, the most wonderful, the most eminent was the annual journey to Rome conducted by the Latin teacher, Maura Briscoe.

Of course, this excursion was restricted to seniors and, moreover, only to those seniors who had survived the truly demanding rigors of a four-year Latin curriculum — which meant, in effect, only the very cream of the student body found themselves sufficiently privileged to go. Yet the effort to survive that program, and the competition to keep up with the other students in the program, was positively fierce — if for no other reason than that the journey to Rome was seen as the consummate experience that St. Mary of Cleophas could provide.

Even the excluded multitudes could participate in this experience in a surrogate way, if only as those who eagerly anticipated what would assuredly be breathless accounts of what had occurred — stories that never disappointed and that quickly accrued to the vast repository of legend about the trip in school history.

And, if that journey to Rome itself were not marvelous enough, the most marvelous of all was the excursion, traditionally taken on the penultimate day of the trip, a hundred or so miles to the south of Rome, to the ancient, once buried city of Pompeii.

Even this excursion itself had its summary moment — its "moment of moments," if we can use such an expression — though a curious kind of silence reigned about what exactly went on in that "moment of moments," as if what happened there was too esoteric, too special, too sacrosanct for anyone to discuss except in the most vague and allusive terms.

It took place during the visit to a roofless ruin of a house at the edge of the city. Here, after a tour of the house, replete with intimate details of the busy life that had once ensued there, Maura would astonish and terrify her Latin students by standing before the hearth of that ancient house and offering up a sacrifice before the apse of the sacred Lar, the household god. For, claimed Maura, this very place was her ancestral domicile, the house where she was living in A.D. 79, when, as a little girl of eight years old named Egeria, Vesuvius erupted and buried Pompeii, and her, and all that was most dear to her, in burning cinders.

Is the story I'm about to tell you a happy story or a sad story, a story of birth or a story of death, a story of regeneration or a story of unspeakable loss? I wish I knew.

But let me tell you a bit more about Maura Briscoe. When I knew her —during those few years I spent as a fellow teacher at St. Mary of Cleophas—she was in her mid-forties, unmarried, living by herself in a small cottage that overlooked a small, solitary lake close to the school. She was about mid-height, slender, vigorous but by no means muscular, an ardent walker, with bushy brown hair and a pert, small-featured face. She was always cheerful, always alert, and always laughed at little things.

She had a master's degree in Latin from Columbia University and had— certainly an unusual gift in modern times—a curious ability to speak it, though what she spoke was not the Ciceronian Latin one studied in the classroom but more the language of characters in the plays of Plautus and Terence. (She claimed, of course, that it was her "native" language.)

She also grew lovely flowers around her little cottage, went for hikes, often alone, in the White Mountains, traveled a great deal in Europe and was familiar with most of the great sites of classical antiquity spread from Asia Minor and across Europe and northern Africa to the coasts of Spain and Britain.

In the schoolroom she was a devoted teacher; she loved her pupils to distraction and yet demanded everything from them (and got it). She was a colorful and animated figure on campus, in the library, at school events, and in the dining hall.

Most fascinating of all, she was a pagan.

I mean a real pagan. You know—Jupiter, Diana, Mars, Minerva, Apollo —that kind of pagan.

Or so she said.

Now, granted, that seems odd in a school such as St. Mary of Cleophas. In a way, yes; in another way, no. The positive reason should be obvious enough—after all, this was a Catholic school that took itself very seriously; the negative reason may be a bit more abstruse.

For Maura Briscoe gave a different version, in its own way more intense for youthful minds, of what was imparted to them day by day in the glowing liturgy that St. Mary of Cleophas made of life itself—and here the pagan and the Christian could vaguely converge and resonate with one another. "All things," as Herakleitos would and did say, are "full of gods"; and St. Thomas Aquinas could add, "God is in all things, and intimately so." But what the students learned at St. Mary of Cleophas, they learned primarily as a sacred ambience imparted by stained-glass color and Eucharistic candles and cheerful bouquets laid at the feet of smiling saints.

Here, by contrast, in Maura's world was something infinitely chiaroscuro—a bronze and verdigris world with darkness and somber golden light and the heavy shadows of the numinous and sad beyond all words. You could say, certainly, that Maura Briscoe was a religious woman—filled with *pietas* for the ancient divinities of earth and sky, of tree and pond and sacred well and mountain. Beyond that, you could speak of her ancestral worship, of her devotion to the household gods who inhabit hearth and bedchamber, of her attachment to the sacral precincts of a homeland and of those hallowed enclaves that lead ever downward to the dusky underworlds of the spirit-voices and the venerable dead.

To listen to her speak, enwrapped as she could become in some ancient text, was to feel a chill in your bones, the hair bristling on your skin, the inexplicable awe at the unfathomable mysteries deployed so palpably around her.

She was also a scholar and led her students assiduously through the tangled mazes of Latin grammar, drilling them in the high exercises of translation and composition, verse scansion and oral recitation and memorization of sometimes lengthy passages from Cicero and Virgil. She taught them to walk in Latin, talk in Latin, play in Latin, and dream in Latin. She unfolded, day by day, the richness of the Latin in the English language and enjoyed illustrating for them how French and Spanish and Italian (in all of which she was fluent and one of which most of her students were pursuing as a second language) were developments of what she called "provincial street Latin." She also regaled them with her displays of classical Greek and her occasional evocation of ancient Sanskrit or Old Irish or Proto-Germanic cognate words and forms. And she taught them to love the ancient past—its architecture and literature, its philosophy and its technology, its sense of law and its reverence for the spiritual in life.

All of this was, in a general way, preparation for the senior trip to Rome. In a more specific way, Maura began to prime her students a year in advance for exploring the city itself. Each girl who would go on the trip was given the responsibility to research extensively a particular ancient site and to act as a guide and a resource for that site when the group was in Rome.

The students also became acquainted with the general layout of Rome, its history in the post-classical period, and with much of Renaissance and of modern Rome as well. A quick crash course in modern Italian, beginning a few months before departure, prepared the girls for an interesting and exciting engagement with the modern city.

Moreover, they studied sites outside Rome itself, such as Ostia and Hadrian's Villa and the Etruscan cities to the north, and would be able to visit them if time permitted. Occasionally, a student group might even seek out Horace's farm in the Alban Hills. And, of course, they studied Pompeii, studied it in detail from someone who, it appeared, knew it as thoroughly and intimately as you could know it.

It was only in my third year of teaching at St. Mary of Cleophas that I was invited, by Maura, to act as one of several chaperones who normally accompanied the students on the trip. It was an honor, of course, to do this; no one who had ever taken the trip came back without having been thrilled by it. It was a marvelous opportunity to see Rome in a way that you could rarely see it.

Maura made the most of it too. Though she managed, in her own way, to have her wards do everything that tourists in Rome usually do, she also managed to have them do it in a way that other tourists never do it. She would enter the usual places and, after the designated student had given her presentation, would then focus attention on some curious nook or cranny ignored by everybody else and give some marvelous account of something that had happened there. The student in question always loved this special reinforcement of what she had presented, and the others were thrilled by the intimate narratives Maura could supply in such a spontaneous and lively way. In many locations, she would, in a sense, "strip away" time, descending to ever and ever lower and older layers of what was in front of them.

Moreover, she saw a Rome no one else saw, a Rome not just of antique buildings and jumbled ruins but of action and interaction. She could point to the spot where and when this and that happened, and who was there and what they said or didn't say. She could show the roost where the sacred geese were kept who warned the guards on the Capitoline Hill of the stealthy approach of the Gallic "commandos" (as she called them); she would stand at the base of the great staircase leading up to the Ara Coeli and relate how Cola di Rienzo, in the Middle Ages, was finally cut down there by the angry Roman crowd; she could lead her charges among the somber pines and tombs of the Via Appia and conjure up for them a Roman legion, standard-bearers garbed in grim wolfskins, marching through an early morning mist and accompanied by the dull thud of drums and the flat blare of enormous tubas.

All of this, of course, added immeasurably to the students' morale since they became so aware that their thoroughness of preparation and intimacy of knowledge so expressly differentiated them from the hordes of other tourists who were carted brainlessly about the city in buses, rather a bit like sides of meat suspended from hooks in grocery vans, rocking them back and forth passively as the buses hurtled through narrow streets.

And all of this is to say nothing of the sites they somehow surreptitiously entered. Such escapades gave an aura of secrecy and danger to the activities that, if sometimes jolting to the adult chaperones on the trip, were invariably wonderful to the girls. They always seemed to be sneaking into places where they were not supposed to go. One year, apparently, they infiltrated the Domus Aurea of Nero in the dark after visiting hours were over; the students, it was said, clambered about with tiny flashlights purchased for this purpose and some even got lost (so they thought) in the great labyrinth of halls and chambers.

I surmised, eventually, that Maura probably knew many of the custodians of these places, had prearranged the visits at unusual times (e.g., gates were left curiously unlocked), and had even prearranged the chase that would cause the group to scamper out of a site with a supposedly enraged guardian hot on its heels. Such an episode inevitably made for a lively dinner discussion at some restaurant off the Campo de' Fiori afterward.

Then, as I was told, there always was a run-in with the Roman police, a tumultuous event in a police station, and the sudden appearance of a short, heavy, balding attorney who looked like Bacchus fresh in from the vineyard (or from the tavern, whichever was most relevant at the time). After a few waves of his arms and a few summary expostulations with the authorities, Maura kissed him on the head and shepherded the group out on the street again to face whatever new adventure might await it.

The year I was there, we stayed in a fairly roomy hotel tucked in between the Palatine Hill and the Circus Maximus. Since there were a number of other student groups from different nations at the same hotel, Maura got the idea of organizing a foot race around the Circus, among teams of four from each nation (the evocation of four chariot horses was all too clear). The point of the race, however, was to win not simply by the fastest running but, by the reinstating of an ancient practice, preventing the other teams from winning. The result among the five "national" teams that raced, to say nothing of their supporters—who at least for a while were patiently cheering on their teams while sitting on the grassy banks around the racecourse—was enough to undo fifty years of work by the United Nations, the European Union, and whatever other organizations exist to promote international peace and goodwill. In any event, the Roman police were soon careening through the streets of Rome, sirens quavering and batons frantically brandished from the windows of diminutive Fiat police cars. Bacchus made his compulsory appearance at the police station, and Maura, her students, and everyone else involved were loosed on the world again, all quite certain, despite a few bruises, that it had been great fun.

But the journey to Pompeii was, as it was meant to be, the climax. Here we did, as was usual, lease a bus and were driven southward toward Naples through the Liri Valley—with a brief stop at Monte Cassino, where Maura gave a brief but impassioned account of its monastic history, focusing on St. Benedict's founding and concluding with the massive bombardment of the monastery during the Second World War. Not long afterward we arrived at the outskirts of the ancient city of Pompeii itself.

It would be fruitless for me to try to explain most of what would and did happen in that visit. Maura made the city alive for us: its origins in the old Sabine and Oscan country folk; its newer Roman, Latin-speaking population; its vibrant textile industries; its rebuilding from the great earthquake of 62; its markets and Odeon and forum and games in the amphitheater;

its busy commerce with the huge Roman naval base at Misenum, not far away—right down to the details of where its bookies and gamblers would cluster, downing goblets of the local wine while waiting for the race results from the Circus Maximus in Rome to arrive by carrier pigeons.

Toward midafternoon we finally converged upon the ruins of a house in one of the far quarters of the city. It was Maura's ancestral home. We entered it and learned of the intricacies of daily life and familial deportment that once went on in those old cubicles and atria, the loggia and gardens, which bore, in their present state, such a heavy witness to the swift and tragic demise of that household. This is where that eight-year-old girl, bearing that quintessential Roman name Egeria, had lived and played by the fishpond in the center of the house. This is where her family had practiced the sacred rites that made them a family and made them proper citizens of a city and of a great world empire. Maura was unusually somber as she explored those chambers with us, and the students listened intently and solemnly.

And then …!

What I—what we—saw would demand the eloquence of a Sophocles to do it justice—and it's upon that eloquence that I shall draw. For we were all abruptly herded into a dark, cavernous alcove, where we were suddenly blinded by a dozen parallel shafts of dazzling sunlight slanting downward at a steep angle through jagged crevices in the fractured masonry. We stumbled and tripped and jostled one another.

When we recovered our sight and our footing, we saw Maura standing in the midst of those blazing shafts as if transfixed by a phalanx of luminous spears. Her hands were lifted and bent backward in some kind of ritual gesture before the apse of the sacred Lar, her fingers splayed and crooked upward like thin, naked talons and her palms filled with a fine ash that now whirled about her in a storm of cloud and sunlight.

She stood there amid that whirlwind, like the ancient Antigone herself, emitting the piercing shrill cries "of a disconsolate bird, its nest despoiled, its kindred robbed and vanquished." Three times in rapid succession she swung her lustral offering of ashes over the shrine and remembered all those unmourned and unmarked dead, whom the chthonic depths of the underworld itself had risen to inter with its fiery deluge and whom the

Roman world itself left immured in its ashy entombment and so rapidly forgot.

The students recoiled with terror, clutching one another, trembling, speechless, eyes riveted on the almost violent rite that unfolded before them and which, for all that they had been led to expect, exceeded anything they had ever imagined.

And I, too, was astonished. I could hardly recognize Maura as the one who stood before me and enacted what I was witnessing. I also, for just that moment, saw, or thought I saw, revealed in front of me—with an immediacy I never considered possible—the loss and suffering, the fathomless and inconsolable despondency, the *lacrimae rerum*, that permeated the consciousness of the ancient world and all its cultic visions.

I envisaged then too, envisage even now, the terrified child, Egeria, groping for the hands of her parents in the panicked crowds as they tried to protect her while holding pillows on their heads against the torrents of pumice and sharp little stones pouring down from the skies; the shoving and pushing through the thick ash, the crying and choking, the impact of human bodies against each other, the collisions with frantic dogs and goats and donkeys, the flapping of geese and squawking hens; the impenetrable blackness brindled by jagged strips of flame crackling through sulfurous clouds; houses and roofs collapsing; the sea off the Porta Marina boiling and retracting from the land like gums from crumbling, blackened teeth; thick, poisonous gases, clothes and hair on fire, eyes burning and clotted by dust, mouth and lungs filling with thick, hot cinders; tears and gasping and blood and fright; incandescent fire waves of enormous temperatures surging at immense speeds down hillsides and roads and vaporizing instantly everything in their path; and the untellable passage of the great rivers of agony and death converging and parting through the dark arsenals of the underworld, of icy Styx and toxic Acheron, of fiery Phlegethon and tearful Cocytus and soporific Lethe (and yet, for this person, this Egeria alone, the memory-effacing submergence in Lethe only partially completed)—and then a scream, an arching, heart-wrenching scream, a scream ripping through the fullness of her flesh, the scream of an awakened life, the deep flush of fresh, invigorating air suddenly sluicing downward and flooding her lungs, hands holding her up, suspended like a

jewel in the bright, cool sunlight of a New Hampshire morning: "It's a girl!"
a voice exclaimed — a girl has been born.

Or so one could imagine in just that moment, somehow, somewhere, in
the depths of one's heart.

Everything was over as suddenly as it began. Within minutes we had left
the house, and Maura and I soon were walking briskly along one of the old
streets well ahead of the students, who hovered in a tremulous group behind
us, trying, as best they could, to calm themselves and to stammer to one another what little they were able about the scene that they had just witnessed.

They knew already that for the rest of their lives the most important
part of this story was sealed up in their memories as a secret too frightening — maybe too serious — to tell; and they wouldn't add it to the lore they
would transmit on to others, making it as much a shock yet again when a
new group would see it.

Maura, meanwhile, hooked her arm in mine, as she sometimes did with
anyone she walked alongside of, and glanced up at me as we walked, her face
smiling and her eyes cheerful but a bit strained in the glare of the intense
Mediterranean sun. All traces of the ferociously tragic Antigone were gone.
She seemed somewhat pleased with herself, as we all do when we feel that
we have accomplished what we set out to do and can savor yet another job
well done.

She looked at me and then away, tugging at my arm, and then looked at
me again and said: "Well, how did I do?" She smiled. Obviously, she didn't
expect me to answer her question. She had done very well indeed, and she
knew that. She was happy, yet she still seemed so oddly pensive and sad.

I was puzzled, of course, by all of this; she must have noted the puzzled
expression on my face, for she added, "How else can I help them make the
connection and take it all seriously, as serious as it really is, as serious as it
really was?"

At the end of the street, in the far distance, I could see the tall gray cone
of Vesuvius, ominously silhouetted against the late afternoon sky. We all had
a delightful dinner later that evening, at Sorrento, in a restaurant surrounded
by an orange grove and overlooking the Bay of Naples, which was golden
and darkly glowing in the fading light.

The following morning, we returned to Rome. The final day of the trip was always traditionally reserved for shopping. The girls had the liberty to wander among the boutiques of the Corso and purchase the fashionable accessories that abound in modern Italy with such finesse and elegance, as well as to collect their souvenirs and gifts for the people back home. Maura was not part of this, however, and went off by herself. The final day of the trip was always her own, her very private day. One wondered where she went and what she did.

Well, you know, it's difficult not to speculate from time to time about a person like Maura Briscoe, and I certainly will not try to do so now; but I knew then in an odd sort of way, and my knowledge was only confirmed again and again in those brief years that I enjoyed her company, that the destination of her final, private foray into Rome was the *sanctum sanctorum*, the holy place of the holy ones, the household of the sanctified — no, not the Pantheon, as you might have presumed, or the remnant of some other pagan shrine but the domicile of that old Pontifex Maximus himself, Builder of Bridges, of the bridge that spanned the ages, that linked an old to a new dispensation, that spoke to the eternal longings of antiquity and that assuaged its immeasurable sorrow.

Previously I posed the question whether the story I was about to tell was a happy story or a sad story, a story of birth or a story of death, a story of regeneration or a story of unspeakable loss. I think, in retrospect, it is all of these things.

I don't know, and I highly doubt, that an eight-year-old girl named Egeria ran along the darkening streets of a doomed Pompeii; and if she did, she was not the same person whom I had the privilege of knowing. She was a fiction after all, a fiction like Sophocles' stalwart Antigone herself, who served a purpose sublime and magnanimous and grave.

But the person I did know was someone who was able, or perhaps to whom it was given to be able, to gather into herself all the pain of that event, and perhaps of all such events that had happened innumerable times before and would happen innumerable times again, whenever a child would find herself suddenly abandoned in a fiery city, her brief life soon to be cut short by the peremptory eruptions of nature or man; and this person could let the rest of us know, through her, about some small portion of all of that, and about the grandeur of life itself that, in other ways, served only to underscore the poignancy of its all-too-precocious and unspeakable extinction.

The Egeria she invented was her way of doing precisely this.

And it worked.

How could any of us who observed that "moment of moments" not harbor in our hearts, for the rest of our lives, that piercing cry of a noble soul face-to-face with the boundless and inexplicable suffering of the entire animate creation, with the sacrificial loaves of the universe itself, with the blood of every sacred vessel that has ever mattered, lifted in lustral offering?

I should say, in addition, that such cognizance gave an ever-new meaning to Maura Briscoe's presence at a school named after a personage, St. Mary of Cleophas, about whom nothing is known except that she stood, a mute witness, at the foot of the Cross. And, if life at St. Mary of Cleophas Academy featured its flowered feasts and sparkling windows and smiling saints, it also displayed at its center the bleeding visage of the figure whom St. Mary of Cleophas gazed upon.

We embarked at the airport early the next day and returned to the academy. Its eager students awaited our triumphal entry, and its repository of Roman lore would again be enriched by a multitude of stories, as it always was and always would be. It's many years now since I've been a colleague of Maura Briscoe. Our ways parted long ago, as I drifted off into the ever-illusory opportunities afforded by the world of schools and education, wondering why I had left my original appointment in the first place, wondering why I had left the company of one of the most genuine persons I've ever known.

But still, after all this time, I can't imagine her being anyone other than the person I knew back then, *nunc et semper eadem, nunc et semper nova*: now and forever the same, now and forever new.

"Three Friends"

"Friends"? And "three" of them? Hardly. At least not with one another. (I was supposed to be one of them but scarcely knew the other two.)

I'm not given, in most circumstances, to casting myself in what some might call "dramatic" roles, momentarily and rather self-consciously assumed, but it does happen occasionally, and it could hardly have been avoided when I visited Dorothea Lindstrom a month or so after the death — reported as the result of an accident while fishing — of her husband Sven.

Part of it was the setting: for Dorothea had somehow managed to fashion a diminutive sitting room in a glassy, closed-in porch whose special function it was to engage presumably select and privileged visitors in precisely the kind of formal conversation we were to have.

The room, so refined and delicate in all its deportment, so filled with light and glowing surfaces, contrasted severely with the rest of the house, which had something dark, massive, and ungainly about it and which deployed its oversized furniture into such a set of obstacles that to get across a room was to engage in a dance of physical distortions not unlike that of a football halfback maneuvering through a tightly congested line of scrimmage.

I was always a bit mystified by that house, frankly, for it was so unlike Sven — the Sven I knew or thought I knew — and the appended sitting room was so like Dorothea: reclusive, translucent, "off to the side," impeccably tidy, fragile but poised as if "bearing up" as ever under some kind of strain I could scarcely be expected to comprehend.

Entering that room (it was the first time for me, as often as I had been in that house) was like making an entrance into one of those small stage sets sometimes positioned to the front and side of the main stage—often a garden bower or some such thing where more intimate relations among characters are entertained, and perhaps resolved.

I had never felt before, in visiting anybody, that I was a "caller" in the old-fashioned sense, that the object of my visit was both ceremonial as well as personal, and that, even as an old friend, I had been somehow prompted to this interview not only by Dorothea's invitation but also by a summons of curiosity and conscience on my part, however obscure that summons may have been at the time.

Was there something important I was meant to know?

Dorothea's role in the interview was as distinctly ceremonial as I had expected it to be. She sat resolutely upright in a small, rigid chair, a tall and chiseled Swedish beauty with blond hair braided in a crown around her head. She had a number of pronouncements to make in that mellow voice of hers, declarations of a sort that would round off and conclude the events not only of the past few months but of the past years of her life with Sven as this had affected both his (and, through him, her) interactions with me—as few, really, as these latter had been.

I no longer remember many of the details enumerated in her carefully rehearsed litany, to which I listened attentively, nodding politely at every affirmation, frowning sympathetically at every negation, and even wondering why she was telling me all of this. Naturally I expressed some concern for her financial situation, but she assured me that all was well in that respect (indeed, almost overwhelming in the unexpected size and scope of the legacy she had been bequeathed).

But there was one point I could never forget, the climactic point at which everything else was aimed and which she quite obviously regarded as urgent to communicate to me. She told me that Sven had said to her, several weeks before his fatal fishing accident, that he had treasured three friends especially in his life—that these three friends were Jaleb Brooks, Martin Casey, and myself, Nat Thompson. Moreover, she imparted this information to me in a most peculiar way: on one hand—let's call it, in the ceremonial guise—she seemed to be conferring some sort of honor upon me, a medal or certificate, as it were, of esteem and recognition; on the other hand—let's call it, in the personal guise—she made her bestowal with an odd tone in her voice while peering at me intently, her head tilted a bit to the side, like a bluejay studying an especially tempting berry of some sort. Was there a question in her mind, both perhaps about herself and about my reaction, that held something in abeyance, that called into doubt just how honorific this honor might actually be?

Furthermore, I was not sure at the time why she told me this. Was there something I should do with the information? Was there a commission involved? Did I now have the obligation to perpetuate something about Sven—for example, by being friends with his former friends? I didn't know the others very well—actually, almost not at all. At the time, I tried to accept her declaration simply as a compliment—as I still do, in a way—remembering uneasily the jostling and pushing that took place when the three of us were among the six pallbearers at Sven's obsequies. The other three pallbearers were Sven's son—called "Winkee," for some reason; Art Bailey, Sven's former partner in his law firm; and Brian O'Grady, Sven's old fishing buddy.

I don't know why all that jostling took place. Too much difference in body types, I suppose, made coordinating movements difficult. But I remember Jaleb Brooks, a huge, broad-shouldered, bearded man, swearing under his breath at Martin Casey, a limp, spiny insect of a man who seemed unable to hold up his corner of the casket.

I also remember when, before the funeral began and I was introduced to the other pallbearers (I already knew Winkee, for better or worse), Jaleb leered at me and muttered insolently "So *you're* that teacher guy!" He stared at me for a moment, laughed, and turned his attention to the hired and nowadays indispensable bagpiper, kilt and all, with the same scorn he had directed at me. I was glad that at least he had delivered himself of whatever pronouncement he thought I merited and that I didn't have to deal with his disdain while the casket wrenched and jolted around in our hands, his powerful grasp constantly pulling the others off balance.

Only Winkee, dressed in uniform—he was on leave from military service—seemed to take pleasure in the proceedings and glanced knowingly at Jaleb from time to time.

My interview with Dorothea concluded, I felt "discharged." Our personal postmortem was over, a psychological inquest brought to a proper finish—or so I thought at the time. Years would pass without much further contact with Dorothea. Eventually she took up a new life, vanished for a while, as much as Sven had vanished, perhaps even more so, for I had been, however indirectly, initiated into a company whose only cohesive point had been Sven himself, or so it seemed—three friends who didn't know one another, who were certainly not friends with one another, but whose presence together was occasionally marked by a fortuitous brush at the hardware store or by the gasoline pumps or at the town dump.

I wondered if the others had been recipients of the same officious declaration from Dorothea, though my guess is that, if they had been, they dismissed it rather quickly and gave it no further thought. I can't say that they came to know me—at least they never seemed to recognize me—but I recognized them, and I think I eventually came to know something about them.

I should say, at this point, that both Sven and Dorothea had not been "natives," as the expression goes, having come from somewhere in the midwest to the township of East Gilead in northern New Hampshire about fifteen years ago. Sven, in addition to being an astute lawyer, was an ardent fly fisherman, and I always imagined that his attraction to the locale was based on the many well-stocked trout streams that flow down into the adjacent valleys from the White Mountains.

He met, it was said, his sudden demise by slipping on a mossy rock close to one of those streams and hitting his head against a jagged shard of New Hampshire granite. Jaleb Brooks was with him at the time and was the only witness.

I should mention that I, too, am an outsider and teach history and languages at the East Gilead regional high school.

About Sven: well, what can I say?

Would that I had a stock of heroic epithets I could apply, something Homeric, something vast and breathless and evocative of boundless space and airy heights, for Sven was an eagle of a man for me, with eyes that could see tiny things at great distances and a mind that could stretch its wings over mountain ranges. Okay, I grant it must appear inordinately strange to engage in such sublime hyperbole; but genuine intelligence is rare enough among humankind, and Sven had it, the real thing, I mean. There was a sort of Odysseus in him—a tall, energetic man, a wave of blond hair setting off a broad, luminous face, steely blue eyes, a man "many-minded," adventurous, destined—if anyone was ever so destined—for roaming over the "wide-bosomed earth" and the "wine-dark sea."

I first discovered all this by chance at an open house at my high school, when, among the milling, ingratiating, apologetic parents (who nevertheless regard teachers as a version of latter-day household slaves), Sven emerged, not with his son (whom, for some odd reason I never did have in class and who avoided me as much as his father later sought me out) but to ask me some abstruse question about a point in grammar. You must know something about the inimitable "tribe of grammarians" to know what discussion of an abstruse point in grammar can lead to.

In this case it led to a great deal.

It turned out that Sven knew an enormous amount about language, about classical and modern languages even, and much more than that. He was a polymath, reading voluminously everything that came to hand. Inquiries, subsequent to our first meeting, would reveal not only that, superior to the teachers who taught them, he had a command of almost all the subjects taught at the school but that he was considered an exceptionally qualified attorney whose persuasive skills made him the man most to be avoided in local legal altercations.

I was able to hold my own ground with him, even surpass him in those things that I knew well; and I could follow him into arenas where we were equals. But whereas I had leisure to pursue matters of mutual interest, he didn't; and hence his penetration to the core of issues—with some of which he had the barest acquaintance—never failed to be astonishing.

Our friendship was based on this.

It's odd that Winkee, his son, had a reputation in the school of being a ne'er-do-well, a bounder, a tramp, a "punk."

It's even odder than Sven didn't seem to care about this.

Sure, Sven and I had so many lunches together I couldn't number them—sometimes at a café near the school, sometimes at his home. Or, standing on the sidelines of a high school soccer game, we would unravel the latest version of the "Big Bang" theory, critique what Chomsky had (or had not) accomplished in linguistics, or consider whether Wittgenstein was all that he was stacked up to be. Sven seemed to know some of the Platonic dialogues by memory, though he was equally conversant with the Devonian rock formations that appeared by the streams when he went fishing up in the mountains. And, of course, we talked history, endlessly, scrupulously, taking apart the strategy (or lack of it) at Antietam or Shiloh, or discussing recent excavations of Viking settlements along the rivers of Southern Russia.

Our infrequent discussion of those redoubtable Norse marauders, whom Sven identified vaguely as his remote ancestors, brought out a brief but curiously rough edge in him, a boisterous guffaw that always surprised me but which I took to be his momentary impersonation of such venerable ancient spirits.

And all of this was mixed in with no little fascination with matters such as the permutation of subjunctive verb forms among the various Romance languages out of their original Latin roots.

Most remarkably, there was never a hint of the trivial, an absorption in a mass of irrelevance, involved here. Sven spoke lucidly, learnedly, elegantly, ever with the slightest touch of humor, with an intellectual detachment as refined as it was gentle. He was a bright light in a world in which almost everybody regards knowing anything as a dangerous extravagance and as a serious flaw in character.

Of course, I knew that I occupied a small niche in Sven's life—I rarely saw him in the evening, or at his work, or on the weekends. In any event, that light went out for me—too suddenly, too prematurely. Whatever else I might come to think about Sven in future years, this much has remained for me an unsullied and irrefragable source of admiration.

But why had I never known these other friends of his, fellow compatriots of the select group, the privileged threesome in which belatedly I found myself included?

Sven had never spoken of them. I had never seen him in their company. When I was introduced to them at the funeral, I recognized them as people I had seen around town. It was difficult not to notice Jaleb Brooks now and then, with his great overbearing stride, his unkempt beard flecked with axle grease and wood chips, his pickup truck unspeakably filthy and belching clouds of exhaust from a broken muffler. I was surprised to see this hitherto macabre but obtrusive figure show up at the funeral of someone like Sven Lindstrom.

Martin Casey was also not totally unfamiliar: a tall, angular man, as thin as a stalk of hollyhock, lethargically sprouting great rangy, insect-like limbs, with a drooping head, a long red nose, and spectacles an inch thick. He ran an antique shop in the center of town, and I often saw him—I hate to use the expression—"slithering" furtively in and out of that curiously malevolent den, jammed as it was with the detritus of a moribund rural culture that he sold to tourists at exorbitant prices.

Beyond that, I had no further impressions. Yet we were the three friends of Sven: honored presumably, revered for that fact, sharing something in common, for Sven, if he was nothing else, was an exceptional man; his friends must be exceptional in some sense too.

Were they ever!

About a year after Sven's demise, I was discussing some points of American colonial history with my senior class. What comes up in such classes is sometimes remarkable, for some of the students are descendants of the earliest families that came to these hills around East Gilead in the mid-eighteenth century, and their familial lore has retained fragments of regional history, though what may be factual and what most certainly belongs to the genre "tall tale" needs to be carefully distinguished. If such students happen to be minimally articulate, they have interesting things to say, and the occasional explosive laughter of the other students helps to differentiate the particular family account from the universally understood fabrication.

Local real estate agents, of course, in their marketing efforts, have so embellished some of these stories that it's now more difficult than ever to know what is true anymore: history is a good selling point for them. For example, the traditional "root cellars" in all the old houses put up for sale in the area nowadays have been retroactively transfigured into pre–Civil War "underground railroad" hiding places for runaway slaves on their way to the Canadian border.

The well-heeled urban purchasers of these houses as summer homes accept this fiction without hesitation, not knowing about a farming family's need to store turnips and potatoes through a cold winter and all too glad to be able to palliate their affluently guilty consciences with this effervescent link to one of the more tragic episodes in American history.

In any case, a year or so after Sven's death I happened to mention to my students something about the famous workshops around Boston in the eighteenth century that produced what is now considered invaluable colonial furniture. I discovered, to my surprise, that some of the students recognized a name here and there, but they were surprised when I told them that such furniture was very difficult to find and expensive to buy. One student even brought up the name of Chippendale: his grandmother had owned a genuine Chippendale chair. I asked him what had happened to the chair.

The student told me: Martin Casey, the antique man, had bought it — bought it for fifty dollars, which his grandmother was happy to get because she was a bit short of cash that year. Other students told similar stories. Martin Casey would come to their houses and purchase furniture of all kinds — cabinets, desks, dry sinks, harvest tables, grandfather clocks, old canopied beds, everything. The families were glad to get the money. I recognized that they obviously had no idea what these items were really worth.

And, oh yes, that lawyer, "Winkee's dad, don't yuh know," always came with him.

Sven?

Yes. Sven and Martin Casey.

I guess I should have left things alone at this point, but I didn't. I decided to visit Martin's dreadful little shop, located in the center of town and hideously named "Knick-Knacks, Gee-Gaws, 'n' What-Not." I wanted to see his furniture.

"Furniture?" he croaked at me from behind a desk festooned overhead with a row of battered tin lanterns. "I carry no furniture."

I stood there before him, surrounded by the most amazing collection of dreary junk the world has ever seen, junk in cabinets, junk hanging from the walls and suspended from the ceiling, junk spilling out of barrels and large wicker baskets and old brass-studded leather trunks, junk originally spewed out in vast quantities by nineteenth-century mills and sold over the past 150 years in five-and-dime stores to a parsimonious rural population. His great red nose pointed at me like the beak of a vulture ready to peck at my entrails, and his almost blind eyes were monstrously magnified by his thick spectacles.

"But I understand you buy furniture from the local farmsteads ..."

He lifted and fanned out a long-fingered hand at me. "Well, well ... I do, we did, that, ahyuh, but no longah. An' I shipped it off, yuh know ... ta New Yark, Bahston ... no market for it heyah, but in New Yark, Bahston ..."

"Where to?" I asked. "To Sotheby's, Christie's, I suppose?"

"It could fetch a handsome price at places like that. They was glad to have it. Sven and I ... yuh know ... it worked very nicely for us, very nicely indeed." His lanky body convulsed in a weird, clucking laughter.

"Sven and you ...?" I repeated.

He rose from his desk, his head bent forward so as not to collide with all the objects suspended from hooks in the ceiling. He slid out from behind the crowded desk and made his way through a narrow corridor of shelves filled with old pottery, canning jars, and glass medicinal bottles. He stooped down and began to sort through a wooden barrel filled with broken metallic toys.

"Sven seemed ta know everythin'. Knew his furniture, he did—could identify the really priceless stuff in a second," Martin mumbled. "Course, I couldn't—couldn't see it anyhows, even if I knew. But even plain old pine furniture became valuable for collectors.

"We got it all. We combed the areah from Centah Alliston right through ta Perry's Junction. Made a small fortune, if yuh wanta know. Sven knew how ta get inta othah people's houses, could spot the good stuff right off, outa the cornah a' his eye without lookin' like he was noticin' it.

"What a line he had! He understood old Yankee psychology ta a tee— 'Ain't nothin' heyah for sale, but go ahead an' make an offah anyhow.' Afta bikerin' 'bout some junk—actin' like it were great stuff an' he were real disappointed not ta get it, he'd turn his attention ta what he really wanted, but puttin' on like he just didn't wanta return home empty-handed. They were nevah ready for this. He sure was good at it. He could talk anybody outa any heirloom they had.

"Great friends we were—Sven an' I. I guess Jaleb Brooks was anothah friend. That makes sense, knowin' the both a' them. There was anothah fellah he hung around with sometimes—some teachah fellah at the school. Don't remembah his name. I guess he was anothah one a' them pallbearers at Sven's funeral. Couldn't see him anyhow. That was a heck of a time, I tell yuh, at that funeral with Jaleb bein' his usual piss-ass self an' pushin' ever'body else around an' that damned bagpihpah-man gnawin' out my middle ears with all that high-pitched squealin' like some damned pig in a poke."

Martin fished out a black Lionel steam locomotive from the toys. He looked like a deformed blue heron plucking a lobster out of a tangled morass of seaweed. Its paint was scratched, and its wheels and wires dangled loosely from its base. He glanced at me: "A fellah who collects Lionel trains called me yestaday. Just tryin' ta help him out. I wonda if I be havin' a caboose somewheyah in heyah. He's lookin' especially for a caboose.

"Anyways—what was I sayin'? Yep, we'd buy the stuff, an' then Sven an' Jaleb Brooks would go out an' fetch it in his pickup truck an' bring it inta my shed. From there I'd ship it off. Didn't want ta be sellin' it around heyah—that's for shuwah. Didn't want the folks 'round heyah ta get wind of what this stuff was worth.

"That Jaleb is something else, let me tell yuh—a good match for Sven. It's funny though; eventually they began ta bring furniture in that I had nevah seen befowah. Great stuff, I tell yuh. I don't know wheyah they got that stuff, but I shipped it on too. Didn't ask no questions 'bout that, an' the people who got it didn't either."

He slid his long fingers back into the mound of toys. "By the way," he added, "yuh interested in old baseball cards? I got a whole shipment a' them this mornin'."

"No," I replied. "Tell me about Jaleb. What do you know about him?"

"Nothin' much. He's rough, all right, an' maybe even dangerous. Yuh wouldn't wanta cross him, yuh wouldn't. But for all his blustah, he's a smaht man, maybe the smahtest man 'roun', 'cept for Sven when he were alive. Much smahtah than that othah fellah Sven hung 'roun' with whom I can't remembah. Sven used to say about that othah fellah that he was like the fool in some Russian folk tale who went ta the county fair an' spent so much time lookin' at the exhibits a' little things, he nevah saw a great big ol' chained bear standin' right in front a' him."

"Oh, really … how like Sven to know a Russian folk tale!"

"Yuh wanta know what else Sven thought a' that teachah fellah?"

"No, I don't think so."

I said goodbye and left the shop.

Weeks later, promptings of no especially beneficent nature, I'm sure, drove me to enter the law offices of what was still called "Lindstrom and Bailey" upon some pretext I no longer remember. Art Bailey was not busy at the moment and had time to chat. He recognized me and invited me into his office. He sat in a large aluminum and leather chair that tipped back rather alarmingly. He was a short man, a bit chubby and bald, with a thin moustache and a curious propensity to tap his head rather loudly with his right index finger whenever engaged in what was meant to be taken as an act of thinking. His head sounded curiously hollow. Sometimes he would grasp his head in both hands and lift that same finger upright so that it looked like a small stubby antenna attached to the top of his skull; he would then waggle that finger around as if the antenna were trying to pick up a signal. As we talked, he did a great deal of that tapping and grasping as well as rocking back and forth in the chair, which at times would suddenly catapult him from an almost reclining position to an upright position so violently that it looked as if it would hurl him right across the desk—in my direction, unfortunately—antenna and all pointed directly at me.

We spoke of what we had in common: our memories of Sven. He was visibly nervous about that but was able to acknowledge how brilliant Sven was. Indeed, the law practice had certainly declined since the time of Sven's accident. But there was a curious lack of remorse in his whole manner of speaking. Late in our rambling discourse, he mentioned something about a "ghastly incident."

"And what was that?" I inquired.

"Well, well," he said. "It was that pal of Sven's, that bearded barbarian, Jaleb Brooks. A few days after Sven's accident, he barged in here and demanded several items of furniture that were in Sven's office. I had assumed they were antiques of some sort. He said they were his, that *he had made them.* Of course, I protested, threatened to call the police, all the rest you know. I was met with language so coarse, so abusive, so intimidating that I decided to let the things go. I thought he was going to kill me. He would have killed anyone over those antiques. What did it matter to me? I just let them go. Sven had seemed rather fond of them, however. They were very nice pieces — completely unlike the grotesque hunks he filled his house with."

"That must have been pretty shocking — after all those years with a gentleman like Sven, to be treated so crudely like that."

Art allowed his chair to come slowly to an upright position. He took his hands away from his head and folded them on the desk in front of him. He looked down at his hands.

"Not really," he allowed. "That was not the shocking part. Sven, you know, always treated me like that too. Sven was a coarse and violent man, given to the most uncouth oaths and violent tempers I've ever witnessed. Surely you knew about that, Mr. Thompson. Surely you knew that about Sven. And he had met in Jaleb a man as violent and coarse as he was, except perhaps a bit more so. If the two of them, for some reason, had gone at each other, the consequences wouldn't have been pleasant."

I was astonished. "No. I didn't know."

"But the shocking part — that was the admission by Jaleb that he had made those antiques — those 'antiques,' if you understand the contradiction in terms."

"He must be very skilled."

"Skilled indeed! I've made some inquiries since then. Only Sven could have figured out all the details of how to do that — the right glues, the right wood and pegs and nails, all extracted from genuine old pieces of no real value, then recrafted to a perfect set of specifications. It took Jaleb to do the actual carpentry, and, yes, he must be very good at that, judging from those pieces we had here in the office. I guess they had quite a business going from what I can reckon, all funneled through Martin Casey, who never had an idea of what was going on. Even the experts were fooled."

"And have you tried to bring this out, expose this ...?"

"There's no point in doing that. I learned a lot about law from Sven. What little success I've had is due to him. Anyway, he's dead. And anyway ..."

"Yes?"

"I wouldn't want to get on the wrong side of Jaleb Brooks. He's too dangerous a man. He wouldn't stop at anything."

I turned to go. As I opened the office door I heard Art Bailey murmur, "And I never believed, never for a moment, that Sven died from hitting his head on a rock. Never believed that, never did."

That evening, hours after my brief interview with Art Bailey, I could swear I saw Jaleb Brooks roar down the main street of East Gilead in his old pickup truck, his beard aflame in the evening sun, his eyes intent with demonic fury, and his truck rattling like an infernal chariot loosed upon the unhappy denizens of this world.

Years later, I happened to go to a teachers' conference in Minneapolis. Such affairs, as anyone knows who has ever been to one, are so dreadful that any excuse to get away for a while is quite welcome. I decided to rent a car and drive out to a pleasant suburb where I had learned that Dorothea now lived. I found a somewhat more robust and happier woman than I had remembered, less tense, living with a new husband amid decorous surroundings. We talked about life back in East Gilead, what had happened to whom, who was doing what, and about her life and what she was doing.

We talked about Winkee, too, but he rarely kept in touch with his mother. He had been in trouble a number of times—a dishonorable discharge from the army, drugs, alcoholism, a short prison term, a short-lived marriage. Dorothea was clearly sad about him.

Toward the end of our conversation, I felt impelled, really in spite of myself, to allude to her pronouncement, made so many years before, about the three friends.

"I knew," she said, "how much you admired Sven, and I thought you might be honored to know what he told me he thought of you. And I am so glad you remembered that."

"I did remember," I answered. "And I was honored."

"I considered telling the others the same thing, you know—Jaleb Brooks and Martin Casey. But I never did. I would have felt just a little awkward mentioning it to Jaleb because in the last week or so before the accident there had been hard feelings between Jaleb and Sven. It was something about furniture in Sven's law office.

"Sven had a few pieces of furniture in his office that I guess Jaleb thought belonged to him and Sven was unwilling to give up. I never saw this furniture. I wonder if it was as awful as what our house was furnished with.

"Anyway, I found out because Jaleb called at the house once—something he never normally did. Jaleb was in a terrible state at the time.

"I couldn't imagine the two of them as having any interest in furniture. Furniture! That's so unlike them. Anyway, they must have resolved the disagreement, whatever it was."

Dorothea tilted her head in a slightly odd way, in that same curious bluejay way I had seen years before, and watched for my reaction.

"Why do you say that?" I replied.

"Because of the fishing trip—when the accident occurred."

"What about the fishing trip?"

"Usually, Sven went fishing with Brian O'Grady. He often spent evenings and sometimes weekends with Jaleb doing I don't know what. But that weekend he went fishing with Jaleb. They wouldn't have gone fishing together if there still were hard feelings between them, would they?"

I was silent. I knew she was testing me. "I mean, they must have resolved that issue about the furniture."

I was still silent. I knew that they hadn't resolved that issue. I knew that she realized that as well.

"And Jaleb was so nice about it." Dorothea dropped her eyes. "He supplied all the fishing gear. Sven didn't take his; I guess his ties were getting old and were not so effective anymore at luring the fish. I didn't even know that Sven had gone off on a fishing trip that day."

Dorothea looked at me again. "I'm so glad you came by. You were such a good friend with Sven. That's why I told you back then about yourself, and Jaleb Brooks, and Martin Casey. I just wanted you to … to know; I just wanted someone other than myself to know. And I knew that you would finally work it out ... that you would put all the pieces together. I gave you the foundation for what you needed to find out."

"Find out what?"

"You know very well what I mean."

"Who ..." I hesitated.

"Yes," she smiled. "Who Sven really was, and ..."

"And ...?" I repeated.

"What he was up to, and ..."

"And ...?" I repeated yet again.

"... what actually happened to him."

Colloquies

(Overheard in a restaurant,
North Conway, New Hampshire)

1.

Two elderly ladies,
in slacks and with permanent waves

Now, did you ever hear that?

What, Cynthia, what should I have heard?

That waitress! That waitress split her infinitive.

Well, no, I didn't notice.

She said, "To quickly get the salad …"

How dreadful!

They don't teach grammar in school anymore. When I was in school, we learned everything about grammar. Every day we studied grammar. We certainly did.

Well, so did I, Cynthia. That's why it was called "grammar school" back then, you know.

They call it "elementary school" now. That's to make people forget about grammar. I'm sure of that.

Really?

Of course, I'm sure. They don't want anyone to know about grammar anymore. They don't want people to know English. They want to make English disappear.

How dreadful!

And look at all the foul language people use nowadays — in the movies, and on television, and everywhere. And the violent way of talking! And the threats! Girls use it now. Even children use it. They hear their parents using it. When I was a girl, if you said a bad word, you would have your mouth washed out with soap. And that was not just an expression. People did have their mouths washed out with soap. It was not a pleasant experience, I can tell you.

Did you ever have your mouth washed out with soap?

Don't tell anyone about this, but, yes, it happened once. I was nine years old, and I used the word … you know … "h-e-l-l."

How dreadful!

My mother washed my mouth out with soap—Ivory soap. Or was it Palmolive? Anyway, it was a lesson I would not soon forget.

Well, nobody is taught good manners anymore.

No correct grammar, no good manners: two sides of the same coin! Roy, my grandson, you know, has the worst manners of all—and he's only six years old. His parents let him get away with anything. When he comes to my house, I try to teach him some manners. I'm the only one who tries.

I admire you for that, Cynthia. Someone has to stand for something.

They certainly do. Well, he wears this silly baseball hat all the time. The other day, I tried to get him to take his hat off when he came into the house. But he didn't want to take it off; he even wanted to eat dinner with it on. I told him: "Take your hat off, Roy. Young gentlemen should not wear their hats in their grandmother's house."

Did he take it off?

No. I had to ask again and again.

Then what did you do?

I finally got angry. So, do you know what I said?

No.

I shouted, "I'm askin' you to quickly get that damned hat off your damned little head, or I'm gonna flatten your damned little nose."

Uh … Cynthia!

But it's the only language they understand.

> *How dreadful!*

I even split my infinitive.

> *Did he take his hat off?*

You're damned right he did.

2.

*A teenaged waitress
and a middle-aged woman*

My name is Janice. I'll be serving you this evening. Our specials are ...

    Do you have anything without onions?

Um ... without onions?

    Onions. I hate onions. I can't eat anything with onions.

Well ... there must be something without onions. I'll have to think. I could ask the chef.

    These medallions of beef tenderloin—that looks good—do they have onions on them?

I think so. They're served with a sauce of onions and mushrooms sautéed in a merlot wine and garnished with ...

    Could you take the onions out of the sauce?

Take the onions out of the sauce? I'd have to ask the chef about that too.

    But leave in the mushrooms. I adore mushrooms, especially if they're portobello.

I think the onion flavor would still be left behind.

    I don't mind the flavor so much. It's the texture I hate.

So, one order of "medallions of beef tenderloin with onions removed from sauce."

    No, I think I'd rather have the grilled salmon with mashed potatoes.

Okay, scratch that. Umm, "one grilled salmon—"

    No onions.

"… without onions." Actually, I don't think it comes with onions, but I'll write that down just in case.

And rosemary on the salmon.

Rosemary? Rosemary on the salmon?

Yes, rosemary.

And "rosemary on the—"

You do have fresh rosemary, don't you? I wouldn't want dried rosemary.

I don't know if we have fresh rosemary, but I'll ask the chef. So, "fresh rosemary—"

Dried rosemary would be all right on the mashed potatoes, but not on the salmon.

Okay.

And no onions in the salad.

How about rosemary on the salad?

Yes.

Fresh or dried?

Fresh.

Would you like some rosemary sprinkled on your onions?

What? What did you say?

Nothing. Nothing at all. One grilled salmon and mashed potatoes coming up.

3.

Two men, in their early forties,
both balding and slightly overweight

Of course, business was bad, but no one knew just how bad it was. The first layoffs were in the shipping department.

How did you find out about that?

Well, rumors, you know how they fly through a building. "They just laid off six people in the shipping department." Everyone was saying it. Everyone was terrified.

What did you do?

I went to my supervisor and asked him if it was true that six people were laid off in the shipping department. He denied it—just flatly denied it. So, I went back to my department and told my staff that the rumors were false. No one was laid off, I told them.

Did that calm them down?

Well, it did for a day or two. Then the rumors were confirmed. Six people had been laid off in the shipping department. I ended up looking like a fool.

Did you go back to the supervisor?

I certainly did. I said, "Why did you deny that six people were laid off in the shipping department?"

What did he say?

Something about company policy, confidentiality, respecting the privacy of those laid off. I asked him if more layoffs were planned. That's what everyone was so worried about. He said not to be worried about that. No more layoffs.

So, were you worried anyway?

Of course I was. And for good reason. The following week the entire international sales department was laid off. We were in a frenzy. People kept storming into my office all day and yelling, "Are we going to get laid off? Are we going to get laid off?"

Did you go back to your supervisor?

Of course I did. I said, "Everyone is in a frenzy. Everyone thinks they're going to get laid off. Are they going to get laid off? You've got to tell me!" But he tells me no one in my department is going to get laid off.

So, I guess that calmed things down a bit?

Well, a little. But ...

But what?

Three of my staff got layoff notices early the next week. They screamed at me, "You told us we weren't going to get laid off, and we got laid off!" Then everyone else is screaming about the chances of getting laid off too.

And ...?

So, I decide that I have to go back to my supervisor. I have to tell him to be straightforward with me, to let me know what's going on.

Did you do that?

I did.

What happened?

I got laid off.

4.

Two men in their mid-thirties,
both in baggy sweaters and with trim beards

We always worked together well as a team, you know, but we've had our little differences. Things get worked out in the end. Not like some of the other labs—they have nothing but hassles. People are forced to take sides. I hate it when people force you to take sides.

Really? Lizzie told me otherwise, told me you guys are always fighting…

Well, that's Lizzie for you—stirring things up, backbiting, tale-bearing, telling the "family secrets," giving us a bad rap.

Lizzie told me you guys got really divided over that Newcomb project…

Yes, okay, we had our little disagreements. It was difficult to decide who was to conduct which aspect of the project. We decided to divide into two teams. Daryl, Austin, Jessica, Lizzie, Glen, and Mark would be on one team; Jason, Ashley, Lindon, Cassy, Tom, and I would be on the other.

What about Doug? You forgot Doug.

Yes, come to think of it, I forgot Doug. He was on our team.

Why did you forget Doug?

Well, I think I forgot Doug because he tried to be on the other team. He wanted to be on the other team because he hates Cassy. He doesn't like to work with Cassy.

Why didn't you just put him on the other team?

Glen hates Doug and refuses to work with him.

So, you could have put Glen on your team and shifted Doug.

Ashley hates Glen, and I couldn't have spared Ashley under the best of circumstances. Anyway, everyone would have gotten mad at me if I'd made that change.

Sounds pretty bad to me!

No! No problem. Just a few little differences to iron out.

Lizzie said it turned into a pitched battle.

Lizzie always says things like that. I don't have much respect for Lizzie.

She said you had some kind of big confrontation.

Well, Daryl, Austin, Jessica, and Lizzie decided to appoint Mark as their representative to meet with me about Glen, since my group had appointed me to meet with them about Doug. But Glen and Doug got together to protest to Mark and me that they were being treated like "pawns" by the rest of the group, at which point Ashley stormed up and said that Glen should mind his own business, and then Daryl, Austin, Jessica, and Lizzie marched up in a kind of armed phalanx to our side of the lab and demanded that Ashley be transferred out of the lab, at which point Cassy screamed at Doug, and then Lindon and Jason joined Jessica in insisting that Daryl and Austin had improperly represented the interests of the group by appointing Mark as their representative, while Lizzie ran out of the lab and down the hall. I don't know where she was going.

Probably to tattletale to me.

I would believe it.

What did you think of all this?

I was furious. First, I was furious at Doug and Glen, then at Ashley; then I was furious at Mark, then at Cassy, Jessica, and Lindon; and then at Daryl, and then ...

What about Tom?

He ducked out. Maybe he went to the men's room. How should I know? He wasn't there.

Maybe he just didn't want to take sides.

Sides? Take sides? There's nothing about taking sides here. I mean, we were just having a friendly discussion. Nobody was forcing anyone to take sides. I mean, what are you trying to say? Are you trying to impugn the integrity of my team? Are you, too, trying to give us a bad rap? Whose side are you on, anyway?

5.

Two women, late twenties,
tanned and athletic, in hiking clothes

I will never climb that mountain again.

It's awful, just awful.

Slippery dangerous paths, trails badly marked and maintained, no switch-backs where there should be ...

Pretty bad, all right.

And too many people on the trail. That guy sitting by the brook with his cell phone, calling his office. All the summer-camp kids with their cell phones, calling their mothers and saying, "Hey, Mom, guess where I am?" It makes me sick.

Me too.

And that stupid cog-railroad engine puffing huge amounts of black smoke into the air. You would think the environmentalists would go after that.

I would.

And that Appalachian mountain hut with its septic tanks stinking like the pits of hell! Every time the breeze blew across them in our direction, I almost died.

I could have keeled over dead at any moment.

Who was that jerk at the hut, anyway, who kept looking at everybody's boots and commenting on them as if he was the God of Hikers rendering some kind of Final Judgment on hiking boots? Did he comment on your boots?

Yeah.

What did he say?

He said I would be lucky if I didn't get a sprained ankle on the way down.

They should get rid of jerks like that.

They certainly should.

Then all those big rocks at the end, no real trail, just go whatever way you can.

That was tough, all right.

And you get to the top, after a long climb, and the summit is crowded with tourists who came up on that railroad or in cars, wearing their silly-looking clothes and hats. Why do all tourists look like obese Bugs Bunnies and insist on having their photographs taken with their buckteeth sticking out and the equivalent of some sort of big carrot in their hands?

It's a pretty ugly show, it is.

And everyone complaining about the price of a bottle of water? Do they think the bottle of water walked up six thousand feet on its own? You shouldn't go mountain climbing if you're going to complain about everything.

I hate complaining.

Me too. That's all some people do — complain, complain, complain. They spend their whole life complaining.

It makes me sick. People who complain make me sick.

The way down wasn't so bad. But I'm so stiff I can hardly move.

I'm having a cramp now and then too.

Don't you just detest the food in this restaurant?

It's awful, just awful.

The Birthday Wish

If you should ever happen to be driving through the Connecticut River Valley between New Hampshire and Vermont and would like to take a slight detour and visit the village of Southwell on the Vermont side of the river, I can recommend a good place to have lunch.

It's called The Cinnamon Stick. My law office is located right next door, so I always have lunch there, and sometimes, when my wife goes off on one of those innumerable conferences of hers, I even have dinner there too. It's a comfortable and cheery sort of place with little niches where you can eat in private and read the newspapers without being disturbed. My favorite sandwich is the smoked salmon and avocado on pumpernickel. It's especially good with the in-house brewed beer. I recommend it very highly.

The Cinnamon Stick used to be called Dottie's Eats back about twenty years ago, when I first came to Southwell. It was the sort of place where the tradesmen of the town had their breakfasts of eggs and home fries at six in the morning and exchanged information about available jobs. In the late sixties, the first great wave of refugees from the cities, as I like to call it, arrived, mainly in the form of "hippies" who thought that rural life was the answer to all their problems. It's funny how old-fashioned that word "hippie" sounds now.

Anyway, a "hippie" couple purchased Dottie's Eats and turned it into an organic food place with all kinds of weird biotic broths and breads made of grains that no one has heard of, since, I guess, the Stone Age, or something like that. It was called The Living Essence.

I don't know what happened to that couple, or even to all the rest of the people who came at that time. They just disappeared, or became like everyone else, but the restaurant changed hands again a few years later, and a young, very fashionable couple from Boston, who affected English accents, gave it the name Chez Tutu and served gourmet French food there. For a while, every Mercedes and BMW and Volvo in the upper Connecticut River Valley showed up parked on our main street at one time or another. The place was especially favored by the people from Hanover, forty miles or so north of here. Then the cars stopped coming, the English accents were dropped, there was a divorce, and the place folded. Afterward, another couple purchased it and gave the restaurant its present name.

Now it serves workingmen's breakfasts of eggs and home fries at six, bagels at nine, organic luncheons at twelve, and gourmet dinners in the evening—something for everybody. So everybody goes there now.

In fact, it was there that I witnessed, one evening, Clara Dodd's twenty-fifth birthday party. It was there that I heard her whisper, among a torrent of heavy tears, that birthday wish of hers that came so soon, so oddly, true.

Mind you, it's only with some reservations that I get into this story about Clara Dodd at all. It's really my wife's story and she's my source for most of what I know, though even much of what she knows is secondhand, at least about recent years, since she got it in turn from someone else; and, with all due respect for my wife, she frequently interprets what she hears in a peculiar fashion that I don't always understand.

Anyway, my wife's name is Harriet, and she teaches at the local school. Her field is working with "special education" children, but she also has important relationships with other children in the school and was very close to Clara during Clara's high school years.

Clara, in fact, often volunteered to be her assistant and, at one time, wanted to get professional training for the same kind of work. That's amusing to think of now, because Paula Dodd, her mother, would have died before she would have allowed that to happen. Frankly, I wouldn't blame her.

Harriet and I don't have any kids, but if we did, I wouldn't have wanted any kid of mine spending a life working with mentally handicapped children.

What has it done for my wife, if I may sound somewhat crude here, except to make her a little strange?

In any case, I was present, as I said, at Clara's birthday party, and I was the only one, through all that din and laughter, to hear what Clara said—to hear, as it was spoken aloud, that birthday wish. So there is something about Clara's story for which I'm the only source—and it's an important thing in that story too, if I may say so—and I was able to tell my wife about it. Harriet sat down on a sofa and cried when she heard it.

But it was an interesting turnaround for a change. Now I was the source. It made me feel close, in a way, to what happened to Clara. It made me feel as if I was part of her story now, and that's why I'm telling it to you.

The reason I was at The Cinnamon Stick that evening was that Harriet had gone to a conference in Burlington. She hates these conferences, by the way, but goes to them only because they're necessary for renewing her teaching credentials. The local school district and the state school board require it. She says that these conferences are forums for people to air the most dubious and absurd hypotheses, which are then taken as proven facts by many of the participants. That's a typical Harriet opinion, by the way; I don't know how seriously you have to take it. She always has to be different, no matter what.

Anyway, I went to The Cinnamon Stick for dinner, as I usually do when Harriet's gone, and there I happened to be seated in a small alcove immediately adjacent to the long table where Paula Dodd's little social circle, which she called Pi Delta (her initials, in case you didn't see the connection), was celebrating Clara's twenty-fifth birthday.

The eight ladies who comprised the club—actually the seven ladies, now that I think of it, because one of them had been, in a sense, recently ostracized—were so intent on their celebration that they never noticed me sitting in the shadows right next to them, so close to them, in fact, that my elbow was almost touching Clara's elbow where she sat as guest of honor at the head of the table.

I guess Clara didn't particularly like the idea of turning twenty-five. But isn't that a problem for many young ladies of her age? She sure was upset that night.

Clara's father was named Jack Dodd, and he died when Clara was six years old. My wife tells me that he grew up in Southwell on the old Nathaniel Dodd farmstead up in the hills, just eight miles or so out of town. According to Harriet, who grew up in Southwell too, and to all the reports I've heard about him, Jack Dodd was just about the most promising young man ever to come out of this township. At the urging of one of his teachers at the regional high school up the valley a ways, he applied for and won a full scholarship to a prep school in Massachusetts—it was Deerfield Academy, I think. He needed that scholarship because certainly the Dodd family didn't have any money to speak of—though they owned a lot of land, which later, after Jack's death, came to be worth a great deal.

Jack must have cut a strange figure at Deerfield, I would have thought—a woodsman, in a way, within that rarefied outpost of suburban affluence. I'm told he was a lean, muscular young man, very good-looking with unruly blond hair, sharp blue eyes, and a taut, bony face always tanned from the outdoor activities he engaged in. He loved to work with his hands—hoeing a patch of fresh spring peas, splitting wood for the winter fire, hauling in hay, or clearing trails through the dense underbrush for the convenience of hikers in the national forests. His sports were mountaineering and canoeing, though at Deerfield he excelled at crew and lacrosse. Intellectually, he was a phenomenon, I'm told: a wonderful speaker and writer, an omnivorous reader who particularly loved the great English classics.

After Deerfield, he went to Dartmouth, again on scholarship, where he became captain of the varsity crew, president of the Dartmouth Outing Club, and one of the most outstanding majors that the English department could remember in decades. Certainly, the whole world lay open before this promising young man; it was his for the "taking."

The problem was, again as I've been told, he just wasn't interested. He wasn't interested in "taking" it. Some people make strange decisions, I must say. If what they say about him is true, he would have made a great lawyer—that much I know. Maybe he could even have become governor. And then what would that have led to?

Don't tell Harriet I said this. She always gets cross when I say things like this. She works with people who have no future. She says we should appreciate people for who and what they are, not for what their futures might be. Harriet is a bit testy about stuff like that.

Now, at about this point in the story, at least as I've heard it, Paula enters the picture.

Jack and Paula met at a reception that followed a collegiate crew regatta on the Charles River in Boston. She was an attractive, lively young woman, brunette with an oval face and petite features, always well-dressed, a fashionable debutante of the finest country-club set in Westchester County, educated in the ways of the *haute monde*—or at least that's the impression she gave; and as ambitious as anyone could be. That's what everyone who used to be in her club said about her, and most people agreed.

Paula was greatly admired in this town by most everyone—except by my wife, who had this really hostile antagonism toward her, and that's why Harriet is not always, as we attorneys would say, the most reliable witness about the things that happened.

Paula, herself, was not at all reticent in discussing her relationship with Jack among her friends in Pi Delta, sometimes at great length, but she was a cagey woman, my wife says, and was careful not to discuss him outside her circle in the same way that she discussed him within it. That's because some of the admiration given to her by the townsfolk was based on the good reputation that Jack had made for himself while he was alive, and she wouldn't have wanted to damage that—the admiration conferred upon her by Jack's reputation, I mean, and not so much Jack's reputation itself.

Belinda Blodget was one of the members of Pi Delta; she often volunteered for work at the elementary school and, during the lunch break, liked to tell my wife all the news and talk that went on in the Pi Delta meetings. Maybe she did it just to annoy my wife, but whatever the reason, that's why Harriet knows the things she does and why I said already that much of her story itself is secondhand.

According to Paula's account to Pi Delta, Jack's strong good looks and articulate demeanor, added to the Deerfield-Dartmouth connection, piqued her interest at once; and, though he was at first rather shy of her, her persistence quickly cemented a friendship between them. She was smart, she was pretty, and any man would have responded to her attention. However, she didn't get seriously interested in Jack until she attended, the following spring at Dartmouth, an afternoon tea of the English department at Sanborn House. That's a great atmosphere to be in, by the way—I mean Sanborn House. It's a good place to be seduced into … well, into whatever one gets seduced into.

On that particular occasion, Jack was able to stay for only half an hour at the tea; he had to get to crew practice but would see Paula later on. She stayed on at the tea and happened to get into a conversation with one of the younger members of the English department.

This fellow, short and heavy with prematurely frizzy-gray hair and fists pushed tightly into the side pockets of his bright but ratty-looking tweed jacket, spared no effort in extolling the virtues and possibilities of Jack's future. He puffed and sputtered for a full half hour in front of her.

By the time he finished, Paula had attained an image of Jack as the future president of some major university, and although she found the whole academic world just a bit contemptible ("tacky," she would say) and would have wished for almost any other professional choice on Jack's part, those prospects were not unappealing to her: just imagine inhabiting a presidential mansion at the edge of some tranquil, leafy campus, entertaining wealthy donors and trustees and famous honorary-degree recipients from all over the world, and watching Jack walk at the head of an academic procession accompanied by the grandest sort of music and by a faculty fully outfitted in their most ostentatious pseudo-medieval regalia. Paula's memories of this incident in Sanborn House, by the way, and the accounts she liked to give of it at the Pi Delta parties, were not always favorable since she became convinced in later years that somehow she had been "taken in" by this blustery fellow with his fists balled up in his pockets.

Of course, in a sense, she had been "taken in," but not in the way she thought she had. What Harriet thinks about this story, having been informed long ago directly by Jack about what was going on in his life at that time, is that Paula heard exactly what she wanted to hear and that she didn't think to question why she was being told all of this.

Also, Paula didn't—and wouldn't—listen seriously to Jack, even though he told her everything: that he, at this point late in his senior year, had already rejected all efforts of the younger men on the English faculty to recruit him into the kind of lives they had framed for themselves—lives in which the study of literature was used as leverage to achieve objectives no different in kind from those of his fellow classmates who were about to enter brokerage houses or business corporations or embark on legal or other kinds of careers. Indeed, as my wife thinks, Paula was the recipient of a speech designed as a last-ditch effort to win Jack over by applying pressure to him indirectly through the influence of a potential bride.

Paula didn't know how important recruitment of this sort is to people who are uncertain about what they have done and need to justify themselves by drawing others into it as well. I also wonder if the young fellow in question thought to shore up his own prospects for tenure by landing a "big fish" for the department who could then represent it favorably in a prestigious graduate school somewhere. But I guess there was no chance of this: Jack's sympathies were with the older men on the faculty, who seemed to do what they did out of the love for it and some of whom even explicitly warned Jack about the hazards of the academic life.

And Jack had never even seriously considered the academic life anyway; he desired only to return to the hills and woodlands he loved, and which he had never really left, and to a life in which his purpose would be to pass his devotion to books and to poetry on to the local populace. In short, Jack's ambition was to return to Southwell, take up farming at the old family farmstead, and become a small-town librarian.

What an ambition—if I can intrude here—and with all that talent! What a waste! Harriet tells me that she can't imagine a more genuine ambition for a person to have in this life. But, you know, that's Harriet for you! Good grief!

Now, Paula just didn't believe that Southwell was all Jack wanted.

It's funny how that works: people tell us exactly who they are and what they're going to do, and we don't believe them. We like to say, "Oh well, they really don't mean it."

But they do. They do mean it.

Moreover, Paula was convinced that even if Jack's intentions really corresponded to what he said he wanted, it was her duty, her prerogative, and thoroughly in her power, to change all that. In her view, the purpose of a wife is to get her husband on the right track. Aren't men like children? Don't they need to be given direction? Don't they have their heads in the clouds and gaze on stars and need to be brought down to earth?

Thus, she pushed for the marriage and veiled her intentions. Her policy was to give him line at first and then pull him in. Consent to what he wants, then do everything possible to make it not work. Jack would come around in time. How was Jack to know?

And, we could ask, how was Paula to know either, for that matter?

We go through life thinking everyone else is just like us. If she could shift and change according to what suited her advantage, why wouldn't Jack be able and willing to do it too? And if advantage is seen as the acquisition of money, status, and power, why wouldn't Jack come to see this also, when he had properly matured under her presumably skillful tutelage?

I would intrude here simply by saying: Why was Paula wrong? (My wife would faint to hear me say that!) But Paula couldn't know. Everything I've heard from people about Jack's character, his self-discipline, his unwavering integrity would suggest that Jack would be the most unchangeable person in the world. Changing Jack would have been like turning Mount Ascutney upside down.

There's only one thing you can do with a fellow like Jack if he happens to be standing in your way: contrive some way to get rid of him.

Or you can hate him.

After a few years, Paula would certainly have liked to get rid of him. It would be easy enough — she could just take off, leave town, be divorced, whatever. But two obstacles arose to this course of action. Clara was born, and, after the death of a grand-uncle, Jack inherited the Nathaniel Dodd farm where they were already living. Hate, after all, was her only option.

She was very good at it.

In later years, Paula would proclaim among her friends in Pi Delta that Clara was born "by mistake" and that, if things had "been different back then," Clara wouldn't have been born at all. Termination of pregnancy was not a legal option in those days. In fact, according to her own account, no compunction ever made her refrain from communicating that same information to Clara too, on occasions when some refractory impulse on Clara's part needed to be countered by the reminder that she had been one of the factors that had contributed to "ruining" her mother's life. After two years of marriage, Paula, naturally, was ready to leave Jack and return to Westchester County, but a moment of "negligent" passion (possible, I guess, even with someone whom you have come to detest), followed by pregnancy and Clara's birth, delayed those plans.

Paula knew how to take advantage of this situation; she had come to know Jack well enough to realize that he could be counted on to take his paternal responsibilities, his paternal love, to the highest point of expression. That was good; his parental affection could be converted into the rack upon which she could exact reparations from him to the fullest extent. Clara would be her instrument of revenge. Her fulfillment of the duties of motherhood, duties that she knew that Jack would be most eager to see carried out, would be at the price of submitting him to a hidden life of ceaseless debasement and humiliation.

I guess I don't need to say that there were obviously no other children. In later years, Paula would boast to her friends in Pi Delta that her husband "had forfeited his rights." She took great delight in imagining how much torment she might have been causing him by denying him any further intimacy. He was not the sort of man who would have sought out another woman, and she knew that. As my wife would say: Paula knew how to exploit Jack's good character to the hilt. Jack's point of view about all of this we will never know; he wouldn't have spoken of it, not to anybody.

Meanwhile, the members of Pi Delta regarded Paula with a kind of awe; they could scarcely but admire Paula's strength of resolve and even what could be taken as the exercise of a heroic, if ruthless and even perverse, "asceticism" in this matter. After all, the women found Jack to be an immensely attractive man. Wasn't Paula herself taking a loss of some kind in such a renunciation?

Apparently not.

All were impressed by her determination, her self-denial, except for one woman, the one who got thrown out of the group, and I'll get to her by and by. But one wonders if such an "asceticism" were even necessary, for times had changed and legal constraints had shifted. Paula, according to her own report, had also decreed to Jack, in what was no doubt her timely and peremptory fashion, that no future pregnancy would be brought to term—a ukase effectively forcing Jack, as we could surmise, into a situation where he had to make sure that such an outcome could never happen. He may have, in Paula's mind, forfeited his rights; yet how, in his own good conscience, could he ever presume to claim them?

The other reason Paula stayed on had to do with the farm that Jack inherited. To Jack, it was an ordinary sort of place because he was accustomed to it — about eight hundred acres of pastures and woodlands on the hills above the river. It had an old, rambling farmhouse and several large barns. Virtually everywhere on the property commanded magnificent views of the Green Mountains on one side and the White Mountains of New Hampshire on the other, with the wide, silvery band of the Connecticut River running in between. There was one spot on the highest rise — a broad and undulating meadow — that was especially lovely and had the finest view in every direction. Jack loved the farmstead, of course, and felt a loyalty to it that came from its being in his family since the time of the Revolutionary War.

But Paula saw more clearly the signs of the times. She read all the fashionable magazines and knew what rich people were buying. She knew that the Dodd farmstead was a potential real estate gold mine. In no sense was she ready to walk away from that, no matter how long it took to reap the harvest. There had to be some reward for her pains. It came sooner than she had expected.

Jack died of cancer in Clara's sixth year — of a brain tumor, as swift as it was deadly. Everyone says that he had done wonderful things for the town; that he educated many young men and women in the love of literature and the love of the surrounding woodlands; that nothing was the same before or after him. He could be counted on to resolve disputes between neighbors, to help anyone who needed help, to make things happen when too many interests had piled up and hampered all decisive action.

Harriet tells me that he maintained his sharp bold gaze, his kindness, his unremitting honesty to the day of his death, though his eyes became ringed by signs of an interior suffering so acute that one could scarcely speak of it. She grieved for him; she grieved terribly at the time of his death — but, you know, she does have a way of taking things too far.

From the very first week after his interment, she looked after his gravesite — there was nobody else doing that: she planted flowers, tended the grass — still does today, especially now that … well, we must not get ahead of ourselves.

Why did Paula not pack up Clara and her belongings and leave Southwell after Jack's death? Belinda Blodget told my wife that Paula never made a secret to her club about how much she despised Southwell. In fact, as my wife would interpret this, part of her prestige resided precisely in that contempt: she was perceived by her inner circle as being from a wider, bigger, better world and, therefore, as having the authority to make that kind of judgment. Her fellow club members were subdued by this authority, especially imparted as it was to the privileged inner circle to which they were admitted by her good graces, to say nothing of the flattery they felt in being made her trusted confidants and apparent advisors. Where else could Paula expect to muster, with such facility, a circle of admirers so unequivocally devoted to her — except, again, for one of them who didn't quite fit in with the rest?

Most importantly, she stayed on because she came into possession of the Nathaniel Dodd farm. Once released, as it was by Jack's death, from a family loyalty to preserve a farmland passed down through generations from the colonial period, the real estate value of the farm became all too apparent to the local developers.

One developer worked out a plan for an ultra-high-scale development — a "gated community" as they say, though why anyone needs gates up here I don't know, except to let cows in and out of pastures. Most people around here still routinely leave their front doors unlocked and their keys in their cars.

Anyway, the plan included manicured and dramatically landscaped grounds, a golf course, and expensive, secluded houses. It was to be called The Kensington Dales. The developer convinced Paula, correctly so, as it worked out in this case, that her maximum advantage lay in going into partnership with the development corporation and selling off the land parcel by parcel as construction proceeded. Paula, consequently, chose to stay in Southwell so that she could observe and help direct the progress of the enterprise over the long period of time it would take to complete.

It was a good decision on her part; she made a great deal of money from The Kensington Dales. Many of us in the town did too, including myself. One has to admire her for that.

Still, my wife doesn't. But, as you know already, she's pretty obstinate in her convictions. When I offered to take her on a vacation to Florida on the money I had made from a handsome real estate closing involving one of the sites in The Kensington Dales, she refused on the pretext that she couldn't enjoy spending "blood money." Really! Have you ever heard of such a thing! Harriet goes a bit far sometimes.

I didn't come to Southwell until about a year after Jack's death. I chose the location rather arbitrarily. I had finished law school and was looking for a place to settle down. One day I just happened to be driving north along the river when I stopped for lunch—yes, you got it—at what was still called Dottie's Eats.

I liked the town—it wasn't the food at Dottie's, I can assure you; I decided to stay. I set up my office a month later, met Harriet, and got married. I still feel like a stranger in the town, even though I've been here for almost twenty-two years now. Business has been reasonably good.

I got to know Clara because she often—when she could get away—came over to our house to read books (Paula hated books with as much passion as she loved her magazines) and to talk with Harriet about all kinds of matters. Sometimes I wonder if Harriet didn't think of her as a daughter. She was a wonderfully pretty young girl, with long, thick, silvery-blond hair and very pale skin; and, just like her father, she had sharp blue eyes. Harriet said she was amazingly intelligent and could read just about anything at a young age. But life was not easy for her; Paula had set out to arrange every detail of her life as much as she could. Paula's overriding concern was that her daughter not make the "same mistakes" that she had made.

Clara was a teenager about the time that the little clique—the miniature sorority in a sense, which I've already referred to and which was called Pi Delta—gradually formed around Paula. It didn't get its name Pi Delta until it had been around for a few years, and I don't know if the name originated with Paula. Or was it the circle of friends who came up with the name, using her initials, precisely because they knew that Paula was the heart and soul of the group? The purposes of the club were several: to listen to Paula's interminable complaints about what had happened to her in life, to be a forum for the reception and confirmation of her multitudinous opinions (most of which were appropriated from those fashionable magazines that Paula read continuously) and, most importantly, to help Paula plan and organize Clara's life.

Indeed, discussion of Clara was the center of every Pi Delta meeting. Clara was to grow up and to blossom unhampered by the attitudes and faulty decisions that had constricted the lives of the various members of the club in one way or another. All of them were college-educated women, and all shared, to some extent or another, the common conviction that living in Southwell had been a betrayal of their "just" destinies, though few ever really showed much of a desire to leave and even fewer expressed much of a sense of what that "just" destiny may have been.

A few members were also drawn by a kind of curiosity into the proceedings, because they were bored; all, however, were affected to some degree by Paula's commanding and, at the same time, flattering personality. They considered themselves to constitute an "elite" — more intelligent, more fashionable, more attractive (to whom? one wonders) than other women in the town. They also engaged in a bit of friendly competition among themselves: who could go on the costliest vacation, who owned the most expensive tennis racket, who had the fanciest car, who played the most golf, and so on.

I've already mentioned Belinda Blodget; the names of the other women would be tedious to list. But it's worth alluding to a tall, gawky woman by the name of Penelope Blake. I've never been able to figure out why Penelope ever took part in Pi Delta in the first place. She was hardly attractive (to anybody, including herself, though I guess her husband must have found her attractive, at least for a while): she had a long, scrawny neck that seemed to hose up endlessly from her narrow shoulders and out of the little sunken cup formed by her collar bones. Her neck was capped by a small oval face with tiny bead-like eyes and a pasty, acne-scarred complexion. She was constantly scratching and rubbing that crane-like neck of hers, making it red and sore, and, when not doing that, covering it with one long, spindly-fingered hand as if she had something caught in her throat. Efforts to conceal the irritated skin in this way succeeded only in drawing more attention to it.

She was mostly silent in the Pi Delta meetings, her little tense eyes darting from person to person as they spoke; but, when she spoke, it was only a few words, and they came out suddenly, impulsively, like a burp or a sequence of burps, after which she clutched her throat with both hands, her back arched and her eyes dazed with embarrassment both at having spoken and usually at what she had said. There would be a brief silence in the group as everyone stared at her, astonished by her tactless interruption, and conversation would begin again as if nothing had happened.

Penelope was also odd because, if she felt that something was missing in her life and that she had taken wrong turns, it was certainly not the same malaise as the others felt. She was odd, too, in that she was happily married, was reasonably content with looking after her four children, and enjoyed life in Southwell.

Her curious and indefinable malaise expressed itself, other than in her peculiar participation in Pi Delta, by her spending much of her spare time polishing the old oak choir stalls in the Episcopal church outside town and helping Father Odenheim with an assortment of ecclesiastical housekeeping duties.

Father Odenheim was an Episcopal priest who had converted from Judaism. People had some serious questions about him, particularly because a variety of malicious rumors (or at least I would call them malicious) seemed to indicate that he was moving toward yet another conversion, but we won't get into that. Anyway, some of Penelope's odd notions might have been attributable to her connection with Father Odenheim.

What I'm trying to say is that she didn't really share either the convictions or the interests of Pi Delta, but I don't think she understood that about herself. Her disagreements with the group—indeed, her unpredictable "burps" of shock and outrage with them—took even her by surprise and always embarrassed her; it was no surprise at all that she was eventually ostracized from the group.

One wonders why Paula needed such a support group in the first place. After all, was it such a problem to bring Clara up in the right way, that is, in Paula's way? Perhaps there was a problem at times. There was resistance. There was, for example, Harriet, who was such a good friend and mentor for Clara. There was, for another example, the occasional effort on Clara's part to strike out on her own, to make her own decisions and work out her own life.

But it was Clara's goodness, her willingness to please, her inveterate courtesy and loyalty that made her so susceptible to Paula's influence—not an influence over her thoughts (that much even I know all too well) but over her actions.

Paula was effective in using Pi Delta as the "voice of the community"—a kind of chorus from a Greek tragedy whose views she was paramount in forming as much as she was prolific in citing, as if it were a source of independent and indubitable social authority in making decisions and resolving personal problems. Against this "weight" of social opinion backing up her mother's interventions in her life, Clara was defenseless.

Clara did, at one time or another, strike out on her own. She went to college at Bennington—located not too far from Southwell, though at the other side of the state—where she immersed herself, like her father, in literary studies, especially in French and German. Paula was able to abide this unfortunate development only because she could conceive of it as a "phase" Clara was going through, one that Clara would outgrow soon enough.

When Clara returned to live in Southwell, she found herself attracted to one of the local young men. His name was Sam Overton, and he was utterly dizzy about her. He had known Jack Dodd when he was a young boy and had learned a great deal from him—being one of the youngsters who worked with Jack in the woodlands and who were part of his library reading group. In later years, Sam went to college upstate at Middlebury but decided, after graduating, to return to Southwell and set up a workshop to make high-quality, handcrafted furniture—desks, tables, and armoires, mainly. I've seen his work, and it's really very good.

Well, as you can imagine, Paula was nothing but disapproval. Clara could, and would, do much better than this, if she, Paula, had any say in it, and she had plenty to say about it. In fact, a number of—I'll call them "emergency"—sessions of Pi Delta were rallied to tackle this problem.

In the first of these sessions, poor Penelope Blake made one of her most infamous "burps" when she declared that it was wrong to interfere with this matter. But to no effect; she sat in mortified stupor, arching her back and clutching her neck, while Pi Delta came to its conclusions. Clara, as a result, was railroaded off to Boston and set up in an apartment there. Everything that could be done to break the relationship was done, and it worked.

My wife and I have sometimes spoken about this matter. She thinks that Sam Overton would have been the ideal spouse for Clara. Actually, for once I agree. I told Harriet that Paula had been somewhat too precipitous in her judgment of Sam Overton. I told her that I think that someday his furniture will be known throughout the world and he will be the CEO of a big company. But, you know, she just scowled at this and said that I had missed her point.

What point?

You should see Harriet scowl. It's quite a scowl!

It's difficult to imagine how Clara's life in Boston could have been arranged so meticulously from the command post in faraway Southwell. But it was even easier to do this than had been the case back home, because now all possible adverse influences had been removed. Paula was perpetually on the telephone, asking innumerable questions, insisting that Clara do this or that, conveying the deliberations of Pi Delta, informing her about what this magazine said about such and such a matter and what that magazine said to do when confronted by such and such a problem. Regulations were passed down about what clothes to wear, what cosmetics to buy, what food to eat, what restaurants to frequent, what kind of job was appropriate, how to meet men and what sort of men were acceptable, how to decorate the apartment, what to do on weekends, how to behave on dates, what sports to take up and what to drop as soon as they became unfashionable, and so on and so on. Naturally, all these injunctions were constantly revised and reversed according to the latest authoritative communications from the world where someone, somehow, decides these things. The members of Pi Delta shared, to their utmost delight, in all of these matters.

The most exciting matter of all, of course, was sex. Clara must have "affairs," and Pi Delta must be involved in every detail of how these affairs were initiated, conducted, and concluded.

The magazines were a source of an enormous amount of information on this — information that could be pooled and assessed and discussed in intricate physiological terms at Pi Delta meetings. The women of Pi Delta were convinced that the "sexual revolution" had come too late for them. Even if it had not, they doubted they would have been part of it. The restraints governing their own lives were still too forceful for that, and they would never consider applying what they read and talked about to themselves, but with Clara as their surrogate they could participate in what had become so current in the media.

With the exception of Penelope, who became more and more confused by this development, they launched Clara's new life with enthusiasm and monitored it, through Paula, with unparalleled curiosity. Clara resisted strenuously at first, but until it was actually done there would be no remission of her mother's inquiries about inviting a young man to spend the night in her apartment.

When it finally happened, as it did — more as a result of the young man's inordinate aggressiveness than Clara's willingness — Pi Delta had something of a triumphal celebration. Penelope Blake didn't attend that celebration, by the way. I guess she had some choir stall to polish. But Paula praised the young man at the party for having broken down Clara's "obstinacy," as she called it, for Clara had informed her mother of her shame and horror about the event. Paula, in turn, passed on this "amusing" information to Pi Delta, and Belinda Blodget told Harriet, who told me, and Harriet was put into such a state as to have hunted down Paula with a shotgun, if it was legal to do that sort of thing. Ah, Harriet!

Pi Delta didn't have as much to celebrate as it thought it did. Clara's "affair" with the young man, whose name was Brandon Thorpe, was the only "affair" she ever had, though it lasted for quite a while and led to cohabitation and finally to an engagement to be married. It would have been much more exciting if there had been a whole sequence of affairs to discuss and analyze, but this one "affair" was good enough to provide all that was necessary for ceaseless conversations about sexual techniques, foreplay, contraception, kinky times, places, and methods to do "it," and all the intricate psychological ins-and-outs of quarrels and breakups and reconciliations.

Though the women of Pi Delta readily disavowed any really personal knowledge of such matters, the periodical literature that they read in consort gave them copious information, and they had a wonderful time with it. The preparations for the upcoming marriage, even if a more traditional source of interest, engaged the group just as intensely.

Paula was pleased with her prospective son-in-law. Brandon Thorpe was ambitious, ruthless, and brash, though it was never too clear exactly what he did for a living. But whatever it was, he apparently worked very hard at it, and nothing would stand in his way. The world was his for the taking, and he would take it, without scruple and without hesitation. He gave the impression that he had already, at his young age, amassed a small fortune of his own, though he always seemed rather oddly short of funds—a fact that Paula attributed to his propensity to channel most of his earnings into long-term investments.

Soon after the "affair" began, Paula felt it was important to make Brandon think that Clara was from an affluent family, and she began using some of her wealth acquired from the sales of The Kensington Dales to promote his relationship with her daughter by sending money for cruises, trips to Bermuda, expensive weekends in New York, and gifts of all kinds for Brandon.

Eventually, it became clear that Brandon supported a costly cocaine habit—a habit into which, he claimed, he was successful in inducing Clara herself. Pi Delta, under Paula's leadership, was, if momentarily dismayed, delighted by this development.

Naturally, it was a bit difficult to reconcile such a discovery with the presumption that Brandon was carefully saving for the future. But Brandon's cocaine habit became part of his "credentials"; isn't this what all important and aggressive people do nowadays? Also, the world of drugs was utterly alien to Pi Delta, and this connection made them feel part of that "bigger" world they seemed to miss so acutely. Now they had this to talk about as well—in hushed and excited whispers, for an enchanting pall of illegality hovered about it. Of course, Penelope just rubbed her long scrawny neck and kept her silence.

The wedding preparations were lavish and complex, and Pi Delta threw itself into the details with passionate energy. Paula had reserved the best building site in The Kensington Dales for her last and most opulent construction project. It was that grassy meadow on top of the highest hill on the original Dodd Farm. Its views were the finest in the region. She resolved to have the wedding take place in the open field on top of the hill under an elaborate pavilion, specially erected for the event, and surrounded by all the glory of the Vermont and New Hampshire mountains.

Southwell would never have seen such a celebration before and would never, most probably, see its like again. Caterers were brought in from Boston and a famous jazz band from New York. The best champagne was ordered;

a wedding dress of the most exquisite design was flown in from a Parisian couturier. The guest list included most of Paula's old friends from college and from her Westchester County days. Paula even wrote out a sizable check to Brandon to cover his expenses and that of a costly honeymoon to Europe, though she felt confident that Brandon would take care of all other financial matters after that. The climactic event of the wedding would be her announcement, at the time of the wedding toast, that the hilltop site at The Kensington Dales would be her wedding gift to Clara and Brandon.

The evening before the wedding, the pandemonium of preparation allowed Clara to slip away for a while from the watchful gaze of her mother and to come over to our house. She spent an hour in Harriet's arms, weeping uncontrollably. Then she pulled herself together, so like her father with his set gaze, and went home to face what she had to face.

The day was splendid: a northern New England August afternoon of the most unflawed brilliance. A gentle southerly wind blew up from the Connecticut River Valley and stirred the bright pennons that fluttered over the pavilion. The food, the music, the flowers, the guests were all in place. Clara was beautiful beyond compare in her silken wedding dress and long blond hair that was braided around her head and down her neck. She wore a lovely crown of blossoms woven from wildflowers that grew in the meadow on top of the hill. Everyone could give Paula credit—even my wife, in a begrudging sort of way—for, despite the obvious extravagance, the whole thing was done in the most tasteful manner.

There was only one problem—a very big problem: the classic nightmare scenario for any wedding. *Brandon never showed up.* In fact, he disappeared permanently from Boston without a trace and with all that money advanced to him by Paula.

Harriet later said that one would think that this event, with its humiliation and shame, might have altered Paula somewhat. According to Harriet, it didn't have any such effect, but I think it did.

It hardened and embittered Paula. She ended up admiring Brandon. He had seen something that he didn't like or had discovered something that was more to his advantage, and that was enough for him to cancel at the last moment. Would that she had had such gumption when she needed it!

As for Clara—well, it was probably her fault somehow. Things were just beginning.

Indeed, they were! What happened next, we didn't hear about for several months afterward, when Belinda Blodget, gobbling down a soggy hamburger bun served up by the school cafeteria, finally told my wife. It's good that my wife didn't hear about it until then because she would have tried to stop it. She would have gone on the warpath: and I would have found that embarrassing. It could even have hurt my law practice. Now it was too late to do anything about it.

According to Belinda, never did Paula's leadership become more powerful, more preemptive, more decisive through the crisis that evolved.

It turned out that Clara was pregnant with Brandon's child. Even worse, Clara intended to have the child and fought all her mother's demands that the child be destroyed. But Paula, in peak form, you might say, after the marriage disaster, would not be deterred. She called another "emergency" meeting of Pi Delta to make plans.

It was then that Penelope Blake made her last and grandest "burp," though it was not a burp; it was a shriek. She jumped to her feet and screamed, "You can't do this! It's murder!"

Pi Delta recoiled as Penelope wrung her own neck with both hands, as if she were trying to strangle herself. She ran from the table, from the house where the meeting had convened that day, from Pi Delta forever.

The remaining seven nodded; they had, somehow, the impression that they had gotten "rid of" her. It was about time. Anyway, she could hardly fit in with what they planned to do. All of them, led by Paula, would go to Boston together and, forming a little impenetrable circle, march Clara into the abortion clinic.

Which is what they did.

Belinda Blodget said so. She was there. She said it was, in retrospect, awful—just awful. She wished she hadn't agreed to help. Many of the Pi Delta women felt bad about it afterward and regretted that they had been part of it. They didn't meet again for a very long time.

Six months later Clara was brought home for her twenty-fifth birthday, and Pi Delta assembled in The Cinnamon Stick for the event. In fact, it was their first meeting since the occurrence at the abortion clinic. They were noisy, boisterous, and obstreperously cheerful, for they saw the event as marking a new beginning, a new episode in the life of their protégé.

Also, a number of them wanted to drown the lingering memory of the abortion clinic in a show of coarse hilarity. Surely, things had not gone as well as planned, they could all argue, but that was typical of life—*didn't they all know!* But Clara was young and had plenty of time to start again.

Paula presided over the gathering with her usual aplomb, telling stories, enunciating capricious and uncompromising opinions that everyone consented to with uproarious acclamations, and talking about Clara as if Clara were not even there.

Clara, as I've told you, was sitting at the end of the table, so close to me that I could hear her heavy, soft breathing. She was no longer the young and beautiful woman she had been. Her face looked ravaged; her eyes were baggy; her hair was thick and knotted. She was overweight and puffy. She sat through the meal in the dimly lit restaurant without talking or even looking at anyone. She hardly touched her food.

They brought the birthday cake in, and Pi Delta all sang raucously and loudly, waving around streamers, and yelling back and forth to one another, one of them addressing Clara now and then by shouting, "Make a wish, Clara! Be sure to make a wish before you blow out the candles." But they were paying little attention to Clara.

I tried to mask my presence by slouching back into the shadows of my alcove and keeping a newspaper well poised between me and the noisy crowd at the table. Occasionally I took a peep at what was going on.

Suddenly I sat up in my seat with alarm. I thought that Clara's face was on fire. But it took just a second to realize that it was only the fiery reflection of the candles in the huge tears slowly gathering in her eyes and rolling down and streaking her puffy cheeks. A tear dropped from her face and sputtered in one of the candles nearest Clara before it put out the candle, slid down the shaft, and made a little crater in the soft frosting of the cake. Another tear plopped into the frosting by itself and made a second crater. The smooth surface of the cake on the side near Clara began to look like the moon, as crater after crater, of different sizes and in different places, appeared one after the other.

She was leaning so far over the cake that I thought her hair might actually catch on fire. I wanted to reach over and grab hold of her and pull her back. I bent over in her direction. Then, even despite the dreadful din that surrounded us, I heard her utter that final, that solemn, birthday wish to herself. "*I wish,*" she whispered, "*I wish I were with my father.*" Then she added, still in a whisper, "*I wish I were with my child.*"

No one else, other than I, was paying attention to her; no one else, other than myself, heard that wish. Of course, it sounded like two wishes, but I knew it was one wish.

A loud voice cried out, "Make a wish! Make a wish! Have you made a wish yet?" Other voices took up a discordant and broken chant, "Make a wish! Make a wish!" "Shush! Look, she's crying!" (At last, they noticed!) "Everyone shut up, don't you see she's crying?" "Poor dear, why are you crying?" "Did she make her wish?"

Amid the hubbub, Paula, obviously mortified by the swollen, tear-streaked face of her unkempt daughter, leaned over the table and shoved a dinner napkin into Clara's face, wiping it as Clara jerked backward and hid her face in her hands. "She's sad; who wouldn't be?" someone shouted. "Twenty-five's not the end of the world!" another added. "Get hold of yourself," Paula hissed at her through the clamor of other voices.

I slid my chair deeper into the little alcove I occupied and away from Clara, turning my head into the shadows and trying not to be noticed when attention was finally being directed toward her. The candles were blown out by one of the women who was close enough to do it. While the cake was being cut, amidst a great deal of hooting and laughing, I contrived to leave the alcove, pay the cashier for my dinner, and leave the restaurant. They never saw me.

When Harriet got home from her conference the next day, I told her about what had happened, and as I've already said, she sat down on the sofa and wept. I don't know why she had to take it so personally.

The newspaper announcement two weeks later didn't have much to say. Clara Dodd had died, "after a brief illness." But we all knew what really occurred. She had overdosed on the cocaine Brandon left behind in the apartment. Harriet got hold of the police report and knew that it was true. She also figured that the overdose had been intentional. I don't know how she figured that out, but, somehow, she did. She said the cocaine had been left there for months, ever since Brandon's disappearance and, in fact, without ever being touched; then it was taken all at once. As a lawyer, I doubt whether her evidence for this presumption could stand up in court.

Pi Delta has never met since, and to this day its former members will scarcely speak to one another. Paula sold the remaining lot on top of the hill at The Kensington Dales — the one that was going to be given to Brandon and Clara. She received a huge price for it and left town after that — to Arizona, everyone thinks, but there has been no further contact with her. Penelope Blake still polishes the choir stalls at the Episcopal church with a fervor and an urgency that suggests she's doing reparations for some terrible and unexpiated crime in the recesses of her heart, or in the hearts of her townsfolk, or in the heart of her nation and the world.

But she's not so happy with the new priest there; he's the kind of guy who accepts anything and everything. Good for him, I say (but please don't tell Harriet I said that). Father Odenheim wasn't like that at all; anyway, he left the parish when he decided to become a Catholic and join up with a Catholic monastic order.

Can you believe that? It shows how zany and unpredictable people are. But I always suspected that Father Odenheim was at the edge, so to speak.

Belinda Blodget doesn't do volunteer work at the school anymore. She runs a shop where she sells scented candles to tourists who think that old-fashioned country people like to have expensive scented candles in their homes.

Harriet goes every week to look after the gravesite where Jack Dodd and his daughter are buried. I think it's a kind of obsession with her. I tell her to "get on with her life." She hates that expression, by the way; she says it's "so shallow."

And she keeps doing what she's doing. I don't think she will ever stop. But she always puts flowers on their graves … even a little flower for the child who isn't there. I guess that birthday wish got fulfilled, so much faster than anyone would have thought, though only Harriet and I knew about it.

Now you know about it too.

I do hope you'll stop by The Cinnamon Stick if you happen to come through Southwell sometime. If it's lunchtime, I'll probably be in there, so drop in and say hi. If I'm not there, remember that I recommend most highly their smoked salmon and avocado on pumpernickel. They use only organic grains in their pumpernickel. I think you'll enjoy it very much, especially if you order their in-house beer as well. It's delicious, I can assure you.

"The Triumph of the Human Spirit"

"Eustacia! Such a pretty name! Don't you think so, Mildred?" Miss Witherspoon tilted backward in her chair and peered over her shoulder at Mildred. Mildred nodded affirmatively and murmured in her deep, throaty voice, "Indeed, it is so, Miss Witherspoon."

Mildred slid the pupils of her perpetually half-closed eyes to the side and fixed them on me. She had a square, blank face with a thick jaw and a wide, lipless slit of a mouth that slanted downward from right to left. Her brows were a single flat band of shaggy hair that stretched from one side of her face to the other and that contracted back and forth, on occasion and for no discernible reason, like an accordion. She always stood behind and slightly to the side of Miss Witherspoon whenever Miss Witherspoon officiated at her headmistress's desk and in her headmistress's high-backed throne.

Mildred was dressed, as ever, in something that looked like a particularly ascetic version of a liturgical chasuble — an oval shaft of coarse woolen cloth, usually brown, folded in half with a circular cutout for the neck and head. Underneath that was a shapeless black garment, a caftan of sorts, sweeping the floor and having a tight turtleneck. On her head was a disorderly flop of gristly hair that seemed to lean, curiously, to one side of her head as if it were about to fall off.

Miss Witherspoon, on the other hand was a bony, petite woman with a sharp little woodpecker's beak for a nose. Her brows, if she had had any, would have bordered the high-arched mother-of-pearl crescents over her eyes that made her look as if she had two oysters on the half shell embedded in the front of her head.

She sat at her spacious desk attired in fluffy white lace and engulfed in a heavy cloud of what smelled like witch hazel. The polished surface of the desk was crowded with porcelain statuettes of birds of all sizes and species—a glittering mute aviary frozen in time and space, though Miss Witherspoon did her best to make up for the fluttering and tweeting that was noticeably absent among her glassy birds.

At least that's how I remember all of it now, almost a half century later.

It happened when I was a student at Foxglove Hall before the war—a private boarding school for young ladies located in eastern Massachusetts. I had been at the school for two years, but this was the first time I had ever entered the headmistress's office alone and under such potentially auspicious conditions.

I had been warned, in some detail by the girls in the dorm, what it would be like. Miss Witherspoon would sit at her desk in her tall-backed chair, erect, nervous, trembling, persistently twittering away and referring every opinion she uttered to Mildred by tilting backward in her chair, peeking coyly over her shoulder, and seeking her approval.

Mildred would stand behind her, half hidden by that chair. She was huge, taciturn, and broad-shouldered, with arms folded and as motionless as a proverbial cigar-store Indian, and muttering her husky approbations from time to time, as was required.

That she always and invariably approved whatever Miss Witherspoon said reinforced the impression that all such opinions had somehow been approved in advance, or even that Miss Witherspoon was simply repeating what she had been told to say and her referral to Mildred was to make sure that she had done that correctly.

It was one of the more delightful, if malicious, rumors among the pupils at Foxglove Hall that Mildred was actually a man in disguise—was, in fact, Miss Witherspoon's husband and the real power "behind the throne," managing Foxglove Hall and making all the important decisions. The speculations upon which these rumors were based, as treasured as they were, didn't attempt to account for the purpose of such an elaborate ruse, except that

Foxglove Hall was known to be, ostensibly at least, devoted to promoting something like an Amazonian ideal in young women, and, accordingly, the board of trustees (Amazonians all, apparently, in spirit if not in fact) insisted on having a single woman for the headmistress.

If any of this were true, it was obviously in Miss Witherspoon's interest that the presumptively duplicitous flop of grisly hair didn't, on some lamentable day, slide off Mildred's presumably balding head and thereby compromise both her and his(?) precarious positions; though if Mildred, as we were all quite convinced, was really the one in control — of the school and of Miss Witherspoon — then he(?) was most likely in control of the board of trustees as well, and there was little to worry about.

I suppose a later and more sophisticated generation of pupils might have expounded a different set of hypotheses, but, in those days, we were just so terribly naïve about everything.

For me, the reason I was summoned to the head office was actually rather embarrassing. I had won the student poetry contest.

First, let me say that I hate poetry. What normal person doesn't? Actually, I don't hate poetry. Sometimes I can tolerate it for a while. I do hate what most people, including most poets, literature teachers, and critics, think poetry is. I hate the abuse to which they systematically subject it.

Secondly, I didn't intend or want to win that contest. I was bored to death in study hall; I didn't want to memorize any more French verb forms; and I was being driven to the brink of lunacy by a fellow student in the music building across the lawn from the study hall who was practicing the first movement of the *Moonlight Sonata* for the thirty-thousandth time, missing notes and then screaming bloody murder and banging the keyboard with her fists every time she did this.

So, inspired as I was by such an inglorious set of circumstances, I decided to write a detestable little poem — you know, just for the fun of it. I tried to make it as overtly self-expressive (or self-obsessive) as I could, shrill with figurative obscurity and with hideously pathological images, arrayed in an incoherent sequence like white worms oozing around in gooey sludge. I tried to make it quite as awful as the creepy dancing of those contortionists whom Miss Witherspoon and her ambivalent consort insisted on enticing up from New York to perform for us and to turn us budding Amazonians forever against all forms of artistic production.

Those lady dancers slithered and rolled all over the gymnasium stage like dying lizards, gasping for breath and moaning and emitting a dreadful odor. Apparently, an aversion to hygiene was taken to be, at that time, a token of protest to whatever needed to be protested.

Consequently, I wrote the poem about just how awful it is to be stuck in study hall, memorizing French verbs, and listening to yet another replay of the *Moonlight Sonata,* accompanied by shrieking and the angry slamming of keys.

In my madness, I submitted the poem.

As a result of that madness, I won.

Hence, the summons to the head office to receive congratulations and my prize. I can't tell you how mortified I was by all of this. I still don't know why I won, but I may have succeeded too well in making my poem like that dancing, and that's why it was chosen.

Well—I guess I don't need to tell you this—Miss Witherspoon just gushed with compliments about my poem. In her high, twittery voice, she said she found it "dark" and "disturbing" and "outrageous." She said I was very brave to follow my impulses into such a "perilous region of the heart" and to pull out of that deep encounter with my "demons" such a resounding "triumph of the human spirit."

She pronounced, religiously and prophetically, that all great poetry was just that, a wresting of affirmation from the forces of chaos, a witness, again and again, to that ever resplendent "triumph of the human spirit." She concluded her kudos by turning to Mildred: "Isn't that so, Mildred?"

In her gruff voice, Mildred responded, "Indeed, it is so, Miss Witherspoon."

I could have died.

I could have died a thousand times over. But I don't know if I would have died of grief or of laughter.

Miss Witherspoon announced my prize (if you really want to call it that). In six days hence, I would be excused from a day of class; and the school chauffeur, Andy, would drive me in the official school limousine to visit a well-known poetess (back in those days they still commonly used that term for a woman poet). It was about a two-hour drive from the school. I would have luncheon with the poetess. We would be able to discuss poetry, and she would be able give me sound counsel about pursuing a career in poetry. Someone as talented as I was should not let such a superb talent go untapped.

Frankly, though I didn't regret the opportunity of getting away from the school for a day, I was horrified by this prospect. The last thing in the world I wanted to do was get trapped with a poetess in who knows what kind of lair and have to discuss poetry with her. I didn't want a career in poetry, and I was quite determined that whatever talents I might have—superb or not—were to go untapped.

Further, there was Andy the chauffeur.

The next to last thing in the world I wanted was to be anywhere nearer than a half mile to him. But I didn't get a chance to express my dual horror. I was dismissed from the head office a bit too quickly for that. As I left the office, Miss Witherspoon looked over her shoulder again and smiled at Mildred, who, in turn, stiffly revolved her head like a self-propelled cork squeaking around in the neck of a musty old wine bottle, and grinned back at her, unmasking, in the process, a maxilla punctuated irregularly by a row of exquisitely tapered tyrannosaurus teeth.

A word or two about Andy. I think every school has an Andy, especially every girl's academy whose function it is to fashion an accomplished, refined, flawless specimen of female humanity, albeit in Amazonian guise. He was the only male around—a scruffy-faced, twisted, dishonest, treacherous, obsequiously arrogant, ill-kempt caricature of a male, but a male nonetheless and, as such, for the students, the perpetual object of fascinated scorn and enchanted disdain.

He was a living model, in adult guise, of the horrifying kid brother every girl would like to have and upon whom shocked contempt and outraged censure can be remorselessly heaped. Every and any new story illustrating something grotesque or perverse about him was received with malevolent rapture. It was widely believed by the younger girls that, for the older girls, he smuggled onto school grounds secret caches of alcoholic beverages and cigarettes; and it was widely believed by the older girls that, for the younger girls, he smuggled onto school grounds copious supplies of the saccharine "romance" comic books so popular back then (you know, the ones with little valentines popping out of the heads of the protagonists as they mutually contemplate the moon and each other). It was supposed, of course, that Andy, pandering to such putative vices, made a small fortune.

I often wonder why such a figure was kept around. Was he meant to be an embodied admonition, a sort of cautionary tale in living flesh, of how awful, generically, men are and that we should assiduously avoid them, now and for the rest of our Amazonian lives?

Was he the only sort of person who would take a job like his — to ferry rich, mainly brainless girls from the train station to the school or back again, as the situation required, each of whom brought so much luggage along with her that, by comparison, the Queen of Sheba and her caravan of a thousand camels would certainly have been put to shame?

Was it that only such a misshapen, surly, groveling caricature of a man would be immune from inspiring the affections of young ladies whose isolation in a heady seraglio of burgeoning femininity could engender all kinds of adverse results? A particularly good-looking, or even just a normal, male might have been intolerable under the circumstances.

I suppose I need not belabor this point; suffice it to say that six days later I was greeted by Andy in person. I was dressed, as I had been commanded to be dressed, in official Foxglovian apparel — a uniform of a sort whose drabness was meant, obviously, to keep me securely in my Amazonian place. Andy stood before me: his wrinkled chauffeur's uniform was olive green with a double row of brass buttons in front (two of which were missing). It reeked of cigarette smoke and some other smell I didn't know yet how to define and was covered with what I took to be dog hair. (Does he sleep in that uniform, and with his dog? — superb debating points for dorm-room pundits!)

The limousine was a LaSalle (a now long defunct relative of the Cadillac, in case you don't remember). It was, of course, filthy, both inside and out; and the dog hair — which was shed all over the interior upholstery — testified that the dog was a frequent passenger in the car and that any other passenger would promptly be garbed in a goodly portion of its furry coat. Why was Andy allowed to maintain himself and the car in this disreputable condition? — another mystery for dorm discussions! In his usual suppliant, yet domineering fashion, doffing his olive-green cap with its torn black visor, he ushered me into the vehicle. I sat in the back seat, as would be expected anyway, but that, at least, was a relief. The farther away from Andy, the better.

The drive took, as Miss Witherspoon had predicted (and Mildred had agreed, naturally), two hours. The weather was nice and the countryside picturesque, though I didn't have the slightest idea at any time where I was or even in what direction I was headed—east, west, north, south? At times I had the odd impression that we were driving around in circles, for either all the towns we were passing through looked remarkably similar or we kept passing through the same town again and again.

Andy seemed to me, at first, to be a cautious, even rather painfully methodical driver, though my initial impressions were altered by the unaccountable swerves and frantic braking that, more and more, interrupted what was otherwise a smooth performance. Being tossed about in that back seat now and then did, I must say, heighten my level of alertness. Back in those days, you must recall, no one had even heard of seat belts.

Also, during the drive I entertained myself with the suspicion that I was being kidnapped. I have to confess that this was not a wholly unattractive suspicion for me, for I dreaded both the luncheon with the poetess as well as returning to the school afterward. I had fun fantasizing about my escape from the kidnapping (which involved galloping on the back of a horse over a "blasted heath," though exactly how I was going to get hold of a horse and where I was going to find a "blasted heath" was, admittedly, rather obscure).

I also held out hope that my ultimate kidnapper, someone at the end of a chain of intermediate kidnappers, would be an amazing buccaneer or someone like that who would whisk me off on his windswept schooner to the dazzling Southern Seas. Moonlight galore but no Moonlight Sonatas down there— of that, one could be reasonably sure!

At the end of two hours, we pulled into a short driveway at the end of which was a church! A church? I wasn't going to church, was I?

It was a morbid Gothic pile in considerable disrepair, more a chapel than a church, made of soiled, orange-red brick and covered with ivy, thorny briars, creepers of various kinds, and other tangled and otherwise uninviting vegetation. The chapel itself bristled with spiny turrets and pinnacles and buttresses and waterspouts and all sorts of other stuff sticking up and out and all over the place, though the overall look was of something crimped and wounded and squashed, like a porcupine run over by a car.

A small legion of tiny gargoyles and wyverns squatted on every cornice and parapet of the edifice and leered at me from above, seemingly waggling their swollen tongues at me in derision. The chapel was ensconced beneath a grove of the biggest, most gnarled, most gloomy oak trees I had ever seen — no sunlight shone through its leafy canopy, and it looked like the kind of place some Druids might be wont to loiter in and sacrifice people or whatever it was they did for fun.

I felt like one of those medieval knights — like one of those female paladins in Spenser, like Britomart or some other ... well, you know, Amazon — arriving at a sinister locale in a dark wood whose baneful inhabitant, having displaced an original but once beneficent presence, now cast a somber, despondent spell over the place.

Andy opened the LaSalle door for me, but I didn't want to get out. Even Andy would be preferable to whatever might reside inside that diabolical chapel. I even began to take some comfort in the dog hair with which, at this point, I was well enrobed. But, true to the Amazonian ideal, I meekly did what I was told. Andy accompanied me to the front door.

The great oaken door creaked open on its massive hinges. A maidservant stood there. She was tall and thin and had a pale, oval, expressionless face that, as I recall, scared the daylights out of me. The memory of it still, after all these years, scares the daylights out of me.

I looked back at Andy and pleaded that he not abandon me. I never thought I could ever be, in any sense, "attached" to Andy and actually desire his company.

In his obsequious sort of way, he promised he wouldn't go. Anyway, I could see he was well supplied with a pack of cigarettes, a newspaper, a sandwich, and a flask of something or other to tide him over. He assured me that he would wait for me right there in the driveway.

I ventured through the gloomy portals and was escorted through the vestibule and into the chapel itself. It was as dark as night inside. It might have been nice-looking once, but now its stained-glass windows were so smudged with dirt and smoke that no color or imagery shone through them. All the pews, altar, pulpit, and railings had been stripped. The apse was hidden by a long velvet curtain draped over a brass pole drawn across it. I later realized that this velvet partition marked off what must have been the sleeping chamber, our poetess's boudoir, no doubt. The sacristy at the side of the apse had been converted into a kitchen or pantry or something like that, and an eerie indigo pallor glowed through the open door that led to it. I couldn't help but think that an assortment of sooty cauldrons was bubbling away in there.

The rest of the chapel was filled with books—thousands, tens of thousands of them, piled unevenly in high, tottering columns. Among the books were bric-a-brac of various kinds; ornate Turkish shawls were draped here and there; and a mangy leopard skin—or was it the shuffled-off coil of some colossal, speckled serpent?—hung from a gothic vault that arched over the center of the chapel.

On the summit of one of the book columns reposed a human skull tipped slightly to the side and wearing a jaunty academic mortarboard cap, its golden tassel drooping over the bony forehead of the skull and disappearing into the left eye socket.

Was I afraid?

Of course I was afraid.

At the center of the chapel was a single floor lamp that shone down over a short coffee table, with a large leather armchair on one side and, on the other, a small seating apparatus of some indefinable sort with an ornate leather cushion perched unsteadily on top of it.

In that leather armchair was enshrined the poetess herself, beckoning me with a thin, long-fingered hand to approach and be seated on the smaller seating apparatus (the deplorable memory and consequent identification of which was triggered, years later on a trip to Egypt, by a camel saddle into which I had scrambled in order to have my photograph taken in front of a pyramid).

But I was glad to be seated on something, whatever it was, because I had feared I might have to spend this interview sitting cross-legged on the floor, facing a similarly cross-legged interlocutor, which, back in those days, was the obligatory ritual form for conducting intense discussions about artful matters between or among intensely artful females.

"Welcome to the Minster," she intoned with a smile as I sat down.

"To the what?" I barked with alarm.

Why a bark? Was I being affected by the dog hair that now covered my school dress? I immediately knew that I had said my first stupid thing.

"To the Minster," she trilled sweetly in her singsong voice. "That is what I call my little sanctuary here amid the darkling woods."

"I thought you said, 'Welcome to the Monster,'" I yelped back, my throat constricted with dread, my voice rising at least an octave, and I being, as I said, still more or less embodied in my canine mode. I immediately knew that I had said my second stupid thing.

"Ah, no, my dear. 'Minster'—a rather old-fashioned word for church—originally understood as a monastic church, as in Westminster Abbey. I find it rather poetic, don't you? There used to be a vicarage here, too, but it burned down many decades ago, and the chapel—a former Episcopalian chapel—was put up for sale. I bought it with my modest funds and have lived here ever since. It's the right sort of place for a recluse such as I am, a sort of modern-day anchoress, you might say." She chuckled. "Yes, I am rather fond of my little minster, under the oak grove, in the dell."

Dell?

Did she say "dell"?

Or did she say "hell"?

I didn't know what an anchoress was, and, at the moment, I didn't particularly want to know. If she was an anchoress, what was she anchored to? Was being an anchoress connected with madness in some way? When she spoke to me, she didn't look directly at me but gazed intently down at the glossy, short-legged table in front of her, as if in eager anticipation of what soon would be there.

"So, your name is Eustacia! Such a pretty name, don't you think, Elly?" she wailed tunefully, turning to consult the tall maidservant with the scary face who stood poised like a narrow, willowy specter near the sacristy door. Elly didn't reply.

My pulse quickened. I now realized that the poetess looked remarkably similar to Miss Witherspoon. She was emaciated and frail, was enfolded in layers of white lace, and smelled like witch hazel.

A sister maybe?

Or Miss Witherspoon herself?

Was I the victim of a particularly demented practical joke?

Yet Mildred wasn't around, and Elly clearly wasn't Mildred, though there were, upon reflection, some uncanny similarities. I relaxed a bit but didn't know why. There was nothing to be relaxed about.

In any event, she must have been able to read my mind, for she began to reminisce a bit about Foxglove Academy, of which she was, I quickly realized, an esteemed alumna. She extolled its lovely campus, its flowers, and "yon sylvan brakes" that bordered its fecund meadows.

Meanwhile, Elly had disappeared into the sacristy and emerged a few minutes later carrying a black-lacquered tray. It had a little railing around it, embossed with gold leaf patterns. This she brought over to the table, on which she deposited two teapots, two teacups, a platter with some diminutive sandwiches stacked in a little circle around a tuft of watercress, and another plate with five or six petit fours adorned with pink and yellow icing, each sporting a little chocolate flower on top. This was the "luncheon."

The poetess wasted no time, rather indelicately pouncing upon her teapot with her tenacious talons, pouring herself what looked like tea, and gulping down the contents of her teacup somewhat vigorously for a lady of her age and condition. She refilled the teacup at once. I should say that I found comfort in the fact that, during our entire session together, she focused a great deal more attention on that teacup than on me.

It's perhaps fair for me to say at this juncture that the poetess in question, whose identity a modicum of compunction forbids me from disclosing, was once rather well known in the American literary scene, though even by the time of my visit her poems were rapidly disappearing from the anthologies and her name from the roster of literary societies, collegiate readings, public library lectures, learned symposia, and the like.

In later decades, I never heard her name mentioned again, except by a doddering nonagenarian gentleman who insisted that we invite her to give a lecture about poetry at our local historical society, being unaware, apparently, that the Minster, and the world at large, had become bereft of its esteemed anchoress a good thirty years earlier.

It's also fair for me to say that my interview with the poetess went reasonably well and didn't last very long. She was a pleasant lady, after all, and the more she drank of that tea, the more pleasant she became. There were a number of long silences, of course—we really didn't have much to say to each other. I nibbled now and then at one of the sandwiches—a salty meat spread of indefinable provenance had been wiped thinly on spongy slivers of white bread and garnished with a bit of mayonnaise and some parsley.

When it occurred to me that the meat spread might conceivably be tinned dog food, a not altogether inappropriate comestible for the occasion, given my disposition and accouterments, I immediately desisted from my nibbling.

I subsequently popped an entire petit four into my mouth but discovered a hardened, stale, quite possibly archaeological piece of cake, which my teeth got stuck in and which I had to loosen up and wash down with the hot tea. I had the rather strong temptation thereafter to lick the chocolate flowers off the top of each petit four, having no further interest in what lay beneath, but my scruples, as well as my fear of the maidservant, got the best of me.

The poetess didn't touch any of the food. My tea, I must say, was very good: steamy and aromatic. Its fragrance blended harmoniously with the witch hazel emanating from the other side of the table and with the scent of the poetess's tea, which I recognized was not too dissimilar from what was exuded now and then from Andy's uniform and the little flask he carried around with him.

Toward the conclusion of our interview, we did finally—and briefly— broach the subject of poetry. As if on cue, she began to warble, in a quavering but somewhat slurred plainchant, the litany of encomia, which in her prime, I was sure, she would recite to inspire and captivate audiences at high-literary revival meetings all across the United States.

She extolled the lonely but prophetic role of poets as they confront the vast forces of darkness and chaos that threaten human destiny. With their imagination, poets create the face of the earth and the meaning of life. They show to the rest of mankind that the human soul is the origin of all things, the maker of its own conditions, the font of all that is vital and significant.

With their genius for figurative thinking, poets trace the mysterious lineaments of eternal consciousness. A poem confers order upon the howling and brutal whorl of insensate reality. A poem is the ultimate victory that humanity can achieve over disorder and meaninglessness. It consoles, it comforts, it reveals the splendiferous and emergent life force that is in all of us.

I interrupted, "But … I mean … what if the poem is a bad poem?"

She glared at me, a little unsteadily. It was the first time she actually looked at me with her small, watery eyes.

I continued, "What if the poem itself is disordered and meaningless?" I immediately knew that I had said my third stupid thing.

Her head wobbled just a bit. Meeting my objection, she declaimed slowly, shakily, but solemnly: "A poem, my dear Eustacia, can never be bad. A poem, my dear Eustacia, is always and ever, nothing less than … nothing less than … a triumph … yes, a triumph of the human spirit."

Her head tilted abruptly to one side, her eyes closed, her mouth gaped. A tiny rivulet of spittle glittered its way down through the wrinkles and folds on one side of her chin. Almost at once the tall maidservant was standing at my side, as if she had been able to predict the precise moment at which this untimely cessation of our dialogue would occur. She informed me that it would now be best to leave.

I have to say that, at the time, I felt intensely sorry for my poetess, partially mummified and precociously immured in this defrocked and desecrated sepulcher, alone, wasted, disconsolate in her declining years, except for the illusory warmth induced by her surreptitious tea and by a coverlet of platitudes that I regarded then—and still do now—as tragically inane.

But I was also glad to go.

Believe it or not, it was a relief to see Andy. He was drooped over the front fender of the car, one leg up on the running board and newspapers spread out over the engine hood. He was smoking and reading the sports news. He was startled and probably upset to see me emerge so soon, for I was interrupting one of those long, lethargic intervals of inactivity that made his job so palatable.

He jumped up from his languorous pose. In his pale green uniform with the row of brass buttons, he looked like a garter snake wiggling spasmodically when suddenly exposed to light. I opened the door and crept into the back seat of the car without waiting for him to go through his chauffeur's routine with its simulated obeisance.

He had just climbed into the driver's seat when I cried out, "Andy!"

"Yes, ma'am," he grunted. (I didn't know what this thus-far-unprecedented "ma'am" business was, but no matter.)

"We can't—we just can't—go back to the school so early. I'll end up in study hall, having to listen to that harridan virtuoso blasting her way through the *Moonlight Sonata*!"

I don't think he understood the allusion, but he was in no hurry to return to the school either. "Comin' to think of it, ma'am, there's a county fair goin' on not far from here. Maybe we could go there. There's some great boxin' matches planned for this afternoon in the main tent."

"Whatever you want," I shouted back. "Just get me out of this damned 'dell' and keep me as far away as possible from 'yon sylvan brakes' of Foxglove Hall."

The car lurched into action with a stupendous roar, bolted forward—practically hurling me through the back window—and screeched to a dead stop—catapulting me forward so that I was about to collide with the front seat when another sudden acceleration flung me rearward again. Did he treat his dog this way when it occupied this seat? Had he misunderstood my reference to "brakes"? With a few more equally enthralling stops and goes, we were on our way.

But to boxing matches!

I'm not really sure why I consented to go along with this. I had never been interested in boxing before, nor have I been interested in boxing since. And I can tell you, even with my limited experience of the sport, that the sort of boxing that went on at county fairs in those gilded ages of yesteryear—so celebrated in Christmas cards and Norman Rockwell prints and other assorted cozy illustrations—was nothing like what anyone thinks boxing is nowadays. Those were punching orgies: no rules, no decorum, no scoring, no defense, attack only, no judges, no refereeing of any sort. Whoever was still standing in the end, whoever was more or less still alive in the end, won. Of course, I didn't know that yet, sitting there in back of the LaSalle covered with dog hair.

We arrived at the county fair. It was the first time I'd ever been to a county fair. As you probably know, one visit to a county fair in New England is enough to question seriously the authenticity of claims made about the so-called Puritan foundations of New England culture. I won't go into the details of this, but just imagine a county fair as—I hate to say this—Andy written large, Andy written on a cosmological scale, the apotheosis of all that Andy is and does.

I soon found myself hurried through a maze of rancid cooking stalls, garish game booths, and grotesque inducements to sordid entertainments of various kinds.

The main tent reeked of cigarettes, cigars, beer, leather, and sweat. A thousand noisy and disheveled men in shirtsleeves and a handful of women capped by mounds of what was called back then "peroxide" hair milled around the boxing ring. As attendants hosed off the surface of the ring, pink, slimy streams slid off its side and into the sawdust below. Other attendants moved through the crowd, selling leaflet programs, hot dogs, pretzels, and beer. Small circles of men clustered here and there, and what to my eyes in those days looked like a lot of money was passing back and forth among them.

Andy was in heaven; he informed me that we were fortunate to arrive just in time for the big fight of the afternoon. A local favorite named Buckthorn was about to square off against a contender from Quebec with the unlikely name of Pierre Le Doux. Andy grabbed hold of my right arm, and after a frenzy of shoving, burrowing, bending, swearing, elbowing, twisting, and squeezing, we found ourselves sitting on a front bench, right next to the boxing ring. What would Miss Witherspoon think if she saw me here! Or, more pertinently, what would Mildred think! (Somehow, I didn't think Mildred would mind at all!)

The match commenced. Buckthorn was introduced, to the cheers of the crowd. He bounced around the ring, waving his hands over his head and basking in the hysterical applause he evoked. He was physically massive with curly auburn hair. Pierre, by contrast, was greeted with boos and catcalls. He was clearly the villain of the match. He was a smaller man, very dark and slightly stooped, with a black moustache. He didn't parade around the ring but went directly to his corner, glowered at Buckthorn, and waited for the match to begin. The bell rang.

In a way, there's nothing much to report about what happened initially. The two went at each other, savagely slugging away, though at first I didn't look. The sounds were quite enough — the smacking and slamming that was going on, the biffs and puffs and gasps, the splat of sweat and spit, the growling and moaning. The crowd was bellowing for what I presumed to be the expeditious and irreversible dismemberment of Pierre, the "Frenchie," as he was being called, whom Buckthorn was urged to "tear to pieces," "rip to shreds," and "smash into smithereens" (among sundry other colorful expressions that common decency constrains me from mentioning).

I must admit, however, that the crowd did indeed wax poetical with its abundance of rich culinary metaphors — a few I recall are "slice," "chop," "grind," "mash," "cream," "scald," "dice," "fry," "crunch," "hash," and "skewer." One patron apparently desired to see Pierre delivered up to him as a platter of French fries, while another called for — albeit unseasonably — the reduction of Pierre into mincemeat.

When, finally, I began to watch, Pierre did seem to be getting the worst of it. Buckthorn was relentlessly hounding him around the ring, pounding him against the ropes, pummeling his head so hard that it looked like, indeed, it could come flying off at any moment. If you can imagine — to continue the culinary metaphors — an electric eggbeater having its accustomed way with an egg, you might get an idea of what was going on.

Was this "the howling and brutal whorl of insensate reality" of which the poetess of the Minster had so magisterially spoken?

Or was this an inimitable conference of poets glorying in their metaphorical acclamations?

The crowd was ecstatic, clamoring for blood. And blood is what it got, or at least it's what I got, for Buckthorn sunk a thunderous blow into Pierre's nose that sent a spray of blood flying out of the ring. It landed all over me, over my face, my school uniform, my dog hair, everything. I pulled a handkerchief out of my pocket and wiped some of it out of my eyes. The handkerchief was streaked with blood.

I looked up at the ring again. Pierre was down, his head (still attached, as I noted thankfully, to his body) lay right in front of me on the floor of the ring, his face bleeding, his swollen eyes looking shocked and anxiously into my eyes. The crowd shrieked and clapped and stomped its feet.

What happened then I shall never understand, and I shall not try to explain. Suddenly Pierre was me, and I was Pierre. Suddenly Buckthorn and his cacophonous retinue of supporters were Foxglove Hall, were Miss Witherspoon and Mildred, were the poetess and her spectral maidservant, were the study hall and the cantankerous pianist and everything else that made, and was making, my life disagreeable.

Suddenly I discovered my authentic poetic voice — yes, I became poet and Amazon all rolled into one. Suddenly it was my sacred task to achieve victory over disorder and meaninglessness in the universe.

I jumped to my feet, pressed the handkerchief into Pierre's face, and peeled it off again. An imprint of blood and sweat was left behind on the white fabric.

I cried, "Go get 'im, Pierre. Make ... make ... make *pâté* out of him!" (I was speaking figuratively here, of course, and hence speaking just like a poet, though it was a pretty poor effort, I acknowledge; but, trying to be poetic at the moment while simultaneously perpetuating the gastronomical expostulations of the crowd, it was the best I could do. I also thought Pierre might, in any case, appreciate the ethnic twist I gave it.) Then I added, "Remember above all, Pierre ... remember the triumph of the human spirit!"

Andy whispered sharply at me from the side, "He don't get none of that, ma'am! He's a Frenchie! He don't know no English!"

I hadn't considered that technicality; nor did I have time, at the moment, to reflect on Andy's string of double negatives. But I had to communicate with Pierre. For the first time in my life, I actually wanted to communicate in French. In French! Yes ... even after all those horrible verb forms! "Pierre ... Pierre," I shouted in stumbling, hesitant words, "remember ... *souviens-toi* ... (did I get that right? no matter) ... *souviens-toi surtout du triomphe de l'esprit humaine!*"

A second later Pierre bounded back on his feet. He plunged at Buckthorn, head lowered like a bull, driving in at him from beneath, bludgeoning him with left and right hooks and uppercuts. Fifteen seconds later a stunned Buckthorn crumpled to the mat, permanently, as far as that match was concerned.

I hate to say it, of course (it sounds so callous), but he did look somewhat like an uneven clump of a most unappetizing *pâté de campagne*, pockmarked here and there by a swollen bruise that resembled a dark black truffle.

The crowd broke into a riot; members of the audience scrambled up into the ring, trampling the inert body of Buckthorn and attacking Pierre. They soon found themselves punched over the ropes and into the swirling throng, their heads limp and limbs floundering as Pierre engaged in combat with what seemed like the entire audience.

One suitably walloped patron (or poltroon?) was entangled momentarily in the ropes, where he quivered like a fly freshly caught in a web, then flipped over and plopped down into the sawdust right next to me. I took that opportunity, being in high poetical dudgeon, as I was (to say nothing of my newly invigorated Amazonian need for decisive action), to deliver a sharp little figurative kick to his ribs.

"Figure that!" I shouted at him. (Actually, the kick wasn't so figurative, and it wasn't so little either, but one tries to contribute whatever one can). At this point, seeing me gearing up for another not-quite-so-figurative act of self-expression, Andy must have considered it judicious to haul me out of there.

Meanwhile a police escort had thrust its way through the crowd and was helping to rescue Pierre from his besieged redoubt on the ring. As he climbed over the ropes, Pierre turned to me, smiled as best he could through that battered face, and waved. I felt happy about that—immensely happy, to tell you the truth.

Andy managed to snake me out safely through the thick crowd, though some fans were blaming me for what had happened and were becoming hostile to me. Many in the crowd had lost a lot of money on that match, and a few lucky ones were cleaning up quite royally indeed. But the few who dared to confront me were quickly intimidated by the blood and dog hair, as well they might be—I would have been scared of me, too, under those circumstances.

In any event, we escaped from the main tent but had time to stop along the fairway on the way back to the parking lot and to purchase hot dogs, dripping with mustard and sauerkraut, a bag of pretzels, and orangeade. I was famished. Andy diluted (diluted?) his orangeade with whatever was left in that flask of his. He also bought a hot dog to take home to his real dog. It was a wonderful drive back to the school, full of sudden lurches and screeching, inexplicable stops.

We returned to Foxglove Hall by the dining hour. Andy garaged the LaSalle and scuttled back, in his own distinctly inelegant way, to whatever scraggy den at the edge of the campus it was that sequestered his mutt, jug, and cot. He had had a good afternoon of it and was content, and I think I had acquired a small amount—a very small amount, I assure you—of respect for him. At least I wouldn't be so ready, in future dorm discussions, to belittle him as much as I had done in the past. After all, we now shared a secret together—a secret I had no intention to divulge until … well, not until now (forty years later, is it?).

I hurried back to the dorm to change out of my ruined apparel before anyone noticed the curious red splotches and the copious dog hair all over it. I didn't succeed, as I'll shortly inform you, in my purpose. In any event, it wasn't easy to get rid of that clothing without anyone discovering it, but I did manage to do that finally. As for the handkerchief—you may find this a bit morbid, I'm afraid to say—I have it tucked away somewhere, with the dried-up imprint of Pierre's blood still appealing for sympathy and support.

I must report, however, that, on my way back to the dorm, it was my ill luck to run into Miss Witherspoon and Mildred as they took their usual early evening constitutional around the campus. I should have been more wary than I was, being familiar with this routine of theirs, and I did consider sprinting for refuge into a patch of "yon sylvan brakes," but it was too late. They came to a stop and stood there, arm-in-arm, staring at me and being as welcome and endearing to me as would the sight of a gorilla and a baboon out for a promenade together.

"O, Eustacia, my dear, how lovely to see you. I do hope your visit was all you had hoped it to be," Miss Witherspoon piped. Then, squinting through the mellow twilight glow, she noticed my attire. "But it looks as if there's been some mishap—your school dress, it's all …"

"… besprinkled with the blushing roses of life and love," I chanted—figuratively, of course, poet that I was. "I have had the most wonderful day."

"Did you hear that, Mildred? She has had the most wonderful day. Isn't that delightful?" She glanced sweetly up at Mildred, who grumbled in return, "Indeed, it is so, Miss Witherspoon; it is most delightful, indeed."

Mildred slid her cadaverous eyes through their narrow slits and peered at me suspiciously. Mildred knew blood when she saw it.

"It was just … Oh, Miss Witherspoon," I cried as I turned to run off to the dorm, "it was … just as you said … it was a triumph of the human spirit after all."

Dumps: A Meditation

Dumps. Town dumps and city dumps. Is this really the time and place to start talking about dumps?

They bring to mind everything that's unpleasant — the ugly, the broken, the discarded, the rotten and the malodorous, the splintered and the dangerous, the contaminated, the spurned. We haul away to dumps what we're trying to get rid of, trying to clear out of our lives, trying to forget.

In some ways, it's even frightening to think about dumps, which may be why dump euphemisms abound. (To date, my favorite is "Resource Renewal Center.") These euphemisms make it easy for us to think that dumps are really not dumps anymore — that, indeed, they serve some vital function in our national life.

Of course, most of us — at least those of us who have, at any time, been immersed in an urban way of life — have never seen a dump. Brisk, resolute teams of specialists, at their appointed times and places, whisk by our back doors, our garages, our alleyways, and feed remorseless banquets of trash into the voracious rearward maws of giant trucks, which crunch and gorge themselves on it and then shamble onward to the next repast down the street.

Where all of this gets terminally and not so ceremoniously belched, we don't especially know, and we don't especially care. We don't have to care. Dumps are someone else's business. We pay the proper custodians, either directly or indirectly, to provide for us in these matters. If the custodians don't show up for work, as sometimes happens …? Then we're in trouble and know it more quickly than we want to know it.

In these enlightened times we, too, are expected to do our part with our trash, however minimal that may be. Some sorting of it, some consideration of our common good, is now mandatory. Yet, even in that respect, I've more than once espied from my kitchen window in what was arguably a well-heeled neighborhood, a dapper gentleman or a fashionable lady furtively skip across a back alley and deposit, ever so nimbly, into someone else's garbage receptacle what has been declared improper, if not downright illegal, to deposit into his or her or anybody else's own.

Not so in the country.

For many rural people, a trip to the town dump is a ritual, enacted more or less regularly once a week, or maybe once every two weeks, depending on how fast you accumulate the sort of stuff that needs to be taken there. It is, we will have to confess, the civic institution par excellence: the only place where everyone, of necessity, has to go. It's the only place where, for the duration of your stay there, you're acutely aware of fulfilling a paramount civic duty.

Dumps observe no distinctions of age, of social class, of ethnic background, of religion, of political affiliation, of sickness or health, of wealth or poverty, of strength or weakness, of knowledge or ignorance, of virtue or vice, or of anything else that otherwise serves to divide the citizenry into distinguishable and often incommensurate and uncooperative factions.

No distinctions of persons matter at the dump: the dump is the great equalizer. Depending on your point of view, the dump reduces everyone to the same common denominator; or, to the contrary, elevates everyone to the same ideal of civic friendship, of common purpose, unattainable anywhere else among the institutions of our society. As such, the dump may be conceived of as the highest manifestation of everything our civilization aspires to, for everyone there is on the same footing, abides by the same rules (more or less), and achieves the same noble end: to dump their stuff.

Bottles, cans, cardboard boxes, rags, newspapers and magazines, old clothes, food refuse, rugs, batteries, refrigerators, building materials ripped off and out of old houses, rusted lawnmowers, furniture, paint buckets, plastic wrapping and containers of all kinds, light bulbs, diapers, lumber scraps, roofing shingles, television sets, fire extinguishers, wires, aluminum gutters, copper pipes, fiberglass boats, scrap metal, water tanks, automobile tires, pumps, mattresses. The list could go on. Many of these things require paying a special fee to leave them there. Other things must arrive in a special way, depending on how scrupulous the particular dump may be. Cardboard boxes must be broken down and flattened; newspapers wrapped in bundles; glossy magazines separated from glossy catalogues and other junk mail (why? I wonder). Paint cans must be empty and their lids pried off. Refrigerator doors must be detached—usually an easy thing to do, though I once required the assistance of a sledgehammer for several hours to get the lid off an old freezer chest.

Also, we're told, over and over again, not to let Freon gases loose into the stratosphere, and yet we're not to show up at the dump with that gas still in the system of our refrigerating equipment. So, what do we do with it? Inhale it into our lungs and keep it there, more or less permanently?

The most recent, and most startling, and, if I may say so, most depressing acquisitions of great dump collections are the computer monitors that now pile up rapidly in jagged glassy mountains at their designated spots—a dreadful witness to how the impermanence of earthy goods has accelerated the parameters of its demolition.

As I've already indicated, all of these disposable items get separated. They go to their separate piles, their bins, their sheds, their compactors. The act of separating, at least in rural dumps, depends mainly upon the cooperation of the citizenry, so that the scene at a rural dump at any given time is one of people scurrying around from pile to pile and bin to bin, carrying cardboard boxes here or metal wiring there.

The mood is a curious mix of hilarity, urgency, and anxiety.

It's *hilarious* because the activity itself has the quality of something farcical: a shopping spree in reverse, where what you bought by darting from one retail outlet to another you are now tossing out by darting from one bin to another; a photographic negative of a bustling consumer culture; a film run backward, where everyone is frantically doing the opposite of what they normally do.

It's *urgent* because you must be quick to get out of the way of others pushing in from behind, though people are cheerful and reasonably patient about the process. That adds to the humor of the situation, for now otherwise fairly dignified human beings are reduced to what look like animated troops of ants, arms like forceps clasped around whatever thing it is they're disposing of, erratically flitting back and forth over sandy mounds, sometimes in little jostling lines and sometimes singly, and not infrequently colliding with one another or suddenly reversing their paths.

It's *anxious* for there's unremitting pressure to abide by the rules, now quite complicated and intrepidly monitored by dour, often unfriendly, and suspicious overseers whose purpose is to enforce the rules and to intervene, rudely and abruptly, when they see something being carried off to the wrong place.

On a few occasions, I've been apprehended with an object that doesn't fit into any disposal category known to man or God. Since it's illegal to take it home and illegal to leave it at the dump, I've been fearful that I might have to spend the rest of my life holding said object in my hands, remaining stationed where I was until Judgment Day — though that would be illegal, too, since the dump closes at 3 p.m. and I need to be out of there by then (and dumps have a way of shutting down with terrifying solemnity).

Often, in these circumstances, some momentarily beneficent overseer will notice, wink his jaundiced eye, take the object out of my hands, and go off somewhere with it — I don't know where. Such persons are allowed to break their own rules, as I've surmised. I have an image of him (or her, for dump bureaucracies now employ women as well) stepping through one of those invisible time-warp barriers so often portrayed in science fiction films and depositing my forbidden object on the thither side of an alternate universe.

I should add, in all fairness to dump attendants, that I've seen them occasionally resort to heroic efforts in fulfilling their duties: once I saw a female attendant allow herself to be gripped at the ankles by a male attendant and lowered into the yawning mouth of a highly erratic and dangerous compactor just to retrieve a metallic tray that some negligent citizen had tossed into the paper receptacle.

As I'm sure is obvious by now, I've lived in a small rural community for a while and am amazed at how much stuff accumulates in the dump and how quickly that happens. Burgeoning mounds of debris are periodically removed, or flattened, or buried, and soon these same mounds reappear.

When the debris is removed, I don't know where it goes. Some of it "graduates" (if I may use such an expression) to higher institutions of putative recycling, I'm told, though many of my acquaintances regard that claim as a pious fiction—one which they're quite willing to accede to without much complaint. I have, at times, likewise suspected that the claim is a pious fiction, and I've heard stories, as well as self-assured declarations, that all that painstakingly separated trash is ultimately mixed back together again. I've heard that some golf courses nowadays are built on top of vast landfills compounded of the undifferentiated trash that gets lugged in from all corners of the surrounding countryside.

How odd that our most arduous efforts to fashion recreational areas in a self-consciously neo-pastoral mode should be lavished over bulging hillocks of waste!

I reconcile myself to such imputed perversities by affirming, nevertheless, the value of separating for its own sake, even if only done as a moral and intellectual exercise. At least in that way you're made aware of what the disposal of trash entails, and you act on this awareness, even if the effort, in the end, is fruitless. In any case, the local dump does occasionally get cleared, and soon enough everything starts up again.

The rate of accumulation of our rural trash can't help but awaken wonder about what goes on in and around the cities. The population of a rural town, I've been led to believe, is about the same as that of a single city block. If that's true, I can't imagine what a contemporary city dump looks like.

Many decades ago, as a college student, I had a summer job in a factory located on the outskirts of a major city. One day, I was asked to accompany a truck driver who was hauling off a very old, ornate, and massive safe to the city dump. I don't know why I was asked to go, but I was, and I did. Maybe my presence in the truck would deter the driver from making some unscheduled stops at local taverns on the way back—on company time, no less.

My brief encounter with that city dump—and it's a long time ago now—defies any descriptive account equal to the experience. It wasn't just a dump. It was a brave new world; it was partially a moonscape marked by vast ranges, deep craters, mounds of indistinguishable rubble; yet, unlike the moon, it featured vast, ashy plains bordered with rivers of flame and billowing smoke.

Was this the vale of Gehenna, the valley of bones, the imperishable fire foretold by the ancient prophets? Isolated figures wandered randomly over this desert, dressed in bulky white apparel, with white hoods fastened over their heads and shiny, dark-tinted plastic masks that concealed their faces while reflecting the wasteland around them, so that what was outside of them seemed also to be inside of them. A few of these ghostly apparitions carried around with them the brass nozzles of thick white hoses that snaked back and forth behind them across the plains for hundreds of yards to water sources I couldn't see.

One of these figures approached my side of the cab, looked up at me, and directed us over to a hill of metal waste—I was surprised to hear him talk in a human, not a robotic, voice. As he spoke to me, I gazed down into my own reflection in his visor, which gave me an uncanny feeling that this strange apparition was somehow a projection of myself; and I, too, might very well be condemned to roam this smoky wasteland until the consummation of the ages and the end of time.

Anyway, we followed his directions and tilted upward the back of the truck, and the colossal safe landed with an earthshaking thump at the base of the scrap-metal hill. We drove back to the factory. A few years later, when photographs of the moon landings were widely publicized, the costumes of the astronauts were discomfortingly familiar to me as the sort of outfits they might really, in the course of time, turn out to be: Someday might the moon itself become the universal dump for planet Earth?

Meanwhile, I regretted at the time (and still do now) the loss of that wonderful old safe. How many payrolls did it harbor in bygone years, just before the weekly funds were distributed to a workforce looking forward to a Saturday-afternoon baseball game, or an evening in a local saloon, or scraping together, from its meager earnings, a "widow's mite" to send back home to the folks in Donegal or Palermo or Vilna?

That's another strange thing about dumps: they're receptacles of the past, of whole ways of life, of moments in time. I suppose that's why archaeologists are so fond of dumps—which they picturesquely call "middens"—and so affectionately burrow around in them with their little trowels and brushes.

Yet is not the past itself—that is, the sort of thing we make an effort to enshrine in our history books—a sort of gigantic dump too? There are those, of different persuasions and for different reasons, who have thought so. Was it Henry Ford who said, "History is bunk"?

Bunk? Junk? Dump?

It all goes together somehow. I've thought so too, at times; for my love of history leads me again and again to those unsavory disclosures that make the past so utterly unlike what I imagined it was or wanted it to be. And that's part of the problem: we know history only as disconnected bits and pieces—the ways things are presented to us at the dump, unfortunately.

Our effort to put them together may configure the noble or the brave, or something so horrible that we can scarcely conform our minds to it. But what is irrefutable, in either case, is that whatever compound we choose to make of these bits and pieces is our production, our synthesis, and reflects whatever we want and think should be.

Yet how easy it is to reconfigure, or have reconfigured for us, whatever configuration appealed to us. Over and over again my wistful longings to live sometime in the past, instigated by this or that minute shard of information, have been rudely trumped by a potentially larger and less attractive picture induced by yet another minute shard of information.

Now some will claim, and have claimed, that I have an obsession with dumps, and I have to admit that maybe I do. I take the responsibility of proper disposal very seriously and expect others to do likewise. I'm subject to compulsive urges that impel me toward cleaning up after other people's irresponsible disposal of trash. I wonder if psychologists have found a name for this behavioral aberration yet.

When I see litter in parks, along the side of roads, or any place where it should not be, I repress, only with a struggle, my need to start picking it up and getting it into the proper receptacles. I do remember being fascinated, as a child, by the public servants who strolled through parks armed with a sack attached to the waist and a stick with a short nail-like pick projecting from one end. They used this item to poke candy wrappers and Cracker Jack boxes and the like and dispatch them into their sacks. Perhaps my obsession began there.

In any event, I've taken things to a much higher level of engagement. On any number of occasions, I've embarrassed a companion and interrupted what was supposed to be a presumably elegant promenade by suddenly stooping to snatch up something reasonably odious from the sidewalk and transporting it to the nearest trash barrel. I specialize in nails, by the way, and can spot a rusty nail at quite a distance. Having once stepped on a nail and punctured, therewithal, the heel of both my shoe and my foot, I'm doing my best to look out for the well-being of others.

On other occasions my yielding to this impulse has practically cost me my life, as I've pulled some object off a public highway that was negligently dropped by someone or other from the back of a truck or a trailer (probably on the way to a dump) and that was causing drivers to swerve and brake at the last moment to avoid hitting it while maximizing the possibility of hitting each other.

My effort to remove the object, though done purely for the public good, is fraught with danger, for drivers don't particularly appreciate what I'm doing, don't help by slowing down, and may even blame the rescuer (me!) for the object's being there in the first place, in which case the danger entailed by the rescue is regarded as justly deserved and is accordingly augmented. Should my heroic efforts someday result in the ultimate sacrifice, I hope that my countrymen would consider immortalizing me with an appropriate monument and the inscription: "He perished while picking up your trash (and you killed him for it)."

It is, of course, not possible to meditate upon dumps without crossing a certain threshold, without entering into what might be called — please excuse the expression — a "metaphysics" of dumps. According to some scholars, various ancient cosmologies postulated the view that all light and airy things rise, and all heavy and solid things fall. If the earth is understood as the center of the universe, as it once was, then every light and airy thing rises from it, and keeps rising until it enters the empyrean, the heavens of fire that encircle the universe. Correspondingly, all heavy and solid things fall down on and into the earth. If you append to this account a certain generic prejudice against solidity, this makes the earth — well, a kind of dump.

I'm not sure how accurate a picture these scholars have framed of older views, but, if we were to turn to Dante's *Inferno*, the famous description of the infernal regions (which lie in the center of the center of the universe), it's not incorrect to see this venue as the imaginative projection of a cosmological dump, where all that is dross, disordered, shut out, contagious, impaired, especially of a moral nature, ends up (and curiously, like our modern facilities, it's all separated into the proper bins and ditches). It's also a heavy place, and everything gets heavier (including your own body), the deeper you descend into it—thick, frozen, sluggish, immobile, numb, mindlessly repetitive, passive, deafening, obscure, unintelligible, and paralyzed. Correspondingly, the further you get away from it, the more velocity and verve and alertness you sense.

I wonder if there is anything to be learned about our earthly dumps by analogy here. I'm not sure there is—not, at least, *about* our dumps.

But *from* our dumps we may be able to be attuned to the same set of features anyway. A dump, whatever else you may want to say about it, is an oppressive thing; it weighs us down. As we navigate the road out of the dump, we feel already lighter, fresher, buoyant, ready again to face the world shriven of an intolerable burden (and to accumulate once more what will bring us, inevitably and inexorably, back again).

It's easy to dismiss the speculations of past ages as ignorant and outmoded nonsense. But what, then, shall future ages think of us? Our forebears expended no little energy in projecting end-time cataclysms, where our earth itself would be imminently hurtled into the great trash bin, the dump, of cosmic time. But such "prophets of doom" have been partially replaced in recent times by, of all people, the savants among us, whose technical and abstruse calculations foretell a variety of looming apocalyptic denouements whose dimensions dwarf the most extravagant prophecies of old.

I've been more than once in my lifetime so sufficiently terrified by the prospect of, let's say, the sun's burning out, that, even though the event may still be projected for several billion years in the future, I've found myself reluctant, for fear of the cold, to throw out my old woolen sweaters. Well, we scoff only at our own peril, the scientists say ... as was also said by the self-appointed wizards of prior ages. Hence, we shall not scoff.

Still, it's curious to note that, if, by positioning the earth at the center of the universe, some could envisage it as a dump, then, by displacing the earth from the center of the universe, others could now envisage the entire universe itself as a dump, as a fractured, random, purposeless, ultimately fortuitous splat of astronomical size and discordant matter, whose space-time coordinates are finally not coordinates at all, for there is nothing fixed, determinate, or substantial for anything to be coordinate with.

Add to this unseemly mix the second law of thermodynamics, and you will conclude that, after all, consuming a second or even a third martini before (and even after) dinner is not such a bad idea. Such an expanded, and expanding, cosmological dump, indeed, must weigh heavily upon us.

I introduce that word "weigh" quite deliberately here, for another esteemed, though apparently converse, tradition in Western thinking uses the expression "weight of glory" to describe what it posits as the best possible illumination that the human intellect can aspire to. Yet what a curious word to use in this context — the word "weight" coupled, paradoxically, with its apparent opposite, "glory"! I shall not try — nor am I able — to explicate these terms as they have been used in the tradition to which I allude. But the expression, as curious as it is, does encourage me to reflect on why dumps so singularly weigh on our consciences, given that weight is not always, and necessarily, a negative attribute. For dumps are weighty places. Dumps are very weighty places.

I had initially promised, tacitly, to myself that there were certain boundaries I would observe as imposing limits for my meditations. But our consideration of "weight" causes me to transgress. I suppose I wouldn't do this, except that I read a memoir of the First World War recently in which the author referred to the "no-man's land" between the opposing lines of trenches as a dump — and not only as a dump, but as *a dump at the edge of the world.*

The expression is strange for a number of reasons: it takes a locale of what can be construed — validly, to some extent, I suppose — as a space for heroic action and sacrifice and redefines it as a ruthless abattoir of insensate and obscene human butchery. For the author in question had to experience, again and again, the act of digging down into the earth to make a protective shelter for himself, only to delve through layer after layer of corpses, stacked horizontally like geological strata and able to be differentiated both by how deep they were and by their uniforms as to who occupied this ground and when and how long ago. And all of these corpses were tangled together with enormous amounts of unexploded ordnance, poised to detonate and fulfill the duty it originally failed to do. A dump, indeed!

And why at the edge of the world?

Well, dumps are usually out at the edges of things, which is where we put stuff we're trying to get rid of. On the other hand, we think of a no-man's land as being, in a sense, at the center between two worlds in conflict. How totally this strange metaphor shifts the conflict from a center to a periphery where all combatants share a common fate—to be, as it were, the refuse of nations, tossed off to the edge, dismembered, disfigured, broken, burned, buried; a squalid and indistinguishable moil of visages, limbs, entrails, and offal known in more polite terms as the "fallen" and the "slain."

Yes, I know, such a composite image is bound to startle and offend, and I know it's not the only image possible. But it's an image, nevertheless, mediated to us by our venerable habitué of the trenches.

And it must make us wonder why nations resort to such practices. After all, one can argue, it's much of the best that's getting thrown away. Maybe that's the explanation. Maybe sometimes the best is exactly what we don't want around anymore.

It has often been contended that governments exploit the weaknesses of their citizenry—their credulity and conformity, above all. That may well be true; but the reverse could be argued just as well—i.e., that governments exploit the virtues of their citizenry: their capacity for courage, for trust, for loyalty, for the willingness to sacrifice self-interest, for endurance in the face of the most extraordinary hardships. All of these can be readily transformed by governments, for their not-all-so-transparent aims, into the instruments of a debased and remorseless savagery.

Those, among us, who are given to identify the broil of historical events and national objectives as a cosmic contention between the children of darkness and the children of light and who assign themselves, with imperturbable self-assurance, to the latter camp, will not agree with what I have to say, of course; that aspect, at least, of our indelibly Puritanical heritage I don't share.

But however much we do, or don't, consent to such a vision, the resulting image is bound to be the same: *a dump at the edge of the world.* Yet such an image is not as dishonorable as it may seem, for the Apostle to the Gentiles, while redressing the contumacious faithful of ancient Corinth, could affirm, even about himself: "We have become like the rubbish of the world, the dregs of all things, to this very day."

Such thoughts, I'm afraid, lead me into a further weightiness about dumps. Of necessity, I shall be oblique, allusive, cursory about such weighty matters. For we have created again and again, all of us, human dumps of inexplicable horror. We have lined roads with the litter of peoples systematically murdered and dismembered and expelled from ancient homelands while being marched into territories they were never meant to reach. We have gathered peoples from disparate ancestral dwellings and concentrated them in one place so they could be bonded together and forever in common funereal columns of smoke. We have depopulated entire regions through induced starvation and disease. We have transformed great cities into smoldering ruins, wiped out their citizenry, reduced them to rubble, sometimes with a single flash cutting a horizontal swath of destruction through the sky. We have filled remote camps with anyone we considered an enemy to our cause. We have shut people down in teeming human enclaves where death and humiliation abound. We have used the instruments and custodians of health to extract and pitch into hungry crematoria the most innocent among us. And this is just our short list.

Countless, innumerable are the dumps we have made. Let it be known among us, that we — we human beings — are the masterminds of dumps. And in this process, as awful as it is, we ignore blithely the most obvious fact of all — that we are, each of us, joint and severally, destined for a dump. The great English poet and divine John Donne spoke about us as "the rags and bones of time"; nor did he forebear for a moment to appropriate the Pauline word "rubbish" to describe us, especially what we will become in what he called our "posthume death," that death of the inanimate body that awaits just beyond the death of the animate body, when the body itself, now shorn of life, gradually, in whatever way is given it, is deprived even of its residual bodily form; where our dust must be "mingled ... with the dust of every highway, and of every dunghill, and swallowed in every puddle and pond; this is the most inglorious and contemptible vilification, the most deadly and peremptory nullification of man that we can consider."

Indeed! Who then will sort us into the right bins? Who will recycle us? Or are we beyond that, well beyond that—not rubbish simply, but rubbish that makes all other rubbish seem salubrious by comparison?

I've promised myself not to end my meditation on dumps with "heavy" thoughts, so perhaps it's best that I recur to where I began, with considerations more putatively bucolic and fanciful. For, in the rural life I adumbrated above, as important as town dumps may be, they're appurtenances of fairly recent origin. Anyone who has driven around our much and grievously despoiled countryside is quite too familiar with the occasional shack surrounded by heaps of refuse—much of it old automobiles, tractors, appliances, and other machinery that have collected around a place.

Much of that, as appalling as it is, is often connected—as I've been led to believe—to a social pathology induced in many cases by poverty and personal collapse. But, even in more normal circumstances, anyone who buys—often for sentimental, though laudably sentimental reasons—an old farmstead will soon discover where the original rural dumps were located: yes, right around the corner of that newly acquired and ever so picturesque house and barn.

It's hard to reconstruct exactly what took place in what we like to conceive of as those blissful and innocent epochs of early Americana. Sometimes I think that it may have amounted to little more than the occasional act of a person—indeed, one of those stern, lock-jawed Yankee farmers, or maybe his thrifty wife—taking an empty bottle or crock or jar to the back door and just plain, good-old heaving it. Where it fell, or where enough of such projectiles fell, was the domestic dump. On the other hand, the concentration of discarded artifacts in some areas suggests much more focus than this.

I've spent quite a bit of time poking around in some of these old domestic dumps—part of my obsession, I suppose. Sometimes I've made an effort to clean them up (here I go again) and move all the stuff somewhere else. It's ironic and curiously perverse to re-dump a dump, but I've done it.

Most of the things we recover from such a dump, if recovery is what we're interested in, are hardly worth paying much attention to: crushed and variously punctured cans, smashed bottles, broken glassware and ceramics, enameled teapots with gaping holes in them, bent-up sheet metal (old roofing?), the iron rims and hubs of wagon wheels (the wooden parts, like all other wooden objects, have disappeared into the soil), the rare axe or pitchfork head or scythe blade, white porcelain doorknobs with big discolored cracks in them, plows and harrows and rakes, brass bedposts and box springs, lanterns, clay jugs, horseshoes, and a multitude of rusty mechanical parts whose original purpose is often impossible to decipher. Of special interest are the colorfully tinted vials that once contained the ointments and balms, tinctures and syrups, unguents and salves, and other anodynes that kept our allegedly robust forbears mentally lithe and physically lissome.

I appreciate the carriage springs (sometimes with the remnants of leather thongs still attached) and the ubiquitous sled runners sticking up long and thin out of the moist composted soil. I've also discovered old boots and shoes, especially woman's shoes with high rows of buttons lining the front or the side. I even once found a pair of gold-rimmed spectacles, still intact. Who read with these, I wondered, and what were they reading?

An especially exciting find is a coin.

Looking specifically for such items is not my lure to rustle around in old dumps, but still, it's fun to date a site by studying the coin, though such a coin rarely is of the sort that has much value among collectors. I found a silver dollar once, but my delight in finding it was almost instantaneously eclipsed by the thought that, a hundred years ago, this may have been a considerable loss for someone, a week's salary perhaps; and I imagined some man or woman searching anxiously for it. I wanted to cry out to them the ever-comforting words: "It's over here. I found it."

For those who may find the prospect of coping with a domestic dump — discovered belatedly at the threshold of their newly acquired cottage — particularly depressing, I should like to lift their sagging spirits by noting that a number of people in my area have transformed a liability into an asset and converted their dumps into flower gardens.

I'm not sure how to explain such a curious phenomenon. It's not altogether unintelligible that a productive civilization such as our own should develop a certain fascination with junk. After all, we keep producing it, and keep producing it at ever-expanding rates of productivity. In the meantime, we curry, collect, and burnish the junk of previous generations, decorate houses with it (the junk style that reoccurs every now and then, mentored and encouraged by the doyens of high fashion itself), and have devoted a not inconsiderable amount of time, resources, and admiration to works of art either assembled out of junk, or made to look like junk, or made to be junk, or simply are junk—on the premise that junk itself can be an object not of beauty certainly but at least of studious fascination. We even make reproductions of junk, so much so that buyers should be ever wary that what they pick up from junk sales may be, however implausible it may sound, fake junk.

I might add here to my discussion of junk, in order to be just to the citizenry of my little corner of the world, that it has become routine hereabouts to call junk of a specific kind "treasures." Those who don't own barns, tractor sheds, and other assorted outbuildings no longer devoted to their original agricultural purpose can have no conception of what can collect in them over a century and get passed down from one generation to the next, and even from one buyer of the property to the next, everyone adding to it in their turn and no one having the moral fortitude even to sort through it and figure out what is there.

Finally, the reckoning must come, in which instance overwhelming collections of junk get transmogrified into the equally overwhelming treasure of Solomon's Mines, and Great Grandpa's pitchfork shall hang, at considerable expense and to the wonderment (both genuine and ironic) of all, over a bank president's desk.

Now, all of this brings us back, however indirectly, to the dump garden. There is something enormously and undeniably poignant about seeing a sprig of forget-me-nots rising up through the center of an old truck tire, or primroses peeking coyly out from a tangle of rusty barbed wire, or wispy columbines, pleasantly swaying in a gentle breeze, having precariously made their way through the shattered panes of a discarded window. Some might even expostulate here over a Zen sensibility of wistful illusion and transitory meditation; others might want to celebrate the noble theme of life itself emerging out of the detritus of time and the fragments of the past. Still others might marvel at the cherished implements of old supporting the fragile roots and tendrils of the new.

Of course, nature itself has often been the gardener, and many a domestic dump has disappeared, partially or wholly, under the cover of brush and woodland that has grown up during the passage of time. I once saw a wagon wheel's iron rim with a sizable tree rising up through the middle of it. I've seen a riot of black-eyed Susans, hollyhocks, and daylilies explode through the tangled coils of old box springs.

Yet the most spectacular sight I've ever seen in an arboreal dump was signaled to me by a curious creaking far over my head. I gazed upward and saw above me the disheveled frame of a Model T Ford. It was missing its tires, its engine, one of its doors, and possibly other parts as well, as far as I could see. For it was located thirty feet above the ground, cradled sideways in the arms of an oak tree that, from the time it was a sapling (and perhaps with the initial assistance of other saplings long since perished in the struggle for survival) had gathered the remnants of the vehicle up in its branches and elevated it higher and higher over the years into the woodland canopy above. The sole remaining door hung downward and squeaked on its hinges as it swung loosely back and forth in the breeze.

I tried to imagine that automobile being driven home from a dealership by a proud farmer, his first internal combustion vehicle probably, putt-putting up a dusty road with chickens squawking and fluttering out of the way, and a dog barking, and children scrambling from the porch to greet their father in his new machine, and a mother peering out the kitchen window with a look of bemusement and maybe some wry skepticism on her face.

Did any of this actually happen this way? Or am I recreating in my mind an advertisement I once saw in an antique magazine I ran across in one of the innumerable junk shops in the vicinity?

But there it is now, that horseless carriage, up in the tree, dangling and abandoned and forgotten, the family prize, that envy and dream of the ages, that harbinger and paradigm of the modern world. *Sic transit gloria mundi.*

Yet did I say glory? Whatever else can be said about it, the old vehicle has been reclaimed by nature, there where the leaves garland it with their seasonal beauty; where the snows gather upon its aged fenders under a wintry moon; where birds build their nests and squirrels scurry to gather their acorns; where, by night, the churning, sparkling stars are reflected in its still burnished fittings; and where, by day, the sun, shining downward at different angles during the flight of its fiery arc, shoots its feathery rays through the morning mists and, at evening, enshrouds the armorial lineaments of that venerable artifact in a priceless cape of gold. Glory, did I say? And lifted up, in the end?

Yes, I said it; and we shall not forget.

Givin' D'recshuns

Outah-state car. Now, what will this fella be wantin'? How's that? Hiram Cooke's place? Why, hell, that's easy ta find. Ever'one 'roun' heyah knows wheyah Hiram Cooke lives. He's been livin' theyah all his life.

Now, yuh jus' go up that road a-piece an' 'roun' that bend. Furst thin' yuh'll see is a white cape tucked back in a grove a' tamarack trees ta yowah right. Now, that ain't Hiram Cooke's place yet but it's on thuh way an' I wanta be sure yuh're followin' thuh right track, 'cuz folks do get lost 'roun' heyah though I could nevah figgah out why. I mean, theyah's only one road, an' how do yuh get lost on one road? Even a stray cow can't get lost on this road.

Anyhow, that white cape belongs ta Ray Piper, an' he keeps it real neat, with a gahden an' everthin'. Yuh'll see his name on thuh mailbox. He's a mighty rich ol' fella an' owns half thuh land 'roun' heyah, which makes him 'bout as rich as ol' King Solomon, though yuh would nevah know it, he lives so simple.

Like ol' King Solomon he's had his share a' wives — they jus' keep a-comin' an' a-goin', in an' out thuh front dowah — "feet furst," as they say at thuh end, cuz theyah ain't any othah reason fur a house ta have a front dowah 'ceptin' ta get newlyweds in an' dead people out.

Thuh last wife were a mighty fancy lady from down Concord way who married Ray fur what she reckon'd were "his fortune," figgahin' thuh ol' buzzard didn't have all that lon' a time ta go befowah he'd be a-wingin' his way down inta thuh depths a' hell, while she'd be a-wingin' her way ta some swanky hayloft in Miamah—yuh know, down Florider way.

Well, he outlived 'em all, includin' her.

When thuh fellas from thuh fiyah-stashun came ta help out—she had flipped ovah in thuh bedroom fur one reason or anothah—I went ovah ta his house ta do some neighborly comfortin'. He were sittin' in thuh parlah an' didn't need all that much comfortin', as fahr as I could tell. Well, one a' 'em fellas comes inta thuh parlah an' tells Ray he might like ta sit fur a spell in thuh kitchun, 'cuz they were goin' ta be bringin' thuh body downstayahs in a moment an' through thuh pahlah an'—as I were tellin' yuh—out thuh front dowah.

Well, Ray just kinda stares at that fella fur a spell, an' then he says, "Heck, I seen a whole bunch a' 'em hauled outa heyah already. Anothah ain't gonna mattah all that much ta me anyhow."

Well, that's Ray Piper fur yuh, thuh ol' son a' a gun.

Next yuh pass a cemet'ry on yuh left with a white picket fence 'roun' it. Josh Bickford—he's dead an' gone now an' is buried in that same cemet'ry, as a matter a' fact; he spent a whole summah paintin' that damned picket fence. Now, yuh'll be wonderin' why, 'cuz it ain't that much a' a picket fence. Town paid him ta do it.

Well, he paints a single picket, jus' on one side, an' then alon' comes some fella, an' they chattah like a bunch a' bluejays fur a spell, an' Josh tells all 'bout what's goin' on in his chickun house an' 'bout some damn raccoon been raisin' hell with his chickuns. Well, yuh know, raccoon talk leads ta skunk talk, an' that leads ta porcupine talk, an' all that talk nevah gets 'roun' ta stoppin' when it should.

Then that fella moves on, an' Josh manages ta paint maybe thuh othah side a' that picket, an' alon' comes anothah fella, an' next thin' yuh know, they're talkin' up a stahm, an' that goes on an 'owah or mowah, 'til that fella finally gets 'roun' ta rememberin' he's got bettah things ta be doin', an' he moves on.

Then maybe Josh gets his paint brush dipped inta thuh pail—at least that's gettin' somethin' done—an' wouldn't yuh know but Maisie Oldham pulls up in her ol' Fowad pickup, an' they go on God knows how lon' 'bout thuh pests in theyah gahdens, though it's hard ta 'magine Josh havin' any kinda gahden, 'cuz he were jus' 'bout thuh laziest man alive, an' all he could get 'roun' ta doin' is talkin' thuh eayah off any passerby.

An' most a' what he says is lies, too, fur what that's worth, 'cuz I don't think yuh'll be talkin' ta him anyhow, now that he's dead an' everythin'.

Well, as yuh can guess, he might get 'bout two or three pickets done in a day's work, an' that's 'bout it. So, it took 'im an entire summah, it did, that job; just lucky thuh town were payin' him by thuh job an' not by thuh 'owah. Thuh ol' son a' a gun, I figgah he's down theyah undah thuh groun' still chattin' away an' not lettin' them folks down theyah get theyah well-deserved rest.

Funny how some folks just want'a talk yowah eayah off, whethah yuh wanta listen or not.

Aftah yuh pass thuh graveyard, yuh'll go up ovah a rise, an' perched on thuh top a' that rise, like a big ol' rooster a-perchin' on a fence, is Milly an' Harry Mudget's house. It's got a big porch in thuh front an' a big unpainted bahn in thuh back, an' yuh jus' might happen ta see a couple a' cows in thuh pasture nearby. Harry is a quiet fella, but he'll give yuh a hand anytime yuh need it—yuh know, jus' in case yuh get a flat tire or somethin' between heyah an' theyah.

Now, Milly is somethin' else. Steyah cleyah a' her, if yuh can help it. I once sore her come a-scramblin' down thuh road full-tilt, shakin' a broom ovah her head with a fox not all that fahr in front a' her, draggin' along one a' her prize ducks in his mouth while it quacked away an' flapped its wings. I don't think Milly would'a caught him, but thuh crittah released thuh duck anyhow 'cuz it were slowin' him down too much, an' I guess he had got it figgahed out by now it were bettah ta go hungry than fall inta thuh hands a' that crazy woman.

But theyah were a big black beyah once, many a year ago, who wern't so lucky. One mornin', Milly had jus' milked her favorite Guernsey an' left thuh pail a' warm milk in thuh bahn while she went ta ansah thuh phone that were a-ringin' its head off in thuh kitchun. While she were talkin' ta her sistah, she heard all thuh cows a-mooin' an' all this comoshun goin' on in thuh bahn. So, she throws down thuh phone—with her sistah still connected—an' races out ta thuh bahn.

Theyah she stumbles on this big black beyah, standin' up on its hind legs, grippin' that pail a' milk in its front paws, an' jus' a-gulpin' down that milk thuh way some fellas pour thuh applejack down theyah throats at Halloween. So, she screams an' shouts like thuh end a' thuh world is come.

Meanwhile, Harry, who's in thuh toolshed, hears all thuh screamin' an' shoutin', grabs a crowbar, an' runs ta thuh bahn. But he's too late ta help, 'cuz thuh next thin' he sees is that big black beyah a-scamperin' outa' thuh bahn an' inta thuh woods faster than yuh can shake a stick at it. An' on thuh head a' thuh beyah are two bald spots, thuh size a' fists, freshly glowin' in thuh mornin' sun. Then Milly come outa' thuh bahn shakin' with angah an' clutchin' some tufts a' black hayah tightly in each hand.

"Hell, Milly," Harry calls ovah ta her, "what did yuh do ta that poor ol' beyah ta make him skedaddle like that?"

"Oh, nothin' much, Harry," she hollahs back. "No different than what I did ta Jenny Burrows in high school when she started a-makin' moon eyes at yuh. I figgahed she learnt ta stay away from what were rightfully mine. It took her a half a year ta grow back that hayah. I figgah that beyah has learnt his lesson. His hayah will grow back too."

Aftah yuh pass thuh Mudget fahm, thuh road will dip down a bit inta a little gully an' head back up an' 'roun' a big bouldah an' a beavah pond an' then past a sandpit. Thuh cottage by thuh sandpit belongs ta Davis Davis. Yuh bet, he's got thuh same furst an' last name, but his mom were a thurd cousin a' his pop, an' they both had thuh last name a' Davis, so when Davis come alon' they decided ta name 'im Davis Davis.

It gets a little confusin' at times, 'specially fur Davis, who nevah knows if someone is callin' 'im by his furst name—an' bein' friendly like—or by his last name—an' bein' not so friendly like; not that it makes much difference anyhow. When I call 'im Davis, I'm usin' his furst name, though sometimes I furget an' use his last name.

If yuh don't recognize thuh cottage, yuh'll recognize thuh rusted-out John Deere tractor with thuh backhoe that's tucked up next ta it. He uses that ta dig in thuh sandpit. Sometimes he spends all day movin' piles a' sand from one paht a' thuh pit t'anothah. I nevah seen thuh point a' it, but some folks jus' gotta do what they gotta do, no mattah how crazy it is.

If yuh're still uncertain about wheyah yuh are, yuh'll see a sign outside thuh cottage that says "Fiyah Wahrden." Yuh see, Davis is thuh fiyah wahrden, an' that makes him 'bout thuh most important person in town. But that ain't ta say he hasn't had his problems. Like when thuh fiyah-stashun burned down durin' thuh fiyah-men's ball. It weren't his fault, but he got blamed fur it anyway. Folks always need someone ta blame.

So, thuh town selectmen figgahed they had ta fiyah him, an' since Davis Davis ware thuh selectman in charge a' thin's like that, he had ta fiyah himself, which ain't all that easy—yuh know, ta write a lettah fiyahin' yuhself. Then he turned right 'roun' an' rehiyad himself anyhow, 'cuz he were thuh only one in these parts who knew how ta do thuh job. Wrote that damn lettah too, he did.

Then theyah were thuh incident on thuh ol' Atherton highway—some folks still call it a "highway" even though it don't go much a' anywheyah anymowah, though some folks comin' in from Maine use it as a shortcut now an' then. Well, theyah were this big ol' fahmhouse up ta theyah, not lived in fur many a yeyah now, which some city folk had bought up an' were fixin' ta restore an' turn inta somethin' that looked like a paintin' or a Curriah an' Ives print or somethin' like that. I dunno who these damned Curriah an' Ives fellas are, but they must be runnin' thuh biggest real estate bus'ness in all thuh narth country.

Anyhow, these city folks were too late, 'cuz thuh place caught fiyah one night, thuh way places like that sometimes do fuh no reason at all, an' burned ta thuh groun'. Well, natur'lly, thuh fiyah squad come out an' did what they could, which were, as usual, 'bout nothin' but get ta take thuh fiyah-truck out fur a spin, dampen down thuh hot coals, make showah thuh fiyah don't spread ta thuh woods, an' have a won'erful, grand ol' time a' it all.

'Course, ouwah fiyah-truck is somethin' ta behold, thuh best an' most expensive piece a' equipment yuh can get on thuh face a' thuh earth. It's gotta be, fur it represents ouwah town, a-flashin' its lights an' a-howlin' its sirens at thuh Fourth a' July parades in ever' village 'roun' heyah. It's thuh one thin' thuh town is willin' ta spend money on, though it's nevah yet been used successfully ta put out a fiyah.

So, at thuh Atherton highway fiyah, everthin' were pretty much undah control, as they say. Thuh ladies' auxiliary were theyah with lemonade an' doughnuts. Now, ta this day, no one understands how it happened, but some ol' son a' a gun puts somethin' or othah inta that lemonade, an' befowah long, theyah ain't a person left theyah—includin' ouwah only policeman, Donny Dunlop—who can eithah legally or illegally drive, 'ceptin' fur a few elderly gals a' thuh ladies' auxiliary who I figgah may a' been thuh culprits in thuh furst place.

Well, thuh condishun a' everone ain't gonna keep 'em from goin' theyah sev'ral ways back ta theyah homes when thuh party's ovah. Thuh problem is thuh fiyuh-truck. No one wants ta be responsible fur drivin' thuh fiyah-truck off thuh road an' inta a ditch somewheyah or some damn thin' like that.

So, Davis Davis takes ovah. Nobody much is on thuh highway that time a' night, but a car—I think it was one a' 'em damned Volvos—comes a-trundlin' alon' thuh road, an' he flags it down. Inside is a fella from New Jersey.

Now, yuh know how fellas from New Jersey look—they got faces that look like overripe peaches, an' they waggle 'roun' these soft white fingahs that look like theyah were made a' vanilla puddin' with little black hairs like chocolate sprinkles all ovah 'em. This fella were kinda bald too.

An' were he evah shakin' all ovah, like we were goin' ta do somethin' really bad ta him! City folk see these crazy movies an' read these crazy books 'bout people in thuh country, an' anytime one a' 'em sees a fella with a few calluses on his hands, some stubble on his chin, an' a few teeth missin', he figgahs thuh fellah's gonna do somethin' ta him that'll require thuh tinkerin' a' one a' 'em head-doctors fur thuh res' a' his life ta get ovah.

Well, Davis makes it cleyah that they jus' need someone ta drive thuh fiyah-truck back ta thuh fiyah-stashun. But this fella wants no paht a' it, bein' that now he's kinda calmed down a bit, an', gettin' a little sassy, he protests. "I don't know how ta drive a fiyah-truck," he says.

Davis says, "Yuh just come in from Maine?"

"Yup," he says.

Davis says, "Yuh know how ta eat a lobstah?"

"'Course, I know how ta eat a lobstah," he says. (City folks are mighty touchy 'bout thin's like that—like knowin' how ta eat a lobstah an' what kinda wine ta drink with it an' stuff like that.)

Davis says, "Well, if yuh know how ta eat a goddamned lobstah, yuh can learn ta drive a goddamned fiyah-truck. Aftah all, they're both red an' have antennahs a-stickin' up all ovah thuh place outa 'em."

"But I nevah drove one befowah," he says.

Davis says, "I nevah drove one befowah neithah, 'til I finally did."

Well, that kinda clinched thuh argument. Good ol' Davis Davis! Thuh New Jersey fella drove thuh fiyah-truck back ta thuh fiyah-stashun with Davis sittin' beside him, givin' 'im instrucshuns, an' one a' 'em elderly gals followin' behind thuh truck, drivin' his damned Volvo. Davis were thuh hero a' thuh day, an' he tol' that New Jersey fella he done real good.

As fur thuh New Jersey fella, why he were soon on his way back ta New Jersey or wherevah, an' most likely feelin' much relieved an' wondahin' maybe like he had been abducted by some sorta aliens or ape-men or somethin' like he seen in a movie. But thuh son a' a gun's probably thinkin' it'll be a great story ta tell at one a' 'em dinnah parties with his pals while he's a-yankin' an' a-crackin' away at some poor ol' lobstah an' a-slurpin' down God knows what kinda wine.

Jus' talk, talk, talk, nothin' but talk.

Some people! All they can do is hang 'roun' an' tell stories an' gossip 'til yuh're blue in thuh face! Ask 'em a simple question, an' they go on a-yappin' forevah. An' then, 'course, yuh can't even remembah what thuh devil yuh was talkin' 'bout in thuh furst place.

What were we talkin' 'bout in thuh furst place?

Ayuh. I was givin' yuh d'recshuns ta Hiram Cooke's. Now, aftah thuh sandpit, look ta yowah right. Theyah's Hiram Cooke's house jus' spittin' yuh straight in thuh eye. So theyah yuh are. If that don't get yuh theyah, nothin' will.

How's that? Yuh still don't know how ta get theyah? Kinda got lost in thuh drift, huh? Fourth house on yuh right. Yuh can't miss it.

(Damn fool! Can't see thuh forest fur thuh trees! I've know'd some cows got mowah sense than these outlandahs! Why, any self-respectin' cow could get down ta Hiram's house without even askin' fur d'recshuns.)

Oh, an' by thuh way, mind yuhself oveh theyah at Hiram Cooke's. He's one a' 'em damned fellas gonna talk yowah eayah off if yuh give him half a chance.

The Stonemason: A Journal

Day One

His name is Anpu. That's what he told me. At least, that's what I think he told me. I don't know what kind of name that is, or even whether it's a first or last name. Rural New England abounds in exotic names, though I never heard that one before. If his name is odd, it's even more odd that he approached us exactly when he did.

How did he find us?

I don't know how he knew we were thinking about having a stone wall built in front of our house. I suppose we may have spoken about it casually with some of our neighbors — they often walk along this lane and have seen me dallying about, studying the front yard, musing, measuring, considering. Naturally, they've asked me about the object of my studiousness, and I've told them. I've also mentioned the prospect with some of the people who had been working on our house recently. And maybe we'd begun to make some initial inquiries, though I don't recall whom I spoke to about that. But obviously the word had gotten around. He came to the door this morning and asked me if the job was available. I was a little taken aback by this query. I hadn't really decided anything yet, and his inquiry was, in a way, forcing me into a decision. So I decided right there and then, and I said, "Yes, there's a job available."

He asked me what I had in mind — where the wall would be located, how long it would be, other such matters. I wasn't quite prepared for this either, despite all my preliminary but vague fantasies. I knew that the wall would serve as a border between our front yard and the country lane that runs by our house, that it would be made in the "dry" fieldstone style traditional in our locale, and that it would be fifty to sixty feet long. It would have a gate or entrance. Other than that, I'd settled on few details of the project; indeed, I knew so little about what was involved that I didn't even know what there was to settle.

As is common in such a situation, I sought his advice, and he was more than happy to explain some of the technical problems that would have to be solved and what some of my options were. He spoke learnedly and confidently about his subject. I said I would give it some thought and discuss it later with my wife.

He asked me where the stones would be coming from. I said I had a plentiful supply of stones. I don't own a lot of acreage, but I own enough to have, as so many landowners in the area do, sizable stone walls of some antiquity running obscurely through dense second-growth woodlands. Such walls once formed the boundaries of pastures that have long since been reclaimed by the forest; now, though often difficult to get to, they're a good source of nicely weathered fieldstones that can be dragged off and used for the construction of ornamental walls in more conspicuous places. Even better than that — since I'd rather not tamper with old walls, even if they're hidden — I have a number of large fieldstone piles located close to my fields. I asked if he wanted to examine the resources I had, and he said it was unnecessary.

I asked about an estimate. How much might it cost?

He looked rather vacantly into the sky for a moment, as if he were doing some calculations. Yet somehow, I don't think he was doing any calculations. I think he was studying a cloud formation that was drifting overhead. Then he gave me a price, not an estimate.

The price was very low. I didn't believe it when he said it. I still don't believe it.

After saying he would come by again in a few days, he departed. I don't know where he lives or what his telephone number is. I don't know anything about him — except for his name: Anpu.

Day Two

So I've made inquiries. Of course, it's difficult to make them because I can't even identify who he is. Anyway, nobody knows him: nobody even knows of him. Nobody has heard of Anpu. I've spoken to a few construction people.

They're acquainted with all the stonemasons around, and since this fellow isn't in one of their familiar groups, he must be a newcomer, which already makes him suspect.

Naturally, they warn me against him. I need to take their admonitions with a grain of salt, for local people warn against everybody and anybody—that's just what they do.

They're all, however, incredulous about the price. A wall of the sort we're planning should cost about four or five times as much. So that makes them really suspicious. Such a low price must mean that he does very low-quality work.

I don't know what to make of all of this. Could he be giving me a low price and then intend to jack it up monumentally as he runs into the supposedly unexpected but inevitable problems? That's a game that all the local construction people know how to play, and he would be no exception in that regard.

How do I get in touch with him?

Day Three

He showed up again this morning. Came in out of nowhere. Has a dirty, crumpled-up-looking van, curiously box-shaped, with indecipherable markings on it. I wonder if he lives in that van.

Was I interested in having him work? Yes, I was interested—that is, interested enough to pursue the issue.

I asked him if there was a stone wall somewhere in the neighborhood that he had built that I could look at. Well, no; he's new to the area. (I guess we all had that right.)

Does he have references? No, he doesn't have any references. He informs me of that in a way that implies that the question is unnecessary and impertinent. Apparently, according to him, he doesn't need references.

When could he start on the job? Anytime I wanted him to start.

Could he start tomorrow? Yes, he could start tomorrow.

I'm a bit confounded. Now, my normal procedure in situations like this would be to get several bids from different masons. But for reasons I can't unravel, I'm willing, in this case, to bypass that procedure.

Why do I have confidence in him? On that first day he discoursed so eloquently about his métier that I was convinced he knew what he was talking about (a dangerous inference to make, under any circumstances). Also, I know I won't get a price like that from anybody else.

So am I just being stingy? After all, I don't know what I'm going to get for that price. Indeed, I tend, by and large, to be susceptible to the dynamics of what people call "value perception"—that paying a higher price entails getting a better product. So I know I'm not stingy, not in principle anyway. I like things of quality and am willing to pay for them what they're worth, though I know that "value perception" psychology can often be deceptive.

In any case, I'm not the obsessive bargain hunter who fills his life with junk, nor the shrewd financier who, more often than not, is the long-term victim, if also maybe the short-term beneficiary, of his own connivance.

I ask Anpu how I should contact him. He doesn't seem to have an address or telephone number yet. He says he'll contact me. As I said, he just came into the area.

In addition to the price, I'm also attracted to the immediacy of when he can begin work. At least I don't have to wait some indeterminate length of time before things get underway. That's a relief.

Sometimes I think I'm crazy. I must be crazy. I offer him the job. I offer him the job on the spot. I've never done that before.

Does he want an advance? No, he doesn't want an advance.

Anpu doesn't want an advance.

Day Four

He arrives early in the morning, and I must interrupt my leisurely breakfast hour to accompany him to the woods and show him the mounds that will serve as the source for the new wall. I also show him the walls that belong to me, and I'm careful to distinguish them from other walls that run close by and that are boundaries between my land and the adjoining woodlots of my neighbors. I don't know who's considered to own walls like these, but I assume we shouldn't touch them, and I don't.

Anpu has no difficulty grasping the logistics of the situation.

When I ask him if the supply will be sufficient, he laughs. There's enough stone there to build a wall ten times the length of the one being planned.

He notes that I have a tractor parked behind my barn and asks if he can use it to haul stones from the forest to the front of the house. I agree to that. We go to the tractor, and I explain a few things about the hydraulics and the clutching system and a few other gadgets, just in case he's not familiar with this kind of tractor. But he doesn't seem to need this information. He's soon at work, and I return to my coffee cup and newspaper. All day long I hear that tractor going in and out of the woods.

Day Five

The fieldstone heap he's created already is amazing. Gigantic. I can't figure out how he's moving some of these stones. The front-end loader of the tractor can carry them, of course, but how does he get them into it in the first place? And stones of so many shapes and colors and sizes? On those mounds up in the woods they all looked more or less the same: grey, rounded, covered with lichens, sedate, ordinary. Maybe I just never looked carefully at them.

Here they have sharp edges, sculpted projections and bulges, flat sides and rounded sides, rectangular lines and pyramidal shapes and brilliant hues, all aglitter with embedded mica or shot through with jagged veins of dazzling white quartz or encrusted with coppery sheaths.

No two are alike.

I don't know how to identify stone, despite that one course in geology I took at college (one of several random "science" requirements), but there must be dozens and dozens of different kinds of stones here. Those glaciers of old must have scooped and gouged deeply into the strata of the earth to yield such a variegated harvest. I can't imagine how he's going to put them all together.

Many of my neighbors, who regularly walk along the street for their daily exercise, are now aware that something fairly dramatic is going on and stop to gape at the huge mound of stones. All day long Anpu keeps adding stones to the pile, slowly and methodically. Sometimes he stands for a while, with that curious vacant look, studying the clouds in the sky, but he gets a lot done, though it's impossible to figure out how he does it.

It's difficult not to watch him at times.

I keep thinking he looks familiar to me, but I don't know why. He doesn't look at all like you would imagine a stonemason should look. He's not hefty, round-shouldered, thick, or rugged like the stones he moves about. He's medium height and slender as a reed and has a sallow, pleasant face; his nose and chin project somewhat forward beneath large black eyes and eyebrows, and his lips are broad and full; his low forehead slants backward into a thin, oblong head that looks curiously canine. He looks as if he had stepped out of some other world.

He wears a strangely shaped cap that hides his ears. I don't know why I think this, but maybe if he took that cap off, I'd see that his ears are tall and erect and have pointed tips. Why do I think that?

Day Six

Anpu dug a trench today, along the entire length of where the wall will be going and has begun filling in the trench with smaller stones. Later in the day we discussed briefly some issues touching upon details about the wall, especially about the ending of the wall, where it will meet the driveway, and about the position and shape of a gateway. He has quite a few suggestions to make, and we'll have to make some decisions. We never discuss the general style of the wall. I assume that that matter is decided simply by what is more or less traditional in the area.

Stone walls around here all tend to look a certain way — at least if you're not looking at them too carefully, though, in recent months while thinking about a wall, I've learned to distinguish several variations of style. For the most part, the fieldstone is fitted together without mortar or any other joining substance or rigging, making what is called a "dry wall." Variations seem to be determined by how careful the fitting is — some walls are loosely fitted; others are precise. Some are thick with broad, level tops; others are only one stone thick with a thin, craggy ridge along the top. It's also amazing how nice these walls look, no matter what variations of style they exhibit or in what state of disrepair they happen to be. Many of the older walls have partially fallen down or settled and flattened out, yet they still look so attractive that people, as I've heard, sometimes instruct stonemasons to build new walls so that they look like these old, partially fallen-down walls.

In earlier days, I was of the conviction that the multitudinous stone walls of New England were simply piles of stone conveniently lined up along the edges of fields. Some of them were, but the most elementary sort of effort to repair one of these walls quickly dispels any illusion that building these walls didn't require a fair amount of skill. The walls were built by people who knew what they were doing. For the most part, they did it well. I've given Anpu no particular instructions about the style of the wall he will build. I assume the stone wall will look like—well, just like a stone wall.

Day Seven

The building has begun.

Stakes and strings have been set up and a row of stones placed along the outside of the base on either side. They look like a jagged little parade of two mountain chains running parallel to and facing one another. The sides of the stones facing outward from the wall are all flat. How can they all be flat? The stones up in the woods were round. They looked to my eyes like cannon balls of different sizes. I know he isn't cutting the stone, so where did all these flat sides come from?

I now think I know where I've seen Anpu before ... seen him a thousand times. He looks like one of those figures in ancient Egyptian paintings, face presented in profile, shoulders at right angle to the face, dressed in a kirtle or short tunic, surrounded by hieroglyphs and papyrus stalks and lotus blooms, wielding tools, building temples and pyramids.

Could his name be Egyptian too?

Anpu? But that name doesn't ring a bell.

And Anpu doesn't seem to be using any tools, though he carries around with him at times a sort of iron rod with a crossbeam and a circle at the end. A crowbar of some sort? I don't know. I never see him actually using it.

I walked up to the woods this afternoon to check out how much of those original rock mounds are left. All of them still seem to be there. It doesn't look as if he's touched any of them. Where did all those stones come from?

In the evening, after he's left for the day, I go out and examine the heap of stones. I try lifting some. Most of them I can hardly budge, even though I'm physically much larger than Anpu is.

Day Eight

Sometimes when Anpu works outside, I'm practicing piano inside. I'm not very good at it and am only trying, desperately, to pick up where I left off about forty-five years ago. If I work at it persistently for a decade, maybe I'll get back to where I was when I was about fifteen. Frankly, I'm embarrassed by the notion of anyone hearing my practicing. Some of my neighbors hear it when they go for their daily walks and have indicated, without my asking, that they enjoy it—I can't imagine why. I think they're just being polite.

Anpu hears my playing (or, as I would put it, is the hapless victim of it) and has mentioned it to me, expressing some appreciation. I reply by saying that I'm glad that Beethoven and Mozart and Schubert and a few others are interred on the other side of the Atlantic so that they don't have to go through the trouble of turning in their graves, should my maladroit renditions of their work happen to assail their ears.

Anpu seems to like especially the second movement of the *Appassionata* (actually, it's the only movement of the *Appassionata* I'm able to play); but in its heaviness and slowness, alternating with sudden divagations into lightness and speed, it's perhaps like the joining of stones. Maybe that's why he likes it; or maybe he likes it because I play it reasonably well (unlike the rest of my belabored and belaboring repertoire).

I've noted of late that my interpretation of the piece has become unusually ... lapidary? Marmoreal? Hmm—like travertine, like huge blocks of limestone fitted and angled precisely in an ascending line pointing directly at a burnished desert sky?

Day Nine

Pouring rain. Black clouds. Thunder and lightning.

Winds roaring and trees pitching fitfully backward and forward, turning their leaves upward in the thrust of the wind like corybantic worshippers raising and flailing their palms to and fro before an ancient idol.

Anpu works all day, unperturbed, in the storm. He carries stones back and forth through lashing curtains of rain. Often, I can't see him unless lightning crackles in the distant skies. Then he looks like a figure in an early black-and-white film moving in clumsily disconnected steps through darkness.

He carries the stones without effort and ignores the turbulence of the storm around him. The heavens thunder over him, but he works without stint—from early morning, when the sun never rose, unto this night that follows upon a day that, for all practical purposes, has been indistinguishable from night. Like a god he moves awesomely, solemnly, through the powers of unleashed elements and the forces of chaos.

Sometimes I have the impression that he's carrying titanic rocks larger than himself.

Sometimes lightning spreads over the far horizon in jagged spires, and I see him suddenly in silhouette, a sinewy presence, etched darkly against the momentary splatter of light, more mysterious than life itself, a face as pointed and black and lean as a shard of glossy obsidian, with arched eyes glowing fiercely opalescent through the darkness, and ears pointing up from beneath that cap, ears lithe and sharp.

At other times I see him on one knee, crouching backward on his heel, the other knee tilted up in front of him, his arms raised and his head bent slightly in his canine way, wondering, concentrated, as he meditates the tongue of an invisible scale, balancing stone upon stone, their sole bond and stay being an invisible gravitational plumb line, the subtle cosmic force that holds the teetering rocks firmly in place.

"I have come unto the House of Him whose dwelling is upon the mountain."

Why did I say that? Where does that come from?

Day Ten

I can't believe how much got done during the storm yesterday. A wall is rising out of the ground, as if it were growing out of the earth. It's a wall such as I've never seen before. It looks like a New England fieldstone wall, and yet it doesn't. It has a sculpted look about it, something architectural and monumental, yet simple and unpretentious at the same time. As is so often the case with arts that one appreciates but doesn't understand, it's possible to perceive differences and features but not be able to explain what accounts for any of these perceptions.

My wife is just as puzzled by it as I am. We've started calling it Hadrian's Wall, for lack of another expression, though it doesn't look at all like Hadrian's Wall. The neighbors walk by, and stop, staring at it in wonder. They can't quite believe what they're seeing. They like what they see, even as we do, but are mystified by it. Cars drive by and slow down as they pass. The town road crew, in several trucks, stops up the road a bit, ostensibly to work on the road, but actually to get a better view of the wall.

I decide to join them. I want to see how they react.

I amble up the road, having deliberately left my partial dentures in the bathroom. I've discovered, through long experience, that a certain measure of edentation greatly facilitates discourse with some coteries of the local gentry. One can loiter about with them, shifting feet, hands in pockets, staring at the toes of one's boots while pleasurably engaged in interminable wheezing, lisping, yapping, blabbering, and whistling through the open fissures of one's mouth. My gums are not quite as discolored as theirs, but that's okay. It would be unreasonable to expect perfection in such a circumstance.

They're laughing.

Of course they're laughing … because they're *always* laughing.

Everything, for them, is funny. What people do and what people don't do is funny. Fauna, domesticated or wild or somewhere in between, is funny. Flora is just as funny. News is funny. Town politics is funny. Accidents are funny. Weather is funny, and extreme weather is extremely funny. And so on.

The new stone wall is funny — that's not a sign of derision; it's a sign of respect. They admire that stone wall, and they've never seen anything like it, as they repeat and laugh about it over and over again. Eventually, they go back to work (if that's what you want to call whatever it is they do) and drive off in their trucks.

Back at the house, with partials restored and now fully dentilated, I sally forth, brandishing checkbook and pen, and offer to make a half payment for the wall. Anpu is not interested. He says he will present a bill when the work is completed. He says that in a very curious way.

Day Eleven

Word has gotten around. Everyone's stopping to look at the wall. Cars pull up, and people get out with cameras and take pictures. Promenading neighbors are ever more astonished. Local contractors are coming by to gaze at it, though I think it's annoying them intensely. But that's their business—to be annoyed by others' work. If Michelangelo were out there sculpting this wall, they would still be annoyed. If Michelangelo were out there looking at this wall, he would be annoyed too.

I am, I must confess, a little disconcerted by all this attention, even though it seems favorable, indeed very favorable. When people work on my place, I always have the curious sense that I'm personally, even somatically, involved, as if I were being operated on by a surgeon, and others are witnessing this event. So I'm jittery, distracted all the time, unable to concentrate on anything else, watching things out of the corner of my eye.

Moreover, it's difficult for me, with Anpu out there, shifting those great stones back and forward, fitting them together with enormous precision, not to imagine myself complicit in some great archetypal event, something that resonates throughout history.

I'm not speaking merely of the stone wall building era in New England through the past few centuries, as amazing as that was: the glacial scree of the last ice age had, after all, to be picked up and stacked somewhere if pastures were to yield hay and orchards were to be planted.

I'm thinking of all that astonishing movement and cutting and fitting of stone that has transpired with time. Anpu himself makes one think of the lofty pyramids and temples mirrored in the waters of the Nile. And then there are the great ziggurats of the Euphrates lowlands, the jungle compounds of Maya and Angkor Wat, the city walls of Minoan Crete and, as Homer would have it, of golden Mycenae itself, perched so high above the coastal plains of "horse-pasturing Argos."

Again and again, I've thought of those ancient craftsmen—a race of giants, as the old Anglo-Saxon bards described them when singing of the Roman ruins at Bath—quarrying great blocks of stone, building tombs and citadels and theaters, castles and bridges and aqueducts, massive fortifications and monastic sanctuaries and elegant chateaux, guild halls and towers and amphitheaters and the retaining walls of marvelous terraced hillsides whose wavelike forms flow upward from valley depths into the skies above.

The world is replete with their work, much of it hidden from our eyes.

And, in my own front yard and at my own behest, another edifice of the mason's art is rising—like a natural wonder itself, carving the most obdurate sculpture of the earth into the most noble of earth's sculpture, arguably mankind's most enduring things. That, in itself, is the most astonishing thing of all, for these things made of rock seem to live, and to breathe, and to sing their existence through time.

Anpu's wall is already like that, even in its unfinished condition. It seems to be alive, to unfold and to transmute itself into a multitude of forms, and modulations of those forms, like a scroll of contrapuntal music, like one of those great cathedrals of medieval Europe as you saunter meditatively around and through them, and they respond to your gaze like partners in a dance, their exquisite recursive figurations shifting from moment to moment, by moving in unison with the dazzle of your eyes.

Now, some may disagree with what I'm about to say, but here it behooves me to pick a bone, or two, or three, in this respect, with our esteemed poet of New England, Robert Frost himself, who, I think, did our regional stonework something of a disservice when he wrote his piece on "Mending Walls." For therein he posits an impulsion that seeks to bring down what human beings have so laboriously put together and to restore, in the process, a balance and rapport conceivably more natural and humane.

"Something there is that doesn't love a wall," he sententiously asserts, and later adds, "that wants it down."

Granted: walls do fall down in time, erode, or just get lugged away (to build another wall sometimes); and there are walls that pen in, or keep out, what should by rights, progress back and forth through welcoming gates. Moreover, I'm not oblivious to the manifold social and moral ambiguities that have affected, through time, the building, preservation, and destruction of walls—even these stone walls of New England.

But I don't know what there might be that doesn't love our fieldstone walls in these latter times. Even the foraging deer, the birds, and the chipmunks love them as much as we do.

And when Roberto (as I affectionately call him — he wouldn't mind) brands his toilsome, wall-repairing neighbor "a stone-age savage armed," he hasn't seen Anpu, or ten thousand of his ilk, deftly joining for us the most adamant of nature's gifts. Nor is that work achieved by uttering spells or turning a blind eye and hoping it will work.

Fie on you, Roberto, you progeny of Rousseau!

Something there is that *does* love a wall and will keep building them, whether you approve or not. What else can bring neighbors in the spring to work together; what else can you lean against or sit upon so commodiously — morning, noon, or eventide — as you chat and smoke your pipe?

Of walls, I sing, and barriers and barricades (begging forbearance for my brief foray into rhapsody) and all they are and represent; of fences, railings, moats, curbs, and hedges; of banisters and balustrades and cloistered galleries; of natural rims and fringes of every kind — of riverbanks and beaches, of mountain ranges and craters and coasts and crested waves and horizons whose multifarious contours distinguish everywhere the earth from sky. I luxuriate in limits, bask in boundaries, delight in demarcations. Edges edify me, embellish me, exalt me, enrich me. Partitions purify me.

I rejoice in perimeters, frames, and borders. I savor distinctness and avow that, ever and ever, distinctness and distinctiveness walk hand in hand through all the aeons of time; for what is distinct is distinguished, and to distinguish is a mark of distinction.

I revel in divisions: in seconds and minutes and hours and days; in sunrises and sunsets and periods of the moon and seasons of the year.

I celebrate all that encloses and envelops and harbors and shelters: the roof over my head, the walls around and inside my house, the bark of trees and the rinds of fruit, furry hides and ornate garb and scalloped shells tumbled inland by the frothy surf.

The measures and movements of music modulate my soul in the rhythms of splendor. I indulge in the beginnings and endings of stories, of symphonies, of poems.

I relish the embroidered entities of speech itself: syllables and words, and phrases, and clauses, and sentences; paragraphs and chapters, verses and stanzas and cantos — all that delimits, all that segments, the flood of speech into tight-knit bundles that glitter like beaded jewels upon a necklace.

I know that wholes, to be wholes, require parts, and that parts, to be parts, require wholes, and that unity, to be unity, requires units.

And the glory of the wall, and all that resembles a wall, is nowhere more manifest than in its own internal divisions, the most important of which are its gateways, its windows, its apertures into whatever lies beyond.

I shall never cease to reflect upon that ancient memory of the Garden of Eden, which was surrounded by a wall, and the universal dream of Paradise, remembering at all times that the word "paradise" itself means, in its original Persian, "surrounded by a wall."

Something there is that truly loves a wall.

Me!

Tonight was a full moon. A pack of coyotes came down out of the woods and respectfully sniffed around Anpu's wall. They scurried back and forth along the wall, jumped over it, and one or two even ran along the capstones, where some have already been placed. None of the coyotes saw fit to "mark territory."

Then something set them off, I don't know what, but they gathered together in the moonlight next to the wall, crooked back their necks, and howled and yapped and clamored to their hearts' content.

A chorus of wonder.

A chorale of praise.

Day Twelve

Sometimes my wife complains about Anpu. She watches him from a window upstairs. He's just standing there, doing nothing, she says. She says he "ain't nothin' but a hound dog." Of course, she's not serious and she's making fun, too, I presume, of a song popular in her adolescent years. But I have noted Anpu's spells of inactivity.

I've also noted that he rarely places a stone in the wall and then takes it out again or moves it around very much. No trial and error. The stone goes from the heap to the wall and is an immediate and exact fit. He doesn't act until all the thinking about acting is done. Everything falls into place. That's what he's doing when he just stands there. He's doing that thinking.

But my wife is right. He does look like a hound dog, sort of. Lean and supple, strong and purposive, his head at times bent resolutely to a scent, his nose in the air at other times to refresh and retune the senses. Yet his face is more like the face of a jackal seen in profile, one great black-contoured eye affixed steadfastly to a far desert horizon, to the boundaries of a twilight world.

Like Anubis.

Like the jackal god.

Like the custodian of the dead, preparing their final passage, encasing them with gold and anointing them with frankincense and myrrh — the sacramental accouterments of entombment.

Like the *psychopompos* — as the Greeks would call it — the escort of souls into Hades, into the netherworld. Like Virgil leading Dante through the realms of the dead. The saying that came to my mind the other day — "I have come unto the House of Him whose dwelling is upon the mountain" — now I remember where it comes from: the Egyptian *Book of the Dead*.

I keep thinking about those coyotes that showed up here last night. Had they discerned a kindred spirit?

Day Thirteen

I've asked Anpu for, and received in turn, some advice on how to conduct a few minor projects in stonework. Not that I really have building a wall in mind, but I'm going to try to put some simple stone borders around the flower beds in the back of our house (where the neighbors won't see them). I can't say I really understood most of what he told me, but I'm setting to work anyway. I have a good supply of small stones, about the size of loaves of bread, to work with. They're not weathered fieldstones but, rather, were recently dug up from the soil in various drainage projects I pursued last spring.

As I work with these stones, I begin to understand, I think, one of the attractions of this métier to those who practice it. I've always been aware that craftsmen love the materials they work with. I've seen carpenters affectionately caress a wooden board and mechanics taking pleasure in the heft and the feel of a metallic bolt.

Musicians, I know, love musical tones—a G, or an F, on a piano, or violin, or guitar: what a lovely thing it is, just by itself. Then add something to it, and it's even better now, for that which is special about it is heightened by the contrast with something different—but not so different that the difference doesn't matter.

Poets love words. Even more, they love syllables, love the way they feel inside the mouth when they utter them, love how they cluster in little bouquets and garlands, love the rhythmic pressure in the throat and tongue as they navigate through those remarkable physiological straits like miniature armadas of vessels laden with spices and gold.

But I never thought that rocks could be lovable, both for themselves and in sequence with others. I soon learned that. Some of the rocks I found so lovable that I wanted to bring them into the house and cradle them in my arms and give them a sudsy bath in the kitchen sink the way you would bathe a newborn child.

So many of them, so different. No two shapes alike.

The astonishing textures—rough and smooth, grainy, soapy, mellow, ridged and sharp and serrated, solid, flaking, brittle, grooved, gnarled and knobby, flat and sometimes wavy and sandy as if an ocean breeze had, once upon a time, carved miniature dunes in a beach that, in turn, some other force petrified and preserved.

Many stones seem to be made up of several kinds of stone blended or molded together, so that they have many different textures in one surface. I love to touch them, run my hands over them, turn them around and examine them from different angles, and let sunlight and shadow play over their folds and furrows and brows.

The colors are beyond all description: thousands of delicate hues whose names I don't know—organdy and lavender and peach and bluish-gray and pastel gold and aubergine, like eggplants or damson plums.

Some stones are artist's palates in their multiform and sequenced richness. Many stones display webs of finely tinted veins, while others exhibit patterns of glacial scratches scored over their gritty surfaces. There are horizontally layered stones that split, even under as mild a pressure as from your fingers, and open up like thick, meaty sandwiches, revealing a medley of interior colors that even the most elaborately gourmet sandwich in all the world could scarcely emulate. There are stones that look like melons and mangos and Brazil nuts and pineapples and exotic squashes.

Why have I never noticed any of this before?

Ribbons of light spiral through the glittering facets of what I clasp in my wondering hands. I'm especially fond of the auburn and ruddy stones. Where do they come from? Did the earth pitch these up from its depths like all this quartz and granite; or did they compact as sediments at the bottom of an ancient sea?

Another stone common in this area is an amazing pale-pink granite filled with millions of small black dots. And then the silvery mica and the deep ruby-red garnets that shimmer in the fissures of the stone!

My house faces across a valley, at the eastern end of which is possibly the largest exploded volcanic caldera in New England. The sun rises directly out of that mountain-ridged kettle every morning, reenacting the blaze of its primeval glory. Is that the cornucopia out of which spouted such abundance, half a billion years ago?

Putting the stones together just in a single line — "pointing" them, or trying to do so, according to my instructions — reveals even more about color and texture and shape. Well, I can't say that I'm particularly successful at what I do — even at such a simple task (I'm not even engaged in putting rocks on top of one another to make a wall, which is the difficult thing to do).

But I am able, now and then, to sense the satisfaction when two utterly different rocks almost "click" into place. It is, I suppose, a little like the experience of finding the combination that unlocks a safe: hearing that subtle little "click" that says, "This much is done." The rocks that so overtly seem to repel one another, to be so intractable and stubborn, suddenly, even inexplicably, attract, invite, align themselves, as if, from the beginning of time, as different as they are, they were meant to go together. And yet a stone asks finally for one thing and one thing only: to be at rest; to be at peace so that it supports another and another and is supported by them in turn — an interplay of force, dynamic, harmonized, and serene —

Is that what we look for too?

In our lives, our relationships, in the course of events that we make happen and that happens to us, locking together our bits and pieces into their own inimitable happenstance? To be at peace, our internal force aligned perfectly with the forces of the earth, the forces of the cosmos around us, the forces of those we know and love?

I once asked Anpu, while observing him at work, if he enjoyed doing jigsaw puzzles. Laconically, without explanation, he said no. Later, and with a little experience, I could understand why the question was absurd to begin with. In a jigsaw puzzle, the pieces press in tightly, seamlessly, and, once in place, have no further function or importance as pieces. They vanish into a whole that finally has nothing to do with them as pieces. In a "dry" field-stone wall the stones retain their independence, even while coalescing into a complex and dynamic set of tensions and pressures. They're contiguous with their neighbors but don't fuse with them. Further, unlike the jigsaw puzzle, where only fit is vital, and not the dynamics of which I spoke, each combination of stones is a special case, for which no prearranged pattern is available. The making of the pattern is the same as finding it.

Well, I enlarge here upon matters about which I'm scarcely qualified. Meanwhile, my wife refers to my stone circles sardonically as "barbarian." Is that a compliment or not? But I know she's glad the neighbors won't see them. Actually, so am I; and I plan to deter Anpu, if I can, from making any exploratory forays to the back of the house to check them out.

Okay, so barbarian they may well be. I'm doing my little thing and feel my solidarity, however fleeting, with the stonemasons of Nineveh and the monument builders of Carnac and Tara and Stonehenge. If I've edged across the threshold of their immemorial guild with only so much as the somewhat disreputable toe of my boot, I shall have done at least that much.

Day Fourteen

Anpu didn't show up today. Or at least I don't think he showed up. I took advantage of his absence to work on and complete my stone circles.

While I was working, a fox clambered up over the old stone wall that borders the back field that rises high above our house, lay down in the high grass, and basked there in the sun, observing me and munching, now and then, on the wild blueberries that grow profusely in the thin soil along the brow of the hill. I could see his ruddy head above the grass, his pointed ears, his little eyes staring intently at me. He seemed to find what I was doing rather amusing.

I had the uncanny feeling that I knew this fox already; further, I had the even more uncanny feeling that I knew who this fox was. After an hour or so, he rose, turned, twitched his big bushy tail, mounted the stone wall where he stood, gazed at me again for a few moments, and then descended on the other side, trotting off calmly into the scrubby underbrush at the edge of the woods.

Day Fifteen

Anpu is back.

More and more people show up. Now they take photographs of Anpu, as well as of the wall. He seems not to notice them. Someone tried to take a photograph of me. Of me! Me—standing somewhere in the background: bemused, puzzled, a little quirky, after all! Ah, I do flatter myself!

At one point during the day, Anpu asked me how my stone circles were coming. I told him they were coming along fine, but I didn't offer to take him around to the back of the house to show him. His amused smile informed me that he knew all about them already and didn't need to see them.

He's putting finishing touches on the gate he created about a third of the way along the wall. He's adorned each side of the gate with small thin triangular pinnacles of stone.

Obelisks?

Day Sixteen

It's done.

Shouldn't there be, or have been, some kind of ceremony?

I knew that Anpu was finishing up because he had been cleaning up around the wall, removing unused stone back to the woods (or wherever it came from), and making some last minor adjustments, so I was keeping a close watch on his activities. He has a way of suddenly slipping away. He never says goodbye.

Meanwhile, I was engaged in a few desultory activities to keep me busy while I waited for the right moment to emerge from the house, inspect the finished product, congratulate him on his work, and present him with a check with the name Anpu (awkwardly) inscribed on it as well as the agreed-upon price (about which I now feel rather guilty). But, as so often these things go, I would watch for a while, then go off and do something, come back and see if things were ready yet, which they weren't, go off again, do something else.

I decided at one point to run through the second movement of the *Appassionata*. It would take only a few minutes. Then I would check again to see what was happening. Somehow, during those few minutes, while I was playing the piece on the piano, Anpu vanished.

One Week Later

Just vanished.

He hasn't returned. No one has seen him.

One Month Later

No one knows where he's gone. People drop in constantly and ask me how they can contact him. I tell them I don't know. He's never come by to collect. He's never sent a bill.

Three Months Later

He never did send that bill.

One Year Later

I've done the unimaginable. I've purchased a grammar of the ancient Egyptian language and am learning how to read hieroglyphs. I don't know how long I'll keep this up — it's a bit over my head. But I've learned something important already.

I have before me a hieroglyphic image. It's one of those hieroglyphs that function pictorially rather than phonetically. It shows a human figure, in profile, sitting on its heels with knees slanted upward at a forty-five-degree angle. Projecting from the knees, at the same angle, is a hand that holds a rod or scepter capped by the sacred *ankh*, which was later reverenced by Christians as the ansate cross, the symbol for life.

The head of the figure is canine with a sharp, thin muzzle and high, pointed ears. Yes, it's the sign for what we have come to know in a Hellenized or Greek variant as Anubis — the jackal deity, the Weigher of Destinies, the Escort into the God-World, the purveyor of Eternity. He's also the god of craftsmanship, of skill, of the perpetuation of the dead. His name is synonymous with wisdom and judgment. But the proper transcription for this hieroglyph is not Anubis. It's Anpu.

Could it be?

It can't be. My wife tells me I'm having delusions. That I've imagined most of this, dreamt it into being.

Maybe I have. But I don't think so. There's a wall out there in front of the house. It was built by a stonemason who said his name was Anpu. And Anpu never sent a bill.

People are coming from far and wide to gaze upon this wall. They've never seen anything like it. It's a miracle. It's a wall that must have been put together by a god. But there is no god but God. Therefore, it's a wall that must have been put together by God.

Last night, as the moon rose above the wilderness, I heard from afar the lonely shriek of a catamount and, soon afterward, the mournful howl of a wolf from the depths of the great forests beyond the mountains.

About the Author

Johann M. Moser was born in Cambridge, Massachusetts, in 1940. He grew up in New York City and later in New Jersey. At Dartmouth College he majored in philosophy and studied with the poet Richard Eberhart. In 1970, he received a Ph.D. in comparative literature from the Catholic University of America in Washington, D.C., where he specialized in poetics and medieval literature. From 1970 until his retirement in 2000, he taught literature and philosophy at St. Anselm College in Manchester, New Hampshire.

Moser published a volume of verse titled *Most Ancient of All Splendors* with Sophia Institute Press in 1989, as well as edited and translated for the press both an anthology of classical Nativity verse and, in collaboration with a colleague, Robert Anderson, an edition of St. Thomas Aquinas's hymns and prayers.

Although familiar with many areas of the United States and having lived several years abroad, Moser spent his early summers in the Lakes Region of central New Hampshire, where he has now resided for over half a century. In these decades, he has formed an intimate bond with northern New England, whose mountains and lakes and lively populace have been a source of inspiration for him, even as he has devoted himself to a sustained pursuit and emulation of world literature in all its dense historicity and its universal aesthetic achievements.